PRAISE FOR JONATHAN WHITELAW'S NOVELS

'A perfectly pruned murder mystery – sharp, surprising and absolutely blooming with charm.'
Jo Middleton, author of *Happy Bloody Christmas*

'It's always a joy to join the Penrith Bingo Club's most proactive member on another mystery. Jonathan Whitelaw's series continues to delight and surprise, with incredible warmth and sparkling wit along the way. The king of cosy crime has done it again.'
Alice Bell, author of *Grave Expectations*

'A perfect read for one of those dark afternoons … wonderfully compulsive.'
J.M. Hall, author of *A Spoonful of Murder*

'A cracking cozy crime mystery – I loved it.'
Marion Todd, author of *What They Knew*

'Sharp … unforgettable … hugely enjoyable.'
Emma Christie, author of *Find Her First*

ALSO BY JONATHAN WHITELAW

The Garden Club Murders
The Concert Hall Killer
The Village Hall Vendetta
The Bingo Hall Detectives

Banking on Murder
Summit of All Fears
Death Do They Part

ALL AT SEA

A DEATH ON THE OCEAN, A KILLER BELOW DECK...

JONATHAN WHITELAW

Harper North

HarperNorth
Windmill Green
24 Mount Street
Manchester M2 3NX

A division of
HarperCollins*Publishers*
1 London Bridge Street
London SE1 9GF

www.harpercollins.co.uk

HarperCollins*Publishers*
Macken House,
39/40 Mayor Street Upper,
Dublin 1, D01 C9W8, Ireland

First published by HarperCollins*Publishers* Ltd 2026

1

Copyright © Jonathan Whitelaw 2026

Jonathan Whitelaw asserts the moral right to
be identified as the author of this work.

A catalogue record for this book is available from the British Library.

PB ISBN: 978-0-00-870594-7

This novel is entirely a work of fiction. The names, characters and incidents portrayed in it are the work of the author's imagination. Any resemblance to actual persons, living or dead, events or localities is entirely coincidental.

Set in Sabon by Amnet

Printed and bound in the UK using 100% Renewable Electricity
by CPI Group (UK) Ltd

All rights reserved. No part of this publication may be reproduced, stored in a retrieval system, or transmitted, in any form or by any means, electronic, mechanical, photocopying, recording or otherwise, without the prior permission of the publishers.

Without limiting the exclusive rights of any author, contributor or the publisher of this publication, any unauthorised use of this publication to train generative artificial intelligence (AI) technologies is expressly prohibited. HarperCollins also exercise their rights under Article 4(3) of the Digital Single Market Directive 2019/790 and expressly reserve this publication from the text and data mining exception.

For Isabella, Rose and Patricia

Chapter 1

'Don't you know who I am?'

Howie was losing his temper. Or perhaps he had never had it in the first place. He hated to fly at the best of times. Airports drove him mad and he absolutely loathed queuing. The thought of being cooped up in a tin can hurtling through the air at thirty thousand feet didn't fill him with confidence either. However, this was the twenty-first century and his work meant he was on more flights than he liked.

If he'd thought he was going to have a restful jaunt from Heathrow, he was clearly mistaken. The grave expression on the flight attendant's face as she hovered over him made that as plain as the nose on her face.

'Please, Mr Temple, could you keep your voice down,' she said. 'We have other guests onboard.'

'Yes, I can see that,' he said, craning his neck. 'I'm a guest too, you know.'

'You *are*,' she said, staying calm. 'Just not in business class, I'm afraid.'

'You've said that already,' he replied. 'There must be a mistake.'

'There's no mistake, Mr Temple.'

'Check your seating plan.'

'We have done, sir.'

'Then check it again,' he snapped.

'It's not going to say anything different.'

'Have you checked it for the right name?' he asked, now getting flippant. 'Howie. Temple.'

If his anger was getting to the attendant, she wasn't showing it. Instead, she was collected, to the point of indifference. Howie wondered if she had passengers like him all the time. People who used to make passers-by do a double take, who used to have a name and face that opened doors, who used to be recognised in the street. People who used to be famous.

At first he had thought she was offering him a complimentary glass of champagne, as was the style. He was settling nicely into his little pod of luxury when the tap on the shoulder had come. He, apparently, was in the wrong seat. Not only that, but indignity of indignities, the wrong end of the plane.

'The names and seats have all been checked,' said the attendant. 'I'm afraid you'll have to move.'

'This has to be a mistake,' he said. 'My agent booked these flights, or at least my agent's assistant's assistant did. And the production company paid for them. I'm *supposed* to be in business. I'm always in business. That's what's *supposed* to happen.'

'What's *supposed* to happen doesn't always happen I'm afraid.' There was steel in her voice, despite the friendly smile. 'And this is what's happening now.'

'So what am I *supposed* to do?'

'Well,' she started. 'You could always go down the cabin to your assigned seat.'

'But I don't understand.'

'It's perfectly simple really,' she said, now sounding like a nursery nurse talking to a toddler. 'You collect your things, take the small stroll down the aisle to the economy section of the aircraft and take the seat that's been designated for you.' She clicked into delivering a speech that sounded like she could deliver it in her sleep. 'Our economy cabin is perfect for cost-savvy passengers. You'll find a selection of hot and cold snacks available for purchase, along with in-flight entertainment and duty-free shopping. We value all our customers, including our budget flyers—'

'No, no, you're not listening to me,' he said, getting flustered. 'I'm supposed to be in business...or first?' he tried hopefully.

The smile on the attendant's face was wearing thin. 'If you'd like to get your things and head down to economy, one of my colleagues can assist you.'

The business cabin was starting to take notice. The time for politeness had passed a few moments ago. Everyone had, at first, been pretending not to notice the scene unfolding in front of them. They had busied themselves with their headphones, their inflatable pillows, the little bags of goodies that came with the expensive seats. Now the prospect of a showdown had kicked in and they wanted to see what would happen. It was the most attention Howie had had in years.

'Do you need mobility assistance at all, Mr Temple?' asked the attendant, stepping to one side to let him get out.

'Mobility assistance? How old do you think I am?'

'I couldn't possibly comment.' She smiled like a well-programmed robot, not quite managing to pass as human.

Howie thought about staying put. They couldn't force him to get up, after all. He could just sit there, delay the flight, get the cops involved and make a whole song and dance about it. Maybe, if he was younger, he would have. Not that this sort of thing happened when he was younger. Private jets, those were the order of the day then. Now this. A far cry from his box office glory years. Still, work was work, after all. His mentors and managers had told him that so often it was etched into his eyelids when he slept.

'Fine,' he said, pulling himself up and out of the business class pod. 'I hope you lot have good lawyers. Because you won't be able to afford a goddamn biplane when mine are finished with you over all of this.'

He was aware of how pathetic that sounded. It wasn't the attendant's fault after all. She was just doing her job. Although he detected a subdued glee in seeing him flounder and flap in the narrow aisle.

'I just hope whoever the charlatan is who's taking *my* seat here chokes on their complimentary olives.'

'You're him, aren't you?'

The voice startled him a little. He looked up, ready to give his standard gracious performance when fans recognised him.

'You're Howie Temple. You're him. The actor.'

The voice, which was unnaturally loud in the confines of the cabin, belonged to a tall, slender woman in giant sunglasses. She was chewing something, or at least looked like it, her glossed lips motoring away between breaths.

Howie looked about to clock who was witnessing his performance. But immediately an icy realisation hit him. Everyone was watching not him, but the woman who now made her way down the central aisle. A giant handbag was slung over one arm, bumping against the seat backs with every step. Her other hand was filled with shopping bags, bottles clinking and clanking as she moved.

'Yes, I'm Howie,' he said. 'And who might you be?'

The young woman looked more puzzled than offended. She straightened up, pushing her chest out.

'It's me,' she said. 'Cassandra. We're on the show together.'

Howie's years of training had taught him how to not bat an eyelid when circumstances demanded. This woman didn't look anything like the grainy headshot his manager's assistant had emailed him. He always preferred to get the measure of someone face to face, anyway. He knew something about people. He'd spent his life imitating them on stage and screen. He'd also been to enough Hollywood parties to know when someone was going to be trouble. First impressions were important in the acting world. And he'd become attuned to sussing them out pretty quickly.

Garishly dressed, covered in make-up more suited to being on camera than real life and doing a heroic job of balancing all her hand luggage while approaching in six-inch heels, Cassandra was clearly a one-woman force of nature.

'I'm afraid I didn't recognise you,' he said, thinking honesty might be the best policy and also that this line was a classic test. Plenty of wannabe starlets found anonymity more cutting than any bad review.

'Don't worry about that, chuck, these things are always the same. Here, hold this for a minute, would you?'

Startled by her relaxed reaction, Howie obeyed her and held out his hand. She handed him the oversized handbag.

The weight almost pulled Howie's arm out of its socket as he took hold.

'Holy hell,' he said, catching his breath. 'What have you got in here? An anvil?'

'What's that my darling?' she asked, producing her phone.

'This bag weighs more than my whole luggage!'

'Keep your hair on, Howie, it's just a few bits and bobs, that's all.'

'Bits and bobs?' He rolled his shoulder.

'I'm just touching up my face, I won't be a second,' she said, liberally spritzing herself, and a few unfortunate nearby passengers, with something. 'Are you on Insta?'

'Insta?' he asked, still feeling the effects of her bag. 'I'm not *on* anything. I don't do drugs – not so much as a sleeping tablet.'

'Are you serious?' She seemed perplexed. She tapped something into her phone while she spoke, her bejewelled talons seemingly posing no problem. 'How old are you, Howie?'

'Old enough to remember when phones had wires that connected them to the ground.'

'You what?'

'Nothing.'

'Come on, give us a smile. It'll get people amped up for the show,' she said. 'I'll pop it on my socials and they'll go wild.'

'All of that social media nightmare is handled by my agent,' he said. 'I couldn't even begin to tell you how to do it.'

'Ha, lucky for you I don't need anyone to tell me how to do it. You're really not online? How do you get your news and stuff?'

'From the TV.'

'Do they still have news on TV?' she asked.

'You're not serious, are you?'

'It's a genuine question. I can't remember the last time I sat down and watched the TV.'

'You know we're about to go and film something for television, right?'

'Yeah, I know that,' she said. 'I also know that demographics have shown fewer and fewer young people actually even own a TV, let alone watch it. It's all there, in the stats. There's a fascinating series of TikToks on it you should really see.'

Howie was surprised that Cassandra clearly knew what she was talking about. But the attendant cleared her throat behind him before he could quiz her further. He suddenly remembered where he was – and that he was being thrown out of business class.

'Smile for the camera, I'll tag you anyway,' she said.

'What?'

Before he could do anything, she had taken a picture of them both. The phone made an artificial shutter sound and, not for the first time that morning, he was questioning his life choices.

'Oh Howie, look at the state of you, love,' she said, showing him the screen. He'd never realised he could manage to look in two directions at once. 'We'll have to take another one.'

She reached over and straightened his shirt collar. She brushed some of his sandy, grey hair from his forehead before he jerked backwards.

'What are you doing?' he asked.

'Smartening you up a bit,' she said, picking fluff from his lapel. 'You look like you've not seen a mirror for a week. Come on, give us a nice big smile or a thumbs up for the camera.'

'Mr Temple, please,' said the attendant, growing more fidgety. 'If you could just make your way down to economy, my colleagues will be able to take care of you.'

'You're in cattle?' asked Cassandra, a wry smile creeping across her smooth-skinned face.

'Mr Temple mistakenly thought he was in business class,' said the attendant.

'Eh, excuse me,' he said. 'I'm standing right here, you know? You don't have to share my business with the whole goddamn plane.'

'Is this a joke, chuck?' asked Cassandra, fluffing her hair. 'I thought you were a big Hollywood film star.'

'I am,' he muttered.

'Then what are you doing all the way back down there?'

'I could ask you the same thing.'

'I'm business, babe,' she smiled. 'In fact, that's my seat just there.'

Howie didn't want to look. He didn't have to. Even before her outstretched finger, capped with a blood red fingernail, had settled on the direction of her seat, he *knew* which one it was going to be.

Cassandra strutted and clinked her way past him, squeezing into her pod with ease. Settled, she took off her dinnerplate-sunglasses and looked up at Howie.

'I'll see you when we get off then?' she asked, perfectly innocently.

Howie didn't say anything in return. He had a terrible sinking feeling that was growing in the pit of his stomach. Like a man being led to his own execution, he felt the attendant's hand on his shoulder, gently but firmly easing him down the gangway. The carpet beneath his feet changed to vinyl as he passed through the galley and into the maelstrom of the economy section. Hollering, shouting, thumping, laughing, crying and untamed chaos met him. And that was just the adults. The kids were all plugged into screens.

Gone was the hushed, exclusive atmosphere. In its place a theatre of unrestrained frustrations and recirculated air. By the time he reached his seat the cacophony had turned into a background buzz he'd just have to tolerate. He slumped down thinking about all the box office flops he had been part of over his career. He thought about his failed stint on Broadway, the two divorces, everything that could have gone wrong that *had*. He wished he'd enjoyed his time in business class more when he was there. It seemed so far away now, even though it was just a few dozen yards up the aisle. He looked out beyond the seat in front, longing for a little taste of that just once more. Then he felt a hard nudge in his ribs.

'You're him, aren't you?'

A large man, sweat on his balding head and bits of lunch stuck in his teeth, was sat beside him. He was nodding, looking over his glasses at Howie, expecting a response.

'You're that actor, aren't you?' he said. 'Howie Temple.'

Howie tried to summon his usual trademark smile and stock answers. But somehow, this time he couldn't.

'Yes,' Howie just about managed. 'I used to be.'

Chapter 2

The Regal Secret was as majestic as its name suggested. Even tethered to the dock and stationary, it was a vessel that looked like it was going somewhere. Dynamic and sleek, with lines and curves more suited to a museum dedicated to the old masters than a grotty harbour in Livorno, it oozed class, sophistication and expense.

Cassandra Troy hadn't had much experience with ships. Or were they boats? She was never sure what the difference was. Watching ferries chug through the filthy waters of the Mersey was about as close as she had come to sailing on the high seas before now. By her own admission she wouldn't know a schooner from a Shih Tzu. That didn't mean she didn't want to learn. She knew all too well that one of the common misconceptions of social media stars like her was that they weren't very bright. Yes, she spent most of her time endorsing clothes and make-up. Yes she appealed to mass audiences with her salt of the earth humour and glamour. And no, she wasn't going to be asked on *Celebrity University Challenge* any time soon. But that wasn't going to stop her from asking questions.

'How big is she?' she asked, her hand over her brows to shield the Italian sun.

'Fifty metres, from bow to stern.'

Cassandra nodded. She didn't really know what that meant in terms of its classification. Still, it was valuable to have these little bits of information stored away. Captain Rolando stood gazing at his charge proudly, like he had built her himself. Cassandra had never understood the sort of strange infatuation people had with vehicles. Plenty of her colleagues from the influencer, model and online celebrity world could be the same. Most had flash cars or private jets and spoke about them like they were beloved pets.

It was good content for social media, of course it was. Who wouldn't want to be posed next to a multi-million dollar lump of metal and grease? But those astronomical price tags had always put her off.

Despite her flawless appearance, from her celebrity-cut hair to her designer shoes, Cassandra Troy knew she was decidedly boring at heart. She blamed her parents for her frugality. Their sensible upbringing had installed a firm guilt when it came to any expensive splurges. She was certain they wouldn't approve of the bottles of limited edition vodka and 15-year-old malt whisky clinking around in her bags.

Captain Rolando said something in his native Italian and smiled. He was older than Cassandra had been expecting, his beard peppered with grey hairs and a knowing experience in his kind eyes. He whistled and hopped up the gangway, heading onto his ship.

'Do you think he's overcompensating for something?' she smiled, nudging Howie in the ribs as he wandered over to her.

The actor didn't respond. His broad face was as blank as a slab of concrete. He'd been like that the whole trip from Pisa to the coast. Barely speaking a word as their limo weaved its way through the busy traffic, through the rolling countryside and down to the docks. Cassandra had to check every now and then that he was still breathing.

'Suit yourself,' she said. 'Have you ever been on one of these?' She nodded at the yacht moored beside them.

'What? A boat?' he asked.

'Yeah,' she said.

'I live in Los Angeles.'

'So?'

'So? The Pacific Ocean is within spitting distance.'

'But you grew up in Canada,' she said. 'Saskatchewan. That's a landlocked province, is it not?'

That comment seemed to catch Howie off guard. So much, in fact, that he tipped his Ray-Ban sunglasses forward.

'How do you know that?' he growled.

Cassandra liked to pull the rug from beneath people's feet. Especially those who thought she was nothing more than an airhead. It was her hobby, if you could call it that. She wasn't cruel or unkind with it. She just liked to keep others on their toes. Seeing the surprise on their faces as they revised their opinions of her.

'People like me – reality stars, influencers – I know we have a reputation,' she said.

'Do you?' Howie asked sarcastically.

'Yeah, we do,' she said. 'A lot of folk think we're thick as two short planks.'

'What?'

'Daft. Idiots. Numpties.'

'I get the picture,' he said.

'Don't get me wrong, some of us are. But no more than in any other job.'

'And what you do is work, is it?' he asked.

'It pays my bills,' she said firmly. 'What I do lets me buy my mam and dad a new house, it's paid off my brother's student debts and I stay in five star hotels wherever I go. Can't be bad, can it?'

Howie fell silent.

'I do my research,' she said. 'I know all about you, all about your career, how you moved from Canada when you were seventeen to try and make it in Hollywood. Course it's easier that practically your whole adult life has been photographed. It's all over the internet, even that slightly dodgy film you made that only paid you a couple of hundred bucks for two days' work.'

'Ssshhhhh!' he tried to hush her down. 'Don't talk about that in public. What do you want me to say? That I was young, that I needed the money?'

'I'm young and I don't need the money,' Cassandra said proudly. 'And I also don't like being taken for a fool.'

'Okay, okay, whatever.' He was sweating now under the Italian sun. 'I don't care, okay? I'm just here for the pay cheque and that's it. You can be what, who, where and when you want to be, I just don't want any part of it. When the cameras stop rolling, we don't have to talk. Alright?'

'If you like,' she said. 'I just thought I'd make some conversation, that's all.'

'Well don't,' he said. 'Leave it until the cameras are rolling and turn it off again when they're done.'

Cassandra took the hint. She was certain she'd won that round of sparring though. And that made her smile. She went back to her phone.

'Good afternoon, me hearties!'

A booming voice sounded out like a foghorn from above. Cassandra squinted into the sun. A tall silhouette was hovering over them, peering down from the bow of *The Regal Secret*.

'How are we both faring today? Have we found our sea legs yet? Suck down some of this rich, salty air. Absolutely wonderful stuff.'

The silhouette glided down the gangway and came into full view. He was smiling serenely, moving with an almost balletic grace as he glided over to them.

'Ed, is it?' asked Cassandra.

'The very same, for my sins,' said the man. 'And you must be Cassandra Troy. Well of course you are. One of the most beautiful women in the world here, on my little show. I'm quite starstruck. A vision of sheer perfection carved by Jupiter himself.'

'Oh you,' she giggled. 'I like you, you can stay.'

Ed gave her a long, warm hug and kissed her on both cheeks. Still smiling, he turned to Howie.

'And your companion,' he said, marvelling at the actor like a sculpture. 'The face of the 1990s, the man, the myth, the legend all rolled into one hulking hunk. Howie Temple, as I live and breathe.'

'And you are?'

'Howie, don't be so rude, this is Edward Wells, the man who made reality TV an art.' Cass nudged Howie with a shove of her elbow.

'Sorry about him, Ed. He's in one of his moods,' she said. 'The airline messed up his seat and he had to spend it back with the plebs. And as you can see, it's been a long time since the great Howie Temple had to spend time with normal people. It's clearly the biggest hardship he's had to endure in recent years.'

Howie muttered something under his breath about the worse thing actually being offered an advert for denture fixative.

'Not at all, not at all,' said Ed. 'It's a long way from home for the big man and I'd have a face like a bear chewing on a bumblebee if I'd just flown in from LA. I'm just glad you're both here. What do you think of her then?'

Ed stepped back and took in the view of *The Regal Secret*.

'She's stunning isn't she, absolutely stunning,' he said. 'She belongs to a prince from Saudi Arabia who's charging the network an eye-watering fortune to charter her for the show. But it'll be worth it when we set sail and you guys are turned loose.'

'Where is everyone else?' asked Cassandra. 'I mean the crew, not the guests.'

'They're on their way.' Ed nodded. 'You've met Rolando, he's the skipper. He's a real sweetie, been and done the lot, he has. In front of the mast, man and boy, so we're in safe hands with him. Then in terms of your fellow celebrity deckhands and galley slaves,' he laughed awkwardly seeing the consternation on Cassandra and Howie's faces, 'you're going to be a part of an all-star international crew, all famous for different things but all learning how to man a yacht for the first time. You'll be working hard to give the guests booked onto this trip the voyage of a lifetime. I like to think it's the fact that you lovely celebrities will be swapping roles and waiting on normal people that will make this show such a hit. Plus of course, I've curated the cast. We've got one crew member coming in from Brisbane, one from Manchester and another from Düsseldorf, or Dresden, I always get those two mixed up.'

'Strange, given they're on opposite sides of Germany,' said Howie.

'There's a strike with the pilots or the air traffic controllers or some such.' Ed ignored him. 'So he'll be here when he's here. You two are my first.'

'What about the film crew capturing all this?'

'You're looking at it.' He thumbed at himself.

'What?'

Howie's shock was enough to force him to completely remove his shades.

'It's me, I'm the crew, Mr Edward Wells, esquire, the commander and chief of this season's *Celebrity Sail or Fail*. I'm the director, the producer, the *auteur*.'

'Just you?' asked Cassandra.

'Yes, this is my vision so it's just me at the creative wheel,' Ed laughed. 'Well, not *just* me literally, of course. Geri is our camerawoman and Ben is about here somewhere, he'll be handling sound.'

'Ben?' asked Howie, a wry smirk. 'And Geri.'

'That's right,' said Ed.

He looked at the director, then to Cassandra. Neither of them smiled.

'Well,' said Ed. 'Belts are tightening across the network and the blazers in the corridors of power reckon a multicamera production on a fifty-metre yacht is a bit excessive. So we're keeping it nice and lean. Don't worry though, Geri and Ben are top professionals, they'll capture *everything*.'

Cassandra looked at Howie. The actor wasn't impressed. She hadn't done a lot of TV in her career but this all sounded a little strange, even to her. Ed, on the other hand, remained positive.

'Everything will be fine.' He batted them away. 'We'll get this great guerrilla documentary feel to the whole thing, proper fly-on-the-wall moments, you know, stolen moments and shaky footage. The kids will love it. You guys will love it. The ratings will love it.'

He clapped his hands together, as if to bring the matter to a firm conclusion.

'Right, let's get you onboard and settled in your cabins, shall we?'

He marched down the dockside. He was a little away when Howie spoke quietly to Cassandra.

'A film crew of three people? You've got to be kidding me.'

'He seems keen though,' she said. 'And like he said, it's only fifty metres. It's not like we can get lost or anything.'

'I've been in films with a cast of thousands, with crews that could fill a village and here I am setting sail with Tom and Jerry,' he grunted, lifting his bag.

Howie started off after Ed. Cassandra juggled her duty-free and her handbag, trying to grab her suitcase.

'You know, the traditional thing would be for you to at least offer to take the lady's bags for her!'

Howie stopped. He smiled, putting his sunglasses back on.

'I don't hold with tradition,' he said, and strode on.

Cassandra thought about swearing. Then she thought much better of it. She lassoed her cases and managed to somehow navigate her way down the dockside towards the gangway. Howie stood waiting for her, Ed already up and on the ship.

'What?' she asked, struggling.

'Ladies first,' said Howie, grinning. 'If you're into chivalry.'

Cassandra looked down at the gangway. It was a narrow plank of metal strips flanked by shaky looking bannisters. They led a steep path up towards the main deck of the yacht, the water of the harbour sloshing around below looking murkier in the shadow of the beast. Everything was swaying gently in the tide, the creaking ropes looking worryingly under strain.

'Bloody Nora,' she said. 'I think I'm feeling seasick already and I haven't left the dock.'

She took a deep breath. Plucking up her courage, she went to take her first step onto the gangway. Ed screamed from above.

'Wait!'

Cassandra wobbled. She thought for a moment that she was going straight into the drink. Somehow she managed to steady herself, hands flailing as they reached out to grab something. In the melee, she let go of her duty-free bag. It dropped straight into the water and vanished instantly, without even as much as a splash.

'No!' she shouted. 'My booze!'

Howie erupted in a fit of laughter. She spun around and gave him a glare that would have frightened the Wicked Witch of the East.

'I don't know what you're laughing at,' she said. 'I was going to offer you a dram. Ed, what the heck is wrong with you?' She turned back towards the director. 'What could I possibly have done to warrant losing two hundred quid's worth of whisky?'

'Shoes,' said Ed.

'Shoes?' she asked.

'Shoes,' he said again.

Cassandra looked down at her feet.

'They're Louboutins,' she said. 'I got them last month.'

'You'll need to take them off.'

'Why?'

'You can't wear shoes on the yacht.'

Howie's laughter stopped immediately.

'What?' he almost choked.

'One of the rules onboard.' Ed shrugged. 'No shoes allowed on ship.'

'Anywhere?' asked Cassandra.

'Anywhere.' Ed shook his head. 'Something about the flooring, it's made of antique wood from Noah's Ark or some such, I don't know. All I *do* know is that it's come straight from the prince and I'm not inclined to go disobeying him. No formal shoes.'

'This is nonsense,' Howie fumed. 'No shoes on a boat. Whoever heard of something so dumb.'

'C'mon Howie, you've heard of deck shoes haven't you? Not that I brought any with me. I'm usually a heels girl, morning to night. At least I just had a fresh pedicure. What's the matter, babe? You got troll feet?' Cassandra asked him with a smirk.

'I have perfect feet, as it happens, they once did a close-up of them walking through sand when I was trying out to be the next James Bond,' he said. 'I just don't like to walk around with no shoes on. It's savage, not to mention dangerous and unhygienic. You could walk through anything.'

'Go on then,' she said.

'Go on then what?'

'Get them out,' she said, slipping her stilettos off. 'Let's see your tootsies.'

Howie's face turned scarlet. He glanced between Cassandra and Ed up on the deck. He hesitated for a moment before finally kicking off his loafers.

'Oh my word,' Cassandra said, laughing. 'Why are they so *hairy*?'

It was Howie's turn to look down at his feet. He wiggled his toes then grunted to himself again. He barged up the gangway, dragging his suitcase behind him. Storming onto the deck, he vanished into the ship. Ed looked back down towards Cassandra on the dockside. She just shrugged.

'Must have been something I said.'

Chapter 3

The crew, as motley as it was, gathered below deck. A small, cramped galley had been set up for them beneath the main bridge of *The Regal Secret*. There were no frills here, everything was sterile and practical. From the hospital-like white walls to the bunk bed cabins and closet en suites, this was *not* what the celebrity crew was used to. In contrast, the guest accommodation and entertainment deck they'd been led past was sparkling and lavish – fit for the prince himself.

Howie looked bored. He felt bored. The bright pink polo shirt he'd been given by Ed was a size too small and made his gut seem bloated. His belly was big, he knew that already. A far cry from the rippling six-pack of his pomp. He didn't need reminding, however, every time he caught sight of himself in a mirror. Then there were the matching shorts they all had on. They were indeed short. And of course, all this set off by his bare feet. He really, really hated bare feet. Not that any of the rest of the crew apparently had any problems. They were all taking it in their stride, quite literally.

He shifted around uncomfortably, leaning on a cupboard door. Captain Rolando was holding court, maps, charts and paperwork scattered across the table in front of him. Cassandra was by his side, all wide-eyed and enthusiastic for the camera. Ed was prowling around the close quarters, Geri the camerawoman by his side. He was directing her, holding his hands up to frame what he could see. Ben the sound operator was lurking behind them both, awkwardly trying to angle the fuzzy boom mic. Occasionally he'd bump into boxes of produce and supplies that had been delivered earlier. Howie despaired. He looked to the heavens but was met with a filthy extractor fan instead.

'Howie, you're going to be my bosun, yeah?'

Captain Rolando's voice snapped him out of his daydream.

'I am?' he asked. 'And what the hell is that when it's at breakfast?'

'You're my eyes and ears on the deck,' said the skipper. 'You're in charge of all things outside – cleaning, maintenance, getting the inflatables and toys out and into the water for the guests. You're my main man for everything on the outside.'

Howie winced at the thought.

'Am I doing all of this on my own?' he asked, only slightly panicking.

'No, of course not,' laughed Rolando.

The others laughed too. Howie failed to see the joke.

'Kelvin will be helping you. He's your deckhand.'

Howie looked over at the broad shouldered figure on the opposite side of the galley who'd arrived only a few minutes after they had, leaving only time for the most cursory of introductions. The celebrities were still all sizing each other up. For such a big man, Howie thought, Kelvin Kamani carried himself with a timid feebleness that made him seem shrunken. He was practically cowering beside Cassandra, looking thoroughly embarrassed that he was here at all.

'And have you done anything like this before, Kelvin?' asked Howie.

'Erm . . . no, actually,' he stuttered. 'Well, I rowed at Cambridge, almost made the first eight, actually.'

'Did you, babe?' asked Cassandra, turning to him. 'My old dad always watches the Boat Race when it's on. He loves it. Although my mam wants him to give up. The dopey idiot went and bet last year that both teams would *sink*. Can you believe that?'

Another rapturous roar of laughter from everyone except Howie. He felt his insides tighten.

'That'll be a no, then, will it?' he said, cutting the laughter short.

'Yes,' said Kelvin. 'I mean no. I don't have any experience as a bosun or anything like this. You tend to not need any seagoing skills to become an MP.'

Polite laughter this time. Kelvin looked quietly pleased that his attempt at humour had been well received.

'Fantastic,' Howie sighed, biting back his urge to ask what skills you did actually need to become a politician these days.

'Don't worry about it, H,' said Ed, dipping Geri's camera down. 'Captain Rolando here will keep you all right. You don't have to know what you're doing, just *look* like you know. I used to say that when I was working with the police way back in the day when reality was new. We made a couple of docs here in Italy and the coppers were really nervous, they were like wooden puppets. I told them to just relax, go with the flow, make it *look* like you're confident, even if you're bricking it. You can manage that, can't you H? You're an actor, aren't you?'

'That's what he calls himself anyway.'

Howie took a long, deliberate arcing glance around the room before settling on the owner of the remark.

'What was that?' he asked.

The middle-aged woman in the long, dangly earrings was sneering, keeping her eyes deliberately turned away from him.

'Nothing,' she said, looking at her blood-red nails and pursing her lips. 'I just think that actors usually perform work from the likes of Shaw and Shakespeare, not spend ninety minutes running around with their tops off blowing up flying saucers.'

'Hey—' He stepped forward.

'Marjorie, be fair,' said Cassandra, interrupting him. 'Howie hasn't had his top off in a film for decades. Have you, babe?'

He had no answer to that. Marjorie-whoever-she-was sat there smirking at him now. She was some sort of columnist or commentator, Howie couldn't remember what he'd been told. Not that it had mattered. He could always sniff out the media when he had to. In his younger days as a Hollywood heart-throb, the media's words, not his, he'd become quite deft at dodging them. Back doors and alleyways of fancy restaurants and nightclubs had become his best friends.

He would have to watch her closely.

'And what exactly will *you* be doing?' he asked her pointedly. 'Sitting around and sniping?'

Before Marjorie could retort, Captain Rolando interrupted her.

'I've got it all down here,' he said. 'Marjorie Bryant and Cassandra Troy are our stewards. They're responsible for looking after our guests when they're onboard. Attending every need, washing and cleaning, but we'll all chip in when it comes to serving meals and restocking. Got that?'

'Sounds pretty easy,' said Howie. 'A bit of simpering and dusting.'

'Easy?' Marjorie snorted. 'Easy is you and Kelvin blowing up beach balls and swimming in the sea. Cassandra and I will be worked to the bone, morning, noon and night, pampering a bunch of overly-rich spendocrats no doubt.'

'Sorry, have I missed something?' Howie asked. 'Didn't you know what you were signing up for? This is a reality show, not a two week vacation.'

'I was just remarking on your ignorance, that's all.'

'I think we can get by without your running commentary, thank you.'

'Can we indeed?'

'Yes we can.'

The rest of the galley was quiet while they went at each other. The stagnant air felt particularly stifling now. Nobody dared to be the first to speak after the war of words. The only one enjoying himself was Ed, who was urging Geri to keep filming. He gave Howie and the others a big thumbs up.

'Well, at least we're all getting along, eh?' said Cassandra.

Nobody acknowledged the joke. Captain Rolando shuffled some papers.

'That's all from me,' he said, standing up. 'Obviously it goes without saying that this is a working ship, it can be dangerous, especially when we get into open water. We have guests who are expecting good service and a holiday of a lifetime, regardless of this all being filmed for your TV show. I'm the captain of this ship and what I say goes, my word is final. I don't expect chit-chat and in-fighting. I expect you all to work together, as a crew. Do that and we'll be fine. You never know, you might actually enjoy yourselves.'

A few murmured agreements followed. Ed was still giving them the thumbs up.

'Alright then,' said Rolando. 'Let's start about our duties – stewards on cleaning and tidying before the guests arrive. Deckhands, I want an inventory of all the equipment and stock.'

He slithered around Howie, not meeting the actor's eye. As he headed for the narrow staircase that reached up to the deck, a thought struck Howie.

'Hey, wait a minute,' he said. 'Who's doing all the cooking?'

'Our last crew member will be the chef,' said Roland. 'Matthias Kreutz, he's a football player.'

'Soccer?' Howie wrinkled his nose. 'What does a soccer player know about cooking? I'd be surprised if he could *find* the kitchen let alone cook anything in it.'

'And you're Michelin starred yourself then?' Marjorie snapped.

'No,' said Howie. 'But I'm pretty sure the guests who are renting out this tub won't settle for a grilled cheese and Gatorade every night, will they?'

Marjorie had no answer to that. Howie could see how mad it was making her. He quietly congratulated himself on a job well done.

'It'll be fine,' said Ed, stepping in front of Geri's camera.

Ben lifted his mic and clattered it off the low ceiling of the galley. He mouthed an apology, the closest either of the film crew had come to speaking.

'You keep saying that but I'm yet to be convinced,' said Howie. 'You haven't shown any evidence that *anything* will work out once we get out there into the ocean. The deckhands know nothing, the stewards are as welcoming as a nest of vipers and the chef isn't even here!'

'That's what makes this such a great TV show!' Ed beamed. 'Drama, darling, drama. The punters will lap up all of this adversity, they'll be rooting for you to get through it all. In fact, I loved that rant, Howie. Can you do it again for the camera?'

Ed nodded to Geri who shouldered her kit again. Howie slumped against the wall. This was what he had been dreading since he agreed to do the show. Revelling in his misery, that was the prerogative of viewers of this kind of programme. But they hadn't even left the port yet. How was he going to survive a fortnight of this?

Chapter 4

'I thought my bed-making days were over.'

Cassandra wrestled with the huge sheet for the fifteenth time in as many minutes.

'My mam always changed the beds on a Sunday. I used to hate it. You'd break your back just trying to flip the mattress over.'

'It's only as hard as you make it,' said Marjorie. 'Talking endlessly doesn't help. And wait until you have kids, then it's up in the middle of the night to change sheets, pillows and anything else they've been sick on.'

The thought scared Cassandra. She was still young, or so she kept being told. Among the celebrity crew of *The Regal Secret* she was certainly the youngest. Thirty, however, was rapidly approaching. She was now counting down to the big three-oh in months rather than years. And with that impending birthday came the awful internal angst – shouldn't she have a 'proper' job by now? A partner? Kids? A mortgage? She steeled herself for the inevitable questions that followed and tried to remind herself that there was no checklist you had to follow for life. Most people were just making it up as they went along.

'You don't have a boyfriend then?' asked Marjorie, mopping the floor.

'No,' said Cassandra. Thinking she could ask Marjorie the same but had the good grace not to.

'Girlfriend then?'

'No,' she said again. 'Just me and my followers.'

'That's not really a family is it?'

'I never said it was. There's my mam and dad, I'm still close to them. I have a brother but I don't see much of him.'

'How come?'

Marjorie was like a shark, Cassandra had decided. The first hint of a sniff of blood and she was circling.

'We just don't get on. We're different kinds of people. It happens. He's an engineer, a good one too. He's been all over the world working on projects that help people out. Bridges, dams, you name it. And I—'

'Flog cheap make-up on the internet.'

Cassandra was used to the barbs. For every positive comment and follower she had, there were a thousand hostile ones. Everything from her weight, eye-colour, waist size and figure had been dissected and analysed by the internet. They had even counted the freckles across her nose and decided, of course, that there were too many. Until the tide turned and instead the internet decided she had no freckles in real life and they were all drawn in by AI.

Criticism for how she made a living was all too commonplace as well. She had learned to adapt and control her temper in situations like this. She was, after all, making good money, being her own boss and had nothing to feel ashamed about. She was always scrupulously careful about the partnerships she took – no dodgy weight loss tea or cosmetic surgery clinics. She wanted her content to be down to earth and funny. Sure she posted pics with freebies and at glamorous locations, but she always tagged them as ads, and made sure to also post the pics where she was at home alone in her PJs on an evening scrolling and wondering what to make for dinner like everyone else.

There was, however, something inherently nasty in Marjorie's tone. For a woman who had announced herself to the group as Australia's 'premier alternative thinker', she seemed ludicrously out of touch and closed minded. In a time of heightened sensitivities, Cassandra had learned that a shouting match was rarely the way to go. But she wasn't going to be trampled over for the sake of keeping her voice down.

'Listen,' she said, hands on her hips. 'We've got to work together here, and in pretty close quarters too. So if you've got a problem with what I do and who I am, then let's get it out in the open right now, okay babe?'

Marjorie didn't look up from her mopping. She took long, lazy strides across the gleaming wooden floor.

'Nothing then?' asked Cassandra. 'Are we all good?'

'Sure,' Marjorie shrugged. 'Touched a nerve there, I think.'

She had spoken under her breath but it was loud enough for Cassandra to hear. She thought about kicking off again. There was something about Marjorie that rubbed her up the wrong way. As she was about to launch into another tirade, the blazing sunlight from beyond the guest suite caught the face of her Rolex. She blinked and smiled. What did it matter what Marjorie and her out of touch readers thought of her. She was proud of who she was. And that was all that mattered.

'Attention all crew,' Captain Rolando's voice crackled over the walkie-talkies they'd all been given. 'All crew to the harbourfront immediately. Our guests are about to arrive.'

There was a short burst of static and the line went dead. Cassandra finished making the bed as Marjorie cleared up. She caught sight of herself in a full-length mirror as she approached the door. She stopped. There, in front of her, was a 'normal' Cassandra Troy, whatever normal meant anyway. No hair extensions (her stylist had said the saltwater would ruin them), no lashes, no lavish make-up nor fabulous outfit. It had been a long time since she had seen herself like this. And there she was – just a young woman making a TV show, earning a living.

She thought about taking a quick picture for her social media. The phone was in her hand but she stopped at the last moment.

For all of her confidence, for all of her thick skin, for all of her courage to stand up to Marjorie and the million others who hid behind keyboards, Cassandra was still afraid. She knew in this business you were only as good as your last show. She locked her phone and put it back in her pocket. She fixed her hair and left Marjorie behind, heading into the sunshine.

The others were on the dockside already waiting. Captain Rolando was at the head of the line. Kelvin the MP was next to him, shoulders bobbing up and down like he was out of breath. Howie was beside him, huge sweat patches under his arms and down his back. Ed was there too, dancing about the harbourfront. Geri the camerawoman was scanning the line back and forth while her companion Ben tinkered with his sound equipment.

Cassandra slipped down the gangway and onto the dock. She lined up beside Howie who threw a flustered glance at her.

'What's the matter with you?' he asked.

The question caught Cassandra a little off guard.

'Nothing,' she said. 'Why? What makes you think there's something the matter?'

'Your face,' he grunted.

'My face? What about my face?'

'You're not smiling like you're selling something.'

Cassandra hadn't realised. She quickly rectified that.

'Give over, chuck,' she said. 'I'm *always* smiling.'

'You are now,' he said. 'That was the first time I've not seen you with a smile.'

'And why would that mean something was wrong? Do I have to smile *all* of the time just to keep you pleased?'

'Here we go,' he droned. 'Just forget I said anything.'

He looked away, huffing again. Cassandra thought he was actually quite sweet, despite the temper. A complete diva of course, he was used to people doing what he asked of them. Most actors were like that, in her experience. No matter how old or young. She supposed it was the unique world they lived in, playing pretend all of the time. Take that away and what did they have?

She imagined it was quite an odd existence. She was about to thank him for his concern when Marjorie bounded down the gangway and stood to attention beside her.

'Not late, am I?' she asked, straightening her collar.

'Right on time, Marjorie,' said Cassandra. 'You'll make a sailor yet.'

A large, sleek limo appeared at the end of the street. It drove along the dockside and came to a halt just in front of them, their reflections appearing in the tinted windows. The driver got out and opened the rear doors. Cassandra held her breath. She wasn't sure who would be guests on an excursion like this. Neither her agent nor the production company had given them any idea in advance.

Howie looked equally in the dark. Cindy, his agent, barely contacted him from one year to the next unless a fat royalty cheque landed – something which happened rarely these days.

An impossibly tall woman was the first to climb out of the limo. Her legs were so long they appeared well before the rest of her.

She stepped onto the harbourside. Her eyes were hidden behind designer sunglasses, dark hair tied back in a neat bun behind her pale, expressionless face. She carried an enormous tablet in one arm and looked about the dock the same way a bodyguard would. When she was satisfied, she took three long, swift strides towards Captain Rolando who could only stand in her shadow and look.

'Good grief,' whispered Marjorie. 'I don't think the beds are going to fit this one.'

Cassandra muffled a laugh. She nudged Howie in the side.

'I bet you've never seen a woman as tall as that, eh babe?'

Howie puckered his lips. 'I've had too many years hanging out with Hollywood models,' he said. 'Six foot women aren't just common, they're the norm.'

'No talking in the ranks,' Captain Rolando hissed.

The skipper shook the woman's hand and Howie snapped back to attention. Cassandra did the same. After an all too brief exchange, Rolando turned to the gathered crew.

'Okay,' he said. 'Ms Sachiko is the agent for the passengers. She's their translator, their executor, everything and anything they want, it goes through her. And vice versa.'

Howie looked at the tall woman standing a few yards away. She was staring out at the harbour. The sun glinted off her expensive sunglasses.

'Just who exactly are these guests?' he asked, losing patience in a hurry. 'And why do we have to go through The Terminator here if we want to speak to them?'

Ben and Geri were frantically moving their camera and boom mic back and forth to catch the exchange. They settled on the agent who had just made her dramatic entrance.

'Howard Temple,' said Ms Sachiko, her voice surprisingly high. 'Actor and part-time drunk. Two divorces, three children, all of them under twenty-five years old. You're here to pay for their college tuition, which is currently red-lining your dwindling savings.'

Howie's mouth was hanging open. Ms Sachiko turned her anonymous gaze towards him. She walked over, everyone else down the line of the crew taking a step back. She towered over the actor, her face expressionless yet oozing a powerful intimidation, like a great white shark.

'My clients have paid a lot of money for this excursion,' she said. 'They employ me to make sure everything goes according to the schedule and plan, regardless of the television show you are so desperately bleeding of its budget with your fee.'

'You know how much he's getting paid?' asked Cassandra.

'I do,' Ms Sachiko said.

'What is it then?'

'I'd rather you didn't share,' said Howie, feebly.

He stared at his reflection in her sunglasses. He looked pathetic, shrivelled. She had made her point. He didn't really want to be in her company any longer.

'My clients are tired from their journey,' she said, turning back towards the limo. 'They are all cruise aficionados, with the highest standards. Having paid an eye-watering sum to enter the ballot to secure these exclusive tickets, they will be expecting top-tier service. And right now, they wish to board, have their cases unpacked and dine by no later than eight p.m. They want to watch the sunset at sea. I take it that won't be a problem, captain?'

Rolando clicked his heels. He saluted. 'It will not, Signora,' he said. 'My crew are a little rough around the edges but they'll look after the guests immaculately. You have my guarantee.'

If Ms Sachiko was impressed, or indeed convinced, she showed no sign of it. Instead she stood to the side of the open door of the limo. Speaking so fast neither Howie nor Cassandra could make out what she said, the guests began to disembark.

An elderly couple were the next out of the limo, pale white limbs almost as bleached as the stone of the harbourside. They looked immediately out of place in the world of luxury yachts and TV shows. They stood awkwardly in Ms Sachiko's shadow.

'Mr Kirkby, and Mrs Martha, Hofstede,' said the agent. 'Celebrating their ruby wedding anniversary with this competition win.'

'Howdy,' said Kirkby Hofstede, his accent thick Oklahoman. 'Pleasure to meet you all.'

He shook the skipper's hand then made his way down the line of the crew. He stopped at Howie.

'Aren't you . . . ' He clicked his fingers.

'Yes,' said Howie with a laboured sigh.

'You're that Stallone fella.'

'What?'

'That's not Stallone,' said Martha Hofstede. 'He used to be a bodybuilder, Kirkby.'

'This is him,' said Kirkby, enthusiastically.

'I'm not Stallone,' said Howie, swallowing some anger along with his pride.

Kirkby tilted his sunglasses up and placed them on his bald, wrinkly forehead.

'Shoot,' he said. 'Neither you are.'

They made their way up the gangplank, Howie spitting bullets.

'Mr Arakawa Shig,' announced Ms Sachiko. 'A winner from Japan, he's very much looking forward to seeing the Mediterranean.'

A neat man in an expensive suit emerged next from the limo. He looked a little perplexed, quite possibly due to the sight of such an unlikely looking crew. He bowed every time he was introduced to one of the line-up then made his way onto the yacht without fuss.

'And finally, Despoina and Thekla Kontoglou,' said Ms Sachiko. 'Sister entrepreneurs from Crete, delighted to have won the European part of the competition.'

The Greek sisters had barely set foot on the dockside when they raced over towards Howie.

'Howieeeeee Temple!' they both screamed.

Completely ignoring the rest of the crew, they batted and fanned themselves, phones in hand, desperate for a picture. Admirers, it seemed.

'Ladies, a pleasure, do please head on board,' he said, trying to remain polite.

They ignored his pleas, pecking him on the cheek and posing for pictures. They giggled like schoolgirls, not the forty-something women they were. Their compliments and excitement, at least that's what Howie hoped it was, rattled back and forth across him like machine-gun fire. Only when Ms Sachiko politely cleared her throat did they leave him alone, heading up the gangway, blowing kisses back at him.

'You're in a world of pain now, chuck,' said Cassandra to him.

'Ladies, if you'd like to show our guests to their quarters. Our deckhands will collect the luggage,' said Captain Rolando.

Cassandra smiled and headed up the gangway after the guests, Marjorie in tow. Howie watched them go. Ms Sachiko stepped in front of him.

'The luggage is in the trunk of the limousine,' she said. 'Have it all brought on board at once.'

Before Howie could answer her back, she was off up the gangway too.

'She's going to be trouble,' he said to Kelvin, who was hovering about him. 'I've got a bad feeling about her.'

'Come along old chap, you've only just met her.'

'I am a good judge of character,' he said. 'And less of this "old chap" nonsense. We're not on a punt sipping tea and eating crumpets here.'

Kelvin nodded. They walked around the back of the limo and opened the door. The driver was hanging around, smoking a little roll-up cigarette.

'I hope you've both been working out,' he cackled.

Howie looked at the bags all piled up in the trunk. 'That's not so bad,' he said, pointing. 'You should see what my ex used to take on a weekend away to the Hamptons.'

'Oh yeah?'

The driver nodded over their shoulders. Two more limos were pulling up behind them. They stopped as Howie and Kelvin watched carefully, confused. The drivers climbed out and opened the doors to the cabins and the trunks. Inside they were jam packed full of bags, suitcases and more luggage.

'I told you, Hollywood,' laughed the first driver. 'I hope you've been eating your spinach.'

Chapter 5

The Ligurian Sea was quiet at this time of night. Nestled in the arc of the Italian coastline that led to France, Howie was enjoying the tranquillity of the place. The hustle of civilization felt very far away here. The twinkling lights of the fishing villages and towns looked tiny in the darkness as he stared out from the top deck of the yacht.

His back was aching. Every joint and muscle felt like it was on fire. The luggage had weighed even more than it looked and it seemed endless. As a younger man, he probably would have scoffed at the challenge. He had been, in his prime, something of a pin-up. Shredded abs and biceps that would put Hercules to shame. That was a long time ago now. Marriage, children and dwindling box office returns matched only by his dwindling bank balance had put pay to things like personal trainers. That, plus he'd had enough years of eating egg white omelettes and ghastly green smoothies to be camera-ready. When the roles stopped coming, he filled the gap with fine dining and even finer wines. He was on the wrong side of his mid-fifties now. The only magazine covers he'd be gracing would be for retirement villages. If the price was right he'd always consider it.

Even the tips of his fingers hurt. He rubbed them, stared at them, tried to make it stop but he had to accept that he was unaccustomed to hard graft these days. At least everyone else was as exhausted as him. His crewmates were all in bed. Even after they'd heaved all the luggage on board the evening's labours hadn't been over. Serving dinner had proved another ordeal. He'd just about managed to stave off the Kontoglou sisters throughout dinner, throwing Kelvin into the lion's den instead to be their waiter. It wasn't that Howie was unappreciative of fandom. There was precious little of it about these days. But the prospect of being hounded, kissed, pinched and pecked by those two for the next fortnight had put him off his own meagre dinner entirely. He thought he was long past his days of being treated like a piece of meat – he was more gristle than prime rib these days, after all, he thought – but it seemed no one had told that to the Kontoglou sisters.

Against all odds, the ship had left the harbour on schedule and sailed into the deeper waters off the coast. This would be their home for the next week while filming took place. They'd stop in Monaco, pick up another group of guests and sail back to Livorno. Then that would be that. Simple. Ed would have his TV show, Howie would get his pay cheque and all would be okay with the world. For a little while at least.

He let out a heavy sigh and sank his head. He felt old and tired. And it wasn't just from the workout with the cases and bags. Life had been weighing heavily on his shoulders of late. How had it all come to this? There had been a time when his wildest fantasies came true on a minute-by-minute basis. Money, women, parties, his pick of Hollywood roles, you name it. That was just a Tuesday for Howie Temple.

Now here he was, out at sea, staring at the lights of the Italian coastline. It should have felt like a magical moment, if it wasn't for the fact that his absurd uniform made it impossible to forget he wasn't on holiday, and that he was playing bosun on a superyacht for some low-budget reality show. There were harder ways of making a living though, he knew that. He knew countless people would give their eye teeth to swap their day's labour for this gig. He tried to hold on to that idea as much as he could. It was a hard pill to swallow though. Especially when he had once thought the days of plenty would never end.

At least it was quiet up here. Ben and Geri had vanished, no doubt filming something more interesting than him lamenting his misspent youth. For a man who had been in front of the camera for a large chunk of his life, he was already finding the whole twenty-four-seven camera thing quite intrusive. Even if he hadn't made it through twenty-four hours yet. And those two – silent, ever watchful – kind of gave him the creeps. Ed had told the celebs, in their opening briefing, that they wouldn't be talking to them and that everyone was to 'pretend they weren't there', which was easier said than done when you were squeezing past them in the crew corridor made for smaller men than him. He glanced at his watch. This was set to be a very slow fortnight.

'Nothing lasts forever,' he said quietly.

His mother had told him that once long ago, on a call one night close to Christmas when he was in his heyday. Howie couldn't remember the year. He probably didn't even know at the time. The days and months and even years had sped by in a whirl and at the height of his fame, even he had started to realise stardom could be like a car with no brakes. In a fit of fear and frustration he had called his mother back in Saskatchewan, hoping for some sage advice. She had offered him what, at the time, he'd deemed were nothing but hackneyed clichés. All it had done was remind him why he'd hitchhiked south to Hollywood as a teenager. There had been precious little for him at home and there still wasn't. He'd hung up that night and gone out, to some party or nightclub. He never spoke to his mother again. Three days later she passed away.

Now here he was, thinking about all of that again and how maybe his mother was wiser than he'd credited. But he'd never been one for looking back. Life, Howie had concluded, if you looked at it the wrong way, was nothing more than one bad memory after another. He always preferred to look to the future. But now he was aware he had far more past than he would have future. Was it any wonder he was so jaded?

'Oh, what are you doing here?'

He looked up as Cassandra stepped out to join him on the small deck at the very top of *The Regal Secret*. He shook his head. 'Couldn't sleep,' he said. 'I'm in too much pain.'

'Do you want a tablet or something?' she asked, leaning on the rail beside him.

'I'm okay,' he said.

'My mam swears by these.' She unzipped the waistpack that hung low on her hips. 'She takes them when my dad gives her a headache from all his shouting at the TV.'

She handed him the foil packet. There had been a time in Howie's life where he'd take anything a gorgeous woman offered him. Not now. *How times changed*, he thought sadly.

'I'm good,' he said. 'I've gone off painkillers, ever since the nineties.'

'That sounds like the opening of a tale of debauchery and mischief if I ever heard one, babe,' she said.

'Not really,' he said. 'I was once at a Haddaway gig in Cancun and I had a thumping headache following a three day bender. I decided rather than do the hair of the dog, again, I'd go to a pharmacy and get some painkillers. I don't know what was in those things but I don't remember the rest of the week and when I came around, I'd bought a timeshare and three Lucha Libre wrestling promotions.'

'Like I said,' she laughed. 'Mischief.'

'Sadly it's a whole lot more than that for many people I know. I've lost many a dear friend to the siren sleep of an opioid. They think because it's "medicine" it's better than doing illegal drugs. But it's just as slippery a slope. Take it from someone who's looked over the edge. The lesson of the story, my dear, is to always know what you're putting into your body. What are you doing up here anyway?'

'Couldn't sleep either,' she said. 'Marjorie is a snorer.'

'She does strike one as the kind of person who can't ever keep quiet – even in sleep,' he said, smiling a little. 'I can always tell.'

'And how does that work?' she asked, sceptical.

'When you've had two wives who snored from dusk until dawn, not to mention a brood of kids who refused to go to bed any earlier than midnight, you get a sixth sense for these kinds of things.'

'I'll bet,' she said. 'I live on my own. It's fabulous.'

'I agree, I've re-embraced the bachelor life in my golden years,' he said. 'Although Thanksgiving and Christmas can be a bit quiet.'

'I go to my parents for that,' said Cassandra, replacing her tablets. 'Christmas at least. We don't do Thanksgiving where I'm from. But we have one of those big raucous Christmases – the more the merrier. If you're ever in the UK over the holidays, consider yourself invited. Have you ever been to Liverpool?'

Howie laughed. He shook his head. 'No, can't say I have,' he said.

'You'll love it,' she said. 'Tell you what – let's make this happen. I'll text my mam just now and tell her. She'll be thrilled.'

'If you insist.'

He didn't have the heart to tell her he was only being polite. Fortunately December was a very long time away. She'd forget, hopefully.

Cassandra drew her phone and began tapping away.

'Is that the picture of us from earlier?' he asked, glancing over at the screen.

'The one on the plane? Yes!' she said. 'Couple of hundred thousand likes and shares already. Can't complain about that, even if you looked like you'd been pulled through a hedge backwards.'

'Yes, not my finest moment,' he said. 'Lowering the tone of your reel.'

'I'm only joshing you, babe,' she said. 'You looked great. A lot of comments say that actually, mostly middle-aged women.'

'That's my demographic, huh?'

'I guess.' She shrugged. 'I'll take a look at the stats later, signal is non-existent out here, no roaming or anything.'

'I'm not sure I know what any of that means.'

'I'm cut off until I get decent Wi-Fi,' she said. 'Must be because we're in open sea.'

'I'm sorry about earlier, by the way,' he said.

Cassandra looked up from her phone. 'Sorry about what?'

'My behaviour,' he said. 'Saying we should ignore each other off-camera. I'm not usually so rude. I was considered charming once. I don't know, it's been a rough couple of days, weeks even. You're a hard worker, you're just doing your job – and if that means photos and "likes" and all that hashtag stuff, then that's fine by me. I've done sillier stuff in the name of my work. You don't need some middle-aged has-been like me telling you what's right and wrong.'

She smiled brighter now. 'You old smoothie,' she said. 'Don't worry about it, chuck. Happens all the time. I'm an easy target for columnists and keyboard warriors. Anyway, you can't help being a moaning old git.'

'A moaning old what?'

She laughed. So did he. He felt better, a little more positive. Even the pain in his fingers seemed to ease a little.

'Tell you what,' she said. 'Why don't we take another picture, a follow-up. The punters will love that. And you can try to smile for this one.'

'Do I have a choice?' he asked.

'No,' she said, lifting her phone. 'Come on. Say cheese.'

But Howie didn't get the chance. There was shouting from somewhere below them. At first he thought he was hearing things – sound carrying across the water from another boat. But Cassandra looked puzzled too.

'Did you hear something?' she asked.

'I thought so,' he said. 'Did you?'

Another shout, this time closer. And definitely from their boat. The sound of raised voices carried up from the furthest level below them. The shouting grew louder until two shadows appeared, stretched out across the deck. Captain Rolando and Ed were in the middle of an argument, pointing and waving their hands at each other. Howie and Cassandra instinctively ducked down a little, watching from between the railings.

'What's going on?' she whispered.

'I don't know,' he said. 'I can't make out what they're saying.'

'They're fighting.'

'I can tell that.' He rolled his eyes.

'What could they be fighting about? We've only been at sea for a few hours.'

Ed and Rolando continued to argue. Their voices were getting more aggressive and their actions more animated but still the night sky seemed to swallow their words. Ed shook his head and that seemed to kick the skipper on. He grabbed the director by the lapels of his shirt and shook him. Ed freed himself and pointed straight in Rolando's face. The captain shouted something before finally walking away.

Ed remained on the deck for a moment. He flattened his hair back and fixed his shirt collar. Then he turned back and stared upwards. Cassandra and Howie shimmied away from the railing as quickly and quietly as they could.

'Do you think he saw us?' she whispered after a minute or two had passed.

'I don't know,' he said. 'I don't think so.'

'You should look down and see if he's still there.'

'Why me?'

'Because you're the man.'

'That's unbelievably sexist,' he said. 'And if even *I* think that's the case then it must be, as I'm as out of touch with modern protocol as you can be.'

'Just take a look.'

Howie grunted. He rounded on his knees, feeling the sting of agony throughout his body. Slowly, he raised his head above the parapet and stared down.

'He's gone,' he said.

Cassandra stood up. She leaned a little over the edge to see.

'He must have gone back inside,' she said. 'What do you think that was all about?'

'I have no idea.' Howie shrugged his shoulders. 'Could be anything, right? Ed is the man in charge, maybe he's had enough of the conditions we're all living in below deck. Or maybe he's encouraging it – thinking it'll fray our nerves and make his show that bit more edgy.'

'He didn't look like he was just asking him a favour,' Cassandra ventured. 'Although Captain Rolando looked pretty angry too, don't you think?'

'He's Italian.'

'What's that supposed to mean?'

'They're passionate, aren't they?' he said. 'Known for their emotions. They're very vocal, very exaggerated with their actions. For all we know he was just wishing Ed a good night.'

'Now who's being stereotypical?' Cassandra raised her eyebrows at Howie. 'You really think he was just wishing him a *buona notte*?' she asked.

'No, absolutely not.' He folded his arms. 'But I doubt it was anything serious, all the same. I've been on enough film sets and location shoots to know when two people are arguing over something dumb. Believe me, it happens every five minutes in this industry. By morning they'll have forgotten all about it and Ed will be back to his usual, charming self.'

'You don't like him, do you?' she asked with a smirk.

'Cassandra, I don't like *anyone*,' Howie said flatly. 'I'm too old, in too much pain and too tired to give a rat's backside about anyone or anything.'

'Nicely put,' she nodded. 'You still want this photo?'

Howie thought about saying no. Right now he just wanted to climb into his tiny little bunk, pull the blanket over his head and go to sleep.

'Come on, it'll only take a second,' she said.

'If you promise to let me go to bed afterwards,' he said. 'Then fine, hurry up.'

Cassandra clapped her hands. She sidled up to him, put an arm about his big shoulders, ran her tongue over her clean teeth and smiled. As she pressed the shutter button, a terrible scream echoed in the night.

The phone flash went off and they were both blinded for a moment. Howie blinked his eyes clear and looked about the upper deck.

'What the hell was that?' he asked.

'I don't know,' said Cassandra, doing the same. 'But it didn't sound good.'

Without thinking, Howie galloped off down the stairs. Cassandra was close behind him. They hopped the steps two at a time and skidded to a halt.

'Where did it come from?' Cassandra asked, realising they had no idea where they were running to. She looked about the deserted deck.

'Well no-one's gone overboard by the looks of things,' Howie said, peering over the rail at the quiet sea. 'It must be someone below deck.' Temple opened one of the narrow doorways into the quiet interior.

It was just as deserted as the deck. The pair tried a small lounge off the main passageway – empty. Another door revealed only a tiny room packed with heaped piles of clean linens. But Cassandra was a woman on a mission. She pushed Howie down the corridor, checking storage cubicles and other small rooms packed with camera gear. They hurried on and soon approached the bridge.

'That scream sounded too near to be from the lower deck. Rolando must have heard it,' Howie said, trying the door. Locked. He knocked on it, hard. 'Rolando?' he shouted. 'Are you in there? Is everything alright?'

'Force it open,' Cassandra said, the note of panic in her voice now growing.

Howie wrestled with the handle.

'Come on, Howie. Kick it down.'

'What? I can't do that!' he shouted. 'You can't just kick doors down, there's probably a reason it's locked.'

'He could be in trouble in there.'

'Trouble? From what?'

'Just open it Howie, hurry up.'

He looked the door to the bridge up and down. Taking a step back, he lined himself up. It had been years since he'd attempted this kind of stunt. Running as fast as he could, he shouldered the door. It gave way with remarkable ease and Howie tumbled through. He clattered onto the floor, every fibre of his body now writhing in agony. Cassandra rushed over to him and stopped. She let out a scream of her own, clapping her hand to her mouth.

Howie rolled over, pulling himself up with difficulty. When he was on his feet, he looked over at Cassandra and then to Rolando. The skipper was sitting upright in his command chair, half turned towards them, his face blank, eyes vacant. Howie thought he was drunk at first. Then he noticed the large kitchen knife sticking out of his back.

'Good god,' he breathed.

'Hi there,' came a voice from behind them.

Howie and Cassandra turned around quickly, terrified. A tall, tanned, handsome stranger was standing in the wreckage of the doorway. Heavy bags were slung over his broad shoulders, a pleasant and easy smile on his face.

'I'm Matthias,' he said, offering his hand. 'Nice to meet you. Is he alright?' He nodded over at Rolando sitting bolt upright in the captain's chair.

'No,' said Howie, feeling the colour draining from his own face. 'Quite the opposite. He's dead.'

Chapter 6

'Would you please stop pacing about like that, you'll wear a hole in the precious wooden floor.'

Howie rubbed his temples, trying to clear the headache that had formed almost as soon as he'd shouldered the door open. Cassandra was walking back and forth in front of him, biting her nails, her spare hand planted on her hip. The rest of the crew had been gathered for an emergency meeting in the galley. Ed had summoned them there, broken the news in a rather perfunctory way then immediately excused himself. A queasy combination of horror and bafflement had settled over the gathered team. Everyone was silent, either with shock or fatigue. Everyone except Matthias.

The former footballer seemed strangely cheerful. He lounged lazily in the corner, trying to start conversations between taking long gulps from an energy drink, his fifth can, Howie had noticed. They were all waiting for Ed to reappear. Howie felt sick. His headache was bordering on a migraine now, his vision blurring and pulsing. The tilt and roll of the ship hadn't been helping. And Cassandra's pacing was making him feel worse.

'Please, Cassandra, just sit down,' he said.

'Sit down? How can I sit down?' she yelped. 'Poor Rolando is dead. We're out in the middle of nowhere at night, Ed has bailed and you're telling me to calm down. What's there to be calm about?'

'Getting upset about it isn't going to do anyone any good,' said Marjorie.

'Upset? Upset? Are you serious?' Cassandra drew her an angry stare. 'That poor man has lost his life up there. How do you think his family is going to feel when they find out? Eh? I think they'll be more than upset.'

'Not our problem,' Marjorie sniffed. 'We're here to do a job not get caught up in some vendetta. Although I imagine the show's been scuppered now. We probably won't get paid a penny.'

'Unbelievable,' said Cassandra, clapping her hands to her side. 'Truly unbelievable.'

'It's just shock,' said Matthias. 'Everyone is in shock. You all knew him, yes?'

Nobody answered. No one wanted to be the first to say they'd only met Captain Rolando a matter of hours before him. Or that none of them knew if Rolando was his first or last name.

'Longer than you anyway,' sniffed Marjorie. 'Nice to see you've decided to join us at last. You're some sort of sportsman I take it?'

'Footballer.' He leaned forward and offered her a hand. 'Matthias Kreutz, I just retired.'

'Were you any good?'

'I'll say,' said Kelvin. For a moment, he seemed to forget where he was, a faraway look in his eyes.

'Yes, Mr Kreutz here gave England a good thrashing about a decade ago at the European Championships. He scored a hat-trick against our boys, if memory serves.'

'Ah yes,' said Matthias, smiling broadly and revealing a set of pristine teeth. 'What an evening that was. Reminded me of why I started playing in the first place. A hundred thousand fans all chanting your name, scoring against your rivals. The stuff dreams are made of.'

'Dreams for you, maybe, not all of us,' said Marjorie.

'My dad lost a fortune that night,' said Cassandra, coming to a stop. 'He thought you lot would crumble under the pressure from England.'

Matthias grinned wolfishly. He sat forward and steepled his fingers.

'Fräulein, we *never* crumble under pressure. From England, Brazil, or anybody else,' he said.

'Alright, enough,' said Howie. 'I didn't sign up to listen to you all blab on about soccer. I get enough of that at home from my kids.'

'Not quite ice hockey, is it?' Kelvin ventured.

'It's not,' said the actor. 'And where I'm from, it's just called hockey.'

That seemed to put the MP back into his reverie. He shrank back into his corner of the galley.

Cassandra finally sat down. 'Bloody awful all of this,' she said. 'I mean, who could do something like that?'

'How do you know anyone did anything?' asked Marjorie.

'He had a kitchen knife sticking out of his back, Marjorie,' snapped Cassandra. 'I don't think he put it there himself, did he?'

'And that reminds me, where were *you* when all of this was happening, eh?'

'What?'

'You heard me!'

'Ladies, please.' Kelvin tried to calm them down.

'Oh shut up you,' Marjorie barked. 'What would you know about anything? You're just a fat-cat politician.'

'I do not see how this is helping,' said Matthias.

'And you know even less!' Marjorie rounded on the footballer.

'Don't talk to him like that!' Cassandra shouted. 'You don't know anything about him!'

'And you do, do you?'

'What's that supposed to mean?'

'Good god! What the hell is going on here then?'

Ed thumped back down the stairs into the galley. Howie was relieved to see him without his camera crew in tow. He looked pale. But there was still that same, annoying energy about him.

'Sorry about that. Touch of seasickness. Now what's all the shouting about?' he asked.

The room fell silent again. He looked about and let his gaze drop on Howie.

'Come on, Mr Temple. You must have been in tighter spots than this?' he asked.

'You've got to be kidding, right?' asked Howie. 'The captain of this ship is dead, murdered it would seem. How do you want us to behave? Post a selfie? Break out Twister, what?'

That drew a little muffled laugh from Cassandra beside him. Ed didn't see the funny side.

'Oh, I'm sorry Howie, I didn't realise expecting a bit of professionalism from an actor of your experience was asking too much,' he said sarcastically. 'Thank for being as useless as the rest of these snowflakes.'

'Don't start on me, Ed,' said Howie, feeling a rush of anger. 'You're meant to be running this shambles and we've been stuck down here in the middle of the night with no clue as to what's going on. How the hell do you want us to react? The man's dead.'

'He's right,' said Cassandra, backing him up.

'Hear, hear,' said Marjorie, much to Howie's surprise.

'We really could be doing with knowing what's going on, Edward,' said Kelvin.

Ed's mood immediately changed. He could sense the room was turning against him. His flashy smile returned.

'Of course, of course,' he said, trying to placate the celebrity crew. 'What am I thinking? It's been a nasty shock for us all. Very sad, very sad indeed. He was a lovely man.'

'He was, and he's dead,' said Howie.

The words seemed to linger in the thick air of the galley. All of the crew bowed their heads. It felt like the realisation of what had happened had only just set in. The giddy worry and shock had worn off. Now there was nothing but the grim reality of what faced them.

'Do the passengers know?' asked Cassandra.

'No,' said Ed.

'Why not?' asked Howie.

'They're asleep.' He shrugged again. 'I didn't think we should be waking them up to tell them something like this.'

'Bloody hell,' said Kelvin, puffing out his cheeks. 'I'm not sure that's such a good idea, Edward. They have a right to know.'

'Of course they do,' said the director. 'But Rolando won't be any less dead come the morning. We can break it to them gently when you serve them breakfast.'

'Hold on,' said Howie, waving his hands about. 'Serving them breakfast? You can't be serious. A man has been murdered here. The police need to get here as soon as possible, or rather we need to get to the police as soon as possible. We need to turn back, immediately.'

'We can't do that,' Kelvin offered. 'The bridge is a crime scene!'

'It's all been taken care of.' Ed palmed him off. 'I've locked up everything upstairs, put the door back on its hinges, everything is secure, ready for the cops when they get here.'

'And when will that be?' asked Matthias, peering out of a porthole hoping to see blue lights cutting through the dark night.

'That's the snag. I've not been able to contact them. No reception out here and dear Rolando hadn't had chance to show me the tech on the bridge. I'm sure we can work it out between us or if not, we can get a message out via a passing boat tomorrow I'm sure. The police will be with us by the afternoon at the very latest,' said Ed.

If the galley had been laced with despair before, it was now positively flooded. Everyone rolled their eyes.

'Tomorrow afternoon?' asked Howie. 'That's hours away.'

'I know how time works,' said Ed. 'I can't raise them myself, like I said I have no signal on my mobile. None of you will either. So we have to wait until I can work out how to use the ship's radio or the satellite phone. Although Rolando told me there's some problem with the signal on that too, something about tides and magnetic fields, I don't know.'

'This might sound like stating the obvious, but can't we just drive the yacht back to port without, you know, disturbing the captain?' asked Cassandra.

'Volunteering to "drive" this ship, are we?' Marjorie hissed at her.

'What's that supposed to mean?'

'It means that firstly, one doesn't "drive' a ship, you pilot it, steer it, sail it; practically anything other than drive it, as you so ineloquently put it,' said Marjorie, enjoying her sneering. 'And if you think you can navigate currents, tides, the complicated computer systems and propulsion units it takes to move something like this, then please be my guest. I'll start inflating the life jackets for when we inevitably sink.'

'I'm just thinking out loud, okay?' Cassandra batted back. 'I don't hear you coming up with any suggestions.'

'Marjorie is right,' said Ed. 'You can't just stick this thing into first gear and put your foot to the floor. That and I don't much relish having to explain to its Saudi owners that we moved it, uninsured, ill-educated and under-staffed. Our insurance premiums would be blown to bits.'

'Surely a dead body won't be looked on kindly by your insurers, either?' Kelvin asked.

'Oh no, they're used to that sort of thing. A superyacht is far more valuable than a human life, at least in the eyes of any loss adjuster.'

'Unbelicvable,' Howie said. 'Truly unbelievable. I've been part of some two-bit operations in my time but this really takes the biscuit. We've got a dead captain with a knife in his back, a group of useless celebrity morons who don't know their asses from their elbows and a director who needs to learn how to work a ham radio. What's next? Jaws chomping at the back of the boat? An iceberg, perhaps?'

He was breathing heavily. The sweat was beading on his forehead and he was starting to feel a little woozy. Cassandra rubbed his arm.

'Calm down, chuck,' she said quietly to him. 'You've gone a funny colour.'

He shook his head. The frustration was too much. His chest felt like it was bound tightly by chains and straps. His mind was racing, thumping against his skull and wanting to break free. He wanted to punch something, anything, just to feel like he was doing *something*.

'I'm hearing your frustrations and I want you to know I share them,' said Ed, calmly. 'But these are the facts. We're anchored in a safe spot, as far as I'm aware, Rolando knew what he was doing, he was an experienced captain. I think what might be best for us all is to try and get some sleep. It's been a bit of a night and we could all be doing with some rest.'

'Are you telling us to try and get forty winks onboard a floating bathtub with a murdered man onboard?' asked Howie.

'I strongly suspect this was a personal matter, not one that should entangle us any more than it has already. An ugly altercation that we do not want to get involved in. The killer will be long gone by now, I imagine. So I expect us all to lock our berth doors to be on the safe side, get some rest and this will all seem much less troubling in the morning.'

Nobody seemed very convinced.

'Why are you so sure? What if we are trapped on this thing with a serial killer? Can't we fire a distress flare or something?' tried Marjorie.

'I think you've been watching too many true crime documentaries. Serial killers are not normally found taking a short yachting holiday. This will be a grubby but conventional grudge, believe me. No point wasting a good flare when anyone watching would likely just assume we were another yacht full of tourists having a firework display,' said Ed. 'No, we're best just to keep the boat locked down until tomorrow and get some rest.'

Matthias was the first to move. He stood up, stretched and rolled his shoulders.

'Well, I don't know about you lot, but I'm beat,' he said. 'That little trip in a dinghy to get here was absolute hell. And dead captains or not, I'm going to bed for my beauty sleep.'

He shuffled out from behind the little table and sauntered off through the galley towards the cabins. Kelvin reluctantly followed him, Marjorie nearby. Cassandra was just getting up when Ed stopped her. He held a finger to his mouth and looked down the corridor, making sure the others were out of earshot.

'Can I talk to you two for a minute?' he said, turning back to Cassandra and Howie.

'Ed, I don't think it's a good idea we're in the same ocean at the same time right now, let alone the same room,' said the actor. 'You're the absolute last person I want to speak with.'

'It'll just take a second,' he said, keeping his voice down.

The final door to the cabins closed. He took a step back and licked his lips.

'Alright, are you ready for this?' he asked them both.

Cassandra looked at Howie. They were just as confused as each other.

'I've got an idea how this can all be saved,' he said. 'And it's going to make you two very, very rich.'

Chapter 7

'You can't be serious?'

Cassandra was beginning to think she was hearing things. A lack of sleep perhaps, or just shock, it hadn't been the first night onboard she had been expecting.

Ed remained perfectly calm in front of her.

'Is he for real?' she asked Howie.

The actor rubbed his face and stood up.

'I don't know,' he said. 'I don't even think *he* knows what he's talking about anymore. If he ever did.'

He slid out from the table and started towards the cabins. Ed stood in his way.

'Where are you going?' asked the director.

'Bed,' said Howie. 'And I suggest you get out of my way before you go for an unplanned midnight swim.'

He moved to push Ed but the director remained firm. Blocking the way, Howie started to get mad.

'I'm serious, man,' he said. 'Get out of my way before I do something that will put me in court.'

'He means it, Ed,' said Cassandra. 'I've seen that look before. My old man gets it when the chippy has messed up his order.'

'Just hear me out, would you?' asked Ed. 'That's all I'm asking of you, both. Just listen to the end of my pitch and if you still don't like it then fine, we can move on.'

'I *have* heard your pitch and I *am* moving on, if you'd let me.' He tried to barge past Ed.

'Just listen a little bit more,' said the director.

Howie grunted something under his breath.

'Two minutes, I promise,' Ed said.

Cassandra stepped forward.

'Maybe we should listen to him,' she said, tapping Howie on the shoulder. 'Keep on his good side,' she added, whispering into his ear.

He grunted his way back to the galley table. Throwing himself down, he folded his arms and looked over at Ed.

'Well?' he asked. 'Go on then. Dazzle me.'

Ed cracked his knuckles and began to smile.

'Like I was saying,' he started. 'You and Cassandra try to catch the killer, here, onboard *The Regal Secret*. And I get Geri and Ben to film everything.'

Howie looked back at Cassandra.

'To answer your earlier question, Cassandra, yes, he *is* being serious,' he said. 'He really wants us to play Holmes and Watson.'

'Can't you see? It's perfect,' said Ed, sliding into the booth beside him. 'A murder has just taken place, under our very noses. Rolando's death is a tragedy, of course it is, but that doesn't mean we can't salvage *something* for TV. It's all on a plate for us, Howie. You, the fading action star with debt coming out of your earholes and the beautiful young influencer, eager to show off she's more than just a one-trick pony. Together you'll be unstoppable and the networks will eat it all up. Not just in the UK either,

I'm talking international here, the world. Just think what that would do for your profiles, eh? Cassandra, it would give you legitimacy, traditional media. And Howie, well, the last I checked you weren't exactly batting away offers from major studios, are you? Plus you've played enough spies and coppers in your time – you'll know all the basics.'

'Isn't what you're suggesting illegal, though? "Interfering with a police investigation" or something?' Cassandra looked horrified.

'Yes, but that's the genius of it all – there isn't a police investigation, or not as yet. We've got hours before they get here. As long as we don't touch the body, there's no harm done.'

'No harm done? Tell that to Rolando!' spluttered Howie. 'Cassandra is right. This sounds like it's against the law of every land if you ask me.'

'But we're not on land now, are we?' Ed was warming to his subject, gleeful even at the prospect of a televisual first. 'Forget detective dramas – or those traffic cop shows, this is breaking new ground – we'll film a murder case being investigated in real time.'

'But what do we know about investigating a murder, though?' asked Cassandra. 'I mean, we're hardly CSI, are we?'

'That's the best bit!' said Ed, a little too excitedly for Howie's liking. 'You don't know *anything*. But you don't have to. This won't be *CSI Tuscany*. You can just run around asking questions until the police get here and then they'll take over. You don't have to solve the case – just look like you're trying – we'll leave the actual case cracking to the boys in blue.'

'Before, you said it was some kind of feud, suggested the killer would have been and gone...and yet just now you said there was a killer on the yacht,' she said. 'I don't know if I much fancy ticking off somebody who's already killed someone already. I mean, it could be anyone?'

'Even *you*,' said Howie.

Ed sat back a little. 'I'm offended,' he said, serious. 'How dare you, sir. Captain Rolando was a dear friend of mine. We've worked together for years. Years and years, in fact. We've never had a cross word in that time and I'm devastated that he's dead. And yes, like I said, I suspect that this is some private squabble of Rolando's, someone with a grudge or a debt who's stowed away and after doing the deed has jumped off ship. At least, that's my best guess. No offence to you two, but most of your fellow crew, and that bunch of wet lettuces we've welcomed on board as guests, well, they couldn't fight a flea. As I told your crewmates, odds-on, our killer is long gone. You're safe, you two, so you can just dash about pretending to be great detectives. You won't get a job in LAPD, but you might just get a BAFTA if we do this right. And like I say, I owe it to Rolando to at least try to see what we can work out before the law arrives. He was such a dear, dear friend.'

Howie remembered the argument he and Cassandra witnessed on the deck shortly before the scream. He was about to ask when she interrupted him.

'I don't know, Ed. I like to think I'm good at taking on new challenges but I've got a bad feeling about this. What do you think, Howie?'

'I think that is the most preposterous TV show pitch I've ever heard,' Howie replied. 'And that's saying something. I've been in rooms where someone's tried to pitch me *Naked Knitting* or *Monkey Driving School*. But nothing as lunatic as *Celebrity Murder Investigation*. You must have a screw loose, man. Unhinged you are – you probably offed Rolando yourself just to be able to float this mad idea.'

'He doesn't mean that,' Cassandra said, rubbing Ed's shoulder. 'He's just upset. We all are.'

Ed's eyes reached up and he touched Cassandra's hand. 'I know,' he said, voice breaking a little. 'It's been a dreadful night, dreadful. I think I'm still in shock. Maybe this wasn't such a good idea. I don't know, maybe I just wanted to do something to honour my friend. I've known him a long time, you know. We worked on past series of this show and we grew close. I'm bereft, Cassandra, utterly bereft that this has happened.'

To Howie's surprise, a tear ran down Ed's cheek. He felt a jolt of guilt stab him in the chest. It didn't help that Cassandra was staring down at him, shaking her head in disapproval.

'Alright, okay,' he said. 'I'm sorry. I didn't know you two knew each other so well. I just . . . I'm just trying to make sense this of this awful business.'

'It's fine,' said Ed, sniffing. 'It doesn't matter. Just forget I said anything at all. We should all go to bed, get some rest. I need to tell the guests in the morning. I don't imagine they'll be happy.'

He went to get up. Cassandra squeezed his shoulder.

'Hold on a minute, chuck,' she said, stopping him. 'Maybe it's not such a bad idea if it's just for 24 hours, is it Howie?'

He stared up at her. He wasn't sure where this was going. But he didn't like the sound of it so far.

'What exactly would you want us to do?' she asked.

Ed composed himself. He cleared his throat and rubbed his eyes. 'I just thought we could do *something* while we wait on the authorities,' he said. 'You two interviewing the other celebs, the guests, trying to find out what happened. We'd do all the forensic stuff in post-production, get nice graphics, that kind of thing. Get you two to talk us through your thoughts, trying to work out who did what tonight, that's all.'

Cassandra nodded. Howie remained stoic.

'And how do you know one of us isn't the killer?' he asked.

Ed snorted. 'Please,' he droned. 'You two? You found the body. Plus I don't imagine you could handle yourself in a struggle with an experienced sailor like Rolando, could you H?'

Howie was strangely hurt by the comment. Whether it was true or not, he still liked to think of himself as an action star. Of sorts.

'And what about me?' asked Cassandra.

Ed smiled warmly, touching her cheek with the back of his hand. 'Someone as sweet as you, my dear, couldn't hurt a fly, much less kill a man,' he said.

Cassandra pursed her lips. 'That's just about the nicest thing anyone has ever said to me,' she told him. 'Did you hear that, Howie. Ed thinks I couldn't hurt anyone.'

'More fool him,' he shrugged.

'That's my pitch, really,' said Ed, sniffing again and taking a deep breath. 'Finding the humanity in an inhumane moment. Like I said, I want to do something for my friend. If the scurrilous excuse for a human being who stabbed him in the back is still going to be tracked down, then I want to have played a part in that. All evil needs to flourish is for good people to sit back and do nothing, after all. And I think you two are the kind of people who want to be on the side of action. Agreed?'

Howie wasn't convinced. Nor was Cassandra.

'That and I'll give you a quarter of the international syndication rights when we sell the series, I can't say fairer than that.'

Cassandra and Howie didn't know much about playing detectives. They did, however, know all too well how successful these kinds of shows could be. Ed offered his hand.

'Do we have a deal?' he asked.

Chapter 8

Cassandra lay staring at the ceiling in her cabin. The loud, overbearing snorts and gurgles of Marjorie Bryant's sleep were all she could hear. She'd be surprised if anyone else onboard, or even in the coastal villages of Italy, could hear anything else. She'd tried everything to drown it out. Eventually she'd given up.

It was all academic anyway. Cassandra couldn't have slept even if she had complete silence. Her mind was too busy. She closed her eyes and tried to stop her whirling thoughts. In the depths of the darkness she was reminded of being back at school in the middle of her exams. That was the last time she had felt like this. She could feel the sense of being at a crossroads, a point in her life where she knew whatever she did next would have a profound impact on her future, and the feeling that whichever path she chose, there would be no way of retracing her steps.

The feeling made her as queasy as the constant gentle rocking of the boat. She opened her eyes again and let the total darkness settle into an inky blue. It should have been comforting, but she imagined she saw shadows in every corner. This wasn't how she had planned these two weeks.

Far from it. The only solace she could take was that Howie was probably feeling the exact same way just a little further up the corridor. At least he was the only one of her crewmates she was sure hadn't wielded the knife.

Among the myriad of questions fizzing in her mind was whether she was doing the right thing. Not only had Ed seemed convinced that a little private, amateur sleuthing would make for a good TV show, he had made it sound like it was a kindness, something valuable. He had seemed genuinely upset about Captain Rolando's death. But Cassandra couldn't ignore that she had, after all, caught him arguing with the skipper a matter of moments before that awful scream. At least, she thought now, that meant Ed was a very unlikely suspect too – surely he'd not want to encourage anyone looking into the murder if it had his fingerprints on it. But that fight, then moments later, that scream – it was hard to forget.

Cassandra could hear that shriek now, in her mind. It was the only thing loud enough to block out Marjorie's snoring. If there was one bonus to Marjorie's sonorous performance it was that Cassandra knew she was asleep. If she *was* the killer, she definitely wasn't waiting patiently to wield the knife at Cassandra right now.

As if on cue, Marjorie let out a particularly throaty glug. It was so loud, so powerful, that it even woke her up. She coughed, turned over and sucked in air like it was her last breath. Cassandra waited for her room-mate to come around or say something. But she didn't. Her cabin-mate's breathing settled again, and she fell back asleep, the subterranean symphony of snores resuming once more.

That was enough for Cassandra. She threw back the thin duvet and kicked her legs over the side of the bunk.

Dropping down slowly, she gave a quick glance into her room-mate's bunk. Marjorie's mouth was hanging open like a chasm, her eyes covered by a sleep mask, arms at odd angles. Australia's 'premier alternative thinker' looked strangely peaceful, despite the noise. If she had been bothered by the night's unpleasantries, she wasn't showing much sign of it.

Cassandra eased the door open. The hallway outside was lit even at this witching hour with the strip lights that lined the ceiling and small individually lit notices that listed emergency protocol. Cassandra stopped to read the small print of the sign on her door. It was full of instructions about what to do in case of alarm, muster points and life jackets. It did not, however, have advice to offer in the event of a murderer running about the vessel. She closed the door behind her and tiptoed out to the galley. To her surprise, Howie was already there, hunched over the coffee percolator.

'We meet again, eh, babe?'

Howie almost leapt out of his skin. He dropped a plastic mug and it bounced next to his feet. The boiling hot coffee inside splashed up his leg and he began to hop around in pain, cursing everyone and everything.

'Bloody hellfire, Howie!' She chased him about the galley trying to help. 'I didn't mean to startle you.'

When the pain subsided, he sat down. 'Not your fault,' he said. 'I'm just on edge, that's all.'

'Aren't we all? Not every night you try to get some sleep knowing someone's just been done in.'

'True enough,' he said. 'How are we meant to sleep when there's chance there's a murderer on the loose? I'm not sure I buy Ed's easy-breezy confidence our killer did the deed then popped overboard. In fact, they could be the one sleeping right beside you.'

'Are you sharing with Kelvin?'

'I'm meant to be,' he said. 'But sleep won't come.'

'Same,' she said. 'And ordinarily I can crash out anywhere. Only Marjorie is my bunk-mate and she's making enough noise in there to wake the dead. Pardon the expression.'

She poured fresh coffee and sat down beside him. Neither took a drink. They just sat staring at the curling vapour for a moment in silence.

'Is this a good idea?' she asked eventually. 'What we've agreed to do. Should we be poking our noses into a murder investigation?'

'No, we shouldn't be,' he said curtly. 'It's literally the *last* thing any of us should be doing. A man has been killed and at best we'll succeed in doing nothing, finding nothing and getting no answers. And the worst? Well it hardly bears thinking about. We'll be upsetting a very nasty individual. No, there's a reason why people like you and I poking our noses in where they don't belong is a very bad idea.'

'So why did you agree to it then?'

'Money, Cassandra. Money, pure and simple.'

'Aren't you just a little bit curious as to what happened?' she asked.

'No,' he replied. 'I've seen almost every variety of human bad behaviour over the years and I'm not hungering after ticking off any of the few remaining seven deadly sins I've not witnessed or indulged in.'

'Is there no tiny flicker of your imagination that wants to get to the bottom of this awful mess before the police do?'

'Absolutely not.' He took his first sip. 'I'm not a cop. I've never been a cop. Not a real one, anyway. And I don't ever intend on being a cop. Leave it to the professionals.'

'But you read about it all the time, don't you?' she pressed. 'Master criminals foiled by rank amateurs, people who are just in the right place at the right time. It's pretty cool, when you think about it.'

'Cool?' he laughed. 'Cassandra, let me give you a bit of free advice I was told when I was a spotty-faced teenager wanting to be an actor. If you're good at something, charge for it. If there's something you *can't* do, pay somebody who can.'

'That's pretty cynical,' she said.

'Maybe,' he said. 'My very first agent told me that. His name was Arlo Spenser and he must have been about a hundred years old when I first met him. He had an old office on Sunset Boulevard that overlooked Whisky a Go Go. The place was worth more than any money he'd ever made as a talent agent. But he taught me that valuable life lesson and I've never forgotten it. Don't give anything away for free and don't waste your life trying to be something you're not.'

Cassandra scoffed. 'Isn't that precisely what you do as an actor – spend every job being something or someone you're not?'

'I said I'd never forgotten that lesson – I didn't say I'd followed it. Attention to detail, Ms Troy. If we're going to be talking to our numbskull fellow passengers then we will have to weigh every word they say. And the ones they don't.'

'Ha!' Cassandra grinned. 'You *do* care, you do want to find out what's going on. You can pretend all you like, but you're intrigued,' she said. 'This is it. Your second career beckons – a gumshoe.'

Cassandra took a drink from her mug and watched him over the rim. When he realised she was joshing him, he relaxed.

'Very good,' he said. 'Pick on the old guy. I get it. You're worse than my kids.'

'I don't cost you anything, babe. You get me for free.'

'I'm not sure I like the sound of that.'

A loud thud came from above them. They both looked up at the ceiling.

'What was that?' Cassandra whispered.

'I don't know,' answered Howie. 'I left my X-ray vision back in LA.'

'I'm serious,' she said. 'That was a hell of a bang. Do you think somebody else has been murdered?'

'Hopefully Ed,' he said.

Cassandra pinched his arm. He yelped and almost spilled his coffee again.

'What was that for?' He rubbed his arm.

'For saying bad things,' she replied. 'My mam used to do that to me when I said something nasty or horrible.'

'Your mum sounds nuts.'

'She is a bit, yeah.'

They both kept staring at the ceiling. The faint sound of footsteps bumped along above their heads.

'Maybe we should go check it out,' she said.

'Really?' Howie was looking at his coffee like a lover about to be separated from his betrothed.

'We're supposed to be investigating Rolando's murder. That could be the killer up there just now.'

'If it is, I'd rather stay down here, thank you very much.'

'I don't think we get paid if we do that,' Cassandra answered in a heartbeat.

Howie thought about that for a moment. Then he nodded. 'Maybe just a quick look, then. I thought Ed only wanted us playing detective on camera but I suppose a bit of research won't hurt,' he said. 'Although whether we're increasing the odds of us surviving past dawn by doing this, I don't know.'

He slid out from behind the table, Cassandra close behind. They quietly made their way through the galley to the crew staircase that led to the upper decks. Howie was about to start up the steps when she grabbed him.

'Shouldn't we go armed or something?' she whispered.

'Armed?' he whispered back. 'What do you think I am, a Texas Ranger?'

'Could you fight off a murderer if it came to it?'

'Could you?'

'That's my point,' she said, looking about the galley. 'We need *something*.'

She reached over to the nearby counter. Grabbing a spatula from the wall, she handed it to Howie.

'Great,' he said. 'What am I supposed to do with this? Swat him to death?'

'Who said the killer was a man?'

'Now who's splitting hairs?'

She nudged him on up the stairs. Howie climbed until he could smell the salty air of the sea. A hot, dry breeze was wafting in from the ocean as the first rays of the new morning spread across the main deck. There was nobody about as he emerged from the stairwell, Cassandra close behind him. They looked about the place.

'Nothing,' he said, turning round to Cassandra. 'It's empty.'

'It can't be empty, we heard *something*,' she said.

The main entertaining area was quiet and still, the long table with twelve chairs dotted around it cleaned and ready for a new day. The sea twinkled in the dawn sunshine beyond that, everything serene and pristine. Cassandra was starting to think last night was all some kind of terrible dream when something caught her attention in her peripheral vision.

'Over there!' She pointed towards the stern.

Howie raised his spatula. Cassandra hid a little behind him as a silhouette moved behind a cotton curtain billowing gently in the breeze. The ripples of fabric distorted the image and neither Howie nor Cassandra could work out who it was, if indeed, they knew them at all. Cassandra edged Howie forward. They moved silently and slowly, but the silhouette wasn't moving. When they were close enough, he reached out to the curtain and tugged it back.

On the other side stood Ms Sachiko, completely naked and striking a strange, contorted pose. Howie dropped the spatula. Cassandra dropped her jaw, amazed at the sight of the woman stood proudly before her.

'Good morning,' said Sachiko, undeterred and unperturbed by the fact she had been caught naked on the deck.

'Good morning,' Howie managed, trying to only look into her eyes.

'Yeah,' gulped Cassandra. 'Morning, chuck.'

'You've interrupted my morning meditation session,' she said sternly. 'The key to a focused mind is a decluttered one. And without wishing to appear rude, I would greatly appreciate it if you would vacate the fore deck to allow me to complete my yogic self-reflection, unless you are here to join me.'

'Self-reflection sounds right,' said Cassandra. 'I'd do nothing but self-reflect if I had a body like yours.'

'While your comments are intended as a rudimentary compliment, Ms Troy, your presence is still nonetheless distracting. The same goes for you too, Mr Temple. I am in a state of flow and unless you are too, please leave.'

'What?' Howie asked, still dumbfounded by what they had seen.

'I think she wants us to go, babe,' said Cassandra.

'Immediately,' said Sachiko.

'Right, yes, of course,' said Howie. 'Straight away. I'll just flow over here, then, shall I?'

He let his grip of the curtain loosen and it floated back between them. Slowly, they turned around and started heading back towards the staircase that led to the lower decks.

'There are things you never imagine you'll ever see,' she whispered.

'Not to mention things you won't be able to *unsee*,' he agreed.

'Before you go,' called Sachiko suddenly.

They stopped and turned back towards the curtain. Sachiko had adopted a new pose now, and Howie was more grateful than ever for the cotton voile between them. He couldn't help but think Sachiko would be getting sunburn in unpleasant places if she kept this up.

'If you were coming to tell me that Captain Rolando has been murdered, there's no need,' she said, with as much emotion as a virtual assistant. 'I've already prepared personalised ways to comfort each traveller. Nevertheless our competition winners will not be pleased when they awaken.'

The silhouette moved again, forming yet another alarming human shadow puppet. Cassandra and Howie stared for a moment at the impossible looking tangle. Then they took their leave.

'How did she know about Rolando?' asked Howie, stepping down the stairs.

'I don't know,' answered Cassandra. 'Ed, I presume. But I wouldn't like to have to be the one to break bad news to her. Or to ask her anything she didn't want to tell.'

'Just as well we're leading the investigation, huh?'

'Yeah,' she said. 'Something like that.'

Chapter 9

'Okay, what's your first move?'

Ed looked every bit the international globetrotter he liked to portray himself as. He lounged across one of the sofas built into the sun deck. Tanned, hair kissed blonde by the Mediterranean sunshine, just a hint of chest fuzz showing as his Hawaiian shirt flapped in the breeze. Cassandra thought he looked very well this morning for a man who'd spent the night knowing a cadaver was threatening to steal the spotlight on his new series. Even Howie reluctantly gave the director credit for his *sang-froid*. The show must go on, indeed.

Ben and Geri were standing behind him, somewhere between minions and henchmen. They were silent, as always and, as always, they were filming.

'Our first move?' she asked. 'What's that supposed to mean?'

'Your first move, in the investigation,' said Ed, lifting his sunglasses.

He squinted in the morning sunshine. The upper deck was still quiet and the waters calm about *The Regal Secret*. The rest of the crew were still down below.

Breakfast was being prepared, or massacred, Howie couldn't tell which.

The Kontoglou sisters had been the first on deck, looking in vain for breakfast. Howie had made sure to stay well away from them. He hoped he'd have at least until lunchtime before he would have to deal with that double-headed monster. Kirkby and Martha Hofstede weren't much later than them, nervously and sheepishly stepping into the sunshine like it might cost them more money. Arakawa Shig was nowhere to be seen, presumably still locked away in his cabin, Howie suspected. Regardless, Ms Sachiko had taken up her mother hen approach and was keeping them distracted – or 'entertained' as she liked to put it, until Ed could deliver the bad news. Howie could hear her delivering a potted history of Liguria to the guests, in such clipped, forbidding tones that they didn't dare interrupt.

Ed had summoned Cassandra and Howie onto the upper deck not long after they'd returned to their quarters after their run-in with Sachiko. Happy to be above deck and in the fresh air where everyone's worries and suspicions seemed to dissipate, the pair had met him just as the sun fully crested over the horizon, ready – if somewhat reluctant – to start their first, and hopefully only, day as amateur detectives.

'We've not exactly set up an incident room,' said Howie. 'I thought you were going to do all of the investigation stuff in post-production anyway.'

'I can't edit a blank page, H, you know that.'

'Yes, I *do* know that, but that doesn't really help us in this scenario, does it? We thought we'd agreed to a bit of gently probing of our fellow passengers,' Howie went on.

'Exactly, we'll start with questions,' said Cassandra, snapping her fingers. 'We'll start by questioning the rest of the crew and meanwhile you can get the terrifying Ms Sachiko's permission for us to interview her guests after. We need to know the basics and I've watched enough crime telly to know what we're looking for: alibis, motives, opportunity. We've only got a few hours so let's get talking.'

'That's good, I like that, hang on.' Ed pushed between them and clicked his fingers at Ben and Geri.

'Can you say that again, darling,' he said, pointing. 'That's a nice piece to the camera to kick things off. Howie, maybe you can pick up the thread, it'll give the viewers something to be anchored by.'

Cassandra cleared her throat.

'We should ask questions,' she said, very rigidly. 'We should ask questions of the other crew members to find out where they were and what they were doing when Captain Rolando was murdered.'

She looked awkwardly at Howie. He did his best not to fold in on himself with embarrassment. It was probably the worst delivery of a line he had ever heard. And he had worked off-Broadway. And off-off-Broadway.

'Fabulous, fabulous,' said Ed, not making eye contact. 'I'm sure you'll warm up to this, Cassie. And what about you, Howie? What do you think you should do?'

'Erm . . . ' he stammered. 'Well, there's the crime scene, isn't there. I know we can't touch anything or contaminate it as such, but we should maybe have a look around the bridge to see if there are any clues as to who the killer is.'

'Perfect! And I was reading some of the ship's documentation last night – emergency procedures and the like. Turns out that as bosun, in the event of the captain's incapacitation, you're in command anyway.'

Ed gave them a big thumbs up. Howie wasn't convinced. Neither was Cassandra.

'Is this going to work, Ed?' he asked.

'Of course it is!' said the director, motioning to Geri to switch off the camera. 'Why?'

'It all feels a bit *Scooby-Doo* to me,' he said. 'That was a kids' TV show in the sixties, by the way.'

'I know what *Scooby-Doo* was, Howie,' said Cassandra.

'It sounded great, *you* sounded great,' said Ed, enthusiastically giving him a thumbs up. 'You two are a great double act too. The young ingenue and the grizzled old timer. Trust me, H, this is going to be great. It might even be better than *Celebrity Sail or Fail*.'

'Grizzled old timer,' he said under his breath.

'Right, I'm going to talk to Ms Sachiko about the guests. You two better get started. Ben and Geri will capture the magic. Cassie, they'll go with you first, then later they'll get your footage, Howie.'

He dug around in the pocket of his Bermuda shorts and found a key. He tossed it over to Howie. 'That'll let you into the bridge,' he said. 'Nothing's been touched since you kicked the door down last night.'

'Shouldered, I shouldered the door,' said Howie.

'Whatever. You should have seen me trying to fit the thing back on its hinges in the wee small hours.' He mopped his brow. 'Head down there and take a look to see if anything stands out. And have a think about what you'll say to the camera. I'll join you down there in, say, thirty minutes? Good. Ciao.'

He was gone before the reluctant investigators could protest. Howie let out a giant sigh. 'This is getting worse by the second,' he said.

'Maybe you'll feel better when you get down onto the bridge,' she said.

'Oh yes, spending the morning with a corpse. That's exactly the antidote.'

They headed down the corridor that led to the bridge, Ben and Geri at their heels. The door was closed, although there was a huge dent in the middle where Howie had hit it. He didn't say anything, but he was quietly impressed with his own handiwork.

Howie stepped forward. He went to open the door and realised that Cassandra hadn't moved. He stopped. 'What's the matter?' he asked.

She was behind him, shoulders bunched up, a look of fearful dread on her face.

'I've got to get on with my interviews. You heard what Ed said. And besides, I don't think I can go in there,' she said.

'What?' he half-laughed. 'Are you serious?'

She nodded. Howie looked at the door then back to her.

'I thought you were all for catching the killer and playing Super Cop?' he asked. 'I thought you wanted the challenge?'

'I do, or at least I thought I did,' she said. 'It's just the thought of . . . well, him.'

'Who?'

'Ben?'

'No,' she groaned. 'Him, Captain Rolando. The body. I don't know if I can be in the same room as him.'

'Come on, Cassandra,' Howie said. 'We can't play detective if we don't get our hands dirty. And look, you're here, our mute friends Ben and Geri are here. Why don't we at least look in on the scene. Nobody is asking you to go dancing with him or anything.'

'I know that,' she said. 'It's just . . . well, apart from last night I've never been around a corpse before. Not since my gran died.'

'And your grandmother had a kitchen knife plunged into her back too?'

'Of course she didn't,' she said. 'She died of old age. Well that and the forty Silk Cut she got through a day. But I remember going to the bit before the funeral when the coffin is open. And she was just lying there, in the box, ready for the lid to be screwed down. I couldn't get my head around the concept of death. I thought she was going to wake up and surprise everyone. She was right there. I just remember looking at her and thinking "that's my gran" – only the more I looked, the more I realised it wasn't. She wasn't the same. She was different. She'd already gone.'

'Of course, she'd gone. She was dead,' said Howie flatly.

'Yes, she was dead, Howie, thanks for reminding me. Ever since then I've not been to another open casket burial. I've said my goodbyes to the person as I remembered them in life, not as they were in death. And seeing Rolando last night made my stomach turn. I don't know if I can go through it all again.'

Howie shook his head. He was no good at knowing what to say in moments like this. That was part of what made him love acting – it gave you a script. He wasn't sure whether he was meant to console or cajole Cassandra. Certainly he was no expert in the deceased. But his grandparents had owned a farm in the Canadian Prairies. Death was just an everyday part of their lives and he'd gleaned enough growing up not to be bothered by the sight of a cadaver. What were people really, apart from big dumb animals?

'Fine,' he said, rolling his eyes. 'Give me the keys, I'll go in by myself.'

'Would you, chuck?' she asked. 'I'd really appreciate it. I'll do the lead on the other bit – the interviews. I don't think the touchy feely psychology stuff would be your strong suit anyway.'

'Yes, fine, just give me the keys and I'll do the dirty work.'

She handed them over without fuss. Howie unlocked the door and was immediately hit with a foul smell. He stepped back, clapping his hand to his mouth.

'What's wrong?' She hovered about him.

'It stinks in there!' he gasped.

Cassandra took a tentative step towards the door. She didn't get very far before stopping.

'Oh god,' she said. 'That's terrible. Is it . . . ?'

'It is,' said Howie. 'I'm no pathologist but I didn't think bodies stank like that so quickly.'

'Maybe it's the heat,' she said, turning away from the door.

Howie wiped tears from his eyes. He pulled the collar of his ship's polo shirt up over his mouth. Taking a deep breath, he went back into the stagnant bridge.

The place was bright, the sunlight beaming in through the bow windows. Howie took his time, trying to take in as much as possible. The various arrays and computer systems were still operating, although there were a few red blinking lights that he didn't like the look of. He skulked around the place, the smell beginning to creep in through his makeshift mask.

'Can you see anything?' called Cassandra from the door.

'Nothing out of the ordinary,' he shouted back.

As much as he had dismissed Cassandra's concerns over the body, he was acutely aware he wasn't keen at looking at the late Rolando either. Now that he was on the bridge, with the stench of death all around him, he didn't feel quite so confident in his capacity to keep cool in the face of slaughter.

He'd look for clues instead, he decided. He checked all of the cupboards and drawers around the main control deck. Nothing seemed out of place or strange. He was no sailor but it looked like nothing had been damaged. The radars and navigational equipment were all still functioning. And as far as he knew, the yacht was in good shape. That gave him hope for getting the radio working – surely they could raise some help.

'What about Captain Rolando?' asked Cassandra.

He'd been dreading that question. There was no escaping it now. He *had* to take a look. Letting in a shallow breath of the pungent air, he spun around quickly to face the dead skipper.

Rolando was sitting looking at him. A few flies were buzzing around which only added to the vacant look. It seemed nobody had touched him since they made the discovery last night. Howie wasn't sure what he had been expecting. He walked tentatively over to the body.

'You were right not to come in here,' he called to Cassandra.

'Why? What's wrong?' she asked from the door.

'This isn't pleasant,' he said. 'I'm going to close Rolando's eyes. Give him a bit of dignity, at least.'

'Are you sure?' she asked. 'Shouldn't you leave him for the police?'

'Give me a break, it's not illegal to help a guy out when he's dead, eh?'

Howie had closed dozens of eyes on his movies. The difference being the person was usually still alive and only *playing* dead. This was a little strange. He closed the captain's eyes and peered over his shoulder. The knife was still sticking out of his back.

Something pricked his attention. Despite the sheer ludicrousness of his situation, and his avowal he was only in this for the money, in that moment, as he took in the situation, he felt the snagging and tugging of wanting to know what had happened.

He looked at the knife handle, glad he didn't have to touch the morbid thing. He tried to ignore the fact that it was sticking out of a person and examine it dispassionately. He'd seen enough actors play corpses and he gulped and tried to pretend Rolando was just an actor, a very, very good one. He looked at the hilt of the blade. At first glance it looked perfectly normal, a standard kitchen knife, nothing out of the ordinary. But as he looked closer, he spied markings on the hard, black plastic.

'Howie? Are you still there? Everything okay?' called Cassandra.

'As okay as you can be next to a body. Yeah, I'm here,' he shouted back. 'I think I've found something.'

'You have?'

'Yes, I think so,' he said, straightening up. 'The knife that's sticking out of Rolando's back. It's from a different ship.'

'You what, babe?' Cassandra asked.

'The knife. The one that killed Rolando. It's got a different name on the handle. It doesn't say *The Regal Secret*. It's from something called *Meridian Sunset*.'

'*Meridian Sunset*?' Cassandra asked. 'How do you know that?'

'It's written on the handle. I'd pull it out and show you if it wasn't stuck in the captain.'

'Please don't do that,' she begged. 'Or take a photo if you must. How do you know that's another ship?'

Howie scratched at his beard. The atmosphere was getting too much for him. He headed for the door and closed it behind him. Locking up, he handed the keys back to Cassandra.

'Everything on this ship is branded,' he said.

He pointed at the plaque on the door that bore the yacht's name. There were cushions scattered about a sofa close by that were similarly branded. Everything, everywhere, from napkins to coffee cups, wore the mark of *The Regal Secret*.

'It must be a thing, even that stupid spatula you had me waving about earlier was the same,' he said. 'What was it Ed said? This thing is owned by a Saudi prince or something. Being on brand, it's important to these guys.'

'Not half,' said Cassandra. 'Branding is what it's all about for *everyone*. Just ask my manager.'

'If you say so.' He nodded. 'So, what's a knife from what is likely another ship doing on here and, more importantly, jammed between Captain Rolando's shoulder blades.'

Cassandra thought on all of this for a moment. In the end, she shook her head.

'I've got no clue,' she said. 'Not a Scooby.'

Howie smiled at her joke. 'Well thank you for that analysis,' he said.

Before they could think any more on it, Matthias appeared at the end of the hallway. He was dressed in chef whites, the corner of his apron distinctly scorched.

'Neither of you knows how to put out a fire, do you by chance?' he asked.

Chapter 10

The kitchen was choked with smoke by the time they all clattered down the stairs. Howie armed himself with a fire extinguisher. Matthias did the same and they attacked the blazing pan before it spat out any more boiling fat and flames. A quick flurry of foam later and everything was back to normal. Even the smoke alarm got bored and stopped its chirping after a moment.

Matthias puffed out his cheeks. He rubbed the back of his head, perplexed.

'I don't know what happened,' he said. 'I was just trying to make some toast for everyone. The next thing I know, the pan has gone up in flames. Strange.'

'Making toast in a frying pan is strange, Matthias,' said Howie. 'You use a toaster for that kind of thing.'

'I couldn't find it,' he shrugged.

Cassandra spotted the device sitting in plain sight in the corner of the worktop, close to the cupboards and chopping boards. She remembered a conversation she'd had with a fellow influencer a few years before. The woman had dated several high profile footballers, many of which Matthias probably knew. The influencer had developed a taste for them. And, being a psychology and sociology graduate, she'd made her own observations about the athletic class.

Chief among them was a lack of responsibility. Everything in their lives was taken care of by someone else. Agents, managers, physiotherapists, everything. And, what Cassandra had found most interesting, was blame. Footballers would blame *anyone* and *everyone* before themselves. It was always somebody else's fault. The thought made Cassandra smile. She liked that sort of thing. Good science proven in the field.

'Just as well we're here, eh chuck?'

She waded through the last traces of the smoke and found a stack of loaves. Filling the toaster, she hunted out more utensils.

'What are you doing?' asked Howie.

'Breakfast,' she said. 'I imagine our guests will take Ed's gruesome news better on a full stomach.'

'I don't know why you're so keen to help the fellow. That's *his* job,' he said.

'Howie, please,' she said calmly. 'We're all in this together. We each need to lean in and bring our skills to this terrible situation. And mine happen to include making a damn good breakfast. And as handsome as Matthias is, he clearly doesn't know an egg cup from an egg timer.'

'Thanks, I guess,' said the former footballer.

'Don't mention it, babe. Grab me some eggs and a bit of bacon. We'll make them a good, old fashioned full English.'

Matthias quickly sprung into action, seemingly relieved to have someone shouting instructions at him. Howie stood watching the pair as they put together the start of the breakfast for the guests.

'Are you going to help us at all?' she asked, dropping more rashers into the sizzling pan. 'Or just stand there looking gorgeous?'

'I have no idea what a full English is, Cassandra,' he said. 'But by the looks of all the fat frying, it's something to do with a heart attack waiting to happen.'

'Just make a gallon or two of coffee, you can manage that, can't you chuck?'

Howie knew when he had been put in his place. He set about making the coffee. It was something he knew how to do at least. And given the past twelve hours or so, he was grateful to be back in any kind of comfort zone, even briefly.

The three celebrities made quick work of the breakfast. Working in unison, they put together the plates and dishes that would feed the five thousand, never mind the guests of *The Regal Secret*. Cassandra popped the last of the slices of toast as Marjorie swanned into the kitchen.

'They're asking for their breakfast,' she said grumpily. 'That Hofstede man looks about ready to have a coronary if he doesn't get some food. Honestly, some people.'

'Yes, we had a feeling that would be the case,' said Cassandra. 'Can you help with the plates please?'

'I'm supposed to be hosting on deck,' she replied.

'Just do it, would you, Marjorie?' said Cassandra. 'I'm not in the mood for your guff this morning.'

'I'm just saying that I'm supposed to be entertaining our passengers on deck. Ed is running around like a bluebottle with a rocket up its backside. I think he's panicking about the news.'

'Did he tell them yet?' asked Howie.

'I don't know.' Marjorie shrugged. 'I can't be everywhere all at once. But judging from the fact that no one is weeping or wailing and their main concern seems to be the availability, or lack of, coffee, then I'd guess not.'

Cassandra slammed the empty pan down with a hard clank. It was enough to bring Matthias and Howie to attention. She blew a stray strand of hair from her face, the rest of them plastered to her sweaty forehead. Howie could feel his stomach clenching in anticipation of what she was about to say. In the short time he had known Cassandra, she had always been calm and positive. But he sensed there was a fierceness about her that he didn't want to get on the wrong side of.

Matthias, however, got his retaliation in first.

'Come on Marjorie.' He clapped his hands three times. 'Three plates, up and back down, then another three plates. *Komm schon*!'

In an instant he was a professional footballer once more. The energy, the intensity, the urgency he gave off made them feel that they were all on the training pitch. Poor Marjorie didn't know what had hit her. Before she could react she had three plates in her hands and was being shoved back out of the kitchen by Matthias. He was barking instructions at her, telling her to pick up the pace. When she was on her merry way, he came back in.

'Well done,' said Howie. 'I don't think I've ever seen her move so quickly.'

'We're a team,' he said. 'And the team can only move at the pace of the slowest member. That's how I won a World Cup.'

Cassandra liked that. And she was liking Matthias even more with every passing moment. They plated up the last of the breakfasts and then headed out to the main deck. The guests were already seated in neat rows along either side of the huge table. As Howie bent over and placed Despoina and Thekla's plates down, they both pinched a cheek and cackled. He subdued a yelp and tried to smile. It was difficult.

Kirkby Hofstede's plate was barely on the table and he'd speared a sausage. Wolfing down his breakfast greedily before the others had started, Martha looked thoroughly embarrassed.

'What?' he grunted.

Nobody answered. Ms Sachiko stood behind her charges, watching like a hawk to make sure everyone was attended to. Ed appeared at last. He looked flustered, face bright red. His camera crew were nowhere to be seen and there was an edginess that hadn't been there before.

'Ladies and gentlemen, a moment of your time please,' he said.

The guests stopped their eating. To Cassandra's surprise, they all seemed to be enjoying what she'd cooked for them.

'It is with the saddest of hearts that I have to tell you our beloved Captain Rolando is no longer with us.'

Ed paused for a moment, ever the dramatist. The faces of the guests all seemed to drop a little.

'Then who's driving this thing?' Kirkby hollered.

'Where's he gone?' Martha asked.

Ed tried another tack. 'He's gone to a better place.'

'Another ship?' asked Kirkby, still nonplussed.

Howie, always one for plain speaking, couldn't bear to watch any longer. 'He's dead, I'm sorry to say. Deceased.'

The guests looked confused, disbelief blurring into horror.

'Last night, two of our crew members – Ms Troy and Mr Temple – made the unfortunate discovery in the bridge.' Ed took up the gauntlet. 'It would appear, on first assessment, that Captain Rolando's death was *not* from natural circumstances. Or by his own hand.'

There was a clatter of cutlery. Despoina made a strange noise, her sister Thekla fanning her with a napkin. Kirkby shot to his feet, fork still in hand with a half-eaten rasher of bacon dangling from it.

'What?' he rasped, flecks of breakfast showering the deck.

'I've already spoken with the crew and they've agreed, as a group, to continue providing you all with the utmost care and comfort as planned on the voyage,' Ed continued. 'At least until the authorities arrive. When that will be I'm not sure, as we're currently in something of a signal black hole.'

That was enough to spark a mass panic. The guests became very animated at once. Cassandra could see Ed turning a little more red as he stood at the top of the table. Kirkby and Martha clamoured for Ms Sachiko's attention, who remained as implausibly calm as ever. The Kontoglou sisters were in tears, wailing like it was the end of the world. Of the guests, only Arakawa Shig remained quiet, although the colour had drained from his face.

Ms Sachiko let them shout and holler at her all they wanted, and didn't say a word. Then when Ed cleared his throat for everyone's attention, she merely nodded in his direction.

'Please, ladies and gentlemen, hysterics won't get us anywhere,' he said. 'Now I understand that you've paid a lot of money for this trip and you were expecting something rather more luxurious than a murder investigation. However, you'll be relieved to hear that there are advantages to having a camera crew on board. Not only will anything untoward likely have been picked up by our filmmakers, but it also means we're in the fortunate position of having experts on hand to start the investigation ourselves until the relevant officials can reach us. I've spoken to Ms Troy and Mr Temple, they have kindly agreed to conduct enquiries while we wait for the police to arrive. And we'll be filming this as they make their progress.'

It was the turn of the crew to appear flummoxed. Cassandra could feel Matthias and Marjorie staring at her. Their glares were icy, cold enough to chase away the heat from the Med.

The guests all turned to face her. There were more looks of confusion and some of anger, Cassandra noted. The Hofstedes were turning from pale white to red with fury.

'Hi,' she said feebly.

Rather than instilling confidence, it seemed to trigger another bout of hysteria. Ms Sachiko continued to be the target for the frustrations, endless diatribes in English, Japanese and Greek being volleyed at her like a besieging army. She was steadfast, standing like a statue, completely unfazed.

Cassandra thought she should do something. It wasn't Sachiko's fault that Rolando had been murdered. She didn't deserve to be the scapegoat for the guests. She took a step forward and a thought struck her. How did she know that Sachiko had nothing to do with the murder? How much did she know about any of them? The very real possibility that *anyone* could be a killer had dropped.

'Bloody hellfire,' she just about managed.

Sachiko seemed to sense Cassandra's disturbance. She cast a cool, emotionless gaze across the deck at her. Holding it for a moment, it felt like the agent was probing her mind.

Complete nonsense, Cassandra knew that of course. But it was hard to shake.

'How much are they paying you then?' Marjorie's nasal voice broke the spell.

Cassandra blinked. 'Pardon me?'

'How much, eh? How much is that wart Ed giving you and Action Man over there? How did you wangle this little number, eh? Are you sleeping with Ed? I wouldn't put it past you!'

'Oi! That's offensive!' Cassandra shouted back.

'What's offensive is you and Howie capitalising off a tragedy!' Marjorie spat.

'We're not capitalising off anything, we've just been asked to help out.'

'Sure,' Marjorie sneered. 'You and Mr Has-been-movie-star are bound to crack the case.' Cassandra went quiet. Marjorie had a point. They would be no one's first choice of detective. None of this motley crue would be. Sachiko was still silent, Matthias looked dumbfounded and Ed had his head in his hands. Even Howie was looking despairing, standing near the taffrail and appearing ready to jump overboard at a moment's notice. Cassandra stood taking in the scene for a few moments more until a loud, piercing whistle brought everyone to a surprised silence. Kelvin Kamani was standing in the entrance to the dining lounge. He was sodden, large pools forming at his bare feet, an oversized life jacket inflated and almost drowning him, ironically.

He pulled the whistle from out of his mouth. He was breathless, eyes wide.

'I'm not sure what's going on here,' he said in his carefully enunciated public school accent. 'But I believe you all ought to know that I think the ship is sinking.'

Chapter 11

'Yes, we're sinking. Just very, very slowly.'

Matthias and the others all stared down at the stern. The rear of *The Regal Secret* was wide and spacious with steps down to where various inflatables and small watercraft could be launched from when the bosuns had readied them out of storage. However those bosuns, namely Howie and Kelvin, hadn't been fully briefed in their roles. They looked down now at the launch area which was sloshing around with several feet of water. The clear Ligurian Sea lapping gently against the expensive plastic and fibreglass of the rest of the ship. Matthias let out a whistle. 'We're definitely not straight in the water,' he said. He took out a coin from his pocket and placed it on the rail, it rolled merrily away, landing in the water with a soft splash. 'Somebody didn't close the launch doors, that's my guess.'

Howie and Kelvin gave each other a suspicious glance. The race was on to see who could deny it first.

'That wasn't my job,' said the actor, not wasting any time. 'It must have been you, Kelvin.'

'We were only in there for a few minutes yesterday on our tour,' said the MP. 'Captain Rolando showed us how the doors open and shut and told us he'd run us through all the various equipment this morning.'

'Well whoever it was, they left the seals open and water has been getting in all night,' said Matthias. 'That's what I think anyway. You two can fight amongst yourselves as to who gets the blame. Blame the captain if you like. But I don't really want to go swimming anytime soon.'

He turned and headed back into the belly of the yacht, pushing past the others. Ed was there, with Cassandra, Marjorie and Ms Sachiko. The agent had managed to tear herself away from the guests long enough to see what was going on. She wasn't impressed, naturally.

'This really is most unsatisfactory,' was all she offered.

Ed remained silent. His face was almost scarlet now. A large vein was pulsing in his temple.

Cassandra was concerned. 'Are you feeling alright?' she asked him. 'Maybe you should have a lie down, chuck.'

'I'm fine,' he said, staring down at the water. 'I'm just a little stressed out, that's all.'

'We should do something,' said Howie.

'Yes, we definitely should,' agreed Kelvin. But the former politician just stood there, staring blankly at the submerged aft of the yacht. Howie let out a frustrated groan and hopped down into the water. He sloshed around and waded up to his waist. Peering down, he spotted the door mechanism.

'Matthias was right,' he said. 'The doors were not fully shut.'

Cassandra held her breath in sympathy as she watched Howie duck beneath the water, his arched back only just above the surface. When he re-emerged, he dusted off his hands.

'There, closed,' he said. 'That should stop us from taking on any more water.'

'The deck is still submerged,' said Marjorie.

'Is it?' Howie snapped. 'Is it really? I hadn't noticed that, Marjorie. I wondered why I was soaked to the skin though. Do you think those two things might be related?'

She tutted her disapproval.

'As flippant as Ms Bryant is, we still do have an awful lot of water onboard,' said Kelvin.

He was right. Not that Howie was prepared to acknowledge that publicly. He climbed out of the water with a dramatic flourish and headed back inside. The others just stood there looking and feeling a little helpless. Howie stepped back out into the sunlight carrying large, empty buckets.

'What are those for, babe?' asked Cassandra.

'Buckets,' he said. 'For water.'

'I don't follow,' said Marjorie.

'We're going to empty the water from the submerged deck and tip it over the edge. That way the ship should rebalance itself and we'll all stay dry for a while, until somebody who knows what they're doing can get here.'

'Won't there be pumps for that sort of thing, old boy?' asked Kelvin.

'That's as maybe, but unless you can find them and make them work all in the next few minutes, I suggest we resort to the traditional method and get bailing. We can faff around with the tech once we're back on an even keel. Speaking of which, had any luck with the radio system, Ed?'

Ed shook his head. 'I haven't tried it this morning,' he said. 'I couldn't quite bring myself to go in there with Rolando. Not until I'd had a strong coffee anyway.'

There was a collective groan from the crew. Howie was almost at his wits' end with Ed. He hadn't liked the man since he'd first met him. And every day, even every *hour* seemed to throw petrol onto the fire of his dislike for him. He swallowed at least some of his rage and began scooping up water in a bucket.

'I'll go just now and have a twist of the knobs and buttons,' Ed said, retiring into the ship. 'It shouldn't be too difficult. I once had to rewire one of those things when I was filming near Monte Bianco. If I can do it in the middle of the Alps with bullets whizzing around my ears, it shouldn't be a problem here, right?'

Howie, ignoring Ed, called up to his fellow crew.

'This will go a lot faster if you all helped, by the way,' he shouted. 'That includes you two as well.'

Ben and Geri looked at each other. They seemed to have a telepathic ability to communicate with each other. But instead of putting down their kit, they returned to filming.

Cassandra was the first to drop down into the water, followed closely by Kelvin. Marjorie hesitated just long enough to draw a damning look from the others. She eased herself down into the water, making sure the others could hear her grumbled protests.

'And what about you, Ms Sachiko?' asked Howie.

'I won't be getting wet, thank you,' she said succinctly. 'While I may not be a part of the guest party, I'm also not employed by the ship or the production company. I can't begin to think of how many legal obligations I would break if I joined you and left the guests to their own devices. Instead, I shall see that my charges are coping in the face of the multiple calamities they've already endured.'

She turned and marched straight back into the yacht. Howie had to laugh a little. Hollywood was full of people who didn't want to graft. He was often one of them. But Sachiko's elegant and unashamed excuses were in a different league.

The four celebrities sloshed around in the water, filling their buckets and tipping them over the side. They worked on mostly in silence as the sun continued its arc in the clear blue sky above them. Howie's back began to hurt. The pain from the previous day's hard labour was still bothering him. He stood upright with a click and rested against the hull.

'You losing steam already, chuck?' asked Cassandra.

She was panting, her arms and forehead glistening with sweat. He laughed.

'What's so funny?' she asked, still emptying the deck.

'You're quite a vision,' he said.

She stopped and looked down at herself. She laughed too.

'Do you think I'll pass for a sailor?'

'Don't ask me, I have as little clue about being a seaman as I do about being a detective.'

She nodded at Kelvin still toiling away. 'At least he's putting some welly into it.'

'I definitely closed the doors to this area yesterday,' Howie said to her, quietly. 'I'm certain of it.'

'I thought you said Kelvin had left them open?' she asked.

'I did, but I was just testing him,' he said. 'I distinctly remember closing them. Rolando showed us how, when he was telling us what to do first thing in the morning. He warned us that if we kept the doors open then water would get in and if we left it like that, first the launch would fill up then the engines would be flooded. And here we are.'

Cassandra shuddered. 'I hadn't thought about that.'

'I imagine they're totalled,' said Howie, pushing himself off the hull. 'If there's this much water here then everything in the engine room will be waterlogged too. We're stuck here, for the time being at least.'

'But who would have opened the doors?' she asked.

Howie looked at her and cocked an eyebrow.

'I don't know,' he said. 'But I'm guessing it's not a coincidence that the captain is murdered and the whole back of the boat is under the sea.'

'You think one leads to the other?' she asked.

'I can't be certain,' he said quietly. 'Although it's what I would do if I was a killer. Make sure the ship can't go anywhere, then you either make your escape knowing you won't be followed or . . . '

Cassandra blanched. 'You don't mean that whoever killed Rolando might really strike again? I mean if they're on board then we've met them, served them coffee or slept next to them . . . ' She trailed away and nodded over at the other two bailing out with them.

Howie eyed them up and down. They were working hard, even Marjorie. Kelvin was still struggling with his life jacket but he was scooping and dumping like a machine.

'I'm not sure either fits the bill of a serial killer,' he said. 'Neither of them seem to have any reason to off Rolando. And they're just as stuck as we are.'

'The best killer wouldn't exactly look like a criminal mastermind though, would they?'

'Yeah,' he said. 'That doesn't make me feel any better, Cassandra.'

'No, nor me,' she agreed.

Howie picked up his bucket and bent over again, wincing. He pushed on through the pain and started scooping water.

'The kitchen knife,' she said, standing over him. 'You said that it had a different name on the handle.'

'That's right,' he said.

'Do you think somebody could have brought it onboard with a plan to use it?'

'I'm not sure, possibly,' he said. 'That's one of the theories we'd need to establish – was this a crime of passion or premeditated? That's what I was thinking earlier, before I realised I'd be knee deep in water rather than interviewing suspects. What's your point, anyway?' he asked.

'My point is, whoever was last in the kitchen might be the person to start with,' she said.

Howie stopped what he was doing. Cassandra waiting as she let Howie see what she was implying.

'Matthias?' he asked.

'He was last here, wasn't he? Delayed en route, that's what Ed said wasn't it?'

'Something like that, yeah,' he said.

She put her bucket down, letting it drift a little in the flooded deck.

'Where are you going?' he asked.

Cassandra splashed her way towards the dry part of the stern.

'Kelvin and Marjorie have this under control. I'm going to ask some questions,' she said.

'Do you think that's a good idea?' he asked after her. 'I mean, he's a big guy.'

'Oh please, babe.' She batted him away. 'I took karate until I was nine, almost got my orange belt too, I can handle Matthias.'

Before Howie could protest more, she was up and away back into the yacht, pushing past the film crew. He couldn't deny her spirit or her tenacity. Cassandra Troy, it seemed, was full of surprises.

Chapter 12

The kitchen still smelt of smoke and cooking. Cassandra wrinkled her nose – the charring mingling with the tang of cooking oil, and with no windows, just an overworked fan, the greasy air felt like it was clinging to her skin. As she lingered in the doorway looking around for Matthias, she was reminded of long summer holidays at her grandparents' house in Kirkby, just outside Liverpool. Hazily warm afternoons punctured by torrential rain, that was the cost of living in northern England. You never quite knew what weather front would blow in next. It was where her granddad had taught her how to do a good fry-up. He'd told her you could cope with almost anything in life if you could have a cup of tea and a bacon butty afterwards.

That all felt like a very long time ago now. Not just because of everything that was happening onboard. Her whole life had been turned upside down, effectively, ever since she'd stepped onto the show that made her name, ScouseWives. Brought into that show as the token single girl, she'd gone from no one to tabloid superstar in one season. She'd made the most of it – posting the perfect content on her socials to go viral. But she'd seen enough other stars burn out and knew her fame was a game she had to play with real skill. For every positive there was a negative and vice versa. She chose her dates and her friends with care, picked sponsors and promotions with an eye on what could blow up. And when things went sideways? You had to make the most of it. This trip, this show was a prime example of that. Only she could go on a reality programme about celebrities manning a luxury yacht and end up amateur sleuth in a murder investigation. She half-expected Rolando to rise from his chair and tell them all it was a grizzly hoax for the cameras.

She would have laughed if it wasn't so grim. The thought of Captain Rolando's body still on the locked bridge just a few feet above her head made her skin crawl and her teeth itch all at once.

'Hello? Matthias? Are you in here?' she called out now.

There was no response. Maybe she had thought too highly of the former footballer. Maybe her idea that he had returned to where he was supposed to be, given everything that had happened, was too much to expect. While he had shown great vigour and enthusiasm in cooking breakfast, he still probably thought he was above doing the washing up.

She stepped into the kitchen. Scanning the place, she saw she'd been wrong. Everything seemed to be in pristine shape. Somebody had obviously cleaned up after the breakfast fiasco. She drummed her fingers on the worktops. Close to the sinks, she spotted a block of knives. She shuddered as she noticed a missing space – the place for the blade that was still sticking in Rolando's back, she thought.

To her surprise, the discomfort moved on quickly. A morbid curiosity replaced it almost immediately. She rushed over and pulled the block out of its spot beneath the cupboards and cabinets.

'Let's have a look,' she said, pulling one of the handles.

A large meat cleaver came free with remarkable ease. Cassandra staggered back a little. The absurdity of what she was doing wasn't lost on her. Here she was, in the kitchen of a luxury yacht, wielding a cleaver big enough to carve up an elephant. If only her followers on social media could see her now.

She quickly regained focus. Cassandra squinted in the hard light of the kitchen. She looked for the badge.

'The Regal Secret,' she said, reading the name embossed in the resin handle.

She put the cleaver down and examined the other knives. She knew her way around proper kitchen equipment thanks to a stint on *Celebrity Chef Race* one year. Every one of them, the boning knife, cheese knife, butcher's knife and even one for tomatoes, bore the branding of the yacht. None had the mysterious *Meridian Sunset* name.

'This is bloody odd,' she said aloud.

'What is?'

Matthias was suddenly taking up the doorway. Cassandra made a little yelping noise. The sound didn't seem to bother Matthias. He just stood there looking at her, staring, a heap of muscle that seemed too large for the confines of the kitchen. Cassandra was certain he hadn't been that big before.

'What?' was all she could manage.

'You said something was odd,' he said, stepping forward.

Cassandra instinctively moved backwards. She bumped into the hob and was stopped.

'Did I?' she said, feeling nervous.

'You did, I heard you.' Matthias was cold and monotonous. 'You said "This is bloody odd", and I wanted to know what you were talking about.'

He leaned on the worktop, bicep bulging. Cassandra looked at his hands. They were large, big enough to manhandle anyone he wanted, she thought. And certainly big enough to take care of Captain Rolando. As for her, it didn't bear thinking about.

'Well it's all so strange,' she said. 'I was just . . . just looking about, that's all.'

She remembered she was holding the butcher's knife. Matthias watched the blade as she waved it about in the air between them.

'Oh, sorry, what am I thinking,' she said.

She slid it back into the knife block with a click. As soon as she had, though, she wanted to kick herself. That knife might be her only defence if it turned out Matthias was the killer. The fleeting confidence she'd told Howie earlier about her investigative skills was now little more than a vanishing dot on the horizon. Her mouth was dry, her heart thumping. She wanted to get out and get out now.

'How is your investigation going?' asked Matthias.

He stood up straight, towering over her. He crossed his arms but was still very much in the way. Cassandra shrugged.

'You know, starting slow,' she said. 'I'm not very good at this sort of thing. It was all Ed's idea, I think he's trying to salvage something from this trip. The poor duck is at his wits' end, I reckon.'

'Wits' end?' asked Matthias.

'End of his rope, end of his tether. Burnt out,' she said.

'Ah, I see.' The footballer nodded. 'It is a strange set of circumstances to find ourselves in. Do we carry on as the crew of this ship or do we try and swim for shore? I'm not so certain what the best course of action is.'

'No,' Cassandra agreed. 'I want to get off this tub but I think we're stuck here. You're probably the only one mad enough to even think about making a swim for it. Anyway, you've barely been here a day. You arrived late.'

'I did.' He nodded. 'I was in England for a charity match. Then I had to circumnavigate my way around Europe to get to Livorno. A shame I didn't spend more time in the city, I could have played there, you know. When I was younger, the move fell through at the very last second.'

'That must have been frustrating,' she said. 'It's a lovely place, from what I saw.'

'Such is the life of a football player.' He offered a sad smile. 'You can live in three or four different places over the course of a year. Or you get lucky and spend your whole career in the one city. The agents, they make all of the money. We're just meat to them and the clubs too.'

'That sounds awful,' she said, wondering at his almost poetic turn of phrase, all tinged with a melancholy she didn't associate with athletes. 'You're moved around like assets, cattle.'

'Yes, I guess so,' he said. 'But I've done nothing else for my whole life. I've played this sport since I was four. I don't know how to do anything else. It's been good to me, of course, I have more money than I know what to do with. My family is secure for the rest of their lives. But I wonder sometimes, what might have been.'

A wistfulness fell over Matthias.

Cassandra couldn't help but feel a pang of sympathy for him. 'You can't change things now, chuck,' she said. 'All you can do is try to make the best of what's ahead.'

'Yes, you are right, of course,' he said. 'That's why I'm here.'

'In the kitchen?'

'No, on this television show,' he said. 'I thought it might kickstart some sort of new career. You don't have many options when you're finished in the game. Coaching is an obvious choice, maybe some commentary. But I don't want to be at the side of a football pitch if I can't be playing on it. I need something new.'

'And you want to be a TV star?' she asked.

The malaise lifted a little. He looked back down the corridor that led from the kitchen. Then he leaned in a little closer to Cassandra.

'You promise you won't laugh?' he asked.

She wasn't sure how to respond to that. Every time anyone had asked that question, she inevitably was primed for hysterics.

'Yes,' she tried.

'Well, I've always wanted to be a singer.'

'A singer?' she repeated. 'You mean like a pop star?'

'No, no, no.' He waved his hands wildly. 'Country and Western.'

'Stetsons, gingham and tassels?' Cassandra knew she wasn't doing a great job of keeping the serious expression she'd tried to fix on her face.

'That's right.' He was smiling too now, flashing his bright, perfect teeth. 'Johnny Cash, Hank Williams, Conway Twitty, all of the greats.'

'Conway who?'

But Matthias had already broken into a rendition of 'Walk the Line'. He held a hand to his heart as he crooned, drumming with his free hand on the kitchen worktop. When he reached the end of the first verse, Cassandra thought the demo might be over but he dropped straight into the next verse.

Cassandra could only stand and stare as the strapping athlete belted out the country classic with passion, vigour and only a passing resemblance to the tune. Who knew there were five verses – Cassandra counted them – to the classic. When he finished he took a step back and bowed a little.

'Well?' he asked her. 'What do you think?'

Cassandra blinked. Wary of telling him what she really thought for fear he *was* the killer she fumbled to find the right words.

'It was . . . different.'

'Good different?' he asked, still smiling.

'You're unique, chuck. I've never heard a version quite like that,' was the nicest Cassandra could manage.

'It's what I've always wanted, Cassandra. To see Nashville, sing at the Grand Ole Opry, where all of the legends have entertained the crowds for generations. It means a great deal to me, a great deal. And I had hoped this show would put me on that path.'

'We've all got to have a dream,' she said, hoping he wouldn't burst into a new number.

'Now the skipper is dead and I don't know what will happen. The dream is over before it began,' he sighed.

Maybe it was the surprise of being in a confined space with a Teutonic Johnny Cash hopeful, maybe it was the strange yodelling note he'd delivered the crescendo with, but something had quelled any fear in Cassandra's brain. She was in no mood to flirt around the main subject any longer. She decided in that moment that the best option would be the direct approach. Surely a man who dreamt of duetting on 'Islands in the Stream' wasn't going to eviscerate her.

'You don't know who killed Rolando, do you?' she asked. 'Because any insight would be *really* helpful to Howie and me. The faster we produce some info, the more we'll have to share with the police and the quicker we all get home – or to Nashville in your case.'

Matthias tapped his chin for a moment, deep in thought. And for the briefest of seconds, Cassandra thought he might be useful.

'No,' came the flat response. 'It seems to me there is a real mystery here. A luxury yacht's captain brutally murdered and left in a locked room. What I would do if I were in your shoes, is establish who is not a team player. Who is the lone wolf here?'

'A lone wolf?'

'Absolutely. Think of why somebody would risk everything, who is more concerned about their own game rather than solving this together. If you work that out then you might narrow down the suspects, of which I am no doubt one.'

'You are?' she asked.

'Aren't we all?' he laughed. 'I was onboard when you found the body. I would have no trouble overpowering Rolando or anyone else on this yacht. And I appeared at the door of the bridge just after you and Temple broke it down. I'm as much under suspicion as anyone else surely. That's what logic would dictate, no?'

'So *did* you kill Rolando?' she blurted, realising this was not the sophisticated psychological probing she'd imagined she'd be carrying out.

Matthias let out a deep breath. He shook his head and stepped to one side, clearing the way out of the kitchen for the first time since he'd come in.

'I did not,' he said. 'With Rolando dead the show is under threat. No show, no Grand Ole Opry for me. It's down to logic, Cassandra. And before you ask, I don't know who else might have cause to murder the captain. Every member of this crew is probably a little – how do you put it – desperate, to have agreed to do this show to begin with. And desperate people . . . '

'Do desperate things,' Cassandra said. He was frank, she gave him that at least. Whether he was being honest remained to be seen.

'Okay,' she said. 'Well, thank you, for the insight and the, erm, song.'

She gave him two thumbs up and moved to leave. At the last moment, he stepped in front of her. He leaned in close, close enough she could smell his aftershave and see tan lines on the crow's feet that framed his eyes. They looked less twinkly than a moment ago.

'I'd watch your step though,' he said, in little more than a whisper. 'If there *is* a murderer on this ship, they won't take kindly to people asking questions, especially ones as blunt as yours. Sleep with one eye open, Ms Troy. It might save your life. If we all make it through another night, that is.'

He lingered a moment, just an inch or so from Cassandra. Then he turned and walked out of the kitchen.

Cassandra waited until he was out of sight before she breathed again. She leaned on the worktop to steady herself. She was shaking, her hands quivering uncontrollably. She felt tears biting at the back of her eyes, her throat almost closed over with fright. The shock had finally worn off from last night – and in its place she felt a deep, blood-chilling fear. Matthias was right. Someone was playing a different game to the rest of the crew, and the stakes were as high as they came.

Chapter 13

The stern deck was finally empty. The Ligurian Sea had been chased back whence it came. And Howie was exhausted. He'd felt like King Cnut leading the bailing out but hadn't dared share that analogy with his crewmates.

He slumped down on the now drying deck and lay flat on his back. The taste of salty sweat was in his mouth, rivulets running down his temples, the back of his neck, everywhere. He scrunched his eyes up tight as the beaming sun beat down from high above him. He was exhausted.

'Howie, I think . . . '

'No!' he shouted, cutting Kelvin off. 'Not a word. Not a single word from anyone. I just want to lie here for a minute, with my empty bucket and my limbs outstretched. I want to bake in the heat and feel nothing but my own sense of satisfaction for a job well done. Is that okay?'

Silence. He opened one eye and looked over at the others.

'Sorry,' said Kelvin. 'Did you want me to say something to acknowledge your request or stay quiet like you'd asked?'

Howie closed his eye and lay back down.

'Silence,' he said. 'That's all I want. Just silence. Back in the nineties, I had a sensory deprivation tank at my place. I only used the thing twice, cost me an absolute fortune. Then I loaned it to Los Del Rio for the Californian leg of their world tour and I never saw it again. So please, just silence, that's all I'm asking for.'

To his surprise, that was what he got. Even Marjorie had fallen remarkably mute as the clearing process had gone on. Howie couldn't really complain about either of them. They had worked hard, they all had. It had taken them hours but all of the water had been lifted and cleared and everything was now free to dry out in the sun.

He knew he would pay for it all, of course. Already his back was tight. The muscles in his shoulders and upper arms were burning. The tops of his thighs were going the same way. In the short time he'd been on this wretched ship, he'd worked out more than he had in ten years. He rued how out of shape he was. His younger self would baulk at the state of his fitness.

But the world had moved on. Action movies were still being made without him. There was no motivation there. He'd never be called on to do his own stunts again, wouldn't have hair and make-up crews waxing and oiling him so he could artfully rip his shirt off. Here he was instead, sprawled out, flat on his back, a man in his mid-fifties gasping for air after an hour or two of physical labour.

He opened his eyes, disliking where his thoughts were taking him. As he had so many other times before, he pushed himself up onto his elbows and tried not to look at his expanding waistline.

Kelvin and Marjorie were sitting down too. The intense heat of the Mediterranean sun had already dried out great blotches of the deck beneath them. Scattered shapes of darkened timber where the water had been sucked up by the expensive wood were dotted about like shadows. More than anything, the job had taken their mind off the fact that they were trapped on a stranded boat with a corpse, no working radio and likely a killer too. Now the hard labour was done, the even harder thoughts returned.

'Do you think we'll ever get off this boat?' asked Kelvin.

The politician was sitting close to Howie, his knees brought up close to his chest, hands wrapped about them. There was something childlike about him, innocent even.

'Of course we will, what sort of question is that?' hissed Marjorie. 'I expect we'll be back in Livorno before dinner, sitting around in some cheap hotel waiting to give our statements. All I want to do is call my agent and give her what for for booking me this ridiculous gig. I'm meant to be a counter-culture voice of the people – not playing Popeye with a bunch of wannabes. No, we'll be back on dry land by sunset and I can't wait.'

'You seem rather confident about that,' said Howie.

She didn't look in his direction.

'I'm confident that idiot Ed will see the error of his ways and find a way to get us off this tub before we have to threaten him with lawyers,' she said. 'I don't imagine our moneyed friends in the guest party have taken his news very kindly. And their chaperone, she looks like someone who'll find us a way out of here even if Ed is too incompetent. So you and that girl might as well give up on your notions of playing Batman and Robin.'

She let out a laugh that was completely condescending. Howie was used to women like Marjorie Bryant. He'd been married to two of her spiritual sisters. The trick was not to react, not to give them the fuel of anger. Everything, every word, every sentence, every notion, was a challenge from Marjorie. She *wanted* an argument, she needed to be stimulated that way. Howie had found that silence or, worse still, agreement, was the best way to handle her.

'You're probably right,' he said, lying back down, hands behind his head. 'I never thought this whole amateur detective schtick was a good idea anyway.'

He counted down the seconds in his head until he thought Marjorie would answer. Surprisingly, she was a whole second early.

'That didn't stop you taking the pay cheque though, did it?' she said.

'No, of course not,' he laughed. 'Why the hell would I *not* take a pay cheque. I don't do any of this for free Marj, it's called capitalism.'

'Don't call me that,' she snapped.

'Call you what?'

'Marj,' she said. 'My first husband called me that and didn't end well.'

'Good grief,' said Kelvin. 'I hope he didn't end up with a kitchen knife in his back.'

Howie cut him off. 'What about you, Kelvin, are you married?'

There was a hesitation from the former politician. 'No, I'm not,' he said. 'A lifelong bachelor, I'm afraid.'

'A clever man then,' said Howie.

'And what is *that* supposed to mean?' asked Marjorie.

'It means that Kelvin here is smart enough not to go down the marriage road at the drop of a hat. If you're divorced, Marjorie, you'll know the mental toll it takes on the two people involved. And that's if they don't have kids. Throw children into the mix and everything becomes a hundred, thousand times more complicated. No, no, Kelvin is the smart one out of all three of us. He's spared himself the heartache, not to mention the expense.'

'Nonsense,' she dismissed him. 'He just hasn't found anyone who'd put up with him.'

Howie remembered his doctrine. Don't rise to the challenge. He hoped Kelvin wouldn't take the bait either.

'I was in love once,' said Kelvin.

The remark was enough to throw Howie off-guard. Even Marjorie was silent. They both twisted to look at the former MP. They'd expected him to come back with insistence that he had paramours queuing around the block for his attentions.

'It was all a very long time ago,' he said, sensing they wanted to know more. 'When I was a much younger man and the world didn't seem quite so frightful.'

'When was that, then?' Marjorie scoffed.

'It was before I took office, I was working in the City. He was a dear friend's brother. We hit it off straight away, but it wasn't to be. A different time, a different age, those sorts of things weren't really thought well of within the workings of the political machine. We decided, for the better of our careers, that we shouldn't go any further. I was heartbroken, but it was the right thing to do at the time. I often think about him. But politics is an ugly game – there's no room for real relationships, only allegiances of convenience. Maybe it's been better this way.'

He bowed his head. Howie wasn't sure if there was anything he could say to help Kelvin. He wasn't sure if that's what the politician wanted.

'Love's a real kick in the teeth, right? Who needs it?' he eventually remarked.

'It's odd, these last few hours,' the politician went on. 'I've thought about him a lot more than I usually do. It must be the shock. Realising we're all mortal has that sort of effect on people, doesn't it? You think about all the what ifs and the buts and wonder if you could have done anything differently throughout your life. Taken a left when you veered right. Said yes more than you said no, all of these things. Strange how the mind works in a time of crisis. I've faced select committees, the House of Lords, dined with some of the most powerful people in the world. And yet here I am, soaked through from bucketing water from the back of a boat in the middle of the Ligurian Sea worrying about an old boyfriend.'

Howie knew where Kelvin was coming from. He'd seen that look on the man's face plenty of times in his own mirror.

'It's his family I feel for,' Kelvin went on. 'Rolando's family. He was a son to someone, a brother perhaps. Even a father, a husband, who knows. We're stuck out in the middle of nowhere while his body sits in the captain's chair and there are people back on land who think he's alright, he's just at work. There's something deeply disturbing about all of that. It's ghastly.'

He lifted himself to his feet. A seriousness that Howie hadn't seen in him now took over. He pulled his life jacket off and unfastened the valve, deflating it. Folding it neatly over his arm, he started off towards the main innards of the boat.

'We should start preparing for lunch,' he said. 'I had no appetite at breakfast but the slog has made me starving.

The guests will be getting hungry too and we still have duties to perform, even if the engine is flooded from my incompetence.'

He didn't hang around for an answer. Kelvin vanished inside. Marjorie puffed out her cheeks.

'What was all that about?' she asked sarcastically. 'A politician who has a conscience. I never thought I'd see the day.'

'Lay off him, Marjorie,' said Howie. 'The guy's clearly going through a lot.'

'And we aren't?'

'I think I can safely say you and I are not exactly delicate flowers,' he said. 'But a bit of sensitivity would go a long way towards your colleagues thinking you're a human being. Ever think of that?'

'How dare you,' she said, getting up. 'I don't need to be spoken to like that by some . . . by some actor. I'm a thinker, a critic, an academic! I've got more degrees than you've had hot dinners!'

'Great, good for you,' said Howie, standing up to meet her. 'Tell it to somebody who gives a crap.'

He walked off.

'How *dare* you!' she shouted after him. 'Don't walk away from me! Come back here! Right this second!'

'No thank you.' He waved.

'I demand you come back here, right now!' She was screaming and stomping her feet. 'I won't be spoken to like that by some half-witted Yank hack!'

That made Howie laugh. He wasn't even going to hit her with the Canadian card. It reassured him that her venom was built on misapprehensions and wild guesses. He stepped into the shade and felt his cotton polo shirt stick to his back and chest. He was going to find Cassandra when Marjorie flicked a switch in his brain.

'Playing detective, don't make me laugh!' she shouted. 'You and that dolly bird don't even know the half of it!'

Howie stopped. There was something in what she said, something in her tone, her sneering, seething voice that made him come to a halt. Slowly, he turned back around to face her.

'What's that supposed to mean?' he asked, cocking an eyebrow.

Marjorie marched straight up to him.

'You two think you're so smart, but you're clueless, lost at sea, if you pardon the pun,' she said, pursing her lips. 'Captain Rolando was no saint. And while you and what's-her-name have been skulking about making back-door deals with Ed to save your careers, I've been doing my research. I've been working things out. I've been fathoming who the killer is.'

All of the brief respite from the case that Howie had managed after clearing the deck was gone in an instant. Marjorie seemed to pick up on this, her fury quickly changing to arrogance.

'Weren't expecting that, were you?' she said, sticking her tongue in her cheek. 'You think you're so smart but you've done *nothing*, Howie Temple. Nothing. What do they say about empty vessels?'

'Who is it then?' he asked. 'If you know who killed Captain Rolando then you should come forward. This is serious, Marjorie, a man has been murdered. Who did it?'

Marjorie cackled, throwing her head back.

'Oh, wouldn't *you* like to know.'

'Yes, I would,' said Howie.

'Isn't it obvious?' she said. 'Who's the biggest, the fittest of all of us onboard? Who has an agent who's been sitting on more secrets than the rest of us put together? Your pal Cassie couldn't keep a secret if she tried – it'd be on social media and trending as fast as she could type. And you, all the secrets of your glory days are old news – tame by today's celebrity standards. No, to have real secrets worth keeping you need cash. And a team of people prepared to build a wall of silence around you. Yes, you need a team.'

Howie's stomach flipped. He swallowed, his mouth acrid.

'Matthias,' he whispered, already backing away from her.

'Our very own blue-eyed boy no less.'

There was a victory in her voice. Howie had no time to berate her. He had no time for anything but panic and to find Cassandra. He had, potentially, waved her off to her doom.

Chapter 14

Howie's heart was racing and a lightning rod of pain in his forehead was sending stabbing fingers across his skull.

'Cassandra!' he shouted, aware of how frantic he was sounding. 'Cassandra! Where are you?'

He checked the galley first: empty. Then he tried the main deck. It was deserted. He sprinted past the locked bridge and down into the crew quarters. Still nobody about. With every passing second he grew more anxious.

'Cassandra! Where are you?'

With every empty room and deserted corridor, Howie's blood pressure cranked up a notch. He began to frantically push doors open, hoping the next one would reveal the young influencer who, he realised as he searched, was the closest thing to a friend he had onboard. He made his way through the bowels of the yacht until he reached the bow where most of the others had gathered.

'What's going on?' he said, his heart thumping in his ears.

Nobody answered him. In front of them were all of the guests, Kirkby chewing on something, his faithful wife wringing her hands beside him. They were huddled and focused on something but Howie couldn't see what. Even Ben and Geri had stopped filming, their silent faces slack and gaunt. If they'd stopped filming, this was serious. As he drew nearer, his imagination warped into the worst outcome imaginable.

'Get out of my way!' he shouted, barging through them. 'Let me see! What have you done to her!'

He reached the centre of the crowd. To his surging relief, Cassandra Troy was nowhere to be seen. Instead it was Ed sprawled out on the deck, Ms Sachiko leaning over him. Howie didn't know whether to celebrate or cry. The relief was immeasurable. It didn't last long though as his concerns turned to the director.

'What the hell has happened to him?' he asked.

'Oh it's terrible, just terrible,' said Despoina Kontoglou.

'It's terrible, Howie,' wailed her sister Thekla.

They threw themselves at Howie. He had the wind knocked from him as the sisters latched on to him like limpets.

'First Rolando, and now Mr Ed,' said Thekla.

'Who is next, Howie? Who is next?' Despoina lamented.

He managed to shrug himself free, kneeling down beside Ms Sachiko.

'He is unconscious,' she said.

'What? How?' he asked.

'I'm not a doctor, Mr Temple, you would need a physician who is properly qualified to make a concise diagnosis.'

Howie shook his head. He was in no mood for her formality. He kneeled down beside Ed who, praise be, was breathing slowly, his eyes closed, mouth clamped shut.

'The quietest I've ever known him,' he said under his breath.

'Pardon?' asked Sachiko.

'Nothing. Who found him?'

Arakawa cleared his throat and put up his hand.

'And you haven't touched him?'

'No,' came the sharp response.

'I believe he's been struck with something, something heavy, on the back of his head,' said Sachiko.

'How do you know that?' asked Howie.

'There's a large haematoma forming close to his crown.' She pointed around to the back of his head. 'In what, albeit limited, knowledge I have of this sort of thing, I would estimate that an impact from something blunt like a club or a bat could be enough for him to pass out.'

Howie stood up, his knees creaking. 'We need to move him,' he said. 'He needs a doctor. Head injuries are dangerous, it's life and death stuff. The longer he's out the worse it could be for him, there's no telling what damage has already been done inside his brain.'

Nobody seemed to move. He looked about the crowd.

'Well? What are you waiting for? Come on, help me check his airways. We'll put him in the recovery position, assess him, then if he's stable, take him down to his cabin.' Howie had sat through endless safety briefings on countless sets. He was surprised now it had sunk in as he gently checking Ed's breathing.

There was another moment of reluctant hesitation before Matthias eased his way to the front. Howie clenched his fists. Marjorie's words were still ringing in his ears.

Matthias didn't seem to notice.

'I don't think you're supposed to move them,' he said.

'We can't just leave him lying here on the deck, can we? He'll have heatstroke soon to add to his woes,' Howie replied angrily.

Matthias mumbled something under his breath. He checked the director's pulse then shrugged. He lifted Ed's feet and Howie took his shoulders.

The others separated for them, watching as they stepped carefully through the clearing. Howie felt his muscles burning under the weight of Ed. They managed to make it down below deck. One of the guest suites was just ahead.

'In there,' said Howie, sweating.

'But somebody is staying in there, it's for the guests,' said Matthias feebly.

'Just put him down on the bed, we won't manage any further.'

They stumbled their way into the room. Clothes were strewn about the place, empty champagne flutes littering the tables and surfaces. A strong smell of deodorant and cologne clogged Howie's nostrils.

They carefully laid Ed down on the unmade bed. Rolling him back into the recovery position, Howie caught his breath. He spotted the large lump on the back of the director's head. He'd been given quite a wallop.

'Damn,' said Howie. 'That could have killed him. What is going on here!'

'I thought you were supposed to be the one investigating,' said Matthias. 'You and your ditzy friend. She could talk her way into some serious trouble, you know.'

Howie thought his heart was going to give out there and then. Thankfully he caught the door handle and managed to stay upright.

'Where is she?' he asked.

Matthias shrugged. 'She's safe,' he said, but the effect was menacing rather than reassuring.

The footballer was gazing down at Ed lying on the bed. Howie could feel a cold steeliness about him now, all the way from across the suite.

'I didn't ask how she was, I asked you where she was,' Howie insisted.

'She's safe, I told you,' Matthias said again.

'And what does that mean exactly?' he asked.

'It means what it means,' said Matthias. 'You don't need to worry about her.'

'What have you done?'

'Hey, watch your tone, Howie,' he said. 'I haven't done anything.'

'Then tell me where she is.' Howie took a determined step forward. Matthias inflated his chest and stood to his full, six-foot plus, height. Howie was undeterred.

'I'm only going to ask you once more,' he said. 'Tell me what you've done with Cassandra.'

'Or what?' the German laughed. 'What are *you* going to do?'

Howie didn't think. If he had, he would have probably backed out of what he was in the throes of doing. And that would have been a much better idea.

He was up and over the bed in a flash, Ed still comatose and unaware of the commotion around him. Howie was relieved the adrenaline had kicked in – his reflexes were much sharper than he had been expecting. The fact he'd managed to ball his right hand into a fist as he did so was even more remarkable. In the split seconds all of this happened in, he had gone from a stationary, middle aged former action star to street fighting man, all with just a few simple steps. Maybe he still had it.

The downside was, whatever 'it' was, Matthias had more of it. While Howie had been quietly congratulating himself on standing up to the giant of a man opposite him, the ex-footballer had seen it all coming a mile off. So, as Howie brought his fist upwards, hoping to catch Matthias under the chin or at least glance an ear, his opponent had taken a small but vital step to the right.

What resulted was a punch that caught nothing but air. Howie's momentum was so great that he seemed to follow his fist upwards, feet leaving the safety of the floor. All of that might have been countered if he was younger, quicker, less shocked. But any chance of salvaging the assault was put firmly to bed by a swing of Matthias' own.

His fist smashed into Howie's cheek with all the force of a runaway train, all the way from Hamburg, first class, with no stops. Howie felt something crack in his mouth. If the whole thing had played out in slow motion, that was corrected quickly as he hit the ground. The world rushed back into normal speed. His mouth was filled with the steely taste of blood and a tooth made a sad attempt at dribbling out. At least he was breathing, he thought as he lay slumped on the floor, battling to cling on to consciousness.

Matthias' bare feet came into his dizzy view. The indignity – what if the last thing he ever saw was a footballer's hairy toes. But Matthias wasn't going in for a kicking. Instead Howie's assailant grabbed Howie under his arms, hauling him upright.

'Don't do that again,' he said, with typical German efficiency.

'Wha . . . ' Howie's tongue was thick and rubbery in his mouth.

'I'm sorry, I didn't want to hurt you Howie,' Matthias went on. 'But you're acting like a crazy person.'

'Whe . . . where is Cassandra?'

Matthias let go of his shoulders. He swayed a little, unsteady on his feet. The German held out his hands, making sure he wouldn't topple over like a tall stack of plates. Satisfied that Howie wasn't going to tumble, he moved around the bed and over to the door of the guest suite.

He popped his head out and returned, closing the door behind him. Howie was confused. Pain was making it hard to think. He rubbed at his jaw and felt it swelling already.

'She's safe, I keep telling you that,' said Matthias, returning, his voice kept low. 'I warned her about your investigation.'

'Warned her? Warned her of what?' asked Howie, still dazed.

'Warned her about the killer in our midst,' he said.

The anxious panic was returning to Howie. He'd been given a brief respite with his aggressive antics. But now it was creeping back.

'Matthias, where is she?'

'I warned her that Captain Rolando's murderer is probably still onboard. And that they won't take too kindly to her poking her nose into their business. It would appear my fears have been confirmed now Ed has been attacked too.'

Howie looked down at the director. He was still unconscious and looked quite peaceful, lying on the bed. Perhaps a little oblivion wouldn't be so bad right now.

'What are you talking about? I have it on good authority who the killer is,' said Howie.

'You do?' Matthias seemed genuinely surprised.

'Yes! That's why I had to find Cassandra. I was told you're the killer.'

'Me?' His voice seemed to leap a few octaves higher than it had any right to.

'Yes,' said Howie. 'Marjorie told me just now, when we were clearing out the aft deck. She said we were looking in the wrong place, that Captain Rolando had more skeletons in his closet than a haunted house but the only person with more was you.'

'Me?' he asked again. 'No, no, you have it all wrong. It's not me. It's Marjorie, I'm sure of it.'

'Well this is convenient, the two of you blaming each other,' said Howie, wincing in pain. 'She was right about one thing at least – she said you were the only one capable of handling yourself. That shiner you've just given me rather proves her point.'

'So what. Show me your evidence? What's my motive? It won't have escaped your attention that I barely fit into these tiny boat corridors – are you telling me I could have been creeping about this place with the camera guys not spotting me? Where's my opportunity?'

'Your . . . opportunity?'

Matthias rolled his eyes.

'Yes, you know, a chance to kill, it's fairly basic stuff, you know. Haven't you read any detective books or seen a cop show on TV?'

'I don't really have the time,' he said.

'No. I imagine you're constantly in the gym or taking on decathlons.' He prodded Howie's stomach. 'Honestly, *unglaublich*, I don't know what Ed was thinking asking you two to be in charge of this probe.'

'Where's Cassandra, Matthias? What have you done with her?'

'She is safe,' he said again. 'Trust me.'

'Trust you? I trust you about as much as I can throw you overboard. Things are getting out of hand. I'm hunting a killer, my right hand woman is missing, our director is unconscious, I've just been socked in the chin, the engines are probably flooded and nobody knows we're here. So if you think you can convince me to trust you, then please, be my guest.'

'What makes you think it's me?' he asked.

'I . . . I . . .'

Howie stammered. The truth was, he wasn't sure anymore. He'd always got through life with an easy certainty – never questioning his instincts, part of what had made him so easy-going when he was younger. Nothing had bothered him, nothing in the least. He had thought it was his strength of character which had given him that but now he could see it was all down to money and fame. It was easy to be carefree when the next opportunity was always just about to come knocking, with a bank balance that made troubles evaporate. With both money and fame effectively gone now, his previously unshakeable self-belief was wavering lik   e a sapling in the wind.

'You're very much mistaken, Howie, I'm not a killer,' he said. 'Yes, I'm strong enough to have done the deed, which is more than I can say for most of the rest of you. But ability is only part of the issue. What possible reason would I have for killing Captain Rolando? Did Marjorie tell you that? The truth is, I needed him, like I needed this show. I told Cassandra all of this.'

Howie winced, and not just from the pain. He didn't like the way Matthias used the past tense speaking about Cassandra.

'Why do you think it's Marjorie that killed the captain, then?'

'She's opinionated, she's selfish. You saw how she reacted when she learned you and Cassandra had been picked for Ed's ridiculous notion of turning the investigation into another TV show. She's a jealous woman, Howie. And jealousy can make people do very risky things.'

'But what's she got to gain?' Howie asked.

'Notoriety, for one thing. She survives an ill-fated cruise, she gives an exclusive interview about the terror and trauma, she could live off that selling that story for the rest of her career. Either that or she is just a genuine sociopath. I'm not ruling that out.'

'Stop, please stop,' said Howie. 'You're just guessing. I don't need your speculation right now. I need you to tell me where Cassandra is, immediately.'

There was a noise at the door of the suite. Both men snapped their heads around to look at it.

'Where is she, Matthias? Tell me, now,' said Howie, his fuzziness all but gone.

'The engine room,' he said.

'What? It's flooded down there!'

'Not as bad as you think. There's only a little water. The equipment is completely ruined, *zerstört*. And it only has one way in and one way out. It's the safest part of the ship.'

'And what's Cassandra supposed to do if the killer finds her in there? She's got no way of escape.'

'If I'm right and the killer is Marjorie,' said Matthias. 'She's not exactly the hardest foe to fight off.'

'Tell that to Captain Rolando.'

That seemed to give pause to the big man. His face went a little slack, as if realising that his brilliant plan might not be so great after all.

'Oh,' he said. 'I hadn't thought about it like that. No, I'm sure she only managed to strike the first time because she had surprise on her side.'

'And what about Ed? Are you collaring Marjorie for that too?'

The door handle was turning now.

'You're an idiot,' said Howie, shoving past him and heading for the door. 'And I'm an idiot too for thinking you'd be capable of murdering somebody and getting away with it.'

Howie pulled the door open. A rather shocked Arakawa met him.

'Oh,' he said. 'Has my room been cleaned? Are you doing housekeeping too now?'

Howie pushed past him and started down the hallway, cursing.

Chapter 15

Cassandra felt ridiculous. Here she was in a dank, smelly engine room, sloshing through filthy water in her bare feet. The engine itself was no company. It was silent, for starters. Cassandra was no engineer but she thought there should be at least *some* form of activity – a back-up generator or something. Occasionally the machinery let out a groan of anguish or a jet of steam. For the most part, though, it was a great slumbering giant beside her.

The water, on the other hand, was much harder to ignore. She could only imagine what she was wading through. Great lakes of multicoloured oil made the surface greasy. And she would wince in pain every time she stood on something loose – a screw, a nut, some sort of bolt. Why she had agreed to let Matthias put her in here was quickly growing beyond her.

She pulled her phone out from her back pocket. No signal, as there had been since they set off from Livorno. Cassandra looked at the dwindling battery life. Even without anyone to call she was still always on her phone – snapping something, editing something else. Still, this was hardly the place for a glamorous selfie. Original content had been hard to come by in the last few hours. Something about a hideous murder onboard hadn't fuelled her creativity.

'This is stupid,' she said aloud, just happy to hear a voice, even if it was her own. 'Here I am, standing talking to myself and for what? Because that footballer is trying to *protect* me?'

Hearing how odd it all sounded out loud spurred her on. She tucked her phone back into her pocket and walked towards the door. Cassandra thought she heard something clanging from the other side. She stopped. Letting the water settle about her ankles, she waited.

There was silence. Even the engine was behaving itself. Cassandra began to wonder if she had imagined the sound. With everything that had been going on, maybe she was losing a grip on reality.

She reached down for the door handle. Pulling it open, the whole thing seemed to give way from a weight on the other side. The metal edge caught Cassandra in the forehead and she stumbled backwards. There was a heavy thud and a splash as something dropped in front of her. Dazed, she rubbed her head where the door had hit her as Marjorie Bryant flapped and floundered in the dirty water.

'Get me out of this!' she squealed.

'Marjorie!' Cassandra shouted. 'What the hell are you doing?'

Australia's self-styled voice of the people coughed and spluttered. She was soaked from head to toe, her straggly blonde hair hanging down around her head making her look like a drowned rat. She threw her hands up then brought them down again, sending plumes of filthy water into the air.

'I hate it here!' she began to sob. 'I hate this stupid boat. I hate the stupid people. I hate Rolando for being killed and most of all I hate *you*!'

Cassandra hadn't been expecting that little outburst. She reached down and offered her hand to Marjorie.

'What are you doing?' the older woman asked, still crying.

'I'm trying to help you up,' said Cassandra.

'I don't need your help. I don't need you for *anything*,' she said.

'Come on, chuck, you just asked for a hand.'

'Well I take that back. And you can stop calling me chuck, babe, and whatever else it is you always say.'

There was an edge to her tone. There always was, thought Cassandra as Marjorie rounded on all fours before getting to her feet. She pushed her wet hair out of her face and lifted her nose into the air, still trying to regain some superiority despite the ridiculousness of her situation. Cassandra begrudgingly admired that in her. Not many people would still be attempting to save face after they've gone for a dunk in a flooded engine room.

'This is a disaster, from start to finish,' she said. 'I'm leaving now, and I hope I never see any of you again.'

'Strange,' said Cassandra.

'Strange? What do you mean?'

'Strange, that you'd say you were trying to leave when you were creeping about outside the engine room door.'

Filthy water was dripping from the ends of Marjorie's hair and nose. Her eyes were darting around. 'If you don't want to see any of us again, why are you skulking around down here?' she asked her. 'Seems like you were looking for something, or someone.'

'You have absolutely no idea what you're talking about,' said Marjorie. 'You're a silly little girl and I don't need to listen to you any longer. I'm Australia's—'

'Foremost alternative thinker, yeah I know, I read your social media profiles,' she said. 'Again, strange, considering you've been nothing but nasty to me about how I make my living since we first met but you seem to be surprisingly up to date on what I post, all my partnerships and how I make my living. I would have thought an academic like yourself wouldn't have time for *silly little girl* stuff like that. Remind me again which university you teach at?'

There was no hint of embarrassment about Marjorie. 'I was hounded out of the mainstream institutions. They're not ready to hear the truth. It's the University of Life for me now. I'm the people's professor . . . ' Her sodden clothes, oil-stained hands and filthy face weren't able to strip away her pomposity.

'Professor of what exactly?' Cassandra asked.

'I don't have to listen to this!' shouted the older woman. 'I'm going.'

'What were you doing down here, Marjorie?' Cassandra tried again.

'Nothing.'

'Cobblers,' she said. 'You were looking for me, weren't you? Or at least, you were looking for something.'

'You don't know what you've stumbled into here,' she said, her voice low. 'You and that imbecile Howie Temple. This is all big, big stuff. You're in danger, both of you. And if you keep poking your noses in, you're going to get us all killed.'

Cassandra felt the same chill that had gripped her in the kitchen with Matthias. While the former footballer had proven harmless, there was a steel in Marjorie's voice that she'd not heard before. That was the thing about a crisis – for some people, it showed the cracks in their bravado, let the scared person inside shine through. For other people, it meant they dropped their harmless act, and showed a far more dangerous inner self. She had a terrible feeling that Marjorie was in the latter camp.

'What are you on about?' she asked, not sure that she wanted to know the answer.

Marjorie stepped forward a little, the water rippling around her ankles.

'This ship, this whole scenario, it's risky, more risky than you could possibly know. Ed doesn't know, Temple doesn't know, but I hope you will see sense at least. We're all in dreadful danger and I, for one, don't want to be the victim of some explosive accident.'

'Marjorie, you're not making any sense,' she said. 'Who's in danger?'

'We are! All of us!'

'I don't understand!'

Marjorie's face flashed anger. She splashed through the dirty water of the engine room and grabbed Cassandra by the shoulders.

'Captain Rolando,' she said, an intensity in her dark brown eyes. 'He wasn't the jolly seadog he liked to play. He has – or rather had – some very unpleasant associates. He was a gangster.'

'Gangster? Rolando? No, you're having me on, chuck, I mean Marjorie. He was hardly Al Capone.'

'I'm deadly serious!' Her voice echoed around the flooded room. She tightened her grip on Cassandra's shoulders. 'This is real,' she said. 'This is the real world, Cassandra, not some Hollywood version of gangland life. We're dealing with serious people and serious money. Mafia-level money. They aren't happy, I can tell you that much. I mean, they can't be, can they? They've bumped off a man while he was filming a TV show. They don't care, they don't need to care. They're above the law!'

'Who?' Cassandra asked. 'Who are "they"?'

Marjorie's head snapped around. She peered out of the engine room door.

'Did you hear that?' she whispered. 'Did you hear that just then? Outside?'

Cassandra hadn't heard anything. Marjorie's grip was tightening on her. She tried to pull herself free but the older woman wouldn't let her go.

'You're hurting me,' she said.

'Quiet,' Marjorie hissed. 'There's somebody out there, in the corridor.'

'I'm sure there is, we've got a boat load of people upstairs and I'd hope somebody might have noticed by now that I've gone missing. I shouldn't have let that stupid Matthias talk me into coming down here. He was babbling on about danger too.'

'He knows nothing,' she dismissed him. 'Another self-regarding footballer with nothing between his ears. Like your friend Temple, all craggy good looks and no substance.'

'Howie is smarter than you think,' she said. 'He's just, well, old.'

'He's the same age as me.'

Cassandra bit her tongue.

'Are you going to tell me what's going on here, Marjorie?' she said. 'We can't just stand here in the water forever. We'll get that foot thing the soldiers had in the war.'

'Trench foot,' she said.

'That's it,' said Cassandra. 'And I don't really want my feet looking like shrivelled prunes. I'm trying to get a deal with Christian Louboutin and—'

There was a sudden shout from outside the engine room. The two women jumped with fright as Howie came charging into the chamber among the froth of the flooded water.

'Don't you touch her!' he shouted.

Marjorie immediately let go of Cassandra.

'Howie, I'm fine, watch out!' Cassandra shouted back.

It was too late. A combination of the deep floodwater and his own clumsiness sent Howie tumbling forward. He clattered into Marjorie and they both tumbled down. They landed with an almighty splash that sent filthy water up as high as the ceiling. Cassandra was soaked and she just stood there while the debacle unfolded in front of her.

'You idiot!' Marjorie coughed and spluttered, surfacing for the second time in as many minutes. 'What are you doing?'

Howie gasped for air. He looked as surprised and shocked as the others, despite being the perpetrator.

'You . . . ' he spluttered. 'Don't . . . You killed Rolando.'

'What? Me? That's absurd,' Marjorie scoffed.

'She didn't,' said Cassandra.

'What?'

'She didn't kill him.'

'But Matthias said . . . '

'Matthias is an idiot,' snapped Marjorie, starting to cry again. 'And so are you.'

Cassandra reached down and offered her a hand. She took it and Howie helped himself up.

'What's going on?' he said.

'I don't know,' said Cassandra. 'But Marjorie here is going to tell us everything she knows. Isn't that right, chuck?'

Chapter 16

The upper deck was warm and comfortable. More importantly, it was dry. It was where Howie had retreated to last night and even in the knowledge of the carnage of the last few hours, it still offered something resembling peace. Being above everything was a brief moment of respite. He thought how he'd looked out at the distant lights of the coast last night, invisible in the daylight. He'd have to wait until dusk to see them again. He had thought how pretty the shimmering villages looked last night, but now the distance seemed ominous rather than freeing.

The old song was true – what a difference a day made. Although the last twenty-four hours felt like decades. If it hadn't been his real life he'd have stolen the idea for a film plot. He liked that idea – maybe he could try to produce something, a new project. Who was he kidding? He had nothing new to work on. He hadn't had anything new to work on for the better part of two decades. Even his last few films had been sequels of ever-worsening quality.

'Watch your back, babe.'

Cassandra eased past behind him. She was carrying a huge, steaming mug of coffee. Delicately, she padded over to Marjorie who was trying to dry out in the sunshine.

'There you go, chuck, a latte, my specialty,' she said, offering the mug down.

Marjorie glanced down at the coffee. She sniffed it.

'Is it soy milk?' she asked.

'Yes, just like you asked.' Cassandra remained cheery.

'And did you use the dark roast beans like I asked?'

'Yes, of course.'

Marjorie seemed almost disappointed that her orders had been carried out to the fullest extent. She took up her coffee and sipped it gingerly. Cassandra, satisfied that her task was complete, rounded and turned back to Howie, giving him a knowing look. He nodded subtly.

'Where's my latte?' he asked.

'You didn't ask for one,' came the reply.

'But she got one.'

Cassandra slapped his arm to get him to be quiet. He begrudgingly obliged. Howie shook his head. He used to have people falling over themselves to make him lattes.

They stood watching Marjorie for a moment. The older woman didn't seem to care. She was sprawled out on the benches that curved around the edge of the top deck, lapping up the rays as she sipped her coffee.

He felt a nudge in his side. Cassandra was looking at him.

'What?' he asked quietly.

'Go on then,' she said, equally quiet.

'Go on what?'

'Ask her what she knows.'

'Why me?'

'Because you thought she was going to kill me ten minutes ago and almost drowned her in the engine room just as she was getting to her point about some kind of mob mayhem we've got ourselves caught up in.'

Cassandra had him there. He was going to protest but stopped before he could start. He coughed and stepped forward.

'And be gentle,' she said to him, holding him back a little.

'What?'

'Gentle, subtle, she's clearly been through a lot.'

'She's not been through any more than we have,' he said.

'Yes, I know, chuck, but that's not the point, is it? My mam always says you get honey from bees if you're kind to them, not go in and smash up their hive.' Cassandra smiled. 'Please, Howie.'

Howie gritted his teeth. He nodded in agreement. There was something about Cassandra Troy that seemed to press his buttons. She was clever, he gave her that. She knew how to get what she wanted but without leaving you feeling as if you'd been trampled. The simple truth was that she was also pleasant. Maybe it was a sad indictment of his career, if not life, that he hadn't been around many people as nice as her.

'Fine,' he grumbled, and walked over to Marjorie.

She looked up at him as he approached. Her eyeliner was a bit more smudged and cheeks reddened from all of her crying. But Howie could see that her usual arrogant smugness was coming back to bear as she dried out.

'Feeling better?' he asked.

'Yes, thank you,' she said. 'No thanks to you. You could have killed me, you know.'

'Perhaps that should have been the plan,' he said under his breath.

'Running in there like a man half your age, half drowning me. You ought to be ashamed of yourself.'

'It was a mistake,' he said. 'Just a mix-up. I got the wrong end of the broom and thought that Cassandra was in trouble.'

Marjorie snorted.

'Typical of you men,' she said. 'Even with the basic facts clearly presented to you, you still make a complete cock up of every situation. I honestly don't know how you ever survived the evolutionary process.'

Howie was doing his very best to keep himself calm. He had to stick to the facts. Their investigation, if you could even call it that, had all been aspersions and suspicions up to now. 'Forget me, it's Captain Rolando I want to hear about, what do you know about him?' he asked, cutting straight to the point. 'And if you know so much about him, how do we know that you're not actually his killer after all? Why should we believe you?'

'Howie,' said Cassandra, joining them. 'Take it easy.'

'I don't think I'm being unreasonable here,' he said. 'I mean, we're all still suspects aren't we? Aside from the fact you and I never left each other's sight between seeing Rolando alive and finding his body, I consider myself not just free to distrust everyone else, but downright wise.'

Marjorie took all of this in. She turned her face to the sun.

Howie just stood there, waiting. 'Hello?' he said. 'Can you hear me?'

'Yes, I can hear you,' she said, laconically. 'In fact I'm just about sick of hearing your voice and all your wild theories.'

'The feeling is more than mutual, believe me.'

'Okay, calm down you two,' said Cassandra, stepping between them. 'I think what Howie is trying to say, Marjorie, is that we'd really like to know what you know about Captain Rolando. You did say you would tell us, after all.'

Marjorie was silent, cradling her coffee. Somewhere, high above them, a gull let out a little croak and flew off back towards the shore. Howie envied it greatly.

'Rolando was a gangster,' she said at length.

'You've already told Cassandra that,' said Howie.

'Am I telling this story or are you?' she asked, tipping her sunglasses down to dart him a glare. 'Rolando was a mob man, or at least he worked for gangsters. Something like this was *always* going to happen. It was just a matter of time.'

'And how do you know all of this?' he asked.

'Not only am I Australia's foremost alternative thinker, I'm also an academic. Do you need me to explain to you what that means, Howie? It means I know how to do my research. Something you'd be familiar with if your roles had ever required even an ounce of creativity.'

He almost crunched his teeth to oblivion as he ground them down. Cassandra, sensing his mounting frustration, took the lead.

'What does that mean exactly, that he was a gangster?' she asked. 'Did he shoot people? Was he running some sort of racket?'

'Of course you wouldn't recognise a gangland player even if they were stood right in front of you.' Marjorie smirked. 'I'm sure you've never come across anyone even remotely dangerous in your line of work, have you Cassandra? Unless you count your waxing technician.'

Cassandra couldn't help but laugh. Marjorie was turning into some kind of pantomime villain right in front of her. All she needed was the wig, the glitter and the chorus of boos from the children in the audience. 'Okay, whatever, babe,' she said. 'We're trying to help out here and you're giving us mixed signals. Either you want to tell us what you know, or you don't. Howie and I are capable of doing this whole investigation without you, you know. Especially if we're going to be the stars of the new show. In fact, we don't need *any* help. More stardom and fame for us. Isn't that right, babe?'

She started to turn away. It was Howie's turn to smirk. Maybe they'd make an actress out of Cassandra yet.

'Now hold on here,' Marjorie said. 'There's no need to be like that, is there?'

Cassandra and Howie stopped. 'Got her,' she whispered to him.

They lingered for a moment longer, letting Marjorie suffer. Then, slowly, they turned back to face her. She'd kicked her legs off the sofa and looked almost approachable.

'I'm sorry,' she said. 'I'm sorry, I'm sorry, I'm sorry.'

She began to cry softly. Cassandra stepped forward but Howie stopped her.

'Careful,' he said. 'She can switch the tears on like a tap.'

'Don't be silly,' she dismissed him. 'She's upset.'

'And literally ten seconds ago she was saying you were dumb as a mule. She can't be trusted. Even if she knows something she's probably holding back until the cameras are on her.'

Cassandra pulled herself free. She sat down beside Marjorie and rubbed her back.

'Come on now, babe, don't be like that,' she said. 'We've all been under stress since all of this happened. Come and tell us what you know and see if it makes you feel any better. If you've got proper intel then we can stage it again when Ben and Geri have turned up again.'

Marjorie sniffed loudly. She put her mug down and then pushed her wet hair out of her face. She wiped away some of her smudged eyeliner.

'Before I flew out here for the show, I compiled a little dossier on you all,' she said.

'Dossier? Who do you think you are? James Bond?' asked Howie.

'I like to know who I'm working with,' she said. 'And the prospect of sharing a luxury yacht with a lot of strangers didn't quite tick all my personal safety standards. I get a lot of death threats, you might be surprised to know.'

After twenty-four hours in her company, Howie was distinctly unsurprised.

'I had one of my assistants pull together information on everyone once Ed had confirmed the guestlist,' she continued. 'Everything about your careers, your interests, social media, the lot.'

'Where did all of that come from?' asked Howie.

'Neanderthal, isn't he?' she said to Cassandra.

'It's everywhere, chuck,' she said to him. 'Personal info, data, it's all online and you don't normally have to look very hard to find it. Especially if you're famous, like us. Newspaper articles, charitable donations, everything, it's all on the internet for everyone, forever.'

'Yes those of us with a public profile, we stand out like sore thumbs,' Marjorie tutted. 'As do those with a criminal record.'

A cool breeze passed over the upper deck. Howie rubbed his bare arms, his still wet polo shirt sticking to his back.

'Rolando had a criminal record?' asked Cassandra.

Marjorie nodded.

'What was it for?' asked Howie.

'Nothing sinister.' She cleared her throat. 'Some petty theft when he was a teenager. He grew up in Bilbao apparently, Basque Country. That's in Spain, Howie.'

'I know where it is,' he lied.

'The usual sad story, abusive childhood, learned to live on his wits in the streets and fell in with the wrong crowd. Only it seems that our dear, departed skipper didn't fully leave his life of crime behind when he enlisted in the Spanish Navy after a string of convictions when he was a teen.'

'What happened?' asked Cassandra. 'Who were the wrong crowd?'

Marjorie sniffed again. Howie could tell she was delighted to be the centre of attention.

'My researcher found a whole pile of companies in Rolando's name,' she said. 'Strange ones, all relating to fishing trawlers and tugs in and around Spanish, French and Italian coastal towns. The companies would start at the beginning of the year and be wound up before the next one began. Financially irregular, wouldn't you agree?'

'If you say so,' said Howie.

'So he was getting creative with his bookkeeping, that hardly makes him a Mafia Don, does it?' asked Cassandra.

'True, and lots of people are at it,' Marjorie conceded. 'But it gets stranger when our dear, departed friend Captain Rolando is spotted at the funeral of a well-known and highly feared crime boss in Florence just a few weeks before we set sail. My researcher showed me the newspaper clippings and the pictures. He was there, front and centre.'

Her eyes widened. She looked at the others expectantly, waiting for praise to be showered on her.

'Well?' she asked, when none was forthcoming. 'Doesn't that all sound cut and dried to you?'

'Erm . . . ' was all Cassandra managed. 'You're trying to tell us you think Rolando was a gangster because he was on the wrong side of the tracks as a kid, was dodging tax and then was seen at a funeral a few weeks ago.'

'Oh Marjorie,' Howie said. 'That was quite the performance. You are priceless. Your real gift is that I think I genuinely believe the nonsense you spout. That's why your acolytes love your mad political views, and that's why you've convinced yourself of your cock and bull story.'

'What are you talking about? Can't you see all the connections?' she blurted. 'The man was clearly some sort of informant for the mob. Or at the very least in their debt. And they've had him killed here, now, on this ship.'

'So who killed him?' asked Cassandra. 'The bridge was locked, there was no way in or out. Howie almost gave himself a heart attack shouldering the bloody thing open.'

'Gangsters,' said Marjorie. 'Other gangsters. These people don't mess around, Cassandra. They're serious. Seriously dangerous.'

'The only thing that's dangerous is your imagination,' said Howie with gallons of venom. 'You've wasted our time, as usual, Marjorie. We thought you might have something concrete for us, something that was conclusive. Instead you've put two and two together and made five. You've spun us a load of garbage about the Mafia and hitmen who've procured keys to the bridge.'

'It might have been a hitwoman,' she said succinctly.

'Whatever.' He waved his hand. 'Unbelievable, truly unbelievable.'

'But . . . but . . . '

Howie stormed away, as far as the small upper deck would allow. Cassandra hurried after him.

'Calm down, Howie, it's okay,' she said.

'She's wasting our time,' he said. 'This whole morning has been a colossal waste of time. In fact this whole venture has been a waste of time – I don't think we've hardly got any good footage either. If I'm not clearing a deck of ocean then I'm helping that moron Ed into bed after he's been hit around the head.'

'Wait, what?'

Cassandra's face went slack. Howie realised then that she didn't know what had happened to their supposedly visionary director.

'Oh,' he said. 'Yeah. Ed was found unconscious on the deck by one of the guests. He's been hit on the head by all accounts.'

Cassandra didn't say anything. She pushed past him and hurried down the stairs.

'What does she think she's going to do?' sneered Marjorie. 'Don't tell me – she was in season three of *Celebrity Paramedic*?'

Chapter 17

'He looks so peaceful, like he's asleep,' said Cassandra.

'Steady on, he's not dead,' groaned Howie. 'He's just unconscious, Cassandra. We don't have to break out the eulogies for him just yet.'

'"Yet" being the operative word,' she said.

Ed was lying in the same position Howie had left him in. He looked calm and serene, eyes closed, a sort of half smile on his face. The rest of the guest suite had been cleaned and tidied. Howie wasn't quite sure who had been hard at work considering he'd been with Cassandra and Marjorie most of the morning. But all the clothes were gone and there was a smell of bleach and cleaning product about the place. Even Ed had been tucked in neatly to the large bed he had left him on. In fact the clinical precision made him suspect the immaculate housekeeping was Ms Sachiko's work.

'Jeez, Ed – you took one hell of a bump!' said Cassandra, clearly hoping she might see his eyelids flicker if she spoke directly to him, but he stayed as impassive as the sphinx. She turned to her friend. 'Who could be doing this, Howie?

Her voice was wavering. For the first time since their amateur detection had begun, Howie saw a fragility in his partner. Until now Cassandra had pretty much taken everything in her stride. Her tough, salt-of-the-earth Scouse humour and warm nature had been invaluable to him. They were, after all, trapped in a fairly precarious situation. Even when he'd found Ed sprawled on the deck, his first thought was that Cassandra would know what to do.

Now she was beginning to crack. Howie couldn't blame her. This morning's attempts at unravelling the truth seemed to have thrown up more questions than answers. Matthias, the footballer, who had been fairly high up his suspect list, was nothing more than a buffoon with dreams of cowboy boots. He had the strength to bump someone off, but Howie wasn't convinced he was a killer.

Then there was Marjorie. She was so self-absorbed she couldn't see anything beyond her own brilliance. Howie had known directors like her in the past. Inevitably their productions had fallen apart due to their unalloyed monomania. Marjorie was the same. He didn't trust her, he didn't trust a word that came out of that spiteful mouth. But was she a murderer? Marjorie may have thought she was an alternative thinker, but she wasn't *that* good. Her overconfidence was her downfall.

'Sorry,' said Cassandra, choking back tears. 'Look at me, I'm a soppy tart.'

'Is that some kind of cake?' he asked.

'No,' she said, wiping her cheeks. 'It's just a turn of phrase, Howie. Don't worry about it.'

They stood in silence again, looking down at Ed on the bed. Howie couldn't help but feel the suite had taken on a funeral home vibe. While he had been at pains to remind

Cassandra that the director wasn't dead, it still felt more like a wake than a visit. Even the bright sunlight and cool breeze wafting through the suite couldn't dilute the sombre atmosphere. He'd been so relieved to find Ed still breathing he'd not given a thought as to what would happen if he never woke up.

He shook the thought from his mind. Cassandra was upset. He raised his arm about her shoulder but hesitated. It floated there in the air, not quite knowing what to do. He dropped it quickly, letting his hand fall to his side. He felt ridiculous. And, more importantly, he hoped that she hadn't noticed.

'You can give me a hug if you want, you know,' she said, rubbing her nose with a balled up tissue.

'What?' He panicked.

'You don't have to be afraid, I won't bite,' she said.

'Oh, I . . . erm . . . '

He broke out in a cold sweat. This was ridiculous. Cassandra was lovely, friendly, helpful. He didn't have to feel awkward around her. If Howie Temple in his twenties could see him now, panicking about giving a young, attractive woman an innocent hug, he would be going berserk. What had he become?

'I could use a hug, actually, chuck,' she said, turning to him.

She turned to face him and opened up her arms. Howie was still sweating. He cleared his throat and nervously leaned down. She wrapped her arms about him and he did the same. She was tiny, thin, his big arms encircling her.

'I needed that,' she said. 'You're like a big, fuzzy teddy bear, really.'

'Try telling that to my ex-wives,' he said.

'Okay, a big, fuzzy, grumpy teddy bear, maybe.'

'That's more like it. They've taken me for every dollar and cent I had. They're the reason I'm saying yes to gigs like this. Me donning a Pepto-Bismol pink polo shirt pays better than art-house theatre.'

'Life's not all about money, babe. You should know that from our last couple of days. Poor Rolando's family are going to find that out the hard way. Anyway, don't try to pretend that if you had the cash you'd be doing Pinter in the West End six nights a week. More like sinking pints six nights a week.'

'Yeah, I suppose,' he said. 'The trouble is, I won't be doing anything, earning anything, unless we salvage some kind of show from this disaster. You don't think there was anything in what Marjorie was saying up there, do you? I don't fancy sleeping with the fishes because we start asking questions about *La Cosa Nostra* on camera.'

Cassandra looked confused. 'What do you mean?' she asked.

'The Mafia, darling. I suspect our Marj is jumping to conclusions but if she's even halfway right then we're on dangerous ground.'

'I'd rather be on any kind of ground right now,' Cassandra said as the boat pitched and rolled gently in the water.

'If we're ever going to get off this boat we're going to need to make that happen ourselves. Ed was meant to be our ticket out of here but we don't even know if he got the radio working, let alone contacted the authorities. No, we can't wait for him to come round. It's time to rev up this investigation. I remember there was a cop on the set of one of my movies in the early nineties—'

'Oh, which one,' said Cassandra, her sadness disappearing. '*Cop Hunter? Cop Hunter Two? Pumped Full of Lead and Left for Dead?*'

'How do you know about those?' he asked. 'They were made before you were born.'

'I told you, I like to do my homework,' she winked. 'Marjorie isn't the only one who likes to do a show prepared. And besides, my dad loved your films. He had them all on DVD. Remember those?'

'I remember when they were video cassettes and laser discs, Cassandra.'

'Bloody hell,' she snorted.

'That's not the point,' he said. 'I can't remember the film. But this cop, he was hired by the studio to come on and tell us actors and the director and producer what would happen in real life. I remembered him, last night, when I was lying awake staring at the ceiling.'

'And what did he say?' she asked.

'I can't remember much.' Howie looked blank.

Cassandra rolled her eyes.

'It's not my fault,' he protested. 'I was young, I was on the cover of every magazine in the world. What the hell did you expect me to do? Take notes like I was in college?'

'It might have helped,' she said.

'Sorry, of course, what was I thinking?' He slapped his forehead. 'There I was, in my early twenties, with the universe at my feet and I thought, yes, let's pay attention because in thirty years' time I'll be leading my own murder investigation on a luxury yacht. That makes perfect sense.'

'You can't remember anything about what he said?' she asked. 'Nothing? No shred of absorbed information you might have accidentally paid attention to?'

'It was something to do with what you don't know being as important as what you do,' he said. 'The facts tell one story, the gaps tell the mirror image.'

'Well on those terms we're doing brilliantly – because we know an awful lot of nothing, Howie. It's making my head hurt. Also, you say we've wasted the morning but just because Matthias and Marjorie had no proof for their wild stories, it doesn't mean some of what they were saying wasn't true,' she said. 'I'm not turning all Team Marjorie here, but if Rolando was at the funeral of a Mafia boss just a few weeks ago, then there could be some truth in it.'

'We don't know the context,' said Howie. 'He might have been the guy's gardener. Or friends with him from school. Just because you're at a Mob funeral doesn't make you a mafioso.'

Cassandra nodded in agreement. She looked back down at Ed.

'Poor Ed,' she said with a sigh.

'Poor Ed nothing,' said Howie.

'Don't be so heartless.'

'I'm not being heartless,' he said. 'He got us all into this mess. And to top it all, he's left us marooned us in the middle of the sea with no means of contacting the authorities. Although he was so quick to come up with his big reality crime gambit, I'm not sure he tried very hard to reach the Italian authorities.'

'So what are you saying – that he deliberately let us think we're stuck here?'

'I'm saying that we've got to go back on that bridge and check out the comms equipment.'

'Hello?'

The door squeaked open behind them. Howie and Cassandra turned to see Shig, the guest who had discovered Ed on deck earlier edging into the room, *his* room.

'Hi there,' said Cassandra. 'Is everything alright, chuck?' she asked him, although it seemed a pointless question – how could anything be alright when you had a victim of what looked like attempted murder comatose in your bed?

'Yes, no, yes, I mean.' He was flustered. 'It's been a very strange voyage. I thought I should get out of the sun for a while. But you're busy attending to Mr Wells so I won't disturb you.'

'Come on in and take a load off,' she said, beckoning the guest in. 'It's your room after all.'

The guest looked back out through the door. Satisfied the cameras weren't rolling, he plodded into the suite and perched on one of the large chairs that looked out onto the balcony.

'I was just coming to check on Mr Wells,' he said. 'I hope he is okay.'

'He's still unconscious,' said Howie. 'And without proper medical attention we can't really tell. It could be touch and go.'

'I'm meant to be your hostess.' Cassandra offered her hand. 'Leading games on deck and serving drinks – not nursing crew in your room. I don't think this cruise is turning out like any of us imagined. I suspect if Ed wasn't out cold he'd be preparing for a whole sheaf of letters from lawyers.'

'Well, that part I could manage.' The man reached out and shook Cassandra's proffered hand. 'Arakawa Shig, solicitor.'

Howie's ears pricked up. He didn't like lawyers. He had a natural fear of them given his past. He found he was instinctively backing away from Arakawa.

'So tell me, how did you find yourself on this boat?' asked Cassandra, determined to actually try to do what she'd set out to and glean some useful information.

Arakawa bowed his head. He stared at his hands, entangling his fingers.

'It's all a terrible mistake,' he said. 'I wish I had stayed at home. This voyage is cursed, I truly believe that. Firstly what happened to the good captain and now what has happened to Mr Wells. I had a bad feeling about it all from the start. We should never have come.'

'You found Ed this morning, didn't you?' asked Howie.

Arakawa nodded.

'I did,' he said. 'Mr Wells had explained to us that the Captain was dead and that we were marooned here, waiting for the police. I retired here, to my suite but I couldn't settle. Once I went for a walk around the deck, I found him, just lying there, still as a stone. I tried to revive him but he wouldn't respond.' He looked over at Ed. 'I didn't know what to do. So I called on Ms Sachiko. She is a very experienced host, a good agent. She has been very helpful to me and my fellow guests.'

'She's quite something,' said Cassandra.

'Oh yes, definitely, we were very lucky to get her for our trip,' said Arakawa. 'Ms Sachiko is something of a legend back home in Osaka. She's very much sought after for travelling parties. Efficient, diligent and expensive. But she's worth every cent.'

'And she helped you with Ed?' asked Howie.

Arakawa nodded again.

'She came immediately. She was calm and collected. Not like me or the others when they found out what had happened. I think we all want to get off this ship as soon as possible. There is a bad aura to this place, a sense of . . . evil.'

'Steady on,' Howie laughed.

'Oh no, there is, Mr Temple, there is.' Arakawa's eyes widened. 'We are all in agreement. There are bad spirits here, an evil presence. You can sense it in everything, everyone. Whoever or whatever is responsible for these terrible acts, they have a wicked heart.'

Cassandra shuddered a little. She looked at Howie who had gone a little grey. He tried to brush it all off.

'There's a murderer on the loose here,' he said. 'But we intend to catch them, Ms Troy and myself. And any information or theories you had would be helpful.'

Arakawa shook his head.

'I don't know anything,' he said sadly. 'I am a lawyer, of course, and I understand the consequences of what's gone on here. As to who may be responsible, it could be anyone. Even you both.'

'What?' Cassandra laughed. 'Us?'

'Oh yes,' said the solicitor. 'Of course it could be. Either one of you could be responsible. My colleagues and I think so, at least.'

'Nonsense,' said Howie. 'We didn't do anything.'

'You discovered Captain Rolando's body, yes?' said Arakawa, innocently. 'You were the first to see him dead.

In my experience, through my profession, the first to find the body is usually the last to see the victim alive.'

'That can't be right,' said Cassandra.

'I'm afraid so,' said Arakawa humbly. 'At least it is back home. The saddest part of my profession, Ms Troy, has been, without doubt, dealing with families often torn apart by the actions of those closest to them. Husbands, wives, sons, daughters, brothers, sisters, mothers and fathers even. Not only do they lose the victim, invariably they'll lose another member to conviction. Although history suggests that this is not a new trend.'

Arakawa seemed to be coming alive. The talk of his work and philosophy appeared to make him relax slightly, despite the morbid subject matter.

'So who do you think is in the frame to be our killer, then?' asked Howie. 'Apart from Cassandra and I.'

The lawyer reclined back in the huge chair. He tapped his chin with a forefinger.

'It is an interesting question, certainly,' he said. 'It would appear that all of your fellow crew are capable of such a heinous act.'

'Now come on, Arakawa,' said Cassandra. 'I don't believe that for a second.'

'It's true,' he said gravely. 'I mean no offence by what I'm about to say but the very nature of celebrity can be likened to a kind of sociopathy. All of you, by the very fact of agreeing to be here in the first place have put yourselves under suspicion. If you are the kind of person who would do anything for fame, then perhaps murder is the ultimate act.'

'Wait a minute now,' said Howie, looking indignant. 'In the last thirty seconds, you've suggested I could be a sociopath, a fame whore and a murderer – even though you've said that very politely, and you speak better English than I do – you've still downright insulted me.'

But Cassandra was fascinated and urged the solicitor to continue. 'So you're saying everyone is a suspect.'

'I wouldn't rule out anyone yet, no,' he said. 'Although one thing confuses not just me, but my colleagues too.'

Howie and Cassandra leaned in a little.

'And what's that?' she asked.

Arakawa steepled his fingers. He made them into a gun shape and pointed at Ed lying on the bed.

'Mr Wells,' he said. 'His attack. It seems very messy, poorly done,' said Arakawa.

'In what sense?' asked Cassandra.

'The captain's murder sounded meticulously planned. Efficient, effective, skilled. But this? A blow to the head that didn't even result in death? That's not a sophisticated attack. Assaulting him in this manner seems like something clumsy, lazy even, from our killer, as if he was taken by surprise.'

'Lazy?' Howie squeaked. 'Cracking a man in the head with a blunt object is lazy to you?'

'Lazy or copycat,' said Arakawa. 'Being able to kill Captain Rolando and leave him in a locked room is *not* the work of an opportunist. The skipper was targeted, pre-determined. That means if Mr Wells was also a target of the same attacker, he would *not* still be with us. We cannot ignore the fact this might be two different assailants.'

Cassandra was terrified by Shig's last statement. 'You really think there could be two perpetrators?'

'Miss Troy, Mr Temple, like I said, in my work we do not discount anything without proof.'

Howie hadn't thought about any of this. He puffed out his cheeks and laughed, turning to Cassandra.

'Maybe Ed picked the wrong detectives,' he said. 'Perhaps Arakawa here would be the better investigator.'

'Oh no.' The lawyer stood up quickly, waving his hands. 'I couldn't possibly do that. I'm a lawyer, not a policeman. I merely deal with facts *after* the arrest, not before it. I wish you both the best of luck in your investigations, but I won't be taking part in anything further.'

He quickly made for the door. Cassandra and Howie followed him.

'If you think of anything else, let us know, would you, chuck?' she called after him. 'Or at least, would you give that speech about two killers again once we can find the blooming camera crew? It's what Ed would want, I know that much.'

'I'm afraid I can't do that, Ms Troy,' said Arakawa almost apologetically. 'You see I am under strict instructions from Ms Sachiko *not* to interact with any of this programme you and Mr Temple are now making. It's not in the agreements we signed before joining the voyage, you see.'

'Programme?' laughed Howie. 'Our director is laid out on your bed, dead to the world. I don't think our little true crime documentary will be gracing screens at all at this rate,' he said.

'No,' agreed Cassandra. 'Getting off this boat with our hides still intact seems like the only win at the moment.'

'Of course.' Arakawa nodded. 'Although I wouldn't stop your investigations. That's my advice at least.'

'No? Why not? She asked.

Arakawa looked back out the door again. He kept his voice low, hushed.

'You're keeping us all safe,' he said. 'You may not think it, but we're all rooting for you, the other guests and myself. If the killer *is* still onboard, they know what you're doing, they *know* you are on the trail. I don't know what happened to Mr Wells. Perhaps he stumbled upon something he wasn't supposed to and he's paid the price. But everyone else is still safer while you both investigate what's happened here. I'd implore you to keep going.'

He offered them a sad but reassuring smile. Nodding once more, he slipped out of the door and headed back for the deck upstairs. Before Howie could close the door, Ben and Geri appeared. The dynamic duo, filming and recording in silence as usual, stood watching him. He tried his best to keep his temper, although it was increasingly difficult. They were only doing their job, after all. He rubbed his forehead in frustration.

'I don't know about you, but I'm more confused than ever,' he said.

'Yeah,' Cassandra agreed. 'Feels like we've made no progress.'

'And Ed is still out for the count.' He nodded at the director.

'He's right though.'

'About what?'

'The killer,' she said gravely. 'They were professional, Rolando was a hit, they knew what they were doing. Whatever happened to Ed, that wasn't supposed to turn out like this, I'm sure. And they're still here, on this ship.'

'How do you know that?'

'I can feel it.' She shuddered again.

'Don't you start with the evil spirits too,' Howie droned.

'I know we've been focussing on the known passengers of *The Regal Secret*, Howie. But I think we've missed a trick. It's not inconceivable that our killer is not on the list,' she said. 'The ship's fifty metres long and there are plenty of places to hide. He could be anywhere right now. Hell, he could be watching us.'

She looked about the suite. The curtains by the balcony door billowed a little as another gust of Mediterranean air blew in.

'So what's our plan?' he asked.

'We redouble our efforts. Rule out as many of the guests and crew as possible first. Who have we not spoken to?' she asked back.

'Kelvin, the politician. We don't know his movements on the night Rolando died. Then there's Sachiko, our nudist yogi who runs a tight ship, pardon the pun. Do you think it's either of them? I don't think Ms Sachiko will be keen on allowing access to the other guests so let's start with Kelvin and her.'

'Sure,' Cassandra shrugged. 'But we need to find out quickly. Poor Ed needs treatment and we need to get off this yacht. You said you were going to look at the radio on the bridge again, see if Ed was right about it being unusable.'

They stood in silence, listening to the breeze whistling as it wafted in from the balcony and both thinking up reasons to delay going anywhere near the bridge. Ed meanwhile lay perfectly still on the bed, his serene half smile etched on his face. Howie swallowed his thoughts. Even unconscious, the man irritated the hell out of him.

Chapter 18

To Howie and Cassandra's surprise, the other celebrities and guests were all gathered on the main deck. They were sitting at the long, main table, eating. In all of the excitement of the morning's work, they had lost track of time. Lunch, it appeared, had been served. And what was more obvious was that far from sending everyone to cower in their cabins, the fear of what – or who – was lurking had brought guests and crew together, divisions of server and served put aside for now.

'Howie! Cassandra! Welcome, pull up a chair!' Matthias shouted, mouth full of food. 'We've just started, tuck in, help yourselves.'

A large spread was laid out before them. Everything from sandwiches to lobster tails, crab and even a steak that looked large enough to have come from a mammoth rather than a cow. The pantry looked like it had been ransacked and the guests were all tucking in. No point in saving fancy chow for later in the week, Howie supposed. Hopefully they'd all be back on terra firma before the pantry was totally bare. Or maybe they were all tucking in with such vigour in case it was their last meal, he thought slightly more grimly. Ms Sachiko, however, wasn't eating, instead sitting perfectly still at the opposite end from Matthias. Marjorie was beside her, silent and defeated. Her plate was half-heartedly filled with food but it was clear she hadn't touched anything either.

The Kontoglou sisters were batting their eyelashes at him. It seemed that even murder wasn't enough to put them off their appetite for him. Howie shuddered.

'No, thank you,' said Howie, waving away Matthias' offer of a plate.

'What? Why?' Matthias asked. 'You must be famished. Please, sit down. We all chipped in and helped out. There's plenty of food to go around.'

'I don't have the stomach for it, sorry,' he said.

'Well I'm famished,' said Cassandra, heading for a seat.

She slipped down beside Arakawa who slid his gaze to Ms Sachiko, then seeing he was under scrutiny, studiously ignored Cassandra.

Howie reached down and poured himself a tall glass of water. He jingled the ice around in the glass and slowly started a circuit of the table.

'How are you getting on anyway?' asked Matthias. 'Have you caught our killer yet? How's Ed?'

'He's still unconscious,' said Howie. 'We really need to get the radios working or the engines back up and running.'

'And I'm sure we will,' said the former footballer. 'But we should all eat something first, it's a terrible shock to us. Terrible.'

'Yes,' said Howie, cocking an eyebrow. 'It really is a priority though, and not just for calling the police; it's the medics we need. Rolando may be beyond help but Ed's future might be hanging in the balance. He's been out of action for a few hours now. That can't be healthy.'

The rest of the lunch party was quiet. Everything had seemed jovial at first when Howie and Cassandra had reappeared on deck. For a brief moment it felt like there was nothing wrong. Kirkby Hofstede was gnawing away at a lobster tail, his wife Martha trying to dab the juice from his chin. He kept batting her off, complaining she was ruining his dinner. Now that Howie and Cassandra had shown up, everyone clammed up, shut down, like teachers returning to an unruly class left unattended. Even Despoina and Thekla were more muted, clearly spurned by Howie's lack of interest in them.

'No, it is not,' said Ms Sachiko. 'There could be untold damage to his brain, especially given the extent of the impact to the back of his head. It may already be too late.'

'Well, thanks for that cheery assessment,' grumbled Howie.

'Does anyone know how to fix a radio?' asked Cassandra.

The table was quiet again. Everyone bowed their head, focussing on their food.

'Nobody? Marjorie, Kirkby, how about you two?'

Both shook their heads, looking as if Cassandra had asked them to split the atom.

'Perhaps I could be of some help,' said Matthias, clearing his throat.

'Really?' asked Howie. 'What do you know about radios? Apart from listening to football matches on them?'

'Not much, I admit. But when I was a young apprentice footballer in Frankfurt, the club and scouts encouraged me to plan for a career away from the game. Sensible, yes?

After all, nobody else from my sporting academy won a World Cup alongside me.'

'Did you win a World Cup, babe?' asked Cassandra with a smirk. 'You never really talk about it.'

'I studied electronics,' said the ex-player. 'Although "study" is probably a little exaggerated. I never was one for studying, I'm more of a, how do you say it? A hands-on person.'

'Anything is better than nothing,' said Howie. 'I said that to Sixpence None the Richer once, when we were at the very first Coachella. They were panicking about some missing amp or guitar or inflatable palm tree or something. And I told them, go onstage, anything is better than nothing.'

'Howie, aren't you a dark horse. I didn't have you down as the festival type,' Cassandra laughed. 'You'll have to join me at Glastonbury next year, we'll have you crowd-surfing in no time.'

'You're about a quarter of a century too late, my festival days are definitely done.' The actor shrugged. 'Even the tiny bunks onboard here are giving me flashbacks to camper vans and Winnebagos.' He turned back to Matthias. 'Could you take a look and see what you can do?'

'Gladly,' he said, getting up from the table.

Howie didn't want to put him off so didn't remind him of the fact that he'd not only be trying to mend a radio, but do so in the presence of a corpse. He slung the keys over.

'I'll be in the radio room then if anyone needs me,' he said, heading in the direction of the bridge.

Howie wandered around the table once more, this time Ben and Geri following him. For the first time since this debacle had started, Howie realised he was starting to become unaware of them. He stopped at an empty seat and leaned on the back, surveying the others. For the first time since the murder, everyone bar Matthias was gathered in one place at the same time. It was the first chance he had been given to see how they all interacted.

Howie wasn't sure what he was looking for. Maybe there was nothing to look for in the first place if Cassandra was right and the killer wasn't sitting around this table but stowed away hiding in the belly of the ship. But whether he was looking at the murderer or whether the culprit was somewhere looking out at him, the assassin was hardly going to be waving a neon sign above their head signalling to him that they were responsible. And that, unfortunately, was the problem. The crew, the guests, they all appeared perfectly normal, perfectly human.

Then it struck him. Matthias was gone, he'd seen that. But there was somebody else missing too. Another empty chair, apart from his own. Howie stood up, his back clicking.

'Where's Kelvin?' he asked.

The others stopped eating. Everyone looked about the table, searching for the elusive politician. They all looked blank and turned back to stare at Howie.

'Did he appear for lunch at all?' he asked them.

Again, more conferring. Cassandra seemed to sense the urgency from her detective partner. She slowly got to her feet.

'When was the last time any of you saw him?' she asked. 'I've not seen him since we bailed out the back deck,' she said. 'After Howie had us breaking our backs to stop the ship from sinking.' Silence from her crewmates. 'And nobody has seen him after then?' Cassandra pressed.

Howie felt another cold sweat forming on his brow. He beckoned to Cassandra, hurrying towards the back of the deck and the stairway down to the galley and cabins, Ben and Geri lugging their equipment behind them.

'What's Kelvin up to?' he called back behind him.

'He might not be up to anything, Howie.' She juddered down the stairs. 'He just might not want any lunch. You didn't eat anything either, remember?'

'But earlier he said he was going to start on the cooking,' he said. 'Where's he gone? The man hasn't done a day's work in his life and now he decides he's not going to stuff his face. No politician I know ever turned down a free meal.'

They barrelled through the galley and thudded into the narrow corridor where the doors to the cabins lined the walls. Kelvin had taken the furthest set of bunks, lucky enough to not have to share with anyone. The door was closed. Howie tried the handle.

'It's locked,' he said.

'So? He might be sleeping?'

'Kelvin!' Howie shouted. 'Are you in there?'

'Kelvin? Is everything alright, babe? Are you wanting something to eat at all?'

'You're not his mother,' said Howie, trying the handle again.

'I know that, Howie. I just thought maybe a friendlier approach might yield better results.'

'And how's that going for you?' He kept trying the door.

'Shut up.'

'Kelvin! Are you in there?' Howie shouted. 'It's us. Open up, buddy.'

There had been no response from inside the cabin. Howie had a sudden sense of dread descend on him. He turned, pale-faced to Cassandra who was on his shoulder.

'This all seems a bit familiar,' he said gravely.

She swallowed and then banged on the door.

'Kelvin! Are you okay, babe? We just want to make sure you're alright. Kelvin! Open up, would you?'

Cassandra bashed her hands on the door while Howie keep trying the handle. The others had slowly made their way down into the galley and were filling up the hallway behind them. Matthias appeared too now, disturbed by the commotion, and tentatively joined them, his towering bulk looming over the door.

'Is he alright?' he asked.

'We don't know, Matthias,' said Howie, straining with the handle. 'He won't answer.'

'How do you know he's in there?' asked Marjorie from the back of the throng.

'Where else could he be?' asked Cassandra, still shouting through the door.

'Perhaps we should force entry,' said Ms Sachiko. 'Although myself and my clients will have nothing to do with any consequences.'

Howie let go of the handle. He pushed Cassandra and Matthias out of the way and lined himself up. For the second time in the space of a few days, he prepared to charge a locked door. Strangely, he felt a lot more confident about it this time around. Perhaps it was the success of his last efforts.

'Stand back,' he said to the others.

'Are you sure about this, babe?' asked Cassandra.

'Get back, stay away,' he said again.

Lowering his shoulder, Howie took aim. He charged forward, carrying all of his momentum with him. Unfortunately, that momentum was his worst enemy. He clattered into the door and, unlike the one leading to the bridge, it didn't move. His head bashed against it and he stumbled backwards, the wind knocked out of him. He would have fallen straight onto his backside if Matthias hadn't caught him first.

'The door . . . the door . . . it didn't.'

'It didn't give way,' said Matthias, steadying him.

'I know that,' said Howie, catching his breath. 'I don't understand it.'

'Now there's a surprise,' said Marjorie sardonically.

Howie ignored her. He rolled his shoulders and prepared for another run at the door. Matthias, however, put an arm out across his chest.

'Perhaps I should have a go,' he said.

Howie was going to argue but the effort seemed too much. His head was still spinning and a steady ache was radiating out from his shoulder.

'Fine,' he said, stepping back.

Matthias took a deep breath and cracked his knuckles. He had a fierce concentration on his face and looked about ready to take on the whole world, let alone the door. He rolled shoulders before giving the door an almighty kick. It rattled but held firm. Another swift boot from the former footballer, a loud ripping sound filling the narrow hallway, and the whole thing collapsed backwards.

'Damn,' breathed Howie.

'Impressive,' said Cassandra.

'Thank you,' said Matthias, galloping through the wreckage.

He tossed the door, or what remained of it, away to the side as they all piled into the cramped bunk. It didn't take them long to come to a stop.

'Oh my god,' gasped Cassandra.

Howie's mouth fell open. Matthias said nothing. Ben and Geri, as ever, said nothing but they kept filming as they squeezed in behind. But the boom mic sagged and the camera cut away as they took in what lay in front of them.

Kelvin Kamani, former British Member of Parliament, was facing them, perfectly still. His face was contorted into a grimace, the kind which could only be born out of terror. His fingers were splayed, the tendons in his hands and arms tight and flexed, his dark eyes staring straight at them. The knife at his throat glistened in the dim light of the cabin and Howie was certain he could see himself reflected in its well-polished blade. But for Howie, even more alarming than the sight of the terrified Kelvin was the realisation it was a stranger bearing the cleaver that was resting its sharp edge on the tender flesh of the MP's neck.

A strange man with a pulled, narrow face was standing behind Kelvin. His spindly fingers were wrapped tightly around the handle of the knife, his other hand gripping the politician's other shoulder. He retreated a little when he saw the others although his blade never moved.

'What the hell is all this?' asked Howie, as he gathered his wits.

'Don't move another inch,' said the stranger in broken English, his accent a heavy Italian. 'Take another step and Kamani here has his throat cut.'

'Okay, okay, just take it easy, chuck, we don't want any trouble,' said Cassandra from over Howie's shoulder.

'Trouble,' Kelvin whimpered, finding his voice, albeit little more than a whisper. 'If you don't mind me saying, Ms Troy. I think we're already in a spot of trouble.'

Chapter 19

Cassandra had never been in a standoff before. She wasn't even really sure that this was what a standoff was. She had read about them all the time in the news. In certain parts of her native Liverpool, and anywhere in the world for that matter, these kinds of incidents were all too common. The police were usually involved, of course. Not a group of clueless celebrities and a bewildered bunch of cruise fans.

Cassandra had grown up in the suburbs of her home city, where the only excitement was when the ice cream van came around on a Saturday afternoon. A perfectly safe, bordering on staid, childhood had been capped off by a much more adventurous time at university. Her joint-honours degree surprised most who ever bothered to ask her. And while the nuances of statistics and psychometrics were hardly rock and roll, they did afford her time to party every night.

Cassandra had enjoyed her higher education, even if it hadn't met with the approval of her demanding father. His expectations of her to follow in his footsteps as a neurologist had been dashed as soon as she'd discovered you could stay out past midnight. Not that she thought much of it now. It hardly mattered anymore. Her dad, as brilliant as he was, was crippled with gambling debts and everything else that went along with his flaws. The family had stuck by him, as much as they could. While the 'Dr Troy' title had a nice ring to it, life in Cassandra's household growing up had been much more grounded. When her near overnight fame had started to bring in the cash, she'd been more than happy to help. Her father knew she'd 'done good' and never complained. He didn't really have a leg to stand on after all.

Now, as an ageing influencer hurtling towards the ripe old age of thirty, she had much bigger fish to fry. And the main one, right now, was the armed lunatic in front of her.

'I think we should all just calm down a little,' she said. 'Maybe take a moment to just breathe and relax, before somebody gets hurt. Does that sound about right?'

Nobody answered her. The knifeman was still holding Kelvin hostage a few feet in front of them. They were pressed against the bunk with nowhere to go. His eyes were darting around the room, back and forth between Cassandra, Howie and Matthias. She could feel her heart racing, the endless drum of her pulse hurting her ears.

Beside her Howie and Matthias were edgy. They both looked like tigers getting ready to pounce. She thought there was something strangely heroic about Howie now. He looked determined, brave even. It was a new side to him that she hadn't seen before. Although she didn't approve of him thinking he could take on this maniac. Relief that they'd found Kelvin alive had turned into a gruesome fear that'd they witness his murder in front of their eyes. Somebody was going to be injured if anyone did anything rash.

Matthias was the leading candidate to be that somebody. He was easing closer and closer to Kelvin and the knifeman, his arms stretched out, fingers flexing.

'Can we just talk this through, please?' she pleaded again.

'Don't move!' the knifeman snapped. 'I'll do it, don't think I won't.'

'We believe you,' she said.

'I don't,' said Matthias.

'What?' she yelped. 'Of course we believe him, Matthias.'

'I think he's bluffing,' said the footballer.

'Me too,' said Howie.

'Gents!' she shouted. 'This isn't the time for theatrics.'

The two men were edging forward. Kelvin was sweating profusely as the knifeman's blade dug a little harder into his neck, a thin bead of blood blooming now.

'Please, do what he says,' he pleaded. 'I don't think he's bluffing at all.'

'He's not going to hurt you,' said Howie, eyes locked on the knifeman. 'Not in front of all of us. He's got nowhere to go.'

'I'll do it!' snapped the stranger. 'I'll cut his throat right here, right now.'

'Go ahead,' said Matthias.

'Matthias!' Cassandra squealed. 'Would you *both* just take it easy? This is going to end in disaster and—'

She didn't get to finish her sentence. Howie and Matthias moved in unison – quick and sharp. It was almost balletic how they approached their attack. Under any other circumstances, Cassandra would probably have quite enjoyed the display. Only now, her heart was in her mouth.

But there was nothing balletic or refined about when they clattered into Kelvin and the knifeman. Matthias went high while Howie went low. The four men collapsed in a giant heap in the middle of the cramped cabin, a jumble of mixed-up limbs. Somehow, through luck more than design, the knife spilled out from the pile and skidded over to Cassandra. She quickly picked it up, holding it out in front of her like it was red hot.

After a breathless moment of struggling, Howie emerged from the pile. He had the stranger by the scruff of his neck, pulling tightly on the man's black sweater. He threw him forward a little as Matthias helped Kelvin to his feet.

'There we go,' said the actor, gasping for air. 'That wasn't so hard, was it.'

He bundled him out of the cabin, past Cassandra. The knifeman almost tripped up but Howie kept him on his feet. Marjorie was staring at everything from a safe distance near the stairwell. The guests, along with Ms Sachiko, had long vanished as soon as the action started.

Howie frogmarched the stranger to the small table and booth off the galley. He thumped him down as Matthias, Kelvin and Cassandra all stood guard.

'We should tie him up,' she said. 'Just in case he tries anything funny.'

'Good plan,' said Matthias.

He scanned the galley and found a roll of electrical tape sitting on a worktop. Howie held the knifeman's hands together as the footballer wrapped them tightly in a makeshift fashion. Whether it would hold or not remained to be seen. Cassandra thought the man looked ridiculous at least.

'I think I might faint,' said Kelvin, rubbing at the little mark on his throat where the knifepoint had been.

'Sit down, chuck, I'll get you some water,' she said. It was only the politician's fearful gaze that reminded her she was still holding the blade.

'Sorry,' she said, putting it down and passing him a glass of water. Kelvin slid down into a seat at a safe distance from his former captor.

'Okay, time for some answers,' said Howie, taking charge.

He paced up and down the galley in front of the knifeman. The stranger seemed unbothered, his eyes lazily following him. His top lip curled into a thin sneer and he snorted a laugh.

'I'm not telling you anything,' he said. 'You're not the cops and you're not my boss. So you can spit.'

'Don't talk to him like that!' Matthias slammed his hands down hard onto the table. Everyone jumped except the stranger. He didn't seem intimidated in the least. Cassandra certainly was. That same sense of dread and menace Matthias has shown her earlier was back. 'You're going to answer our questions, got that?' he hissed.

'You don't frighten me,' said the knifeman. He gave Matthias a defiant look. Then he stopped. His dark eyebrows raised.

'Hold on,' he said. 'Aren't you Matthias Kreutz?'

The former footballer stopped. He straightened up. 'Err . . . yes,' he said.

'I knew it was you,' said the knifeman, pointing with his taped-up hands. 'I thought I recognised you when you came at me just there. You played for Germany.'

'I won the World Cup, yes,' said Matthias.

'That's right. You beat Italy in the quarter-finals. I was at that match, you played well. Too well.'

'That's very kind of you.' He rubbed the back of his head. 'But it was a team effort. Everyone pulled together that night. Italy were a good team, that perhaps should have been the final.'

'Oh yeah, of course,' the knifeman flashed a mouthful of rotten, stained teeth. 'You know I remember that night so well. You played much deeper than you normally did. You were unstoppable, nobody could get past you. It was like the ball was stuck to the end of your big toe. I watched you from the stands and I said to my brother, this boy, Kreutz, he's going to be a big star.'

'Oh that's very kind of you.' Matthias sat down beside the knifeman like they were old friends. Cassandra was stunned. Howie was silent. Kelvin was rubbing his throat and Marjorie was still hovering close to the exit.

'Sorry, hang on, here,' said Howie, shaking his head. 'I'm sorry to break up this little fanboy moment, but this man had a knife to Kelvin's throat a matter of moments ago. Now we're swapping sporting anecdotes.'

Matthias and the stranger both looked up at him and then to each other. They both blushed.

'Sorry,' said Matthias, standing back up.

'*Scusa*,' said the knifeman.

'Okay,' said Howie seriously. 'Thank you.'

Cassandra leaned in close to his ear.

'How do you know what a fanboy is?' she asked him.

'It's a long story,' he replied under his breath.

'Gotcha.' She nodded.

'Right, back to the matter in hand,' he said loudly, taking command once more. 'We want to know who you are, what you're doing here and why you had poor Kelvin by the throat. And we want to know now.'

The knifeman sniffed rudely. He sat back in the booth, resting his taped-up hands on the tabletop.

'Well?' asked Howie. 'We're waiting.'

'Wait as long as you like, I'm not talking to you,' said the stranger.

'Oh yes you are,' he said, leaning forward. 'We want answers, and we want the truth.'

'And we want it now,' said Cassandra, getting in on the interrogation.

The knifeman just laughed. He winked at her.

'You know, that was quite good. You almost had me going there for a second,' he cackled. 'Have you ever thought about becoming an actress?'

'Hey, watch it gobby,' she said. 'You don't know anything about me.'

'I know that you lot are lost at sea without a clue, I know that much,' he said.

Cassandra was beaten there. They all were. This knifeman wasn't stupid. How could he be? He'd somehow slipped onboard without any of them noticing, stayed hidden despite a camera crew roving the halls, and now had held Kelvin hostage. His hands might be tied, literally, but he was far from helpless. And he knew it.

'Who are you?' asked Howie again.

'No comment,' said the stranger.

'What are you doing here?' asked Matthias.

'No comment,' said the stranger.

'Why did you almost kill Kelvin just there? And did you kill Rolando?'

'Never heard of the man,' the stranger sniffed.

'You'd better start talking,' said Matthias, trying to ramp up his intimidation levels again.

'Or what?' the knifeman gave a throaty laugh. 'What will you, the old man and the dizzy girl do? You're small-time celebrities, vaguely famous people, you don't know anything about the real world. Even your political friend over there. You're all out of touch, out of the loop. You don't know what's going on. And I spit on you for being so ignorant.'

He literally spat on the floor. Cassandra took a step back, disgusted.

'It's all bravado,' said Howie. 'And he'll talk soon enough when the cops get here.'

'You've fixed the radio then?' the stranger asked.

Matthias' face dropped.

The stranger snorted. 'Didn't think so.'

Just then Marjorie stepped over to the stranger. He looked at her oddly, like she had three heads, as she rolled up the sleeve on his right arm. The knifeman was covered in tattoos, some old and faded, others much darker and new. She picked out one in particular, a huge, black scorpion, its venomous tail raised high and ready to strike.

'*Scorpione*,' she said, tapping the ink.

The stranger tried to wriggle free but Marjorie's grip was tight.

'*Scorpione*,' she said again.

'What does that mean, babe?' asked Cassandra. 'And don't say scorpion – even I can work that part out. I mean why are you prodding it?'

'It's just a tattoo,' said Howie.

'The scorpion.' Marjorie cut him off. 'It's a symbol, a marking, a stamp of belonging.'

'Belonging? To what?' Cassandra asked.

Marjorie couldn't hide the huge, satisfied grin that was stretching her well-tanned face.

'The Serafina crime syndicate,' she said, almost boasting. 'They're a family from the southern tip of Italy. A Mafia family.'

She let the knifeman go and he pulled his arm away. Marjorie drank in the looks of shock from the gathered crew, lapping up the attention and the acknowledgement that she had been right all along.

Chapter 20

'I told you so, didn't I?' said Marjorie.

In the few moments it was taking everyone to digest this latest revelation, Marjorie Bryant had returned to her old, obnoxious self. She made sure that Ben and Geri were filming her, ever the professional. Howie would have been impressed in her turnaround and recovery. Just as the humble, defeated, more reserved Marjorie was beginning to endear herself to the group, she was gone. Replaced by the all-knowing, all consuming, power and attention hungry Marjorie.

Nobody was happy to see this Marjorie return, except maybe the film crew. They were, after all, looking for material. Now here Marjorie the Tyrant was, lording it over the rest of the crew as Scorpione sat sullenly in the galley booth.

'This doesn't mean you were right about Rolando and the Mafia,' said Howie, trying to salvage something. 'We don't know if this guy is behind that too.'

'Oh come off it,' she laughed at him. 'You're trying to tell me that it's just a coincidence that Rolando was spotted at a Mafia funeral, a Serafina funeral at that, I may add, just a few weeks ago. And now we have a hitman from the *same* family tied up on the ship? If you're truly being serious, Howie Temple, you're dumber than I gave you credit for.'

'I'd normally agree with you, chuck,' said Cassandra, arcing her eyebrows. 'But this is all a bit too convenient to just be a coincidence, don't you think?'

Howie frowned. He folded his arms like a petulant toddler. If there was one thing he hated more than being wrong, it was being *told* he was wrong.

'Judas,' he hissed at Cassandra.

Thankfully she ignored him. She leaned on the table.

'You're a Mafia assassin then?' she asked Scorpione.

'I'm not saying *anything*,' he said, equally miserable.

'We'll take that as a yes,' she said.

'Take it however you like, I'm not saying another word.'

'You don't have to,' said Marjorie. 'That tattoo on your arm speaks volumes.'

'And what would you know, lady?'

'I think you'll find she knows a great deal,' said Cassandra, tempted to hold the lapels of her polo shirt like an Old Bailey lawyer. 'I think you'll find Ms Bryant here is something of an expert when it comes to the criminal gangs and organised crime of Italy. Isn't that right?'

She cocked an eyebrow. Marjorie, however, was much less confident.

'Well, I don't know about expert.' She fumbled for her words. 'But I certainly know that the tattoo on our friend's arm here is the marking of the Serafinas.'

'And they are who exactly?' asked Howie.

Marjorie looked a little nervous. She was trying to ignore Scorpione, who was now glaring at her from behind the table.

'They're a fairly dangerous, prestigious crime family from the Calabria region,' she went on. 'Nasty too, if you believe the police reports and books that have been written about them over the years.'

'Why the scorpion?' asked Matthias.

'Because a chihuahua wouldn't look very cool.' She shrugged. 'But this, a deadly beast, always ready to strike, is about as aggressive a symbol as you could imagine. Easily replicated, lots of variants. These mobsters, they like to conjure up a sort of fantasy around them, to try and emulate fictional heroes and mythology. But at the end of the day, they're just petty criminals, crooks, thieves and murderers. There's nothing at all glamorous about what they do.'

'*Ti ucciderò, mi hai sentito?*' Scorpione hissed.

Everyone looked at Marjorie for the translation. She wasn't very keen to share it.

'Either way, I was right,' she said. 'Rolando was mixed up with this family. Although I have no idea how. I told you that he was seen at that funeral a few weeks ago. I imagine our friend here was there too.'

Scorpione went back to his silent fuming.

'Anyway, it hardly matters. We've found our killer,' she said.

'Yes,' said Howie. 'He can handle a blade. And we all saw he had a knife to Kelvin's throat. It's pretty much an open and shut case, we just need to link him to Ed's bash on the head.'

That drew a snort from the knifeman. Howie turned to him.

'Something funny there, buddy?' he asked him.

'You lot think you're so clever,' he said. 'You think you've figured all of this out, don't you? Well you're nowhere *near* knowing what's going on here. You're clueless, like I said. You've got no evidence, no proof I was anywhere near this Rolando character, whoever he is. As soon as the police get here, I'll be free before dawn. You wait and see.'

There was a confident inevitability about his tone. None of the others seemed to have the knowledge or the conviction to challenge him.

'He's right,' said Kelvin. 'Without proof, we can't link him to the other crimes.'

It was the first he had spoken since being rescued from Scorpione's clutches. Howie and the rest of the crew turned to face him as he sat in the corner.

'Without evidence, he's no murderer, he's just a thug who pulled a knife on me,' he said, rubbing his throat. 'We probably shouldn't even be holding him now, like this, like a prisoner. I'm sure it's against his human rights or something. The Swiss would have a field day if they were here.'

'Kelvin,' said Howie, stepping forward. 'This guy had a blade up to your neck!'

'The rules are rules and the law is the law,' said Kelvin.

'Yes, listen to your friend,' smiled Scorpione. 'He's right. I have my rights. You can't hold me here like this.'

'I think you'll find you're no longer in a position to argue,' Howie threw back at him.

'Untie me at once!' The stranger held up his taped hands. 'I haven't done anything wrong.'

'You almost killed Kelvin and you probably killed Rolando!' Cassandra shouted.

'No I didn't,' Scorpione said coolly. 'You've got no proof.'

'I don't believe I'm hearing this,' said Howie, looking about the galley. 'You're all serious about turning this lunatic loose again? He had a knife up to Kelvin's throat not ten minutes ago. Was I the only one who saw that?'

Nobody replied. Scorpione was sat there, laughing loudly now.

'The rules are the rules, fat man,' he said.

'Then to hell with the rules,' he said.

Howie moved quickly. He was around the table and on Scorpione before anyone else could react. Hauling the knifeman out from the booth, he dragged him up the hallway and towards the stairs.

'Howie!' Cassandra shouted after him.

The others followed her. Scorpione was hollering, shouting loudly at the top of his voice as Howie forced him up the stairs. They emerged onto the main deck of the yacht. Everything was a warm, golden yellow, the sun starting its final arc towards the horizon, burnt out for the day.

Howie manhandled Scorpione all the way to the stern. The whole place had dried out by now and there was no sign it had been flooded – more of the knifeman's handiwork, Howie assumed. He brought him to a stop at the edge of the deck, the water of the Mediterranean gently lapping against the fibreglass hull. The rest of the crew and Ms Sachiko had gathered above them, watching on curiously.

'If he's not going to talk then he's not much use to us, is he?' Howie asked them.

'Howie, babe, are you feeling okay?' asked Cassandra.

'Perfectly fine, better than fine actually. I feel like I've got clarity for the first time since I set foot on this damn yacht.'

He was holding Scorpione at arm's length, a fistful of the knifeman's jumper. The thug was twitching, nervously looking back and forth between Howie and the depths of the ocean beneath him.

'Hey, what are you doing, man?' he asked, no longer laughing.

'Rules are rules,' said the actor. 'But not out here. Out here we can do whatever we want. It's the open sea, it's the Wild West. And if you're not going to admit to killing Rolando and attacking Ed, then I don't really see we've got much of an option.'

'Option for what?' he asked, his sallow skin turning grey.

Howie smiled. He turned back to the gathered crowd.

'What do you say? Should we send our Mafia friend out to sea for a little swim?'

Nobody said anything. They were all shocked by what was being implied.

'You're crazy,' said Scorpione. 'You won't drop me in the water. You wouldn't do that. You're famous.'

'Ah, that's where you're wrong, pal,' Howie tapped the side of his temple. 'I *used* to be famous. Now I'm washed up and broke and having to spend my time making crappy reality shows on glamorous yachts that don't belong to me. So yeah, maybe I *am* a bit crazy. Do you want to take that risk?'

'Let me go!' Scorpione tried to wriggle free, the fear in his voice now.

'Not until you tell us what's going on here and why you're on this boat.'

'Let me go! I'll drown if I go in there.'

'Then justice will be served, a life for a life.' Howie shrugged. 'I'm going to give you until the count of three and then it's so long Mr Scorpion. One!'

'Howie, babe, you need to bring him back onboard!' Cassandra shouted.

'Two!'

He loosened his grip on Scorpione's jumper. The knifeman was trying desperately to break free but his taped-up hands left him flailing.

'Please, don't do this, I won't be able to swim!'

'Howie! For God's sake let him go!' Marjorie shouted.

'This isn't a very good idea, Mr Temple,' said Sachiko coldly.

Howie ignored them all. It was just him and Scorpione. He dragged out the last second, offering the knifeman a way out. And when it wasn't forthcoming, he spoke.

'Three!'

There was a split-second where everything seemed to slow down. Time came to a tired halt. Scorpione's face was wide open, terror in his eyes. Howie felt proud of himself. He'd managed to put the frighteners up a Mafia hitman. All those years playing chicken as action stars clearly hadn't been put to waste.

'Alright! Alright, I'll talk!' Scorpione shouted. 'I'll tell you whatever you want to—'

His foot went from under him, polished shoe slipping on the edge of the stern. The sudden shift in weight was too much for Howie's grip. There was a loud tearing as a panel of Scorpione's jumper came away in his hand, the knifeman tumbling backwards into the sea.

He crashed into the water in a fountain of froth then promptly sunk like a stone. Time had accelerated again and Howie was suddenly very aware of everything that had just happened.

'Oh,' was all he could manage.

There was a scream from somewhere behind him. He turned to face the others, feeling completely helpless. All he could do was shrug, his hand still gripping the ball of fabric from Scorpione's sweater.

'Well . . . ' he stammered. 'I wasn't expecting that!'

'Get after him!' Marjorie screamed. 'The poor man will drown! He can't swim after you tied his hands together.'

Howie couldn't shake the shock. He just stood there gawping, his limbs like concrete, feet glued to the expensive wood of the deck.

Thankfully Matthias was much more competent. The former footballer had sprung down from the main deck and darted into the water like a swordfish. All Howie and the others could do was look on as the precious seconds ticked by.

Matthias burst through the surface of the sea with an equally spectacular splash. He gasped for air as he pulled something heavy behind him – Scorpione.

'Help me onto the deck,' he asked politely.

Howie found he could move again. He reached down and pulled the knifeman back onto the safety of the yacht. He coughed and spluttered and rolled onto his side, hands still firmly taped up. He opened his eyes, dark hair plastered over his forehead.

'You could have killed me,' he growled. 'I could have drowned, *idiota*!'

Howie straightened up as Matthias climbed back onboard. The former footballer was looking at him with a frown. The others, including Cassandra, were all doing the same.

'What?' he asked them. 'It was an accident.'

A few murmurs of disbelief rippled around the gathered crew. Howie found he couldn't really care less, not when he really thought about it. The opinions of the others had meant less than nothing to him up until this point. And the job had been done, regardless of whether he had meant it all or not. He'd spent too many years chasing public approval to still play that game now. Except there was something gnawing at his stomach as he looked up at Cassandra.

Her brow was furrowed, her eyes firmly locked on his. She had folded her arms and was like a concentrated beam of disapproval.

'What?' he asked her again.

But she didn't reply. She turned away angrily and disappeared into the boat. Howie couldn't help but feel the gnawing getting worse.

'What should we do with him?' asked Matthias.

Howie was back in the real world. Cassandra would have to wait.

'We better get him dried off,' he said, thinking on his feet. 'Take him up to the common area and give him a towel – leave the others guarding him. You better try and get that radio working quickly. I don't think what Mr Mafia here is about to tell us is going to be for the faint of heart.'

Matthias gave an obliging nod and helped Scorpione to his feet. He led him away from the stern and left Howie on his own. He looked out across the Ligurian Sea, the gold and amber rays of the dying sun making the water look like a copper and brass sheet, rippled and buckled as the tides moved in and out. It was a beautiful sunset, another day over. But he knew that the coming darkness would bring no rest.

Chapter 21

Everyone was milling around the communal area of the main deck. Everyone except Matthias, taking up his duties in the radio room. Howie wasn't hopeful that his limited electronic expertise would be of any use. But it was something. A little hope had never hurt anyone. That's what his mother used to say.

Hope, it seemed, was in plentiful supply this evening. With the exception of Ed, the crew and guests were filled with an excited, if slightly terrified, sense of the stuff. The elusive killer had been caught and was now sitting in the centre of them, dripping over the expensive white leather of the main sofa. The relief sprang not only from the fact they could all stop fearing for their lives, but also that they could stop doubting each other.

Everyone was taking their seat, everyone except Howie. He was finally quite enjoying the role he'd assumed of main investigator in this sordid affair. Cassandra hadn't even looked in his direction since they had all gathered.

'Any chance of something to eat?' Kirkby Hofstede asked.

'Be quiet, Kirkby.' Martha batted him. 'This is serious, can't you see?'

Howie had a strange sort of nervousness about him. On the few occasions he had trod the boards in live theatre, he had almost been incapacitated by the fear and the jitters before curtain up. And each night he'd vowed never to set foot on stage ever again.

Yet here he was. Not playing a role as such, not reading from a script, he was live, unfiltered and very, very much in the real world. He looked straight down the lens Geri had trained on him. Was this why Cassandra had appeared on so many reality shows? The adrenaline? He had half thought that the familiarity of being on camera would have helped. It didn't. Maybe it was them, the silent duo.

He tried to push all of this from his tired mind as an expectant hush fell over the gathered crowd. Scorpione looked miserable, shoulders sunken, hair at untidy angles, his long face the picture of misery. Gone was the cocky, over-confident hitman. In his place was a man who had almost met a grisly, if accidental death in the depths of the Med.

'Ladies and gentlemen, good evening,' said Howie, trying to sound important. 'Thank you for gathering together like this, before dinner. It's been another exhausting day, I know. But I think it's important that we all remain steadfast, together, as a crew, as guests, as a ship. To honour Captain Rolando.'

'Oh lord.' Marjorie rubbed her forehead.

'Is there a problem?' asked Howie, broken from his little speech.

'Can you get on with whatever it is you're trying to get on with please,' she droned. 'You almost drowned a man earlier and now you're giving us the old Hercule Poirot turn. And not doing it very well, I may add.'

'I'm trying to explain why we're all here tonight.'

'We all *know* that already,' she said. 'Just get on with it.'

Howie looked over to Cassandra for some support. There was none there. She coldly turned away when she spotted him, pretending to be distracted by something out at sea. He swallowed, humbled.

'Err . . . yes, right, where was I?' he stammered.

'You were telling us how wonderful it was that we were all gathered together,' said Marjorie. 'Something about solidarity.'

'Right, of course, yes.' He shook his head, trying to regain focus. 'Yes, solidarity. We've had a rough time of it since we set sail. In fact, it's been a damnable nightmare from start to finish. Which is all down to you, Mr Scorpione.'

The crowd's attention was shifted to Scorpione, sitting in the middle of the gathered group. He was shivering, from shock more than the cold, Howie suspected. He walked over to the knifeman and loomed over him.

'I hope our little conversation earlier has changed your mind about speaking with us,' he said, trying to sound intimidating.

Howie held his breath for a second. He was gambling here, gambling that Scorpione would play ball. He hadn't intended to almost kill the man, that had been a pure accident. But it was no guarantee that Scorpione would talk now. If he decided to stay quiet, what could Howie do? He'd already upped the stakes and used his ace by accident.

Everyone was looking at them. He could feel the sweat on his top lip, feel the pulse in his neck. Suddenly he was back onstage on opening night. The beaming lights, the hushed expectation of the audience. His knees were getting weaker and weaker as they tried to support his concrete legs.

'I didn't kill him,' said Scorpione.

Howie was so relieved he had said something, it took him a moment to realise what he'd said wasn't what he wanted to hear. He thought that he might just crumple like a deflated balloon.

'What do you mean you didn't kill him?' asked Howie. 'Of course you killed him.'

'No, I didn't,' said the knifeman. 'I didn't kill Rolando. That is to say, I was supposed to. That's why I'm here. But I didn't do it.'

'Wait, hold on,' said Cassandra, getting up from the sofa. 'You were here to kill Rolando, but you're saying someone else beat you to it?'

She stood up beside Howie but didn't acknowledge him. He was certain he could feel the chill in the air between them.

'That's right,' said Scorpione. 'He was my mission, my target. But I didn't kill him. I came onboard here to do a job. But the job was already done for me.'

'How did you get onboard?' asked Marjorie. 'There was footage of lots of us boarding.'

Scorpione sniffed. He looked about at the guests and Kelvin. Then settled back on Howie and Cassandra looming over him.

'The footballer,' he said. 'When he was dropped off. I stowed away on the little tug that brought him to the yacht. When nobody was looking I climbed aboard. You lot were in bed, and the German, he's hardly the most observant, is he? *Idiota*.'

There was a venom in his voice. Howie was glad Matthias wasn't around to hear the insult.

'So you're trying to tell us that Rolando was already dead when you found him?' asked Cassandra.

'Yes.'

'Garbage,' said Howie. 'How did you get into the bridge, the door was locked.'

Scorpione drew him a look. It was one of contempt and disbelief, making his pulled face twist. 'Are you serious?' he asked him. 'I'm an assassin, for a crime family. You think a locked door is going to keep me out?'

Howie felt his cheeks flushing at how stupid he had been.

'So, what, you expect us to believe that you broke into the bridge and he was just there, dead.'

'Yeah,' said the knifeman.

'That's it?'

'That's what happened.'

'And you think we'll believe that?'

'I don't care what you believe, that's what happened. I opened the door, had my knife at the ready, and he was just there, slumped over the controls.'

Howie felt something pang in his mind.

'Wait a minute,' he said. 'Slumped over the controls? That's how you found Rolando.'

'Yeah,' said Scorpione, talking like he was putting together a shopping list. 'He was just there, lying on all those buttons and keyboards and the like. He was dead. I checked his pulse.'

'But he had a knife in his back,' said Cassandra. 'A knife not from this ship, I may add.'

Scorpione shifted a little uncomfortably on the sofa.

'Yeah,' he said, grunting.

'Well?' asked Howie.

Scorpione sniffed. He licked his lips, looking furtive.

'See, the thing is,' he began. 'The people I work for, they have very high expectations. A strong emphasis on delivery.'

'The Mafia?' Cassandra laughed a little. 'You make them sound like a Fortune 100 company.'

'Please,' Scorpione snorted. 'Those firms make pennies compared to my bosses. And with that comes a certain expectation that when they give you a job, you do it, to the letter.'

'You mean murder,' she said. 'Murder is murder. Don't try to dress it up as something on a to-do list.'

'You have your job, I have mine, I'll live with the consequences,' he said nonchalantly.

'Why did they want Rolando dead?' asked Howie.

'Hey, I don't ask those kinds of questions, okay?' said Scorpione. 'I get my money, I get a name, that's all. You don't ask my bosses how their day was, how the family is, that kind of thing. They tell you to do something and you do it, end of discussion.'

'Except you didn't do it, did you?' asked Cassandra, snapping her fingers. 'You didn't kill Rolando, he was already dead when you arrived. And that means you're in trouble. Big trouble, by the sounds of things.'

'I'll be alright, a stiff is a stiff. Don't you worry about me, Bella, I'll be fine.'

Howie picked up her thread. 'Except you won't be, will you,' he said. 'If your bosses, what are they called again?'

'The Serafinas,' said Marjorie.

'Yeah, them,' said Howie. 'If the Serafinas find out that you came to kill a guy who was already dead, they're going to want their money back, right?'

Scorpione's face had turned to thunder. He was chewing over his words now.

'That's why you stabbed him in the back,' said Howie. 'That's why you propped him up. So the police report would make it sound like you'd done your job. But he was dead already when the knife went in?'

'Like I said, fat boy, I don't need to answer to you,' he spat.

'Why Rolando?' asked Cassandra again. 'Why him?'

'I don't ask questions,' said Scorpione. 'He probably owed the Don a load of cash, something like that. These guys, with their lavish lifestyles, they spend more money than they can ever earn. And Rolando, he was doing okay, clearly. Driving a tub like this, going on TV shows, he wasn't short of money. But that doesn't mean he was paying his bills. And like I said before, my bosses, they aren't the kind of guys you want to owe any money to. Believe me.'

Howie could feel the heat of satisfaction and smuggery radiating off Marjorie behind him. He deliberately didn't turn around.

'You're clearly somebody who's been around more than a few dead bodies,' he said. 'What do you think happened to Rolando?'

'I'm not a doctor,' said Scorpione.

'We know that,' said Cassandra. 'But you must have a theory.'

Scorpione shrugged.

'Could be anything,' he said. 'Poison, overdose, he could have done that to himself. It might just have been his time – stroke, heart attack, embolism – there are a hundred ways to die. Or perhaps an accident – maybe he choked on his pasticciotto before bedtime, I don't know.'

'An accident?' asked Howie.

'How the hell am I supposed to know? I was sent here to kill the guy and he had the bad manners enough to be dead by the time I got here. I wasn't hanging around to perform an autopsy. I've got my own problems to deal with without working out what happened. Okay?'

Howie couldn't really argue with that point. He straightened himself, ran his hands through his hair and puffed out his cheeks. In doing so, he made the mistake of catching Marjorie's eye.

'I told you,' she said, bobbing her foot up and down. 'I said Rolando was mixed up with the mob. And here we are, hearing it straight from the horse's head.'

'Hey, that's offensive!' Scorpione shouted. 'It's not like in the movies.'

'No, real life is much worse,' chimed Cassandra. 'And the fact that you're almost revelling in it is utterly deplorable. A man has lost his life and you tried to save your own skin by stabbing his *corpse*. What does that say about *you*?'

Scorpione swore under his breath. Howie could see that Cassandra was upset. He wanted to console her but she was still not even meeting his eye. He couldn't really blame her. She'd watched him almost drown Scorpione, by mistake or not. The others didn't seem to care quite as much.

'What a mess,' he said aloud.

'You're telling us,' said Marjorie. 'What are we going to do with him now, then?

Howie hadn't thought that far ahead. Once again the gathered guests and crew were looking to him for an answer.

Kirkby piped up. 'He claims not to have committed murder on this occasion but it seems clear to me this isn't his first rodeo.'

Howie knew he'd set out to find who had killed Rolando and if it wasn't Scorpione, then who had poisoned, drugged, choked and ultimately murdered the skipper? But all of Scorpione's revelations, even if he chose to believe them, had raised more questions than they'd answered. 'Hold on,' he said, turning back to face Scorpione.

The knifeman looked up, Cassandra beside him.

'So what do Ed and Kelvin have to do with all of this?' he asked. 'Why did you attack them?'

'Who's Ed?' asked Scorpione.

'Edward Wells. Our director,' said Cassandra. 'The guy responsible for us all being here. Tall, blonde, English, handsome in a sort of haggard way.'

'Haggard?' Howie cocked an eyebrow at her.

She shrugged.

'I've never met the guy,' said Scorpione.

'Come on, cut the crap,' said Howie. 'The game's up, we know who you are and what you've been up to. You may as well come clean.'

'I'm not lying,' he said. 'Yes I read the ship's manifest before I came aboard, my bosses expect me to do my research so I've seen his name. But I've never met this Ed guy. If he's hit his head, it's nothing to do with me. I prefer a blade, anyway.'

'And what about Kelvin?'

That drew a smile from Scorpione. He leaned back, hands still taped up, his wet clothes squeaking against the white leather sofa.

'That's something you need to ask him,' he said with a satisfied gurgle. 'What I will say though, if you want my advice. Never trust a politician. If you think I'm bad, wait until you see what they're capable of.'

It took a moment, too long a moment, for Howie to process what Scorpione had said. Almost immediately after he'd worked it out, the panic set in again and his chest clamped up. Cassandra, by the look on her face, was feeling the same way.

'Hey,' she said, voice quivering. 'Just where *is* Kelvin?'

Howie and the others looked about the deck area. The former MP was nowhere to be seen.

'He was just here a moment ago,' said Marjorie. 'He came back here with the rest of us after Howie tried to drown our mafioso friend.'

'Where is he now, though?' Howie said, all too aware of the desperation in his voice. 'We're stuck on a fifty metre boat, he can't have gone far.'

A spluttering, high pitched zipping sound drifted up and over the deck from the rear of *The Regal Secret*. Howie and Cassandra hurried over to the rails that lined the edge of the yacht, almost knocking Ben and Geri overboard in the process. A murky shape whizzed through the inky darkness, the sun now long set. Even without the light, they both knew who it was.

'Kelvin,' said Howie, gritting his teeth. 'Kelvin! Come back here!'

The politician couldn't hear him over the sound of the water scooter. Even if he did, Howie didn't think he would stop. Kelvin was making a bid for freedom. And he was slipping straight through their fingers.

Chapter 22

'I didn't know those jet ski things worked,' said Cassandra. 'Weren't they flooded with the engine room?'

'I thought so too,' said Howie. 'They must have dried out. I'm starting to suspect that Kelvin knew more about all of that than he was letting on. I'm not sure they're meant for long distance travel but Kelvin seems pretty confident. If we'd known we would have been able to get help or the police or something. Instead of sitting adrift for these past days.'

They hurtled through the yacht, heading for the cargo compartments at the stern. The doors of the cargo compartments were lying wide open again. Kelvin hadn't bothered to close them. Water from the Ligurian was already sloshing into the bay. Howie cursed loudly.

'Damn,' he said, wading his bare feet through the cool floodwater. 'We only just got this place dry and it's going to flood again.'

'What are you doing?' asked Cassandra, waiting by the door.

Howie nudged and bumped his way through the disorganised mess of the cargo hold. The roof was sloped and he bashed his head off the fibreglass more than he wanted to. Throwing inflatables and toys out of the way, he at last reached the second water scooter wedged into a corner in the back.

'Help me get this thing out before it floods again,' he shouted back to Cassandra.

Pulling on one side of the handlebars, Howie heaved with all of his might. Slowly but surely, the water scooter eased its way free of the cargo hold and out onto the launch area.

'Now what?' she asked.

'I'm going after him,' said Howie, grabbing a life jacket from the mess that had been dragged out along with the jet ski.

'What? You can't do that.'

'Why not?'

'Because . . . ' She faltered. 'Because you don't know what he's capable of.'

'That's why I have to catch him,' said Howie.

He examined the controls. There was a starter button and he pressed it. The water scooter roared into life, sending up a huge spray of the floodwater from its rear. Howie tentatively climbed onboard. He nudged the vehicle forward and around, using the flooded deck as a way into the sea.

'Have you used one of these before?' she asked.

'Have you seen my films?'

'That doesn't answer my question, babe,' she replied.

He didn't respond. He stared out at the darkness of the open sea ahead of him. *The Regal Secret* had been gently drifting around its mooring. The Italian coastline was somewhere beyond the bow of the ship and he'd have to be careful clearing it. At least doing this at night meant he had the lights of the coast to aim for – by day, the haze obscured the horizon and any sign of civilization. Sitting on the scooter as if he'd climbed onto a bucking bronco, with the engine chugging away between his legs, he suddenly didn't feel very confident.

'Cassandra, I'm sorry,' he said.

The words were out of his mouth before he knew he was going to say them.

'What? What for?' She seemed genuinely surprised.

'I'm sorry for what happened earlier,' he said. 'With the Mafia fella. I didn't mean to drop him in the water like that. I was just trying to intimidate him, to get some answers. It was a mistake, honestly it was. I'd never deliberately hurt someone.'

'I know that, chuck,' she said, reaching out and rubbing his arm. 'I know.'

'You were disappointed in me. I could tell. You've barely spoken to me since it happened, you won't even look me in the face. I'm surprised you're here, now, actually. And I don't blame you. It wasn't pleasant, for me either.'

'Howie, it's fine. We're all just trying to get through this nightmare.'

'I know we didn't get off to the best of starts, you and I. But this whole investigation, this murder, it's actually brought us closer, I think. And your opinion matters to me. I hated to see that look on your face. That disappointment. And I'm sorry.'

'Howie . . .' She bowed her head.

He wasn't sure why he was saying all of this now. It had just felt right, somehow. The ocean looked intimidatingly huge. And even if he didn't drown on his way to catch up with Kelvin, what would he do when he got there? None of this had factored into his thinking as he'd given chase. Only now, as it all became very real, did it all seem incredibly perilous. Foolhardy, even.

'I've said my piece,' he said, revving the engine. 'And if I don't make it back, thank you.'

'For what?' She looked at him, a little glassy eyed in the darkness.

'For thinking an old dog can learn new tricks,' he said.

If he'd been much braver, he would have reached over and hugged her. If he'd been thirty years younger, he probably would have kissed her. Instead, he revved the engine again and pulled the throttle. Hoping for a hero's exit, the scooter lurched forward. Then it lurched again. And before it could reach the end of the flooded deck, it sputtered, coughed and stalled.

'Damn,' was about all Howie could manage.

Of course, the rest of the guests and crew had assembled on the upper decks, watching this debacle unfold. Nobody said anything, they kept their criticisms politely to themselves. But Howie knew they were judging. He half-heartedly thumped the handlebars as the sound of Cassandra's footsteps came sloshing over through the water.

'Need a little help?' she asked.

In the dimness of the night, Howie could see that she was smiling wryly at him. She had pulled on a life jacket and was buckling it up. He didn't say anything, just shuffled backwards and let her climb onto the seat in front of him. She restarted the engine and kicked the scooter forward. He held her around her waist as they sped off the yacht and out into the open water.

'Where did you learn to do that?' he asked, catching a mouthful of her hair and spray from the sea.

'Dubai,' she shouted back over her shoulder. 'Any self-respecting influencer has been there. And you're nothing if you haven't learned how to ride one of these.'

'Just as well I'm old and out of touch then.'

'Something like that!'

Howie laughed. She couldn't hear him over the roar of the engine, the white noise of the ocean. Cassandra rounded the scooter about *The Regal Secret*. The yacht still looked magnificent, a pleasure palace that gave no outward clue that it had been the site of gruesome violence. As they passed by its long, sleek body, Howie allowed himself to gawk a little at it. He hadn't seen it properly since they had arrived at the harbour, and not at all at night. The whole craft was majestic. Hard to imagine, he thought, that it was effectively a floating tomb for now.

That thought sobered him immediately. The romance of the yacht, the dazzling splendour of its smooth lines silhouetted against the night sky, all paled into insignificance. He suddenly felt glad to be off the ship and speeding across the sea even if it was in perilous pursuit of a person of interest.

Chapter 23

La Spezia's harbour opened its arms like a kindly mother, welcoming Cassandra and Howie as they bounced and bobbed their way over the sea. As a major port, the place was still busy, even after dark. Tall, ominous tankers and freighters loomed over them like great cumbersome giants. Howie had spent the whole journey in fear of the engine failing, or the fuel running out, leaving them adrift in the sea, but the relief of seeing land in reach was quickly replaced with fear of getting mown down by a supertanker. Towers of shipping containers stacked almost as high as the ships that would carry them lined each side of the dock. They passed unnoticed through this myriad of haulage, the beating heart of Liguria's industry indifferent to the tiny jet ski.

Cassandra had no idea where she was going. She'd just been following the lights of the coast, imagining they'd land at some little fishing village or beach bar – not having to cross commercial shipping lanes. They knew roughly what direction Kelvin had raced off in. But where he was heading, if even he knew, was anyone's guess. He'd soon been swallowed up by the darkness, and neither she nor Howie could see another jet ski as they zigzagged towards land.

'It's strange, seeing all of this activity,' said Howie in her ear. 'I had kind of forgotten what civilisation looked like.'

'We've only been at sea for a couple of days, babe,' she shouted back over her shoulder.

She guided the water scooter towards a smaller jetty close to the harbour walls. Little boats with sails flapping in the evening breeze bobbed and swayed in each of the berths. Cassandra pulled up and switched off the engine, the last of the fuel gurgling away.

Howie let go and climbed off with a pained grunt. She joined him on the jetty, unbuckling her life jacket.

'Come on,' she said, looking around for sight of their shipmate.

'Hold on, wait,' Howie shouted.

'What is it?'

'Shoes,' he said, pointing down at his bare feet.

'What?' she yelped.

'We don't have any shoes.'

'So?'

'We can't go running around a city without any shoes on, Cassandra. We're not savages.'

'You should have thought of that before you gave chase, shouldn't you?' She grabbed his hand. 'Anyway, what choice do we have?'

Reluctantly he followed her. They hurried along the jetty until it reached the high wall of the harbour. There was nobody about here, the private moorings left undisturbed overnight. Climbing a tall staircase that cut into the slimy walls of the dock, they emerged onto a busy crossroads.

Scooters and cars whizzed by. A chorus of honking horns and beeps met them as the lights dazzled Cassandra.

She took a step back, bumping into Howie. He steadied her.

'Wow,' she said, blinking and trying to refocus. 'I don't think I was expecting this much humanity.'

'A bit unsettling, isn't it?' he said. 'I kind of wish I was back at sea.'

'Steady on, chuck. It's not that bad.'

There appeared to be no order with the traffic. None of the drivers stuck to the lanes, instead choosing to whizz, duck, dive and weave between each other. It was hypnotic, in a strangely dangerous way. Cassandra cleared her head.

'We need to think,' she said. 'If Kelvin *is* here, where would he go?'

'I don't know,' said Howie. 'I don't know anything about the man or why he's absconded. He's kept himself to himself the whole trip.'

'I never thought anything of it,' she said. 'I just figured he was the quiet sort.'

'Still waters run deep and all that.'

Cassandra looked up and down the street. She had absolutely no idea where to start. There were a few road signs but nothing that screamed 'haven of a desperate former politician'.

One sign did catch her eye though.

'*Centro Storico*,' she said. 'How's your Italian, Howie?'

'Non-existent,' he said. 'I grew up in the cold and the ice. The only Italian I know is Mario Lemieux and he's a hockey player.'

'Sounds more French than Italian,' she said. 'Let's start there then, it's probably a square or the city centre. Everyone seems to be heading that way, anyway, and if we can't see Kelvin then we need to find the police station. We've got a lot to tell them.'

Cassandra hadn't taken two steps before Howie started making strange noises. She stopped and turned to face him. He was jumping on the balls of his feet, patting his life jacket, his face a mix of shock and puzzlement.

'Howie! What's wrong with you, babe? Are you having a heart attack?'

She reached out to him but he was a flurry of activity. He was bouncing around, arms flailing, furiously searching his own torso. At last, he pulled something free from the pocket of his shorts.

'My phone!' He waved the device in front of her.

Cassandra took it from him. The screen was flashing furiously, the device buzzing in her hands. A string of notifications all appeared at once, signal returned to the device.

'Of course!' she said. 'We're back in signal range. Damn, I've left mine in my cabin.'

'I thought I was going crazy,' he said, staring at the device. 'I wondered what the hell was happening. That stupid thing was rattling away in my back pocket. I thought a snake had crawled up there or something.'

She waited a moment until Howie's notifications started to slow. Emails, text messages, updates, everything was all flooding in at once. If this was what Howie's phone was like, she dreaded her own. She had multi-million followers across all of her social channels. They'd all have been watching her scheduled posts that she'd set to run while she was filming but keeping content flowing was like feeding an ever-hungry beast.

'I didn't miss that,' he said, pointing at the screen. 'Being out of contact was actually quite pleasant. Reminded me of the nineties when you'd have to go through my agent and manager to get hold of me.'

'Sounds grim,' she said, the messages slowing.

'To you, maybe,' he said. 'But at least back then I was able to hold a conversation with somebody. If they really wanted to reach me they had to try. Not like now. I can't work out which messages I need to actually read they're so well hidden in the rising tide of spam and nonsense I get.'

'It's more complicated than that, chuck,' she said, handing him the phone. 'Unlock the screen, would you?'

'What for?' he asked as they started towards the city centre.

'If I can get logged on to one of my accounts I can try and get help in finding Kelvin.'

'How are you going to do that?'

Cassandra tilted her head and drew him a long, unfavourable look. 'Really? You want me to explain it right now?'

'I'd like to know what you'd going to do with my phone before I turn you loose on it.'

'Howie, babe, there's absolutely nothing I could do on that ancient rock you call a phone that could cause you any harm.'

Reluctantly he punched in the four-digit code and handed the device back to her. After a short walk, the splendour of La Spezia's Centro Storico opened up around them. The classical buildings with their terracotta roofs stood on every side of the square. Cafes, restaurants and eateries were busy, tables with umbrellas and cast-iron tables and chairs all filled. Strings of bare bulbs with soft glows gave everything a warm feel, welcoming to strangers and locals alike. Even the traffic that had reached here seemed a little calmer, the mass of loud, obnoxious vehicles diverted away leaving only those happy not to mar the frivolity of the square.

Several modern sculptures were dotted around the place, punctuated by more historic ones – serious faces of oxidised copper staring blankly out into the night.

'Wow,' said Howie, marvelling at the place. 'This is stunning.'

'Yeah,' said Cassandra, busy furiously tapping with her thumbs and fingers on his phone.

'See, this is another problem with kids today,' he said. 'You'd rather look at pictures of a place on your phone than see it for yourselves. Your eyes are the best camera you're ever likely to get. You should enjoy it.'

'I don't need a lecture, chuck,' she said, irritated. 'I'm trying to get a clue as to where Kelvin Kamani has gone. Finding a needle in a haystack is hard work, you know. We can't all be tourists.'

'You're onto a hiding for nothing with that one,' he said. 'There's no way we can find him. He might not even be here in the city. The coastline stretches for hundreds of miles around to France and then some. He could be anywhere and—'

'Got him,' she said, finally looking up.

'What? Nonsense,' he said, disbelieving.

'It's not nonsense, babe. I know where he is. He's here in the La Spezia.'

'How the hell could you possibly know that?'

Cassandra grinned from ear to ear. She held up his phone to him.

'Millions of followers, from all over the world,' she said. 'They hang on my every word, or at least they used to. After I updated your phone and about a million apps, I logged in and asked if anyone had seen Kelvin Kamani. He's got a public profile of course, people know him.'

'As much as they know me?'

Cassandra was polite enough not to answer that.

'The world at your fingertips,' she said, tossing the device back to him. 'You've just got to know how to use it, that's all.'

'So where is he?' he asked.

'It took a couple of minutes, but somebody came forward saying they thought they saw him heading towards the railway station. That's about a ten-minute walk from here so we need to hurry.'

'Is this real?' he asked as she started to jog through the square. 'I mean, couldn't it be anyone giving you false information.'

'I have a very loyal fanbase, chuck,' she said. 'If somebody says they've seen Kelvin while they're here on holiday, I'm inclined to believe them. Some of my followers are very helpful that way. Others just send me abuse.'

'And you did all of this on my phone?'

'That's right, it's not all brain rot you know.' She threw a smile back over her shoulder. 'It's pretty helpful, this technology lark. You should try it sometime, chuck, you might learn something.'

Howie didn't reply as they power-walked in the direction of the station. He just hoped this wasn't for nothing. Pounding pavements barefoot was not something he'd recommend but there was no time to complain. Time was one thing that was in short supply – not just for him and Cassandra in their search for Kelvin but for their shipmates back onboard *The Regal Secret*.

Chapter 24

Howie had always liked trains. Why on earth hadn't he found a reality show on a train rather than a wretched boat, he thought as they approached the station. The solid-looking building reared itself out of the night with a quiet, dignified trustworthiness. Stations were portals, gateways, places of connection and possibility. Perhaps trains were not as glamorous as their airborne cousins but certainly not as arduous or as much work as driving. There was an old worldliness to trains and railways stations that offered him a sense of reassurance.

If this was how he was thinking, he was definitely tired. In his five decades and more, Howie Temple had never been the sentimental type. Quite the opposite. It had taken him barely any time to shake off his prairie accent and Saskatchewan heritage as soon as he'd landed in Los Angeles. He had been happy just to fit in, to be another generic face in the throng of actors all looking for their big break. And when that break had come, a tertiary role in a Stallone action romp, he had always had his eyes on the next role, never looking back.

As the years and decades had worn on, he hadn't really mellowed. The thought of the next job was always enough to spur him on. And he might not have the cameras on him right now, but if nothing else, the plot he'd found himself caught up in was much better than the last five movies he'd made put together.

'Do you think Kelvin did it?' asked Cassandra as they quickly headed for the main doors of La Spezia Centrale.

'What?' he asked, just waking from his daydream.

'Kelvin. Do you think *he* murdered Rolando?'

'I don't know,' said Howie. If the past twenty-four hours had taught him anything it was that supposition was not just useless without evidence, but positively dangerous.

It was a new approach for Howie, admitting he didn't know something. Certainty had been his MO for years, or at least until his divorces and children had cleaned out his once substantial bank account. And at one point he'd worried he wouldn't see the end of the week without going bankrupt. His story was hardly a new one. Stupid investments, a lack of foresight and a tragic dedication to lining solicitors' pockets had pretty much been the end of the era of him feeling the certainty of his own conviction. He'd packed that away with his scruples. The only people who had stuck with him through this lean spell were his bloodsucking management. While Howie Temple's box office value had sunk quicker than a boulder in a lake, they still touted him out to any bidder, not even the highest one. He'd done Japanese adverts, corporate awards gigs, panel shows – they all paid the bills. And now reality television, where the money was good but the credibility was non-existent. He hadn't just checked his shoes in at the harbour in Livorno. It had been his sense of self-worth too.

Strange, then, how he'd come not just to respect Cassandra for being a veteran of so many of these shows, but he'd also come to understand the satisfaction of being on one. Admittedly, he would have preferred for his introduction to the genre not to feature a murder but even so he'd finally grasped what Cassandra had told him. You went on to these shows a clueless celeb, and if they worked well, you left with a new skill, better self-knowledge or new friends. He'd seen stars go on everything from *Gearing Up: Celebrity Mechanic* to *Sofa, So Good: Upholstery Live*. He'd roundly mocked them until now and yet he realised he was going to have to eat his words. Nobody was more surprised by that than Howie. A year ago he would have baulked at the idea of even a murder mystery party, and now he was attempting to catch a killer in real life. Here he was – soaked to the skin, feet filthy from the streets, on the hunt for a disgraced politician who may have had murder on his mind.

'Here we are,' said Cassandra.

Howie pushed the glass doors of the station open and was met with the relieving coolness of the air conditioning.

'It's not very big,' said Cassandra.

'What were you expecting? Grand Central Station?'

'I've been there, you know,' she said, looking about. 'Tommy Hilfiger paid for me to attend a number of their events during New York Fashion week. I got some lovely pictures actually, the reach on them was huge.'

'Reach?'

'I'll explain later.' She shook her head. 'He must be here somewhere.'

'If your follower was telling the truth,' he said cynically. 'There are only four platforms here and I can't see him.'

Cassandra silently agreed with him. The platforms were almost deserted. A couple were embracing in the corner closest to them, the odd person lurking in the darkness across the tracks. None of them were Kelvin Kamani. She cursed.

'Damn,' she said. 'I thought we were on to something.'

'Hang on,' said Howie.

He spotted the departures board mounted on the wall above the main entrance. A digital clock was ticking towards nine, the arrivals and departures lined up on digital screens below it. Doing some quick maths, he snapped his fingers.

'There's only one train leaving here in the next half hour,' he said, pointing to the screen. 'It's heading to Pisa and it's here in three minutes. If Kelvin is here, I'll bet he'll be going for that.'

'Good call,' she said. 'Platform three, that's . . . '

She looked about for the numbers. The third platform was across the tracks. It was empty from where they were standing, no sign of Kelvin. A small ticket office was just behind them. Cassandra nodded over to it.

'He could be in there,' she said. 'He'll need a ticket after all.'

'Let's move,' said Howie.

'Wait, hold on.' She grabbed him. 'We can't just go storming in there, accusing him of all sorts. He's got connections. And look at the state of us, he'll call the cops and have us detained or arrested or something.'

'Then what do you suggest?' he asked.

She spied a row of seats mounted on the wall beyond the ticket booth door. Nudging Howie towards them, they sat down, flush against the wall. Anyone leaving the ticket office wouldn't see them.

'What do we do now?' he asked.

'Wait to see if he's getting on that train.'

'There's only two minutes left,' said Howie.

'Then he'll have to hurry up. As soon as he steps out of the office—'

'*If* he steps out of the office.'

'If he steps out of the office, we nab him before he gets to the platform. Simple.'

'Sure.' Howie shrugged. 'Simple.'

They fell into silence. The clock was still ticking. The train would arrive in ninety seconds. Still no sign of Kelvin. Howie found he was bouncing his knees up and down on the balls of his feet. Anxiety? Nervousness? Or just aching feet? He couldn't be sure. What he did know is that he'd kill for a pair of flip flops. As he looked at his ruined feet, in one way he *really* wanted Kelvin Kamani to come sauntering out of the ticket office, a sense of satisfaction about him that he'd got away. On the other hand, he hoped the former MP would never appear. It would be up to the authorities then to track him down – guilty or innocent. And their part would be finished. He could check into a hotel, have a bath, and try to switch his mind off for the next two weeks, undisturbed.

Less than a minute. Howie could feel Cassandra getting twitchy beside him.

'He's not here, is he?' she asked.

'There's still time,' he said weakly.

'We've been sent on a wild goose chase. I'm sorry, Howie. My followers are usually very reliable.'

'Reliable at what?'

'Finding things.'

'What things?'

'This and that, you know? Gig tickets, lip gloss, expensive, limited-edition trainers, that kind of thing.'

'Great.' Howie rolled his eyes. 'Just when I thought we might be dealing with amateurs, we—'

'It's him!'

Cassandra almost burst out of her skin. She grabbed Howie's arm so tightly that it took all of his effort not to scream.

Kelvin Kamani, former MP for Mid-Kent and Faversham, was there, just in front of them. He walked with stiffness across the main lobby of the station, heading towards platform three.

Howie and Cassandra were frozen. They sat like statues on their seats. It was only the announcer over the public address system saying that the Pisa train was now approaching the station that kicked them into action.

'Come on!' Howie shouted, taking the lead.

They both padded across the concourse, following Kelvin as he made his way to the platform. He kept up his brisk pace, climbing the stairs that led to the gangway across the tracks. The walls of the walkway were high, high enough that it was impossible to see over. Howie nudged Cassandra as they reached the top of the stairs.

'Kelvin!' he shouted.

His voice was loud. The high walls seemed to channel it, amplify it, the name barrelling and bearing down on their former crewmate.

Slowly, he turned. His face was etched with worry. 'How did you find me?' he asked.

'That doesn't matter,' said Cassandra. 'What matters is that we found you. We need answers, Kelvin. We need to know why you ran, what you know. Don't get on that train. You'll just cause more—'

Kelvin didn't give her a chance to finish. He turned on his bare heels and bolted along what remained of the gangway.

'Great,' said Howie, picking up his feet again. 'More running.'

'We can't let him get on that train!' shouted Cassandra.

They reached the stairs on the other end of the walkway. Kelvin was already down on the platform. Two bright lights, shining out of the darkness like the eyes of a predator came into view up ahead. The train to Pisa.

Kelvin was out of breath. He was shuffling to the furthest point of the platform as Howie and Cassandra arrived. The train came screeching to a halt – a huge, long series of silver boxes, the colours of the Italian flag painted on their sides.

'Get him!' Howie shouted.

The automatic doors slid open with a bleep. Only a few people stepped off but it was enough to put more obstacles between them and Kelvin. Cassandra had the edge, she was swifter and more lithe for dodging the disembarking passengers. She weaved through the crowd, never dropping her sight of Kelvin up ahead.

The last passenger stepped off the carriage as Kelvin was outside. He reached up for the handle beside the door and pulled himself onboard. But he hadn't been quick enough. Cassandra had him by the collar of his yacht polo shirt uniform.

She pulled it with as much might as she could. He tumbled backwards off the train, landing on top of her in a heap.

They both lay there for a second. Cassandra's ribs were agony. Pushing Kelvin off her, she gasped for air as Howie arrived, skidding to a halt and hopping in pain from his bare feet.

'Please,' pleaded Kelvin. 'You have to let me on that train. I beg you.'

'No chance partner,' said Howie, dragging Kelvin to his feet. 'You're going nowhere.'

The doors of the train bleeped again. They closed, hissing as the locks were put in place. Slowly but steadily, the engines started up again and the silver boxes rolled onwards, heading for Pisa without Kelvin Kamani onboard.

Chapter 25

Kelvin sat with his head in his hands. He hadn't said a word since the railway station, and the tears hadn't stopped either. Cassandra and Howie had gently ushered him out of the building and into the night. Neither of them knew where they were going, so they followed the traffic back to the square.

They found a quiet little cafe tucked away in the northwest corner and sat down. A miffed looking waiter had taken their order in a huff, determined to close early had it not been for them. A few minutes later three coffees had been thumped down onto their table. Howie didn't speak Italian but he'd heard enough cursing on the roads of La Spezia since he'd arrived. And he was sure what the waiter had said wasn't pleasant.

Now they were alone. 'Quite a Friday night we're having, eh?' said Howie.

'It's Saturday,' said Cassandra.

'Is it?' He was genuinely shocked. 'Damn. I've been at sea too long.'

'We all have, and it was only a couple of days.'

'Quite a couple of days at that, though. Am I right?' Howie took a sip of his drink. It was probably the best coffee he had ever tasted. And it burned the end of his tongue.

'Damn,' he said, flapping about. 'That's hot!'

'It's supposed to be,' said Cassandra, trying not to look embarrassed. 'Otherwise we would have got you an iced latte from Starbucks.'

Kelvin, for the first time since the train incident, looked up at him.

'There are no Starbucks in La Spezia,' he said, rubbing his eyes. 'The local government are quite adamant about supporting local business owners. They've made various tax credits and allowances to try and encourage more entrepreneurs to invest in the area.'

Local economics and business growth had not been the first thing Howie and Cassandra expected to hear from Kelvin.

'You know a bit about that then?' asked Howie, hiding his surprise and keen to keep Kelvin talking.

'There was a feasibility study done by the government,' said Kelvin. '*Our* government, back when I was a member of parliament. It was very interesting actually, if you like that sort of thing.' He looked almost wistful. 'That was when I was really part of things. In the thick of the action. Cabinet meetings, briefings from MI5 and MI6, security details, everything.'

'Not anymore,' said Howie sarcastically. 'Now you get to spend your summer with the likes of me and Cassandra and Marjorie Bryant. Lucky you.'

He sipped from his cup, relieved that it had cooled slightly.

'Yes,' said Kelvin. 'Lucky me.' He stared off into the distance, his eyes red and glassy from crying. Cassandra glared at her friend to get his attention. She nodded over at the former MP, hinting at what should come next.

'Did you kill Rolando?' he asked.

Cassandra almost dropped her coffee cup. It clattered on her saucer as she tried to compose herself.

'What?' Howie shrugged. 'You wanted me to ask him.'

'Yes, I did, Howie,' she said. 'But maybe with a little more tact and subtlety. Not just blurting it out like you're bidding on a Gauguin.'

'Go-who?'

'Never mind.' She turned her attention to Kelvin. 'What the esteemed Hollywood hard man Howie Temple is trying to say, Kelvin, is that we're concerned you ran off and tried to flee just as we were getting to the bottom of things. Is there something you'd like to tell us?'

Kelvin didn't react. It was like he was lost in a trance. He just sat there, staring, thinking.

'I've made lots of mistakes in my life,' he said quietly. 'I know it's such a cliché to say so, but I do regret them. I regret all of the misery and the heartache I've caused. I regret the people who have been left hurt, left without a penny because of the actions of one man and the people around him. They don't teach you that kind of responsibility at university. And you certainly don't learn it when you get eaten up by the party political machine. You just go along with it all, get swept up in the fame, the power, the fact that people know your name and you don't know theirs. You pose for the photographs beside potholes and mended traffic lights in the constituency. Then the next week you're shaking hands with the leaders of the free world. It's intoxicating. Then you find yourself convinced that it can last forever, that you're unstoppable. But you're not. Far from it, in fact. You are just as susceptible, just as flawed as the next man or woman who will take your place. Just like you did to somebody else. I've felt all of those mistakes, in these past few days. I'll feel them for the rest of my life.'

'What mistakes have you made, Kelvin?' she asked him gently. 'You can tell us.'

Kelvin blinked. He took up his coffee cup but didn't drink from it. He spun the cup around in his hands, one thumb pushing the handle one way and the other pulling it back.

'When you're a cabinet minister, you're vetted and briefed before you get the job. What they don't tell you is how you'll eventually leave the post. Some lucky buggers get to go out in a blaze of glory, defeated at an election. There's no fuss there, no shady back dealings. The people speak and their word is final. Then there are those of us who have to go out through the back door, have to give the humiliating statement on your own front doorstep, reading words you didn't write and trying to save face the whole time. Do you have any idea what that does to your esteem? Your psyche?'

He tapped an angry finger against his temple.

'No,' said Cassandra. 'I don't, Kelvin.'

'No,' said Howie. 'You'll have to forgive me though, I've not read up on my British politics. What exactly are you talking about here?'

Cassandra tutted loudly. She reached over and squeezed Kelvin's hand.

'Kelvin had a little problem a couple of years ago,' she said, trying to be as diplomatic as possible. 'There was a scandal, if you can call it that. He was sacked from his job as, what was it you did again, babe?'

'Secretary of State for Defence,' he said glumly.

'Yeah, that's the one,' she went on. 'I can't remember the details, I tend to switch off with these things. But there was some funny money, something like that. Cash in off-shore accounts that were linked to arms dealers or tank builders, is that right?'

Kelvin's shoulders slumped. The mere mention of his indiscretions seemed to sink him further into a depression.

'Mistakes were made,' he said at length. 'I'm not proud of what I did. And the newspapers and media had a field day, as you might expect.'

'That's kind of their job though, right?' said Howie. 'I mean, if you're doing dodgy stuff under the table, the public has a right to know.'

'He has a point, Kelv,' said Cassandra. 'Live by the sword and die by the sword.'

'Of course,' he sighed. 'I just thought I would be different, when I got there, into the corridors of power. I thought I could make a difference. Nobody enters politics for their own gain, not really. I mean, who in their right minds would put their whole lives, their history, their family, in the public spotlight like that if they weren't getting some sort of higher gratitude, some chance to do greater good? I don't need to tell you both that, you know all too well what I mean.'

'We're not all politicians, Kelvin,' said Howie with a hint of defensiveness. 'And I don't use my position to leverage cloak and dagger payments and corrupt bank accounts.'

'Perhaps you're right,' Kelvin sniffed. 'What am I saying? Of course you're right. No use complaining now, eh? All done, all water under the bridge, as I said in my autobiography.'

He finally took a sip of his coffee. When he placed the cup back down, he looked up at the others.

'I didn't kill Rolando,' he said flatly. 'I may have questionable ethics, but I'm not a murderer. I would never do something like that, I'd never *dream* of doing something as awful as taking a life. For all of my problems, for all of my issues, I am not a killer. Plus it would have squandered any slim remaining chance of me getting a knighthood.'

Howie glanced over at Cassandra. She was focused on Kelvin, intently watching him.

'Then why did you run?' she asked. 'Why did you flood the engine room? Why did you flee when we'd caught Scorpione? You can see why we think you might have something to do with all of this, babe.'

'I don't, I assure you,' he said.

'Well tell us your reason for scarpering, then,' said Howie, sounding urgent. 'Our next stop is the cop shop so we can either turn you in along with our statement or you can tell us whatever it is you're holding back. For god's sake man, give us *something*!'

'Easy, calm down, chuck,' said Cassandra, reaching out to Howie.

'I ran because I'm frightened,' said Kelvin.

'Frightened, of what?' asked Howie.

Kelvin looked about the cafe and the square beyond. He was sweating again, great dark patches under his armpits.

'This is much bigger than either of you think,' he said. 'There is more at stake here than you realise.'

'Then help us realise,' she said. 'If you're in trouble, Kelvin, then we can help. We can tell the police, the authorities—'

'No!' he shouted. A look of untamed fear made his whole face open up. Cassandra and Howie both blinked with fright at the sudden outburst.

'No police,' he said. 'We can't involve the police. They're worse than the criminals.'

'Oh come on,' said Howie. 'We can't leave Rolando's body out on the bridge any longer, and as for Ed, if he's not come round by now, he needs more medical help than our first aid kit can offer. Added to that is the fact that this so-called live investigation Cassandra and I are meant to be filming is a complete washout, we need real detectives, not reality ones. It's time to call in the law.'

'No, I'm serious,' said the former politician. 'Deadly serious, Howie. If we go to the police, we're effectively signing our own death warrants.'

'It can't be *that* bad,' said Cassandra. 'You make it sound like we're in some sort of gangster film.'

'I'm being completely serious, Cassandra,' he said. 'We shouldn't even be sitting out here, in the open.'

He stood up quickly, the legs of his cast iron chair squealing on the cobbles.

'We have to move, we have to go,' he said.

Suddenly, his whole body went stiff, arms outstretched, fingers flexed.

'Kelvin?' asked Cassandra. 'Are you alright?'

Slowly, Kelvin raised a quivering hand. He pointed across the square, Cassandra and Howie's eyes following him.

'It's them,' he said. 'They've found me. I don't know how but they've found me.'

Before the others could ask what was going on, Kelvin hopped over the table and started sprinting.

'What the hell?' Howie blurted.

'Get after him!' Cassandra shouted.

They set off from the table of the cafe, once again running after Kelvin Kamani. Across the square there was a commotion as a car barrelled onto the pedestrianised cobbles, screams and hollers going up as people frantically tried to get out of the way.

By the time the disgruntled waiter realised that they had gone without paying, it was too late. All he could do was shout obscenities after them. Howie, Cassandra and Kelvin couldn't hear him. They were already sucked into the hidden world of La Spezia's back streets.

Chapter 26

'I really need to get a pair of shoes,' gasped Howie. 'This is absolutely ridiculous. Who the hell goes running in the middle of the night, in a strange city, without any footwear on? That goddamn Ed will pay for this, if he ever wakes up.

'Shut up and keep running, babe,' Cassandra replied, equally breathless.

They had no idea where Kelvin was running to. Only that he hadn't stopped since he left them at the cafe. They had ducked and weaved down alleyways and back streets for what felt like hours. Howie knew it couldn't possibly be that long. Once again he cursed his shocking lack of fitness. There was little solace to be taken from Cassandra's flagging. If a woman half his age and ten times healthier couldn't keep up the pace, what chance did he have?

'Kelvin!' she rasped, barely enough breath to yell. 'Please stop, babe! Whatever's happening, we can help you! There's no need for all of this running away lark. We're here to help!'

Kelvin didn't stop. He kept running, barrelling down a hill that appeared to be heading back towards the harbour. The cobbled street was slippery and damp. Howie felt his muscles twisting and straining just to stay upright. He put up a brave fight, still running, but the inevitable happened. He felt his bare heel slip from beneath him and down he went.

There was a crack somewhere. All he could do was groan as the biting sting of pain reached around his ribs. Cassandra had carried on for a few more yards before she realised he had fallen.

'Howie!' she shouted.

'I'm alright.' He pushed the words with great strain past his teeth. 'Just keep going. Catch him up. We can't lose him.'

Cassandra faltered for a moment. She took a step back towards him and he waved her away.

'Go!' he shouted. 'I'll find you. Go! Catch Kelvin!'

In the dim light of the back street, Howie could see she was panicking, torn between what she should do. Stay behind and help him, he was clearly hurt? Or keep chasing after the disgraced politician? Howie didn't envy her. At least he had an excuse now to stop all the running.

He forced himself to sit upright. The pain was unimaginable. A few seconds of total agony before it subsided. All he could do was grimace and try not to show it. Now *that* was acting, he thought, clutching his side.

'Quickly!' he shouted. 'I'll be fine. Just catch him, Cassandra, otherwise our goose is cooked!'

That seemed to be enough to jolt her into action. She gave him a concerned nod and fled down the street. Howie watched her go, vanishing around a corner close to the waterfront. When he was sure she was gone, he lay back down, flat on his back and let out an enormous groan.

Holding himself together in front of her had taken all of his effort. And now that she was gone, he could just lie there and let the pain take over.

It wasn't just the fall that was making him suffer. Ever since that awful flight he'd been wracked with aches and niggles. The whole trip had felt like a test of his resolve, of his patience and, most of all, his age. He wasn't an old man, not by a long shot. But he'd felt that way on this trip. Now, here he was, lying flat out in the middle of the street. He wasn't even drunk.

The roar of an engine stirred him. The back street's dinginess was chased away by the searing white brightness of a car's headlights. Howie forced himself up, remembering he was lying in the middle of the street. He rolled over as the motor came thumping over the crest of the hill at speed.

'What the—'

He just had time to roll away as the car whizzed past him. He landed among old boxes and bags of garbage, the sound of the engines still buzzing in his ears. He was about to pick himself up when the car screeched to a halt a few yards down the street.

Howie clambered upright, banana skins and old newspaper tumbling off his shoulder. He winced as he stood up straight. His cracked ribs were the least of his problems.

The front and back doors of the sleek black car opened quickly. Three burly looking men in immaculate suits and dark sweaters got out and immediately charged towards him. They did not look like they wanted his autograph. All he could do was hold out his hands.

'Wow!' he said. 'Take it easy fellas, I don't know what you want but—'

None of them said a word. Two grabbed him by the shoulders and started dragging him toward the car. The third, the tallest of the men, remained behind, head looking about the alleyway, presumably for witnesses.

'Watch it,' he shouted. 'What's this all about?'

They threw him carelessly into the back of the car. One climbed in beside him, another joining the waiting driver. The last got into the back on his other side. He was squashed between the large men, squeezed by their sheer bulk and muscle.

'Where's the girl?' asked the driver, a woman, not turning around.

'Hey, listen, who are you guys?' Howie asked.

'Where's Kelvin Kamani too?' the driver asked.

Howie began to panic a little as the sheer forces of his predicament became abundantly clear. The two lumps of muscle on either side of him were staring intently. Their hands rested on their knees but they looked ready to react as soon as he made a bad decision. Howie's life felt like one great, big, bad decision at this point. Especially agreeing to this stupid programme in Europe.

'Look, if it's money you're after, I can assure you that I don't have a dime,' he said. 'And I highly doubt my management would pay any ransom.'

'*Stai zitto*!' shouted the driver.

Her eyes shone through the darkness as she watched him in the rear-view mirror.

'Where is Kelvin Kamani?' she asked again. 'And the girl? We saw you with them.'

Howie Temple could be accused of many things throughout his life. He had a fondness for card games and drank too much. He was an absent father to his children and he'd failed not once but twice at being a good husband. His morals had been iffy in the past and there was no doubt that he could have, and should have, been a better human being. Especially at the height of his fame and fortune. However, he was a great believer in second chances, when they were afforded. In that moment, he felt like the universe was handing him a lifeline, a chance to do something noble for a change. Surrounded by thugs and a mysterious ringleader looking for his help, he had one of two choices. Sing like a canary and point these people to Kelvin and Cassandra, regardless of what their intentions were. Or, stay quiet, just sit there and take the consequences, whatever they may be.

It was a huge risk. And one that most certainly would put him in mortal danger. Images of Scorpione, the mob, dodgy weapons deals and everything else flashed through his mind on those seconds he was thinking about what to do. In the end, he decided that enough, perhaps, was enough.

'I've got no idea who you're talking about,' he said, sitting back in the seat, watching the driver carefully in the mirror.

She didn't say a word. Kicking the car into gear, she took off down the street, hurtling around the corner in the opposite direction Cassandra and Kelvin had ran. As they sped off into the night, Howie looked back through the rear window. There was no sign of his companions, no sign of anyone at all.

He had done the right thing. So why was he terrified beyond all belief?

Chapter 27

Cassandra was scared. She didn't like this. She didn't like it one bit. And she could feel every atom, every fibre of her body screaming at her that this was a bad idea.

She was on her own, in a strange city, at night. Out of breath, no money, no shoes, no phone, chasing after someone she didn't completely trust. She shouldn't have left Howie. He needed help, he was hurt. But what could she do? He'd told her, shouted at her to keep chasing Kelvin Kamani. In those split seconds where she had to make a decision. She knew Howie had been correct to send her after Kelvin. Now, here she was. And there was no sign of Kamani.

The back streets and lanes had opened up to the harbourside. It was quiet here at this end of the bay. Tall stacks of commercial containers were piled high down by the waterfront. A long road stretched around the curve of the harbour, the busier end of the port blinking in the distance.

The road she was on was empty and poorly lit, old streetlights offering a weak orange glow every few hundred yards. The buildings that looked out onto the water were all dark, windows and firmly closed. She was alone in every sense of the word. So she stopped.

Bent double, she tried to catch her breath. She looked down at her feet and wriggled her toes. The nail polish she'd applied a few days ago, before she'd flown, was almost non-existent. Chipped, cracked and mostly long gone now. When she'd painted her nails, she had felt like a different person. Cassandra Troy wasn't naive enough to think bad things didn't happen in this world. Far from it, no matter what her critics accused her of. But experiencing them first hand was a completely different matter.

She looked about the empty street. Still no sign of Kelvin Kamani. There was no sign of anyone. She walked a little to get out of the dark, settling in a large pool of the sickly streetlight.

'Hello?' she shouted, not expecting an answer. 'Kelvin? Are you there?'

Silence, as she thought. Her breath was starting to slow as her energy came back. There was nowhere to run to though. The disgraced MP could have gone in any direction. She'd lost him.

'Bugger,' she said.

Cassandra tried to think logically. Logic had always been her best friend, even when she was at school. One of the benefits of having an academic for a father was that strict regime and diet of problem-solving and attention to detail. She'd never lost her hunger for that kind of thing. Even as her star rose, her profile and profits too. Logic, science, good common sense, they'd kept her feet on the ground all this time.

When things were tough, when she was bombarded with foul messages of hate and worse, she had always resorted to logic to give her a sense of perspective. When revenues started to dip, and she wasn't asked to as many events and high profile gigs, she resorted to logic to reverse things. Vacuous celebrities and hangers on had come and gone over the years. But logic had always stayed true. That was its thing, Cassandra thought. Now she hoped it wouldn't fail her again.

'He didn't kill Rolando,' she said aloud, taking comfort in hearing her own voice. *What would Kelvin have to gain from Rolando's death?* she thought. They were strangers to each other, thrown together through circumstance and nothing else. Yet Kelvin looked pretty scared when he saw that car in the square. And he definitely didn't want her calling the authorities. What was he scared of? Who was he scared of? Who was he protecting?'

None of it made any sense. She pinched the bridge of her nose.

'I shouldn't have come here,' she said. 'This was a bloody stupid idea, no matter what it does for my profile. I should have stayed at home, gone back to Liverpool, bought a new coat, something, anything but set one foot on the gangplank of that boat.'

She looked up and down the street again. Putting her hands on her hips, she felt something. Then she remembered. 'Oh for goodness' sake,' she sighed, pulling Howie's phone out of her pocket. 'Why didn't I think of that before?'

She quickly searched for the number of the local police. Her mother would be proud, she thought. She was, after all, always accused of 'having her head in that bloody phone' all of the time. And here she was, forgetting she had one at all.

'That'll show her,' she smiled, flipping through pages of information.

She found something official looking, a seal of the *La Spezia Polizia di Stato* – the main police force for the city – at the top. There was a phone number underneath and she pressed it with her thumb.

Before Cassandra could even lift the phone to her ear, a hand lurched out of the darkness and smothered her mouth. She was pulled backwards with an incredible force. She tried to scream but the hand was clamped over her mouth tight enough that only a muffled whimper came out.

Cassandra thought the absolute worst was happening. She could feel her head thumping as her heart rate accelerated again. The darkness of a doorway swallowed her up in one gulp as she was forced against the wall. In the gloom, Kelvin Kamani's face appeared.

Kelvin held a finger to his mouth, imploring her to be quiet. He peered around the edge of the alcove, checking the street.

'Don't make a sound,' he whispered.

Cassandra nodded. Slowly, he let her go, taking away his hand. She thought about screaming, thought about doing the opposite of what he'd asked. He had, after all, scared the living daylights out of her.

She didn't though. She stayed quiet. Kelvin's hand hovered over her mouth for a second longer as he made sure she did as he asked her. When he was satisfied, he relaxed, pressing himself against the opposite side of the doorway.

'Were you followed?' he asked her, voice silent.

'No,' she said.

'Where's Howie?'

'He's back up the one of the streets,' she said. 'He fell and hurt himself. He told me to keep chasing you. We should go get him.'

'No.' He reached out to stop her. 'We can't leave. We have to hide.'

'Hide? Kelvin, I'm a twenty-seven-year-old millionaire influencer. I don't and won't hide from anyone.'

'Please, Cassandra, I'm begging you. Please just stay hidden,' he said, the veins bulging in his neck.

Cassandra wasn't convinced that this was a good idea. She was worried about Howie. She knew they should get him, he might be seriously injured. And if Kelvin was right with his paranoia, then he was in danger too. Perhaps more so.

'Look, this isn't right,' she said to him. 'You can't expect me to go along with everything you're asking when you won't tell me what's going on. This has been very bizarre behaviour from you, Kelvin. I'm worried you might be out of your depth or you need some help. This isn't normal, chuck, hiding in the shadows.'

'We have to stay out of sight,' he said. 'Please, I'm begging you. Stay hidden until we know it's safe.'

'Safe from who?' she asked.

'Them,' he said.

'Them who?'

'Please.' He was close to tears again.

The distant sound of an engine made him jump. He pushed her back against the wall and pressed himself further into the darkness. He was breathing heavily, his eyes closed firmly shut. The engine was drawing closer. It was high-pitched and nasal. Cassandra thought it sounded a little like Marjorie.

A scooter trundled past them, gliding between the pools of streetlight. The driver didn't notice them, continuing on down the road that ran alongside the containers and the harbour. When they were far enough away, Kelvin began to breathe again.

'Thank god,' he said. 'I think they've gone.'

'Who, Kelvin? Who's gone?'

He rubbed his eyes. Slowly, sticking his head around the edge of the doorway, he looked up and down the street.

'I'll tell you everything,' he said. 'I promise. But we have to get off the streets. We have to go somewhere safe.'

'And where would you suppose that is?' she asked.

'I think . . . ' he said slowly. 'I think we have to go back to the yacht.'

Chapter 28

The harsh lights of the interrogation room were hurting Howie's eyes. He sat staring around the dingy room. He'd counted the ceiling tiles several times – there were thirty-six and a half. The game had lost its appeal quickly. A filthy mirror took up most of the wall to his right. He knew there were people behind it, watching him, trying to work out his tells, his body language, what he was hiding. Howie had been in enough cop movies to know there was nothing he could do or say that would change their mind and let him walk out of here. Wherever here was.

The car had sped quickly through the night streets of La Spezia, cutting corners and hopping over the cobbles with reckless abandon. Had it not been for the slabs of meat on either side of him, Howie was sure he'd have hurtled out of the back windows.

The journey had only taken around ten minutes. While his orientation was knocked off, the tiredness now firmly holding onto his brain, he reckoned he had been taken further into the city, away from the harbour.

The car had come to a halt outside a dingy-looking building. The masonry was cracked and creepers were reaching up from the ground like long, spindly fingers. He'd been bundled out of the car and taken down drab corridors and left here in the room, alone. Nobody had been in to see him, not even the hired muscle he'd had for company in the mysterious car. The driver hadn't spoken again since he was first grabbed. And she hadn't joined them in the building. In all, Howie was no more knowledgeable about where he was and who had brought him here than he had been before.

He stood up from his chair and stretched. A single table was in front of him, the surface scratched and old. Another chair was on the opposite side, much like his own. That's what let him know this was an interrogation room. If it was a cell, he'd have no need for two chairs. He was proud of that deduction.

He sauntered over to the mirror. The surface was filthy, large blotches of grime making it almost impossible to get a clear view of his reflection. He hunkered down and found a small patch. Although he instantly regretted it.

'Good grief,' he said aloud.

He looked ancient. Huge bags hung under his eyes, heavy and cumbersome. His eyes themselves were bloodshot. He hadn't shaved in days and the designer stubble he normally insisted on maintaining was now a beard. He stuck out his tongue and immediately popped it back in, disgusted at the sight. His hair was salt-stiffened and matted. Trying to pat it down into some sort of respectable shape only made him notice the filth on his hands and then his feet.

He thought about Arlo Spenser, his very first agent, and what he would have said about the way he looked. Image was everything in showbusiness, Arlo had taught him that.

As soon as he'd signed his first contract, he'd been given a thousand dollar advance to go out, get a haircut and a new suit that actually fitted him. Dress for the parts you want, not the parts you're getting, that had been Arlo's sound advice. The only part he'd be offered on his current look would be tramp or hobo.

Remembering his first mentor made Howie smile a little at least. They'd had a falling out and parted ways just before Howie made it big. They hadn't spoken for years after that, a degree of bitterness that outlasted their memories of what the dispute was actually about. Only now that he was older, wiser, poorer, could he see that old Arlo had known every trick in the showbusiness playbook. And he'd tried to impart some of that knowledge on the no-good punk, teenage Howie Temple before he was swallowed by the Hollywood juggernaut.

'History is for teachers,' he said, another of Arlo's favourites.

He stretched and winced, the pain in his side still there. He straightened with difficulty and sighed.

The door of the room swung open. Howie briefly thought about trying to escape. The thought was among the briefest he had ever had. Even if he had the mobility, the stealth, the competency to attempt such a thing, where would he go? And he was hardly going to fight off those three henchmen if he came across them again.

Instead he stood primly to attention as a woman came striding into the interrogation room.

'Sit down,' she said to him.

Howie recognised the voice. She was the driver, the same cool, dark eyes he had seen in the rear-view mirror were now staring at him head on. He tentatively walked back over to his chair and sat down. She waited until he was settled before doing the same with the other chair.

She was severe looking, a sternness that seemed to radiate out from her. Howie reckoned she was about the same age as him, although she was faring much better than he was. Her suit was immaculately tailored, her whole body language neat and orderly. Her dark hair was cut in a curt bob that moved as she walked, keeping just enough humanity about her to convince him she wasn't some kind of AI android. In fact, Howie found he couldn't take his eyes off her.

'Thank you for helping us, Mr Temple,' she said, her English immaculate, with only the slightest hint of an Italian accent.

'Helping you?' he said. 'You make it sound like I'm here through choice.'

The woman didn't twitch. He immediately regretted his tone.

'That is to say, those three gorillas you had helping you pretty much stuffed me into your car without as much as asking who I was.'

'We know who you are, Mr Temple,' she said.

'Okay, well, that kind of puts me at a disadvantage then, doesn't it?' he said, trying to remember lines from his movies. 'You know who I am but I don't have the faintest idea who you are. That's not really fair, is it? Are you Mafia? CIA? MI6? Who am I dealing with here?'

'Where are Cassandra Troy and Kelvin Kamani?' she asked.

Howie felt strangely brave. He wasn't sure where that confidence was coming from. But he was happy to ride it out.

'Come on now, honey,' he said, leaning forward on the table. 'You know I'm not going to say another word without my lawyers here. And I'm certainly not going to rat out my friends.'

The woman pursed her lips. Businesslike, to the point of frosty, she remained perfectly stoic.

'Any chance I could get a coffee?' he asked, leaning back, playing his role. 'Something with a caramel flavour would be great.'

That seemed to draw some reaction from the woman across the table. She laughed a little to herself. Reaching into her pocket, she drew out a small, black wallet. She placed it down on the table with a loud whack. Howie flinched at the noise. Sliding it across to him, she nodded down at the wallet.

'My credentials, Mr Temple,' she said.

She withdrew her hand. Howie eyed the wallet with suspicion. He reached down and opened it up. A warrant card stared back up at him.

'*Ispettore Superiore* Dorotea Sal,' he said, reading her name aloud. 'You're a cop?'

'Senior inspector,' she said.

'But . . . you kidnapped me off the streets?'

'You were escorted to one of our official police residences, Mr Temple.'

'Escorted? You call that escorting?'

Sal remained cool. She reached down and took back her warrant card. Howie wasn't sure if he should be outraged or terrified. If this was how they treated him and he was innocent, what would they be like if he was a criminal?

'Am I under arrest?' he asked.

'Mr Temple, please, try to remain calm.'

'Am I under arrest? It's a simple enough question.'

'We're hoping you can help us with our enquiries.'

'Yes or no?'

Inspector Sal let out a quiet, collected breath. She folded her arms across her chest, watching him with her mistrusting eyes.

'No, you're not,' she said. 'But I'm hoping you can be of some help to us as part of a much wider investigation.'

Howie stood up. He walked around the room, rubbing the back of his head.

'This isn't right,' he said. 'You can't treat me like this. I need medical attention, I could have cracked ribs, or worse. You've abducted me. You've not arrested me or charged me. And you have the gall to sit there and ask for my help. What kind of circus are you guys running here? You're supposed to be a police force!'

'Sit down!'

Sal's voice boomed around the close, claustrophobic room. It was enough to stop Howie in his tracks. She levelled a look of sheer contempt at him. He did as he was told.

She gave him a moment of grace to settle. Howie was thankful for it. All notions of being the bold and brilliant Hollywood star were now firmly packed away. And they weren't coming back.

'Now, I acknowledge, Mr Temple, that our methods here in La Spezia may not be to your liking,' Sal began. 'But we are hard pressed for time. You might even say it's of the essence. I need you to tell me exactly where Cassandra Troy and Kelvin Kamani are, right now.'

'I don't know,' he said.

'I'm afraid you'll have to do better than that.'

There was something ominous in the inspector's tone.

'I can't do any better. I don't know, it's as simple as that.'

'We know you came ashore with Ms Troy earlier this evening. And we know that you were in a cafe with Mr Kamani not long after.'

'Yes, all of that's true,' he said. 'It's also not illegal.'

'No, it's not,' she said.

'Then if you're not arresting me or charging me, I'm free to go.'

Sal didn't reply. Howie stood back up. He watched her carefully as he rounded the table and made for the door. The inspector hadn't moved. Howie was growing suspicious. Slowly, he opened the door but stopped immediately. The two lumps of muscle and flesh who had sandwiched him in the back of the car were waiting on the other side.

The better light of the police station was not kind to them. They seemed almost feral in a way, despite their expensive suits and fashionable haircuts. They both stared down at him as he closed the door again.

'It's like that, is it?' he asked.

Sal didn't respond. She waited for him to return to his seat for a second time. He did so.

'Satisfied?' she asked him.

'Not really,' he said sullenly. 'But it'll have to do I guess.'

'Where are they, Howie?' she asked him. 'Tell us. You've got nothing to fear if you work with us on this.'

'Work with you on *what*?' he asked. 'That's the problem, Inspector. Nobody seems to be willing to tell me what the hell is going on here. One minute I'm filming a second-rate

TV show on a luxury yacht, the next I'm being bundled into police cars in the dead of night. I've got overgrown baby footballers to nursemaid, mouthy pseudo-intellectuals, a disgraced politician with an inferiority complex and a young woman who knows more about the world than I do despite being half my age! And on top of all that, a dead body and an unconscious director to deal with.'

'Body?'

The first hint of emotion crept across Sal's face. Howie was too furious to delight in the little victory he'd achieved.

'What body?' she asked, leaning forward a little.

'The body,' he said, deciding that Rolando couldn't get any more dead and despite Kelvin's warning about avoiding the police, this seemed like the only way to get help to Ed. 'Our captain. He was killed onboard the ship. We couldn't raise land – or at least thought we couldn't. So Cassandra and I were investigating until help arrived. We thought we had our killer, we thought it was all tied up when we discovered some Mafia hitman had crept onboard but he fed us a wild story about not being the culprit. Then Kelvin took off and we chased him. And now here I am.'

It was all out before Howie had a chance to think. Hearing it all back to himself, he was astonished he was still going. The fumes he'd been running on had evaporated a long time ago. Everything from here on in was just instinct.

Sal had heard every word. She considered it all for a moment, then gave him a curt nod. She pushed herself up from the table and raced to the door, barking instructions to the goons outside. They both looked terrified. Howie couldn't make any of it out, only Rolando's name. He just sat there, feeling like a spare wheel.

'I'm sorry, Mr Temple, you're going to have to come with us, immediately,' said the inspector, returning to him.

'Go with you? Where?' he asked.

'Please, we don't have a lot of time.'

'Inspector, you're going to have to tell me what's going on here if you want any more of my help. Ed, the director, he's lying on that boat in a coma or something. And the rest of the crew and guests are stranded. They need help.'

'They'll be seen to, I promise you. But please, we have to go.'

'Go where?'

Sal grumbled something under her breath. She looked up to the grotty ceiling of the interrogation room, as if searching for divine inspiration or patience. She flexed her hands and turned back to face him.

'Rolando,' she said. 'The captain of *The Regal Secret*. He was an informant, a spy, for the police.'

'What?'

'Yes,' she said. 'He had some previous issues with the mob and came to us for help. The fact that he's dead means that other people's lives could be in danger, Mr Temple. He was feeding us information that could lead to some very high-profile arrests, arrests that could shake up the whole organised crime situation from here to Monaco and Nice, maybe beyond.'

'Information? On who?'

'Mr Kamani,' she said, then paused. 'And . . . '

'And?' he asked.

'Ms Troy.'

Howie couldn't quite get his head around what he was being told. Rolando had been working for the police?

What the hell did that have to do with him? Just what had he walked into here when he'd stepped on that yacht?

'We have reason to believe that Ms Troy may have something to do with all of this,' said Sal. 'That she may be aiding and abetting Kamani.'

'Bloody hellfire,' he said, not thinking.

'What?' Sal screwed up her face.

'What? Oh, nothing,' he said. 'Just something that a friend always says.'

His mind was racing, his head thumping. He tried to concentrate, tried to pull himself back into the dingy interrogation room, back to reality. This all sounded so bizarre. Cassandra? Involved in all of this?

As if reading his mind, Sal reached into the inside pocket of her blazer. She pulled out a folded piece of paper. Carefully, she handed it over. Howie took the paper, staring down at the fuzzy pictures printed on the sheets.

The first showed a group of around twenty people. They were all wearing similar pink sashes. Middle-aged women, young men, the group was as varied as it was busy. At one end, with a beaming grin, stood Kelvin Kamani. He looked younger, slightly thinner, glasses magnifying his eyes to an alarming degree. At the other side of the group was a fresh-faced but still highly recognisable Cassandra Troy.

Chapter 29

Cassandra had been following Kelvin at a safe distance. They'd been wandering around the dock for what felt like hours. She was beginning to think that the former MP wasn't quite as assured or competent as he was trying to make out.

'I was sure I parked it around here somewhere,' he kept saying as they moved from one jetty to another, searching for his stolen water scooter.

Cassandra wasn't quite sure what to think anymore. The evening's activities had been traumatising to say the least. From high-speed chases to now being led through the darkness by a disgraced politician. She knew that the life of internet stardom would have its ups and downs. But never anything like this.

She was starting to feel cold. Her basic uniform had been fine onboard the yacht. Walking the streets of La Spezia was a completely different matter. She rubbed her arms and tried to stay warm.

'I think it's the next one,' said Kelvin, pointing randomly up the harbour at the next moorings. 'Yes, it must be the next one.'

'You said that about the last one. And the one before that, chuck,' she said.

'Yes, I know. I wasn't expecting to have to come back. And it's been a rather stressful day.'

'You're telling me.' She rolled her eyes.

They reached the next jetty. Several small boats were tied up and moored along the creaking wooden bays. Kelvin checked every one of them, counting them down with his index finger. Then he spotted the water scooter he had stolen from *The Regal Secret*.

'Ah, here we are,' he said. 'Just where I left her.'

He stepped onboard and twisted the key in the ignition. It started up, kicking out water from the rear end. He gestured up to Cassandra to join him. She didn't budge.

'We have to get going, Cassandra,' he said. 'We have to get back to the yacht with the others. It's not safe here.'

'I'm not going anywhere until you tell me the truth,' she said. 'I need to know what's going on here, Kelvin, what this whole thing is all about. I can't abandon Howie without good reason. Tell me, what's so dangerous here?'

'I will, I promise, when we're back onboard the yacht. Now please, get on.'

Cassandra narrowed her brow. She didn't like his tone. She didn't like being told what to do at the best of times. The way Kelvin was flitting between paranoid maniac and bumbling politician was disconcerting.

She motioned to step onto the water scooter. He opened his arms to help her. But at the last moment, she reached down and snatched the keys from the ignition. The engine juddered and then stopped, bubbling beneath Kelvin. She was back on the jetty and holding the keys above her head.

'What are you doing you silly girl!' he shouted. 'We have to go, now!'

'I'll throw them away, don't think I won't,' she said.

'We don't have time for these games, Cassandra. The others need us, their safety as well as ours depends on us getting out of here.'

'Don't give me that old pony,' she snapped. 'Don't you dare sit there and try to convince me you give a toss about the others. I'm not stupid, Kelvin, once a politician always a politician and I know what you're capable of.'

'We don't have time for this!' he shouted. 'Get onto this contraption right away! I demand it!'

'You can demand all you like, chuck, but I'm not going anywhere with you until you start telling me what I want to know. Or so help me, I'll throw these keys into the sea and you'll never see them again.'

Kelvin closed his eyes until they were just slits. He measured her up and down.

'You won't do it,' he said. 'You're bluffing.'

'Bluffing am I?' she said.

She curled her hands around the keys and pulled her arm back. She was just about to throw them away when he yelped from below.

'No!' he shouted. 'No, please, don't!'

Cassandra stopped herself, just. She steadied her feet on the smooth wood of the jetty and turned back to face him.

'What's going on here?' she asked. 'What are you involved in, Kelvin?'

'It's all happened so fast, I can't quite believe it myself,' he said.

'What has?'

'The unpleasantness that cost me my role in the government,' he started. 'It was the start of a slippery slope. I mean, when you ascend to one of the very highest offices of state in the land and then come crashing down less than a year later, it's no wonder I did what I did.'

'What did you do?'

Kelvin bowed his head. 'The reports in the newspapers, the media, everywhere, they were all true,' he said, shamefully. 'When I was the defence minister, I was paid by certain lobbyists, people representing forms and others to secure contracts. It was highly illegal and a complete abuse of my position of power. I got away without jail, Cassandra, but only thanks to the good grace of those still in the corridors of power. My public resignation and humiliation was the price I had to pay. That and knowing I wouldn't ever again sit at the top table. I was grateful at the time. Just glad I was spared prison. But the people involved in all of this, they make jail look like a holiday retreat in the Seychelles.'

'Who are these people?'

Kelvin seemed to be building himself up to what he was about to say next.

'Mobsters,' he said. 'The Serafinas.'

'You took payment from the Mafia when you were a Secretary of State?' said Cassandra, in disbelief. 'What's the matter with you, Kelvin. Are you bonkers?'

'A moment of madness, yes,' he said. 'Like I tried to tell you before, when you have as meteoric a rise through the party ranks as I did, your head is swimming. You're effectively told you can do what you like, with who you like. I got used to accepting favours, donations, support, whatever you want to call it, from all kinds of groups of people and middle men. Pretty soon you get lazy about doing your research on who's really behind the money. By the time I realised whose dollar I'd taken, it was too late.'

'Greed is what I'm hearing,' she said. 'A habit of relying on bungs so much until you can't afford to say no.'

'Yes!' he exclaimed. 'That's *exactly* it! You meet people at various functions when you're in the government. Well-wishers, supporters, and people who want something that seems innocuous at first – a contract tender, an introduction, a phone number. Through friends of friends I was put in touch with the Serafinas. One of their companies was happy to supply munitions and body armour for our troops at a fraction of the cost the Americans were charging us. It was too good a deal to pass up. You would have done the same in my position, *anyone* would have. A global recession, the safety of our soldiers, it was perfect.'

'Too perfect,' said Cassandra. 'When did you find out the Serafinas were behind the suppliers?'

Kelvin's face went a little blank.

'You always knew, didn't you,' she said. 'You always knew it was them behind this weapons company.'

'As I said before,' he whispered. 'Mistakes were made. I was naive enough to assume the Serafinas had some legitimate businesses alongside their less official enterprises.'

'So what? Now they're looking for their favours to be returned, is that it? Is that why Rolando's dead? Did you murder him?'

'No, I didn't kill him,' he said. 'I absolutely didn't kill him. When the whole scandal broke, the media, they knew nothing about the mobsters. I don't know if they had something to do with it, I don't really care. I was disgraced enough and retired to the back benches. I've spent the last eighteen months trying to rebuild my career, my profile. Then I get a phone call one day, from someone with an Italian accent. It's them, the Serafinas. They said I owed them for everything, the discounted weapons and armour, covering up the worst of the scandal, everything. And they needed me to act for them.'

'Act in what way?' she asked.

Again Kelvin fell silent. He was staring off into the distance again, lost in his own thoughts.

'Kelvin, what did they want you to do?'

'They wanted me to keep influencing the government, to make sure their contracts were upheld, even though I was out of office.'

'And did you do it?' she asked. 'Have you been winding the new ministers up from behind the scenes?'

'No,' he said. 'Absolutely not. I wouldn't dream of that. Despite what many people say about me, I wouldn't drag others into this dreadful business. I said no, but I knew they wouldn't like it. I had to get away. I've lost everything but my profile. And that was to my advantage. When I heard that a new series of this dreadful programme was being made, I insisted on my people getting me onboard *The Regal Secret*. If for nothing else it would get me out of the country for a while to somewhere the mob couldn't get me, or so I thought. I was actually glad about the prospect of having cameras following me around. I have friends in Monaco, they would have put me up if we'd ever reached there.'

'Bloody hellfire,' said Cassandra, puffing out her cheeks. 'So why did you flood the engines of the ship? You must have known they would get fixed.'

'It was stupid,' he said. 'But after Rolando was killed I needed time to work out who the mob had onboard. You have to believe me though, Cassandra. I didn't murder him. I had nothing to do with his death.'

Cassandra had listened intently. Politicians, contracts, the mob. No small part of her wanted to be back in her apartment with her laptop and her ring light, talking about the latest cut-out dresses and cloud slides.

'This is a mess, Kelvin,' she said. 'You need to go to the police or your lawyers or something. You can't keep running like this and putting other people in danger. Poor Howie is back there somewhere. He could be dead for all we know. And the same goes for Ed on *The Regal Secret*. It's not fair.'

'I know,' he said, bowing his head again. 'I know. It's shameful. I've tried my very hardest not to involve others. I should have stayed in London. I should have come clean to the authorities. But these people, Cassandra, the Serafinas, they have people everywhere. That's why I need to get back on the yacht. At least there I can see them coming.'

'Like you saw that assassin,' she said sarcastically.

'I know,' he said. 'I hadn't expected that. But if you and Howie hadn't followed me, I'd be in Pisa by now and on my way to Monaco. But I'm not sorry you pulled me off that train. I just want this nightmare to end.'

'Then let me contact the police,' she said. 'Let me get help to the others on the yacht. Ed doesn't deserve to be hurt because of this. Marjorie, Ms Sachiko, the guests, they're stuck out there and relying on us to get them back to shore. It's not just your life in danger, Kelvin.'

The former politician nodded solemnly. She looked at the keys in her hands and handed them back to him.

'We have to do the right thing. There's still time.'

'You're right of course,' he said. 'You should call for help. You have a phone, yes?'

Cassandra patted the pocket of her shorts. There was nothing there.

'Damn it,' she said. 'It's Howie's phone, I must have dropped it when you grabbed me back there. Not cool, by the way.'

'Sorry,' he said feebly.

Cassandra started searching the floor and looking back towards the harbourside. She was just scanning the route they'd taken from the road when she heard the engines of the jet ski starting up. Peering through the darkness, she saw Kelvin pulling out of the berth. He'd already spun the scooter around and was heading for open water. It was too late even to shout after him. Hopefully he'd run out of fuel before he got back to the ship. It would serve him right. She thought about finding the other jet ski and tailing him but this time at least she knew where he was going. She was needed here more – to find Howie, find his phone, find answers.

Chapter 30

'Do we have a lock on the phone?'

Inspector Sal had decided to leave the driving to someone else now. One of the meatheads that had intimidated Howie was in the seat, throwing the patrol car about the late-night streets of La Spezia with abandon. A blue flashing light was sending its glow out across the quiet buildings as they whizzed through the city. Everything felt a lot more official this time. And less like a kidnapping. But he felt no less confident that the trip might end in his own demise.

Howie had at least been afforded his own seat in the back of the car. He hadn't spoken since they'd left the police station. Light conversation didn't appear to be the order of the day here. Sal had been constantly on her phone, her serious expression lit up by the glowing screen. Whatever it was she was doing, she was concentrating hard. Howie didn't want to disturb her.

In the short period of time he had known the inspector, she had struck him as the no-nonsense sort. He supposed that was the bare minimum it took to take on the mob. Severe, uncompromising, steely; he wasn't inclined to ever be in her bad books. Not that it would have been hard. He suspected Dorotea Sal was a woman who didn't suffer fools lightly and criminals even less. Remarkably, she'd grown even *more* severe since he'd said that Captain Rolando was dead, murdered on his own bridge.

Marjorie had been half-wrong, half-right he thought. Most of their time on *The Regal Secret* seemed wreathed in half-truths, he realised now. A Mafia informant. Howie still half wondered whether it was all some terrible dream. He would wake up in his bunk, the rest of the crew, including Ed and Rolando, all fawning over him, like the end of *The Wizard of Oz* when Dorothy returns home.

'We're triangulating now, ma'am,' said the goon in the front seat.

The muscular officer's brooding tones were enough to confirm that this was no dream and that Howie was, in fact, very much awake. Even his imagination couldn't come up with as blunt an instrument as that man.

'Keep on it,' she said. 'They can't have gotten far. We might still catch them before they make a break.'

'Yes,' he said, turning back to the tablet in his lap.

'I think you're mistaken, inspector,' he said. 'Cassandra Troy has got nothing to do with this. She's too good-hearted, for one thing.'

'Don't count on it, you saw the picture,' said Sal. 'We've got reason to believe she's just as up to her neck in the Serafina operation as Kelvin Kamani. Not to mention some other high-profile people.'

'Other high-profile people? You mean celebrities?' he asked.

Sal's grim face told him he shouldn't be asking those kinds of questions. Not now at any rate. Howie's head was thumping. He had no idea what time it actually was. But he felt like he'd been awake for weeks, if not months. He stared out of the window at the streets zipping past. A throng of squad cars were snaking behind them. This was serious, he thought. He began to worry what lay in store for Cassandra.

She couldn't be involved in all of this – whatever this was. Could she? Howie still wasn't sure what was going on. But the idea that Cassandra was somehow connected to the Mafia, to big time crime syndicates, it just didn't make sense. She had proved all his preconceptions wrong about influencers, she seemed so genuine, so real, for want of a better expression. It had been a long, long time since Howie had ever come across someone as authentic as her. He realised then, sitting in the back of the police car, that she had been a breath of fresh air, not just throughout this debacle, but his life in general. It made his heart hurt to think she might have been playing him all along.

'Inspector, please,' he said. 'You have to let me talk to Cassandra when we find her.'

'Absolutely not,' said Sal, not looking up from her phone.

'Please, I'm begging you.'

'I can't risk your safety, or that of my officers.'

'Safety? What do you think she's going to do?'

'I don't know what she's going to do, Mr Temple, that's the problem.'

'She's not a master criminal,' he said. 'She's a social media star, or whatever it is they call themselves.'

'Got it,' shouted the muscle-bound officer in the passenger seat. 'The phone was last seen at the docks.'

'Go, move!' Sal thumped the driver's seat in front of her.

The car accelerated, pulling Howie back into his seat. He held on tightly as they raced towards the harbourfront. He had a sickening feeling in his stomach. With every passing street, every alleyway and road that sped by the window, he knew he was getting closer to Cassandra. And then what?

The sirens blared from the motorcade behind them. The endless expanse of rippling black ocean opened up ahead as the car screeched its way around the corner and came to a sudden halt. Before he knew what was really going on, Inspector Sal, the muscular officer and driver were all out and running. Howie thought he should do the same – he just didn't know in which direction.

The squad cars had all stopped behind them. Uniformed officers in their droves were piling out onto the concourse that ran alongside the docks. Enough officers to take down a small army rather than arrest a politician and a twenty-something petite woman. Howie was barged and pushed out of the way as they all followed their fearless leader. He hurried to get past them, his feet burning. Up ahead he caught sight of Cassandra.

'Move!' he said, forcing his way to the front. 'Let me through!'

He reached the front of the throng. Cassandra was standing in the middle of the road, her hands held up high.

'Cassandra!' he shouted.

'Howie!'

He'd never seen a person look so scared. Her head was flicking from side to side, scanning the crowd. Tears had started to mark a path down her filthy cheeks. She looked like a child, a scared, lonely child who'd been caught being naughty.

'Ms Troy, please, lie down on the ground, with your hands behind your back,' said Sal.

'Howie?' She looked at him.

'Let me go,' Howie tried to rush forward but he was being held back by a pair of officers. 'This is ridiculous. She's done nothing wrong!'

'Howie, what's happening babe?'

'Don't worry, it's all just a mistake,' he said, still struggling. 'Just do what they say, Cassandra.'

'Please, Ms Troy,' said Sal, more firmly this time. 'On the ground, with your hands behind your back.'

'What? I haven't done anything.'

'Where's Kamani?' asked the inspector.

'Kelvin? He's ditched me and headed back to the yacht.'

'He's what?' blurted Howie. 'Why the hell has he gone *back* to the ship?'

'He says it's the only place he's safe,' she said. 'He says that the Serafinas want him dead.'

'On the ground, now!' Sal barked.

Cassandra flinched. Her arms were shaking, still held above her head. Howie heard the clicking of guns all around him.

'What are you doing? She's not a criminal!' he shouted. 'You can't shoot her!'

'Shoot me?!' Cassandra's eyes went as wide as dinner plates.

'Get down!' Sal screamed.

'Howie! What's going on?'

He didn't know where the energy came from. He'd read about ordinary people gaining great strength when extreme circumstances occurred. Maybe that's what happened. He couldn't be sure. Somehow he was able to pull himself free of the officers holding him back. He ran as fast as he could and threw himself in front of Cassandra. He held up his hands.

'If you're going to shoot her then you'll have to shoot me first,' he said.

Even at a distance, Howie could see the contempt and anger on Inspector Sal's face. She hesitated for an excruciatingly long moment. He didn't think she would order her officers to shoot. Not really. But for those agonising seconds, there was more of a chance than he had given credit for.

'*Merda*!' she shouted, throwing her own hands up in the air. 'Stand down. Everyone, stand down.'

The massed officers all eased up. Their weapons were dropped. Sal rounded, still cursing. Her slab of an assistant glared down the street at Howie. But he ignored him, turning and hugging Cassandra close to him.

'What's going on, Howie?' she asked, sobbing into his chest.

'I don't know,' he said, trying to calm her down, holding her tight. 'Remember when we were just a couple of clueless celebrities on a trip to Monaco?'

She laughed a little between her sobs.

'No,' she said sadly. 'That feels like a very long time ago now. Another world.'

'I know,' he said.

She pulled away from him, wiping her nose and cheeks.

'Am I in trouble?' she asked him.

The police were walking towards them, collected footsteps getting closer and closer. Howie felt his throat tightening up. He didn't know. But how could he tell that to her?

'Ms Troy,' came Sal's voice. 'Can you come with us please. We have a few questions.'

She looked up at Howie. He felt the stinging bite of tears behind his nose.

'I'm sorry,' he said.

He slowly let her go. Cassandra nodded quietly, resigned to what was about to happen. She sniffed and nodded again.

'Okay,' she said. 'Let's get this over with.'

Chapter 31

A thump from above. That's all it took. Marjorie Bryant had always been a light sleeper. She'd spent her formative years growing up in a house with three older brothers who liked to play practical jokes. Sleep for too long, or too soundly, and you'd wake up with a face full of shaving cream. Or worse.

Her eyes were wide open now. The ceiling of her cabin was in touching distance, the top bunk uncomfortably close. She knew what she had heard. She wasn't stupid, despite what her detractors said. She definitely didn't believe in auditory hallucinations. She was a thinker, she was all about facts, particularly ones she claimed to have discovered. No, she knew what she had heard: someone was out of their bunk and up on deck.

To confirm this, another thump reverberated through the hull. Then another. And a fourth. It was enough for her to prop herself up on her elbows, only just avoiding hitting her head on the ceiling.

She checked her watch. A little after three. Everyone had been in bed for hours by now. At first, after Rolando's death, sleep hadn't come easy. The potent cocktail of shock and fear was enough to keep them all tossing and turning. But humans adapted to even the most unthinkable of traumas. The strains and stresses of the last few days had taken their toll and everyone had been keen to get some rest. Marjorie always tried to be in bed no later than ten at night anyway. She'd even had it written into her contract for this show. The contract that wasn't worth the paper it was written on now.

The show was in ruins and she doubted Ed's madcap scheme to replace it would work now he was unwittingly the star turn, playing victim number two. How could they have just left her like that – Howie and Cassandra? She'd been right in her theories all along and they'd just abandoned her. If this stupid detective series of theirs ever aired, she wanted her fair share of the earnings. They were hopeless, clueless – running after the Mafia lead that she'd uncovered. Why hadn't Ed asked *her* to be the star of his new show? She had worked it all out from the start.

The thought made her angry again. That boiling, all-consuming anger that overtook her sometimes. Especially where money was involved. She'd spent her whole career fighting for equal pay, a chance to have her contribution to modern thought leadership recognised. Art house cinema, countercultural vloggers and weighty political talk shows were one thing. They had given her a platform for the last two decades. But she wanted more. She wanted worldwide fame and recognition that she'd been foretelling the downfall of mainstream media for years. If making a deal with the beast she railed against was the way to get that, then so be it. That's why she was here, on a reality show.

Three more thumps from above. They were getting louder, more intense, and deliberate. She tried to listen for some other clue as to what was going on, who it might be. That Sachiko, she couldn't be trusted. Nobody could be so dedicated to their job as she appeared. Endlessly, she scurried around after those guests of hers. And for next to no thanks, as far as Marjorie could see. Was she involved with the Mafia too? There was every chance they *all* were. Except Howie Temple and Cassandra Troy. Those two morons couldn't spell gangster, let alone be on their payroll.

A prolonged moment of silence. Marjorie was sitting up in her bunk now, in the darkness, waiting. She waited and waited and there was nothing else. That wasn't right. She should do something.

'Wake up,' she whispered. 'Wake up. I think there's somebody on the deck.'

The lump sharing her bunk didn't move. She gave it a good whack with her fist.

'Ow!'

Matthias yelped.

'What was that for, Marjorie?' he asked her.

In the darkness she could still make out his broad shoulders, strong, domineering. Holiday romances had never really been her thing. But these were extenuating circumstances.

'There's somebody on the main deck, up above us,' she whispered.

'So?' He rubbed his eyes, a deeper sleeper than her.

'So, it could be someone here to rescue us.'

'Nobody knows we're here,' he said, lying back down.

'Howie and Cassandra will have fetched help.'

'Maybe,' he groaned, already trying to get back to sleep. 'In that case, it can wait until the morning.'

'It can't,' she said, nudging him.

'It can, *fräulein*.'

'Don't you *fräulein* me,' she said angrily. 'Get up and go see what's going on.'

'*Nein*,' he said.

She was going to shove him out of the bunk. But she thought better of it. What was the point? He clearly didn't care. He'd gotten what he wanted tonight. She gritted her teeth.

'Fine,' she said stroppily. 'I'll go myself. But if I'm murdered, it's on your head, Matthias.'

As if to mock her, he let out an ugly snore, fast asleep. She'd deal with him later.

Clambering over his massive frame, she dropped down from her bunk. She threw on her dressing gown and eased the door of the cabin open. The stern light of the galley hurt her eyes but she pressed on, climbing the stairs that led to the rest of the ship.

The night air was colder than she had been expecting. Up on deck the breeze had picked up. The velvet blanket of night was all around the ship as it gently rocked and groaned, still at the mercies of the tides and waves. Marjorie peered about the deck, looking for an explanation for the thumping.

The place was deserted. No sign of life or even anything that could have remotely made the noises. She didn't like that. She knew what she had heard. It was deliberate. Somebody was up here. Or had been. She was determined to get to the bottom of it.

'Hello there,' she said, as firmly as she could.

Marjorie wasn't sure if she was expecting a response. Surely anyone skulking around on deck at this time of night was up to no good. They were hardly going to answer her back, were they?

Something rattled from behind her. She spun around quickly, searching for something, anything, that would tell her what was going on.

'I know somebody is there,' she said, gathering the collar of her dressing gown about her neck. 'I know you're up here, whoever you are. So just come out and show yourself. You're not frightening anyone.'

More silence. Marjorie could feel her pulse racing, her heart was beating faster than it had in years. This wasn't her world. Maybe the thought of being an amateur sleuth wasn't such a good one after all.

'I'm serious!' she shouted, the desperation bleeding into her voice. 'Get out here, right now. Nobody should be up here at this ungodly time of the morning. Show yourself. I demand it!'

Marjorie held her breath. Her demands seemed like a good idea when they were still in her head. She remembered what her father had taught her, about standing her ground. Never back down, she'd been told. And here she was, all these decades later, doing exactly that.

'Well?' she shouted. 'Aren't you going to show yourself?'

There was a clink and then another thump. This time she was ready. She spun around, fist clenched, flailing wildly into the darkness. Nobody was more surprised than she was when she actually hit something.

'Ow!' came a horrible howl.

Marjorie's momentum carried her through the punch. She narrowly avoided falling flat on her face. When she was steady, her dressing gown flapping wildly about her, she surveyed the damage.

'You punched me!' said Matthias, holding his face.

'Oh my god, Matthias!' she said, going to comfort him. 'I didn't realise it was you!'

'You punched me, Marjorie,' he said with a whimper. 'Right in the face.'

'Please, let me help you, I'm so sorry, I thought you were . . . I thought you were whoever it was who's up here.'

He was bent over, clutching the right side of his face. She faffed and floated around him, like a mother hen attending to her chick.

'Let me get you some ice,' she said.

'Ice! I think you've fractured my skull!'

'Oh don't be so dramatic!' she shouted. 'How could I fracture your skull, I'm almost old enough to be your mother.'

'You are?'

He stood up and looked at her. Even in the darkness, Marjorie could see the bruising and swelling around the former footballer's right eye. She did her best not to wince but it was difficult. She'd given him quite a whack.

'Ice, that should do the trick,' she said.

'I've got a photoshoot with a men's magazine when we get to Monaco,' he said. 'I can't turn up looking like I've been brawling, can I?'

'Ice, that will do the trick,' she said. 'Let's go back down to the galley.'

She began to guide him back down the staircase that led below deck when she stopped suddenly. A dark figure was standing in their way.

'Who are you?' asked Marjorie.

The figure didn't move. They just stood there, features obscured by the dark. Marjorie and Matthias were frozen. Something glistened against the dark outline. A blade, the stars shining off its dirty, blood-stained surface.

'Oh no,' said Marjorie.

'Oh no, what?' asked Matthias.

'I think we might be in a spot of bother.'

Chapter 32

Howie woke with a fright. He had a cramp in his neck that sent a bolt of pain across his shoulders. He cramped up and, jolting upwards, bumped his head against the roof of the car.

He didn't know how long he'd been asleep. Ten minutes could easily have been ten hours. The offer of a chance to lie down, albeit in the back of a squad car, had been all too tempting. He had snatched it with both hands, stretching out across the rear seats of Inspector Sal's motor. Even the neon police jacket had served him well for a blanket.

Now he was awake, everything came flooding back to him. That precious moment after rest before the weight of the world came rushing back was all too fleeting. Howie would have loved it to have stretched out all day, unaware of the hell unfolding around him. He knew that wasn't possible. Reality had a way of making its presence felt, however hard you wanted to ignore it.

He sat for a moment, just staring into space. He was grateful for the chance to close his eyes and switch off his brain. Not that it had happened of course. He had suffered bizarre dreams about running through treacle and trying to beat a clock. His therapist would have her work cut out for her when he got back to Los Angeles.

The thought of home struck something deep inside of him. He'd only left LA a few days ago. But, as Cassandra had said, the whole idea of his 'normal' life was like something viewed from across a chasm – close but unreachable. With everything that had happened, in such a short space of time, he didn't feel the same person. Maybe he wasn't. Maybe this was something that *should* have happened to him a long time ago. Despite the pain in his feet, his neck, his back, his arms, his legs and joints, he felt mentally invigorated. Then he remembered Cassandra.

'Damn,' he said, furrowing his brow.

He closed his eyes and could see the young influencer standing in the middle of the street, terrified, guns pointed at her. She'd just stood there, with her hands in the air, like a statue. He opened his eyes again. He didn't want to be reminded of that. He felt, in some way, that he had failed her – again. But what else could he have done? Sal was the police, they were in charge. And if they suspected Cassandra was involved in some way, he couldn't interfere.

'Damn,' he said aloud, again.

This whole voyage had been a disaster. Worse still, it didn't look like it was going to be over any time soon.

He opened the door of the police cruiser. It bumped against something hard. Then it gave way. Howie climbed out, only to be met by one of the mountains of meat officers who had virtually kidnapped him before.

'Morning,' he said.

The cop didn't say anything. He just stood there, hands crossed in front of him, standing like a bouncer to a nightclub.

'We never really got introduced, did we?' said Howie, feeling cheeky. 'Howie Temple, I'm an actor.'

The officer didn't say anything. He didn't even flinch. The faintest rays of the morning sun were beginning to creep over the terracotta roofs of La Spezia. The officer's ridiculously square jaw was stark and sharp against the early glow.

'You know, you could be a model,' he said. 'With good looks like yours, you'd be a hit on the catwalks in LA.'

Still nothing.

'That's where I live, by the way, Los Angeles. I'm a US citizen, dual citizen, actually, I was born in Canada. Saskatchewan, ever heard of it?'

The cop was starting to get irritated. Howie could see the tendons in his neck tensing.

'It's not like here, it's much flatter. We're landlocked too, with no ocean to go swimming in. Plenty of lakes though. It's not the same. I like the sea, I like living next to the Pacific Ocean. Good to get that salty air in your lungs.'

He took a comically large breath of the morning air.

'You should come out sometime and visit when all of this is over,' he said. 'I'll show you around the sights, the Hollywood sign, and introduce you to some people I know in the fashion industry. You'll probably have to grow your hair a bit, and get some gaudy tattoos. But I reckon there's enough to be getting started with. Oh, and you'll need to work out more, put some beef on those puny arms of yours.'

That did it. The cop was lightning quick. He had Howie by the collar of his polo shirt and pressed against the cop car before anyone could protest. He was snarling, cursing in Italian as Howie held up his hands, a wry smirk on his face.

'What?' he said. 'I'm only trying to do you a favour. You're wasted as a cop.'

'Gianluca!'

The cop kept his grip firm around Howie's neck. He peered around the mountainous shoulder and saw Inspector Sal walking over to the car. She had emerged from the fleet of cop vehicles that had taped off a large section of the harbourfront. Like some strange mythical goddess emerging from the flashing blue lights and incident tape, she snarled at the officer he now knew to be Gianluca.

'What do you think you're doing?' she asked him.

The bulky officer finally let Howie go, but not without a forceful little push that winded him a little. He did his best not to show he was hurt and remained standing, using the police car behind him to prop him up.

'It's alright, Dorotea, we were just having a friendly little chat,' he said, still smiling at Gianluca.

'Inspector Sal to you,' she admonished him.

'Yes, of course,' said Howie. 'What time is it?'

'Five thirty-four,' said the inspector.

'Where's Cassandra?' he asked.

Sal turned to Gianluca. She spoke to him in Italian, her words so quick that Howie couldn't keep up. The policeman nodded and then, with a final sneer at him, he made off towards the gathered vehicles and police scene.

'Come with me,' she said to Howie.

She didn't wait for him. She set off around her police car and Temple followed like a lost dog. The harbour was already busy, the waters clogged with freighters and ships criss-crossing to various parts of the bay. Huge cranes were moving slowly, lifting and removing the massive containers from those frigates that had already docked.

Howie couldn't remember the last time he'd been awake at this time. Strangely he found he was quite sharp and attentive. Adrenaline maybe. Or perhaps a freshly honed sense of your own mortality made every second count.

'Have you arrested her?' he asked Sal.

'No,' she replied. 'And we won't be.'

'I thought you said you had reason to believe she was involved?'

'We did,' said the inspector. 'Even the police can be wrong at times. It wasn't worth the risk if she *was* an asset to an organised crime gang.'

'Like Rolando and Kelvin Kamani?'

Sal remained tight-lipped at that. She led him through the blockade and towards a series of small, plastic tents that had been set up at the edge of the blocked-off road.

'Is she alright?' she asked. 'She didn't deserve that last night, you know. She's just a kid.'

'I wasn't taking a risk with my team,' said Sal. 'The Serafinas are dangerous people, Mr Temple. And I didn't know if she had been compromised.'

'I told you she hadn't. That should have been enough.'

'Perhaps you think too highly of yourself,' she said bluntly. 'I don't take my orders from you, or Ms Troy, or indeed any citizen for that matter. But I *am* in charge of all these policemen and women you see here. Their safety and that of the people of this city, the country even, are my priorities. If I thought she was dangerous, which I did, then I was right to act the way that I did. There will be no lasting damage.'

'You're a psychiatrist now too, huh?' he said sarcastically.

'You can speak with her, alone, for five minutes.' She extended her hand to the flap of the nearest tent.

'Why, what happens after five minutes?'

Sal didn't answer him. She turned and marched off back towards the main throng of vehicles and officers still standing guard. Howie shook his head.

'Impossible woman,' he said.

He reached out for the flap of the tent. Something stopped him at the last moment. He couldn't be sure what it was – fear? Guilt? Shame? All three? The same nervousness he'd had before, like when he was about to step on stage, it was there, sitting in the pit of his stomach like a brick.

'Come on, pull yourself together, man,' he said quietly to himself.

He took hold of the flap and pulled it back. He had stepped into the tent before he really knew what he was doing.

To his surprise, Cassandra wasn't alone. She was sitting on a makeshift examination bed, another woman shining a light into her eyes. When she saw Howie come in, she looked a little surprised.

'Oh,' said the strange woman. 'Are you Ms Troy's father?'

'Father?'

'What?' Cassandra yelped.

'Father?' he said again.

'He's not my dad,' Cassandra was quick to add.

'Father?' Howie said for a third time.

'Yes,' said the woman.

'No,' said Howie.

'Definitely not,' added Cassandra.

The woman looked between them and shrugged. She clicked her little pen torch off and checked behind Cassandra's ears and beneath her chin.

'You're fine,' she said. 'A few bumps and bruises but nothing that some good rest and recuperation won't mend.'

'Thank you, doctor,' said Cassandra.

The medic picked up a small bag and gave a little courteous bow. She eased past Howie and out of the tent.

They stayed in silence for an uncomfortable moment. Howie didn't really know what to say. Cassandra was the same. She kicked her legs lazily as they dangled off the end of the examination bed.

'I was—'

'You were—'

They both interrupted each other. Then more silence.

'I was just going to—'

'You were going to—'

They did it again. This was awkward. Howie could feel the sweat seeping into his already disreputable polo shirt. She had her head bowed, staring down at her feet. He took a deep breath and noticed something.

'Oh,' he said, pointing down. 'You've got shoes.'

Cassandra twirled her feet around.

'Yes,' she said, a happy smile lighting up her face. 'They gave me a pair when they questioned me earlier.'

'They're bright,' he said.

She looked at the brilliant white trainers.

'Yes, they are,' she said. 'Immaculately fashionable of course. But what would you expect, here in Italy? I quite like them, actually. I hope they let me keep them.'

'Do you think they have any for me?'

'I wouldn't hold your breath, chuck,' she said. 'From the way that Inspector Sal talks about you, you'll be lucky to be allowed out of the country. Straight to the Colosseum lions in Rome for you, babe.'

'Yeah, she's a bit of a sour candy, that one,' he said, easing up onto the table beside her with a groan. 'Still, she seems to know what she's doing.'

Cassandra waited for a moment, then raised her eyebrows.

'You fancy her, don't you,' she said.

'Fancy her?'

'Have a crush on her.'

'What? Inspector Sal? Are you kidding me?'

'You do,' she said. 'You're starting to blush.'

'I do not.'

'You do, I can always tell these things. When I was at school, I always knew when one of my friends had a crush on one of the boys, or girls, for that matter. There's a different air about you, you seem almost . . . jovial.'

'Jovial?' He wrinkled his nose. 'I have never, ever, in my life, been described as jovial, Cassandra. Joyless, certainly. Jealous, a few times by my ex-wives and girl-friends. But jovial, never.'

'Well, I'm describing you as it now, chuck.'

He looked over at the flap door of the tent. A little gap showed the chaos of the outside world, the gathered police, the crime scene, the investigating officers. There was no sign of Inspector Sal.

'She's not without her charms,' he said. 'In a sort of serious kind of way. Better than those two sisters we left onboard. I kind of feel bad for Matthias, he's the only living, breathing man left on the ship. He'll be as good as gone by the time he's rescued.'

'Aww, bless.' She clapped her hands to her chest. 'I love it when old people find romance.'

'Old!' he coughed.

'You know what I mean.' She nudged his shoulder.

They fell back into silence. It was different this time though, much more comfortable, almost warm. Howie didn't want to ruin it by asking about the photo of her with Kelvin and why Sal had had her pegged as a Mafia pawn.

'Was she okay with you?' he asked Cassandra.

'Yeah, she was fine,' she answered him, staring down at her feet again. 'She's a police officer. They have to be hard. Especially if they think you're some sort of gangster's moll.'

'You're not, are you?'

'Not what?'

'A gangster's moll? You're not working with these Serafinas, whoever they are? You're not in cahoots with Kelvin and Rolando and all of that.'

'Of course I'm not,' she said. 'I'm an influencer, from Liverpool who's way out of her depth getting guns pointed at her. As pathetic as that sounds, it's the truth.'

'I told them that,' he said.

'That I was out of my depth and pathetic?'

'No, I . . . '

He realised she was joking with him. He laughed it off.

'You know what I mean,' he said.

'I do. And thank you.' She squeezed his arm. 'Thank you for standing up for me and making sure they didn't shoot me.'

'Least I could do,' he said. 'Why didn't you tell me you knew Kelvin before all of this?'

'She showed you the picture then,' she said.

Howie nodded silently, looking at his feet.

'I'm not going to tell you lies, babe, because the truth is simple,' she said with a sigh. 'I didn't know I already knew him.'

'What does that mean?'

She rubbed the back of her neck. 'That picture, the one the police have, it's from about seven years ago, maybe longer, I can't remember,' she said. 'It's a charity ball, a gala. It was raising awareness for cancer research good causes in the Liverpool area. We all got trussed up, limos to the Liver Building down at the riverfront and enjoyed a night of plonk and banter.'

'But Kelvin was there. Didn't you know him? Didn't you speak with him?' he asked.

'Howie, I was twenty,' she said. 'I'd just been handed a cheque from a cosmetics firm that had more zeros that I could count on it. My social media channels were breaking all kinds of records and I couldn't keep up with the offers and endorsements that were being flung at me. Not to mention the abuse and the trolling. Believe me, babe, the very *last* thing on my mind was the dusty old world of politics and MPs.'

Howie felt a wonderful sense of relief wash over him. He remembered his own dizzying heyday. Elections, Olympics, even the end of the world could have come and gone during those years and he wouldn't have known the difference. On that they could both agree.

'I gave a speech, wore my pink sash, with pride by the way, and smiled for the cameras. He gave some speech but I'd probably left by then. And he clearly didn't recognise me either.'

'I can believe that,' Howie agreed. 'He was there to be seen rather than see, I bet.'

'Something like that. Not that I cared at the time. Although I should have. Maybe knowing that seven years later I'd have armed coppers accusing me of Mafia dealings because I was in the same room as the bloke, would make last night a bit easier to handle.'

'You managed to find him though, our needle in a haystack.'

'Yeah, Kelvin.' She rolled her eyes. 'The man is a menace and he can't be trusted.'

'Do you think he killed Rolando?'

'It looks that way,' she said. 'Nothing else explains why he's been the way he's been. He's up to his neck in this gangster business, they have him by the you-know-whats.'

'And Scorpione?' asked Howie.

'He must have been sent to finish Kelvin off.' She shrugged. 'At least that's what Dorotea thinks.'

'She lets you call her Dorotea, does she?' he asked. 'Very cosy.'

'Strictly professional,' she said with a smile. 'Although I can't say I saw Rolando being an informant coming, did you?'

He let out a whistle.

'No, that was . . . unexpected,' he said. 'I wish I could be there when Marjorie finds out. That'll teach her, the old know-it-all.'

'Hear, hear,' said Cassandra. 'I think they want us to go back onto the yacht with them.'

'Yeah, I figured,' he said.

'Sal told me they're planning on storming *The Regal Secret*. They're worried Kelvin has taken hostages.'

'It would kind of make sense,' he said. 'His cover is blown now. He's got nothing to lose.'

'She reckons if we go first, we might buy the police some time. It's risky, she's told me as much.'

'And what do you think we should do?'

She looked at her hands. They were filthy; dirt under her nails. The long strands of her dark hair weren't much better, hanging like raggedy old curtains. She shook her head.

'If my mum and dad could see me now,' she said. 'I think they'd have a right old chuckle. Howie Temple, Hollywood star, asking me for my opinion on how to avoid a hostage scenario.'

'You know, we don't have to go back on that boat. We could probably sneak out of here and nobody would notice,' he said quietly. 'Inspector Sal seems to have her hands full working out what to do next. All the cops are busy. We could be off and away up to the station before anyone knows.'

'Quick train to Milan,' she said, picking up his thread. 'Tour of the shops. You can buy me a Dior dress.'

'We could go dancing tonight,' he added. 'Cocktails, take in the sights, really live it up in one of the fashion capitals of the world.'

'And then New York tomorrow,' she said. 'Los Angeles after that.'

'I can make you a star.' He made an arch with his hands. 'Name in lights, the newest great export from the British Isles. Cassandra Troy – the face of a generation.'

'Doesn't sound too bad, actually,' she laughed.

'Agreed.'

Then he snapped his fingers.

'Shoot,' he said. 'Sorry, I can't.'

'You can't? Why not?'

'I've already promised to make that lumbering ape Gianluca a model when I get home.'

'Darn.'

'I know,' he said. 'You can't call too many favours in all at once in this industry. You'd know that if you were part of The Biz like I am.'

'Really?' She scoffed, laughing. 'So I'm just a yokel from rain-soaked Merseyside. What do I know?'

'It's a hard life.' He smiled.

'Tell me about it.'

She rested her head on his shoulder, her eyes closed. Howie let her sit there. Just for a moment, a precious few seconds, where the world hadn't gone to pieces. Two friends, together again.

'You know we have to go back on that boat, really, don't you,' he said at length.

'I know,' said Cassandra sadly.

'It's the right thing to do.'

'I know,' she agreed again. 'Doesn't make it any easier to swallow though.'

He nodded. The flap of the tent opened and Inspector Sal walked in, purposeful. She paused when she saw Cassandra leaning on Howie.

'Am I interrupting something here?' she asked pointedly.

'Yes,' sighed Howie. 'But it's alright, inspector, you're only doing your job.'

'We're ready,' said the inspector. 'Follow me.'

She stood to one side, holding the flap open. Howie and Cassandra slipped off the examination bed and walked back out into the growing brightness.

Chapter 33

A thin plume of smoke was rising from *The Regal Secret*. Cassandra felt the dread bloom inside her. Was there a fire onboard? Was everyone safe? Just what had Kelvin Kamani done when he returned last night? She looked over at Howie on the opposite side of the police speedboat. He was just as concerned, his brow wrinkled as he squinted at the horizon. But this time, they weren't facing the problem alone.

The waves crashed and thumped into the underside of the boat as it blasted across the Ligurian Sea. Cassandra felt like she was being punched every time they thundered down onto the surface of the choppy water. A team of six officers was with them, all armed, all looking like they meant business. At the front, leading the charge, was Inspector Sal. Cassandra thought she looked like Napoleon or Nelson up there, the fearless leader ready to step into battle.

'You okay?' Howie shouted over the racket of the engine and crashing waves.

'Yeah,' she lied. 'Just a bit seasick, that's all.'

'Have you seen the smoke?'

'Yes, I have,' she answered him. 'That's a little bit more than burnt toast, isn't it?' She eyed the curls of dark smoke wreathing and dispersing in the azure sky.

He reached out and squeezed her hand. She squeezed back. She was glad he was here, heading with her to whatever waited for them on the yacht.

The very worst thoughts had been flashing in her mind since they'd left La Spezia harbour. Howie was right, Inspector Sal *was* severe. She treated everything with the same regimented dedication. There was no comforting pep-talk, no assurance that everything was alright. She was a woman who lived relentlessly in the real world. And her reality was one of organised crime and deadly consequences rather than the TV definition Cassandra was used to: rolling cameras, rivalries and love triangles.

Cassandra was fine with that. Of course she was. There was no use laughing and joking about what they were about to do. A bow wave sloshed over her like a bucket slung at a panto. It was brutally refreshing and forced her to stop staring at the smoke. She blinked and gulped in a big breath of salty air. The splash had soaked her through again, her hair plastered to her forehead. She pushed the stray strands out of her face and tried to stay calm. Sal had briefed them already that her and Howie would be invaluable – they knew the crew, they knew the layout – and the trust the inspector had placed in her was keeping her focused.

The sleek hull of *The Regal Secret* was drawing closer by the second. And the nearer they got, the thicker the smoke coming from the deck was becoming. The billowing tower hadn't gone unnoticed by the others. Inspector Sal looked back toward the skipper. She waved her hand around in quick reverse circles. The officer piloting the boat immediately began to slow it down. The engines were cut.

'Listen up,' Sal shouted at the gathered group. 'It looks like there's some kind of fire onboard *The Regal Secret*. We don't know what's going on up there. But we have to be careful. The safety of ourselves and the guests and crew is paramount. Do you all understand that?'

There were grunts of agreement from the officers. Cassandra and Howie remained silent at the back.

'We take things steady, slowly, and react to the changing circumstances,' she said, emphasising every point with a fist to her palm. 'Remember there are innocents on that yacht. Lots of them. Our target is Kelvin Kamani, you've all been briefed on what he looks like. We know he's absconded before so he's a flight risk now. We bring him in alive, unless we have reason to believe he's going to strike.'

A terrible finality clung to her words. And the gravity of everything that was going on hit Cassandra like a knockout punch. She felt her legs going numb, her hands starting to tremble. She clutched them, trying to hide her fear from the rest of the group. She had to focus. Logic, she reminded herself, pure unadulterated logic.

'Ms Troy and Mr Temple will climb onboard first,' said the inspector. 'They're going to try to buy us as much time as they can as a distraction. If Kamani is on board, he'll hopefully be too focused on them and we can board behind them. Five minutes, that's all we need. Five minutes.'

'Five minutes,' said Howie, trying to sound confident.

'Five minutes,' said Cassandra, barely longer than an Instagram video, she thought.

But five minutes could be an eternity. A lifetime. Never had it seemed so long and short all at the same time. Five minutes. Just five minutes and then it could all be over.

'Good luck,' said Sal, before sitting back down at the prow of the speedboat.

The police all patted each other's shoulders. The nearest to them did the same to Howie and Cassandra. It felt odd, being part of this team.

The Regal Secret reared up in front of them. This was it.

The air was thick with the smoke. A heavy haze had engulfed the ship. The wind swirled and kicked the plume down and around the length and breadth of the yacht. It had at least given some cover for their approach. Cassandra hoped it had been enough.

The skipper eased the speedboat alongside the huge hull. Bobbing up and down, the rear deck of the yacht was just a step away. Howie went first, leaping onboard. He held out his hand, gesturing to Cassandra to join him.

They caught each other's eyes. It was only a moment, a split second. But it felt like centuries passed in that single second. There he was, Howie Temple, the man she'd come to rely on over the space of just a few days. Did she trust him? In that moment she knew.

'Come on, chuck,' he said with a smile.

Cassandra stopped thinking. She leaped from the speedboat and into his steadying grip. There was no time to waste. Now that they were on the ship, they had to go to work.

'You have five minutes,' said Sal, still on the speedboat. 'Five minutes and we'll act.'

'Okay,' said Howie. 'You ready?'

Cassandra nodded. She wasn't, of course. How could she be? How could anyone be? That didn't matter now. Here she was, back on the yacht, with a mission more critical than likes or follows, ratings or reviews.

Howie started up the broad steps that led to the main deck. She was right behind him and then stopped suddenly.

'Howie!' she whispered.

'What!' His face was slack with fear. 'What's the matter?'

'Shoes,' she said, pointing down at her feet. 'We're not allowed shoes onboard.'

He cursed under his breath and grabbed her hand, pulling her up the steps, trainers still firmly on her feet. 'I think your trainers are the least of our worries.'

The wind had changed direction. The whole deck was consumed by the soot and dust of the smoke. Cassandra felt it burn her nostrils, scratching at the back of her throat.

'I can't see a thing,' she said, pawing through the murk.

They crossed the deck towards the stern and reached the staircase that led to the bowels of the yacht. Ducking down, they carefully checked their way ahead. The air was clearer down below – the smoke can't have been a fire below deck, at least. But bright red beacons were flashing, casting everything in a bloody haze that felt almost as ominous as the acrid smoke on deck. The galley lay abandoned, food packaging, clothes, maps, papers, garbage scattered about the place. Every cupboard was open, every drawer pulled from its bracket.

'Looks like a tornado ripped through here,' said Howie, surveying the damage.

'I don't like this, babe,' she said. 'I don't like this one bit.'

They moved through the galley and up towards the guest suites. The doors were all open, rocking back and forth on their hinges with the movement of the ship. Beds were unmade, suitcases opened and ravaged. With every step they took, Cassandra was getting more and more terrified. Everything seemed forced and violated. This had been a beautiful place just a few days before. Now it was a shambles. And a worryingly empty one at that. Cassandra had been used to bumping into guests or crew every few metres, and yet the place was deserted now.

Arakawa's room was the last one at the end of the corridor. His suite, where Ed had been left to recover, was still shut, the door firmly closed. Howie pressed his ear against the door.

'Nothing,' he said. 'Silent as the dead. Sorry.'

'Quickly then, we need to check on Ed.'

Howie grasped the handle. He gave her a nod and opened the door quickly. They both hurried in, only to be met with an empty room.

'Where is he?' asked Howie.

The bed was empty, the covers thrown back. The faintest crimp and crumple of sheets was the only sign that Ed had been lying there, unconscious from his knock on the head.

'I don't like this, Howie,' she said. 'I don't like this one bit.'

'No,' he said. 'I'm beginning to think this wasn't such a good idea myself—'

A loud shout from beyond the suite cut him short. He looked at Cassandra and then moved carefully over to the door. Shouting was coming from further up the corridor.

'The bridge,' he said.

'I think that's Kelvin's voice,' she whispered.

'How long have we got left before Sal's SWAT team move in?'

'It can't be long,' she said, eyes wide. 'So if we're going to do something, we had better do it fast.'

Howie nodded. They left the suite and made their way along the corridor, past more debris. The repaired door of the bridge loomed ahead. There were raised voices coming from the other side. Crying too. Cassandra suddenly felt her mouth turn dry, an unquenchable thirst coming over her. She couldn't work out if she felt relieved to have heard a human voice, or terrified as to what the weeping behind the bridge door signified. They carefully stepped up to the bridge door and listened.

Kelvin was shouting and somebody was arguing with him. There were intermittent sobs and what sounded like pleas from another two voices. In all it was a grim picture.

'What do we do?' Cassandra asked Howie, grim memories of the first time they entered the bridge and found their captain.

'I think we have to go in,' he said. 'There's no other way in and out of the bridge but this door. We have to do something.'

Cassandra knew he was right. That didn't make it any easier to stomach.

'Okay,' she said. 'After three.'

'After three what?' he whispered.

'After three we go in.'

'And do what?'

'I don't know.'

'That's not much of a plan,' he said.

'It's all we've got,' she said. 'Didn't you ever improvise when you were on set, chuck?'

'This is slightly different, Cassandra,' he said sarcastically. 'On set, we usually didn't have a maniac former politician with nothing to lose who'd taken hostages. Although that said, I did see Vanilla Ice sort of take a runner hostage once as he hadn't had his morning Frozen Caramel Macchiato yet. He refused to join the rest of us until he'd had it. He was very adamant. His real surname is Van Winkle, I don't know if you know that.'

'Focus, Howie, focus,' she said.

'Right, sorry,' he said.

She reached down and took hold of the handle of the bridge door. In a reversal of roles from the first time they'd stormed this room, she pressed her shoulder against it, letting it take her weight.

'I push, you go in,' she said.

'Gotcha.' He nodded.

'Okay. Here goes.'

'I thought we were going on three.'

'I was just about to start the countdown,' she tutted. 'Ready? One.'

'Ready.'

'Two.'

She tightened her grip.

'Three!'

Cassandra pushed the door open. It swung inward with relative ease. Howie charged past her, the pair of them spilling into the bridge.

All shouting and sobbing stopped immediately as they righted themselves. Cassandra was the first to react. She'd never seen anything like it before. Kelvin was standing in the middle of the room, the bloody knife that had been sticking in Rolando's back hanging loosely from his hand.

Marjorie and Matthias were in the far corner, crouched down, hugging each other tightly. Ms Sachiko was beside them, Arakawa and the Kontoglou sisters close by. Kirkby and Martha Hofstede were quivering wrecks, knees pulled up to their chests to try and protect themselves. They were all crying, frightened eyes looking over at Howie and Cassandra as they arrived on the bridge. Scorpione was gagged and hogtied as he lay flat on his belly. When he saw Howie and Cassandra enter the bridge, he started to writhe around, voice muffled by what looked like a sock stuffed into his mouth.

Ben and Geri were there too. It was the first time Howie and Cassandra had seen them without their filming equipment. They were, however, as silent as usual.

On his knees in front of Kelvin was Ed. Fully awake, his hands clasped together like he was praying. When he saw the others arrive, his face brightened.

'Bloody hellfire,' said Cassandra.

'Howie! Cassandra!' he said with his usual chirpiness replaced by a fearful tremor. 'You're back!'

Chapter 34

'Good, we're all here, at last.'

Kelvin Kamani appeared to be in charge. He was, after all, the only one who was armed. He waved the knife around like the bloodthirsty conductor of some macabre philharmonic orchestra. He paced back and forth around the bridge, murmuring to himself.

Howie and Cassandra remained by the door and had a clear line of sight down the hallway. When the police arrived they'd know it long before Kelvin. And they wanted to keep it that way.

'Good to see you both again,' said Ed, still on his knees.

'I'd like to say it's good to be back, chuck. But I think I'd be lying,' said Cassandra. 'How's your head?'

'Oh, you know, a bit sore,' he said. 'Still. Could be worse. I heard you looked after me, Howie. You and Matthias. Thank you for that, mate, I appreciate it.'

'Don't mention it,' said Howie, still watching Kelvin walking backward and forwards. 'You can buy me a beer when we get to Monaco.'

'Monaco!' said Kelvin.

The mention of Monaco seemed to snap him out of his mutterings.

'Yes, we should set sail immediately,' he said. 'The sooner we can get to Monaco, the better. Yes, quickly, let's go.'

'Eh, Kelvin, are you feeling alright, chuck?' asked Cassandra.

'I am now, Monaco was always the plan.'

'You know the engines are flooded, right?' asked Howie. 'You did that.'

'We'll get there. They'll be dried out by now, I'm sure.'

'No, babe, you don't understand,' said Cassandra. 'It's all over, not just the show, the yacht, your schemes – none of this is going to work out. Why don't you give me the knife and we'll just . . . talk.'

She edged her way closer to him. He thought about the proposal for a moment before a flash of anger made him snarl. He lashed out with the knife and Cassandra hopped backward, narrowly missing the blade.

'Stay where you are!' he shouted. 'Just stay where you are. Let me think about this.'

'Kelvin, mate, you're acting crazy,' said Ed, still on his knees. 'You can't take us hostage like this. It's madness.'

'You're not my hostages,' he said, becoming more and more furious. 'Okay, he is.' He waved the knife at Scorpione. 'But the rest of you, you're my associates, my crewmates, that's what you are. And we're all going to head to Monaco like we were supposed to.'

He started furiously mashing buttons and pulling levers on the huge control console of the yacht. Lights blinked red and there were angry-sounding bleeps and buzzers. Howie looked back down the corridor that stretched from the open door of the deck. There was still no sign of Inspector Sal and her officers. But someone else was missing too.

'Where's Rolando?' he asked.

The bridge fell instantly silent. Marjorie and Matthias couldn't lift their gaze from the floor. And the usually unflappable Ms Sachiko, for the first time since Howie had met her, looked utterly devastated. Scorpione was still writhing around on the ground, trying to speak. It was Ed who spoke first.

'You know all that smoke, H?' he said solemnly.

'Yeah,' answered Howie, unsure where this was going.

Ed looked back at the others. Marjorie resorted to tears, much like the guests.

'I have to tell them, guys,' he said shamefully.

'Tell us what?' asked Cassandra.

The director let out a sheepish laugh like he was trying to find the right words. It was the first time Howie had ever seen him lost for what to say.

'Yeah, the thing is,' he said, rubbing the back of his head and wincing at his lump. 'It seems that our friend here, the right honourable Kelvin Kamani has made something of a funeral pyre for the late, departed Captain Rolando.'

'Funeral . . . pyre?' Howie said slowly.

The smoke took on a whole other meaning now. The clogging, choking fumes were distinctly more sinister knowing what was on fire somewhere.

'He means he burned the body you dunce!' Marjorie shouted at Howie.

'I know what he means!' Howie snapped back.

'You burned the body?' asked Cassandra. 'Why would you do that, Kelvin? Why would you do something like that? It's destroying evidence for one thing, it's risking the whole crew for another, and it's well, sacrilegious!'

The disgraced politician leaned back on the command console. The knife was loosely hanging from his right hand. He was staring off into some other world, some place far from the trappings of *The Regal Secret* and what he had done.

'I thought it was appropriate,' he said gloomily. 'The poor man had been left to rot here, on this wretched ship. He didn't deserve that, he didn't deserve to just be left there, sitting like a broken marionette. We deserve as much dignity in death as we do in life. He should have been given a proper send off. I did the best that I could.'

'You burned his body, and you could have killed everyone else lighting a fire like that,' said Howie. 'How is that a proper send off?'

'I put him in one of the lifeboats, tethered it to *The Regal* and set fire to that. I thought it was quite Viking, actually.' Kelvin seemed unabashed. Howie felt sick. The smell of the fire was now filtering in through the main door, the wind whipping it in and about the yacht. Everyone else felt the same as the horrors of what was unfolding in front of them became all too real.

'You're going to be in trouble for this, Kelvin,' he said slowly. 'This and everything else you've done.'

'I know,' said the former politician. 'I know. Things just got out of hand, that's all. What was it Macbeth said again? "*Will all great Neptune's ocean wash this blood clean from my hand*"?'

Everyone instinctively turned to Howie, expecting a reaction from the actor. When there was none, Marjorie groaned.

'I doubt he can spell Macbeth, let alone perform it,' she said.

Howie noticed how for once Marjorie's habitual sniping had no impact on him. Instead he wondered how long they had left before the police stormed the yacht. Was it minutes? Seconds even? He wished they would hurry up. The thought of spending another rotten minute breathing in the cursed air of this place made him feel utterly sick.

In all of the drama, he'd failed to notice Cassandra. She had been standing beside him the whole time, or at least that's what he thought. Only she wasn't anymore. While everyone else was distracted, she had been edging her way closer to Kelvin. She was only a foot or two from him now, her aim the knife in his hand.

When he'd wished for all it to be over a moment ago, he hadn't meant like this. As she reached down to snatch the knife from Kelvin, he hurled himself forward.

'Cassandra!' he screamed at the top of his voice.

Howie's sonorous roar was enough to snap Kelvin out of his guilty daydream. He blinked, and saw Cassandra reaching for the knife and recoiled. Then it was Howie's turn to move.

By the time he'd blundered forward, Kelvin had the blade up to protect himself. The two men collided and there was a scream. Howie couldn't be sure it wasn't from himself. He felt Kelvin's strength resisting him and he tried to grab something, anything. The thought of the knife was constant. Where was it?

They tripped and fell. An odd noise in a humbling moment, Howie half thought it might have been his hip. Just what the hell did he think he was doing here? An actor too old for action movies trying to create a real-life one? Wrestling with an armed man in front of a group of celebrities and bewildered cruise guests. This was the definition of madness.

Then he felt it. Something he'd never known before. It was warm, uncomfortable, swelling from somewhere around his belly button. The pain started as a thin, long line but it soon grew to an uncomfortable burning. Then to agony. He stopped the wrestling and rolled over, instinctively reaching down to his stomach.

'Blood,' he said, suddenly now wishing he could have summoned a bit more Macbeth if they were to be his last words.

A large patch of claret was staining his polo shirt. He gasped, looking down as his shirt grew damper and damper, the fuzzy expanding outline darkening to almost black at its centre. He was beginning to feel dizzy. He slumped backwards, losing strength in his arms.

'Howie!'

Cassandra appeared above him. She cradled his head, nervous hands wiping his brow.

'Are you alright?' he asked. 'He got me.'

'It's okay, it's okay,' she was saying over and over, her face crumpled as she knelt above him. 'It's okay, you're going to be okay.'

A sudden eruption of noise came from somewhere beyond his feet. He couldn't see it but he knew what had happened. Time was up. His and Kelvin's it would seem. Inspector Sal and her armed officers had stormed the bridge.

He sensed rather than saw the movement all around him. All he could focus on was Cassandra. If this was to be his end then he was happy she was here. The pain was getting worse, reaching all the way up to his chest now. He lifted a quivering hand and wiped a tear from her cheek. It left a streak of red behind.

'Thank you,' he gurgled.

'Thank you for what?' she asked.

Her voice was close, like a whisper. The din of the police, Kelvin, the others, it was nothing, melted away. The smell of the fire had vanished too, along with the flashing lights and alert signals from the control console. Then the whole world, it felt, had just evaporated, blinked out of existence beyond him and Cassandra. Was this peace? Was this what it finally felt like to not have worries, not have responsibilities? What a bummer if his only route to it was to get stabbed by a lunatic. There had to have been an easier way but Howie couldn't think of it, not right now.

For the moment, it was just him and her. The person who had taught him more in a week than he'd learnt in a lifetime. And he wanted it to stay that way forever.

'Thank you,' he said.

Then the darkness took him.

Chapter 35

From a distance, *The Regal Secret* had lost none of its glamour, despite the damage inside. The superyacht still looked the part as it bobbed and swayed gently in La Spezia harbour. Even the police tape and armed officers that dotted its decks and the jetty could not take away from its elegance and panache. Not that its elegance was enough to hide the fact that this was a crime scene. And it had been almost since it left Livorno earlier that week.

Cassandra Troy was alone. She couldn't quite believe it. The events of the last few hours, and days, had been a lot to take in. Too much. She knew there would be countless bits of paperwork, statements, documents to sign and approve. And that they would make it all feel real enough, soon enough.

For the moment, at least, she could just stare at the yacht and wonder how naive she'd been embarking a few days ago. But although hindsight was a wonderful thing, Cassandra thought now sometimes it was best not to know what was around the corner, and to accept life as it came, and as it went. The morning was wearing on now and the sky shone with a deep azure that made her feel that little bit more alive. She thought about taking a picture, maybe sharing it to her social channels. The thought soured long before she could reach for her phone. There was no comfort to be had there today. She'd had to turn it back onto silent as the endless streams of messages and notifications flooded into the device.

That was a world she wasn't quite ready to go back to yet. The last few days had taught her many lessons, about trust, about life, death and the importance of being with the people you care about.

So she was happy to stay here a little longer, in this sort of purgatory. Not quite in reality, not quite in the digital echo chamber of her work. Cassandra Troy, for the next little while, could just be.

The morning was beginning to heat up. The medics and police had checked her over again and given her a blanket. Wrapping it about her shoulders, nobody had noticed when she'd just wandered off from the others to sit on a wall overlooking the harbour. Inspector Sal and her team were busy processing the guests and the crew. Ed and Ms Sachiko were at the centre of it all, a strange set of parents looking after their equally odd, rag-tag brood.

Cassandra looked down at her hands. They were covered in dried blood, Howie's blood. She shivered at the thought. He had risked his life to save hers. She had been stupid thinking she could grab Kelvin's knife. She had no idea where that recklessness had come from. Never in her life had she tried anything as clumsy or dangerous. Where was pure logic when she'd decided to try to be a hero?

Maybe it was the sea air. Maybe it was the sense that someone had to face up to Kelvin, maybe it was the confidence Howie had given her, he had taken her seriously, made her believe she was a good person who did good things. She couldn't be sure. She wasn't sure she would ever know.

What she *did* know was that Howie had tried to save her, tried to make sure she was safe. And he'd paid the price. Lying in her arms, bleeding all over the floor of the bridge. All she could do was cry. She had felt so helpless, useless.

'Ms Troy.'

Inspector Sal cleared her throat. Cassandra turned a little to see the policewoman standing rigidly straight, hands neatly tucked behind her back. She was still wearing her protective vest over her suit, the walkie-talkie flashing incessantly on her shoulder. 'Would you mind coming with me please,' she said solemnly. 'You can see him now.'

Cassandra nodded. Despite the heat and the blanket, her arms were rippled with goosebumps. She swung around and slipped down from the harbour wall. Padding across the street, following Sal, it felt like her legs, her body, had been taken over by somebody else. She was on auto-pilot, blindly hoping that the inspector's apparent faith in her to handle this was merited.

This had been the part she had been dreading the most. When the armed cops had stormed the bridge, everything had happened so quickly, Cassandra hadn't had a chance to think about it. Kelvin had been arrested, guns trained on him. He hadn't resisted, he'd just lay there after the scuffle with Howie and been handcuffed.

Several police officers had crowded around Howie, giving him the best medical treatment they could. He'd been taken out to the waiting speedboat and hurried back onshore while the rest of them had waited. A tug had been dispatched to pull *The Regal Secret* to the port. And here they were.

The walk seemed endless as she was taken through the chaos and confusion of the police scene. The whole street along the harbourfront was cordoned off. Through the flashing lights and mayhem Cassandra saw tourists and locals, all ogling the action from the safety of the barriers. She envied them greatly – spectators.

Cassandra was trying to busy her mind, putting off the inevitable. A large ambulance seemed to rear up out of the crowd and chaos ahead of them. She slowed to a stop, Inspector Sal continuing for a few paces before realising she was no longer beside her.

'What's the matter?' asked the detective.

'I don't think I can do this,' said Cassandra, her voice broken. 'I don't think I can see him . . . see him like . . . like that.'

Cassandra was prepared for what she had come to expect as the usual, stoic, robotic response from Sal. But instead, a warmth exuded from her as she stepped back to join her.

'This will be difficult,' she said softly, almost motherly. 'These kinds of things are never easy. I have been a police officer for almost twenty years. And every time I have to deliver this kind of bad news, this sort of incident, it is always the same. You have to trust yourself, know that it's alright to be emotional, know that it wasn't your fault and hope, pray if that is your thing, that one day you'll be able to live with it. Like we all do.'

Cassandra nodded. There was a comforting strength in Sal's words. More so, perhaps, for the fact that it was coming from her. But then, in a flash, that warmth was shut away again. Inspector Dorotea Sal was once again the hard-nosed officer dealing with gangsters, killers and injustice. She stepped to the side and ushered Cassandra onwards.

They reached the ambulance, its rear doors closed. Sal knocked twice, firmly. A door swung open and a paramedic with bad skin poked his head out. He was surly, ready to chastise whoever it was disturbing him. That was, until he saw who had knocked.

'*Scusa* inspector,' he said, opening the second door. 'Please, this way.'

Sal stood to one side. She gestured for Cassandra to step up and into the waiting ambulance. She waited a moment, looking up at the paramedic, trying her best not to see what was beyond him. There was no stopping it now. This was it. The moment of reckoning. Cassandra Troy had to do what was right.

'Okay,' she said to herself, climbing up the small steps and into the ambulance.

Howie was propped up on the gurney. He was grey, almost white, so pale that he could have been transparent and she was looking at the sheets of the bed beneath him. His eyes were closed, lips apart slightly. But he was breathing. It was heavy and laboured, but he was alive.

Cassandra felt her chin and bottom lip wobbling as she stared at him.

'Can he hear me?!' she asked the paramedic.

Howie's eyes flickered.

'Cassandra Troy,' he said, voice weak. 'You look good, chuck. Better than me, I expect.'

'Oh you,' she said, laughing and crying at the same time. 'You always know just what to say to the girls.'

'I wish,' he croaked.

The paramedic excused himself and climbed down and out the door. Sal flashed five fingers, letting them know how long they had. She closed the door gently. The sudden silence was heavy, the maelstrom outside shut out. Cassandra reached out and took Howie's hand, avoiding the drip line that had been fastened to him.

'How are you feeling?' she asked him.

'I've had better holidays,' he said, eyes heavy and glassy. 'I can't quite remember, but I think they said I'd lost a couple of pints of blood. Seems Kelvin managed to carve out a nice chunk of meat from my waistline.'

He lifted his free hand that had been resting on the gauze and bandages wrapped around his stomach. A large patch of bright blood had seeped through and Cassandra knew that he would need treatment and time to recover. She didn't want to keep him.

'I just wanted to say thank you,' she said, slowly, deliberately. 'Before you're whisked away and I might not see you again.'

'Thank you for what?' he asked.

'For saving my life. For saving *all* of our lives. Kelvin, he's not a well man, that's clear enough. He's got issues. I hate to think what he would have or could have done had you not wrestled him like that.'

'I was only doing what you were going to do,' he said. 'That was a pretty dumb idea, by the way.'

'You're a fine one to talk,' she said, smiling now. 'I think maybe I'd watched too many Howie Temple movies.'

He squeezed her hand weakly and offered a smile in return. Another knock at the door and Sal appeared on the other side.

'Time for him to go,' she said.

Cassandra stood up. Howie let go of her hand and she bent down and kissed him on the forehead.

'You look after yourself, understand, chuck?'

'I'll try,' he said.

'I'll send you some grapes and a bottle of Lucozade.'

'What's Lucozade?' he asked.

That made her laugh. She stepped down from the ambulance as the paramedic took her place. He was about to close the door when Howie called to her.

'Hey!' he shouted, voice hoarse. 'We didn't do too badly, did we?'

'No.' She smiled. 'We did alright, chuck. We did alright.'

The door closed and the red and white lights flicked into action. The siren blared as the ambulance took off, a path cleared through the barricades. Cassandra watched it move off and disappear.

Chapter 36

Monaco in summertime was a very special place. The principality was extraordinary all year round. But there was something particularly glamorous about it at the height of the warm season.

Everything seemed rich and fruitful, bursting with life. The mish-mash of architectural styles, combined with the glistening Mediterranean Sea on one side gave an almost fantastical feel. Those who walked the streets knew how lucky they were. From all over the world, hosting guests of every language and background, this was a playground – an international dreamland.

Cassandra felt privileged indeed as she sipped her chilled champagne. She was alone, again, standing by the high, immaculately polished glass rails of the penthouse terrace. The sun was comfortably warm as it arced down towards the west, casting a welcoming glow on everything it touched.

As wrap parties went, Cassandra had never been to anything as extravagant as this. Apart from the stunning vistas, the venue itself was lavishly suave. An art deco design, the old and the new met all at once with effortless ease. From the minimalist furniture to the specially selected fauna, the penthouse suite and terrace of the hotel were everything she had expected and hoped for from her first visit to Monaco.

She had dressed for the part. She could almost hear her mother's tutting a thousand miles away as she'd handed over her credit card in the Dior store. The notion had been put in her head by Howie when they'd plotted their escape. And she'd treated herself to the elegant gown that was now her outfit. It beat the regulation issue polo shirt, at least.

The terrace was busy. A nervous excitement hung in the balmy air. A week had passed since the crew and guests of *The Regal Secret* had been rescued, Kelvin Kamani and Scorpione arrested on the spot. While the police worked out all the details, Ed had insisted on pushing on with their intended schedule, culminating in this party to mark the end of the series. No expense had been spared, it seemed. The food was moreish, the drink flowing, the setting immaculate.

Cassandra thought about how much a bash like this would cost the network. Ed didn't seem to care. He was convinced that the show, the footage, everything that had happened, would be a stonking success. There was just the little matter of legal sign-off. And that, he had assured her, it would be a smash hit, meaning more fame, fortune and glory for her.

The thought turned her stomach a little. She stared down at the bubbles fizzing away in her glass. Everything that had happened, with Kelvin, Scorpione and Rolando, it had made her question what she was really looking for in life. What happened if she climbed so far up the ladder that there were always more people waiting to knock her down, or worse, like Kelvin, offer her the kind of money that left you ruined? That wasn't her. She was a straightforward girl, from Liverpool, who'd made it. Fashion and parties, those were her MO. Not bloody murder and political intrigue.

She was glad that it was all over now. And yet, something nagged at the back of her mind. Something just didn't fit, didn't make sense. There was no closure there, despite what Ed, Inspector Sal and everyone else had told her. The pieces all felt like fragments, half-heartedly put together to form something of a complete picture. But it wasn't all there, and she couldn't work out what was missing.

Her taste for the champagne had dwindled. She tossed the last of the drink over the edge of the terrace balcony. Turning around to give her glass back, she stopped with a fright. Ms Sachiko was standing there, looming, face blank.

'You gave me a fright,' said Cassandra.

'I'm sorry,' she said, with about as much emotion as a pocket calculator. 'Are you having a nice evening?'

Cassandra was a little disarmed by the question. There had never been any sign of interest from Sachiko in anyone's well-being before, other than the guests she was paid to care about. Yet here she was, dressed in her same immaculate outfit, hair slicked back behind her ears, asking how Cassandra was doing.

'Yes, thanks, babe,' she said. 'It's a fairly swanky place. I've never been to Monaco before. I don't know if it's always like this.'

'It is,' she said flatly. 'In my line of work, I've visited many exclusive principalities and private islands. They all take on the same guise, expensive and cutting edge. Monaco, I find, is exactly the same. Except for the smell of damp.'

'Damp?' Cassandra wrinkled her nose.

Sachiko did the same. She looked about the terrace, the faintest of sneers on her blemish-free face.

'Yes, damp,' she said. 'The proximity to the sea gives everything a reek of the stuff. They really should do something about it.'

'They?'

'The people in charge.'

Cassandra hadn't noticed any smell about Monaco in the few days she had been there. She afforded herself a quick sniff and still nothing. Rather than argue with Sachiko, she simply agreed.

'I guess you're right.'

Sachiko nodded. She stood silently. Cassandra wasn't sure if this was a personal or professional visit. She decided to take the lead anyway.

'When are you guys going home?' she asked, the only thing she could think of in that moment.

'Two days,' she answered. 'My company has chartered a flight from Marseille to Paris. From there the guests will take their leave, heading to the different corners of the planet. I, however, won't be joining them.'

'No?'

'No,' she said. 'My services have been hired for another party onboard another excursion, a Baltic and Scandinavian cruise.'

'Blimey,' said Cassandra. 'A bit of a change in temperature I imagine.'

'Yes,' she answered. 'But work is work, right?'

Sachiko didn't elaborate but in that one line Cassandra realised that although she'd felt the inscrutable Ms Sachiko and herself, with her tendency to wear her heart on her sleeve, had always been poles apart, there was perhaps more in common than she'd thought. Work had brought her onto the ship, and it would take her to the next one.

'Ms Troy,' said Sachiko. 'May I speak candidly with you for a moment?'

'Yeah, sure,' she said. 'What's on your mind, chuck?'

The guests' liaison remained silent for a moment. Her chin puckered and she dropped her gaze.

'I would like to offer my sincerest apologies,' she said. 'I feel like I have failed both you, Mr Temple and the whole production.'

'What? Failed us? What are you talking about?' Cassandra didn't quite understand what she was saying.

Sachiko was clearly finding all of this difficult. The words seemed to be catching in the back of her throat. Cassandra imagined apologising wasn't something she had to do often. A woman like her was always organised and disciplined. Even with her naked yoga first thing in the morning she had taken a strength and confidence that only being correct and proper all of the time afforded.

'I should have been more of a help,' she said. 'I should have assisted yours and Mr Temple's enquiries more than I did. At the very least I should have tended to those who needed attention.'

'It was a hard couple of days for us all, babe. I wouldn't beat yourself up over it. We got there in the end, didn't we?'

Sachiko bowed her head further. 'In all my experience as an agent for international travellers, I have never once come across circumstances like those we've endured,' she said. 'And I am ashamed to admit that I did not know what to do. The enjoyment and safety of my clients was paramount. And yet you and Mr Temple were exemplary investigators, even without my assistance.'

'That's very kind of you,' Cassandra smiled warmly.

'Without you, I doubt the outcome of our unpleasantness would have been anywhere near as positive as it has been. And for that, I will eternally be grateful.'

She offered a sleek, pale hand. Cassandra's smile broadened.

'Handshakes are for businessmen, chuck,' she said.

She opened her arms and wrapped Sachiko in a huge hug. The much taller woman was stiff like a corpse but she remained there, not pulling away while Cassandra held her. When she was finished, the corporate agent returned, all emotion banished for eternity.

'I hope you enjoy the rest of the evening's frivolities, Ms Troy,' said Sachiko.

'I certainly will, Ms Sachiko.'

She turned sharply on her heels and walked smartly back towards a cluster of the guests who were demolishing the buffet. Cassandra clicked her tongue.

'What a strange woman,' she said to herself, but hoping that one day, their paths would cross again.

The light was beginning to fade, the sun now setting behind a set of towers closer to the waterfront. Soft lights had glowed into existence all around the terrace as the guests continued to mix and enjoy the company. Ed was at the centre of it all, laughing loudly in intervals between more of his stories.

Cassandra took a casual stroll around the outer edges of the main bulk of the party. People she didn't know offered her reassuring and polite nods. Everyone, she was sure, would know what happened by now and her part in it all. She didn't feel much like a hero. Quite the opposite in fact. Especially with the nagging doubt that wouldn't go away.

'What's a good-looking girl like you doing in a dive like this?'

Cassandra didn't have to turn around to know who it was. And she'd never been more relieved to hear someone's voice in all her life.

Chapter 37

Howie came sauntering around to meet Cassandra. Decked out in a fashionable tuxedo, his hair cut, beard trimmed and scrapes and bruises fading, he looked every bit the movie star that he used to be.

'Well, well, well,' she said. 'Look what the cat dragged in.'

'Backwards,' he noted. 'I don't look too bad though, eh? Amazing what a bit of spit and polish can do for an old man.'

'And there was me thinking I'd been stood up.'

Howie looked about then took a step forward. He took her hands in his and gave her a peck on her cheek.

'Darling, the man who stands you up is the dumbest guy alive.'

Cassandra let out a little yelp and leapt forward, hugging him tightly. He flinched as he held her and she pulled back.

'Sorry,' she said. 'Still sore?'

'Just a bit,' he said, patting his cummerbund. 'I'm all stitched up, bandaged and filled with somebody else's blood. It's remarkable what a near death experience can do for one's sense of life and purpose.'

'I'll bet,' she said. 'It's good to see you, babe.'

'I'm very glad to be here.' He gave a quick nod over to the gathered group. 'I see Ed pulled out all the stops for the wrap party. Pity he couldn't do the same for a competent, non-murdery crew on his TV show.'

'Stop it.' She playfully hit his arm. 'It still feels odd to be partying after everything that's happened. Plus I think Monaco knows how to party in a whole new league. It's not my usual thing.'

'Speak for yourself, Troy,' he said. 'I'll have you know I've partied the nights before, during and after several Monaco Grands Prix in my time.'

'Oh yeah? Who won?'

'Who knows,' he shrugged. 'I don't think I saw a car move in all of those times. I've never been one for motor-sport.'

She laughed. He adjusted his bowtie and fixed the cuffs of his shirt.

'Shall we retire to the bar? It seems that everyone is trying to drink their body weight in free single malt,' he asked.

'Not for me, thanks,' she said. 'But you go ahead, I'll join the conga line when it starts behind you.'

'Perhaps it's good that I'm strictly off the booze until the pain wears off and I'm not on a million tablets.'

'Mineral waters all round it is then.'

'We're *so* rock and roll.'

'Aren't we just?'

He bent his arm and offered it to Cassandra. She gladly took it and they glided through the crowd, heading for the art deco bar at the rear of the terrace. They ordered their waters, much to the barman's surprise, and settled in, surveying the bash. Occasionally other guests would come up to them to offer their congratulations. The Hofstedes, still looking and acting like fish out of water, passed on their eternal thanks for the millionth time.

'We're off on the Titanic cruise next,' said Martha. 'You get to sail right over it. It'll be our twelfth month of consecutive cruises,' she explained when Cassandra and Howie looked shocked at their choice of holiday. 'Dry land is overrated, if you ask me. Kirkby and I are at sea more than we're not these days. Where else would you get served breakfast then watch a real-life murder get solved. Terrific! Now, come on Kirkby, I can see new appetizers . . . '

She dragged her husband away and Howie smiled. 'We overlooked those two. With that many cruises under their belt they could probably have repaired the engines for us.'

'Either that or arranged a game of deck quoits,' said Cassandra, watching the couple merge back into the crowds.

Then it was time for the Kontoglou sisters.

They had stolen the show at the party in their matching sparkly gowns and tiaras. Cassandra admired them for it. It took a lot of guts to waltz around a Monaco terrace party looking like they owned the place.

'Oh Howieee, we knew you'd save us in the end,' said Thekla.

'Yes, we just knew it, you big action man,' added Despoina. 'You were always such a hero to us. And now you're an *actual* hero.'

'That's very kind of you ladies but—'

Howie was cut off. The sisters pounced on him, almost knocking him off his feet. Thekla planted a huge kiss on one cheek. And, as he went to move, Despoina did the same on the other side. They both retreated, fanning themselves and adjusting their tiaras.

'Our hero,' they said in unison, before retreating to the bar.

'Look at you,' said Cassandra. 'Mr Action Movie Star.'

'I was going to say that you'd helped me out,' he said, adjusting himself and patting his hair back into place. 'But they kinda left me speechless.'

Cassandra wiped the smears of lipstick from his lips.

'I must say,' said Howie, draining his glass. 'Even the water tastes like it costs a small fortune.'

'Quite,' she said, sipping her own and grabbing a canape from a passing tray. 'And the food's not bad either. Guess it beats hospital grub?'

'Yes,' he said. 'The food was awful, the bed was hard and I had journalists crawling all over me like flies on ... well, you know. No, after I got discharged last night, I just wanted to forget the last few days so I tried my hand at a casino who, rather generously, still remembered me from thirty years ago, although I've got a feeling that was because I blew most of my salary from my latest movie in one night.'

'Sounds like you've had quite a time of it then.'

'It was just nice to be in a room that wasn't in a hospital,' he said. 'The last time I was in one for as long was when I had my teeth knocked out at Pee-Wee hockey.'

'Sounds painful.'

'It was.' He nodded. 'But at least it meant I had a Hollywood smile long before I hit Hollywood.'

He flashed his teeth at her. He might have been a bit more craggy than back in the day, but he still could flick the movie icon switch when he wanted with a megawatt smile and eyes crinkling at the corners.

They watched the party for a little longer. Marjorie seemed happy to be holding court beneath a lavish canopy of flowers, not noticing her audience checking their watches every few seconds. Cassandra could hear something about 'premier alternative thinker' drifting across the crowd, and smiled to herself as she thought Marjorie's captive audience looked like they were looking for alternatives, all right.

Her and Howie scanned the guests for their other friends. Howie nudged Cassandra when he spotted Matthias. He looked like he was very much enjoying himself. Howie thought with his reputation and history, he would be perfectly at home in an environment like this. Then the opening lines of 'Your Cheatin' Heart' by Hank Williams boomed out of his mouth. A few of the other guests winced. Perhaps Matthias was a little too at home. He sounded like he was singing in the shower.

Even Ben and Geri had scrubbed up for the occasion. They looked lost without their equipment, stood over towards the edge of the balcony, not speaking to each other.

'What is it with those two?' he asked Cassandra.

She rolled her eyes. 'What's wrong with them?'

'I just don't get it,' he said, sipping from his water. 'After everything we've been through, I've never heard them speak. Not even to each other. And now look at them, over there, still looking like they've come to a wake rather than a party.'

Cassandra giggled. 'The stoic, silent types,' she said. 'Not like us, chuck. We're too loud, too brash, too bold. We wouldn't be able to hold our water if we did something bad.'

'Hold our water?'

'You've never heard of that one?'

He shook his head. 'Sounds painful.'

'You've got a lot to learn, chuck, a lot to learn.' She smiled. 'You can speak Hollywood, but you need to learn Scouse.'

They spotted Ed, moving through the party like a shark on the prowl. He stopped every few seconds, recognising someone new and regaling them with his patter. Howie grunted.

'I see the knock on the head hasn't changed Ed's personality too much,' he said.

'No, he's made a miraculous recovery,' she agreed.

'Did we ever work out who attacked him and left him for dead?' he asked.

'The police have charged Scorpione. I've not heard from Inspector Sal since I left Italy but I know she believed that Ed must have disturbed him hiding out and he paid the price. He was lucky not to be killed actually. And even more lucky that he came round before Kelvin could dispatch him on another of his floating funeral pyres.' Cassandra grimaced. 'And he won't shut up about it now. His brush with death in the name of art . . . '

'I don't have to imagine,' said Howie cynically. 'I could hear him from the street below as I came up to the terrace.'

On cue, Ed let out a riotous laugh, throwing his head back. When his hilarity was over, he patted an old man on the shoulder and spied Howie and Cassandra by the bar.

'Oh lord,' said Howie. 'We've been spotted.'

Ed immediately made his way towards them, scything through the party guests on a collision course.

'Be nice,' she whispered.

'I'm always nice,' he replied.

'No, you're not.'

'No, you're right. I'm not.'

'Howie! Cassandra! My two favourite people in the whole world!' Ed shouted, loud enough to be heard in Nice. 'How the hell are you both? So good to see you up and about H, you gave us quite a scare back there, what with your heroics. What did I tell you about this guy, Cassandra. He's the real deal, an action star on the big screen and in real life too. He's the complete package!'

He threw his arm around Howie's shoulders and roughly joshed him back and forward. Howie did his best to smile but he hated this kind of behaviour. It reminded him of being back at school and trying to fit in with the cool kids. Cassandra could only watch on and stifle a laugh at her friend's expense.

'Are you having a great time? Have you had enough to eat, enough to drink. Barman! Champagne for these two please, bottle each, Dom Pérignon!'

He snapped his fingers and one of the bar staff hopped into action.

'That's very kind of you, chuck, but there's really no need,' said Cassandra.

'No need? Are you mad? There's *every* need my dear,' said Ed. 'We're celebrating, living life to its fullest. We've come out of the shadow of adversity and we're reaping the benefits. Eat, drink and be merry!'

Howie was pretty sure how the rest of that verse ended. He didn't say anything.

'How are you feeling, Ed?' Cassandra asked.

'I'm okay,' he laughed. 'It's all a bit blurry though to be perfectly honest. I remember being on the deck and then whack, I went down and that was it I'm afraid, until I came around in Mr Shig's cabin. Strange business, that whole being unconscious lark. Reminded me of rugby at school. No concussion protocols in those days. The teacher would dust you down and send you back out into the scrum as soon as you opened your eyes. Madness.'

'We didn't play rugby at my school,' said Cassandra.

'Nor mine,' Howie added.

'Probably for the best,' said Ed. 'The English public school system is a vipers' nest of aggression. In and out of the classroom. Still, it's not steered me wrong down the years. In fact, I'm probably not supposed to tell you this, but I've got a bit of good news.'

He looked about to make sure they weren't being listened to. Ed leaned in a little closer.

'It seems your antics on the high seas have attracted the attention of the media at home and abroad,' he said.

'You mean newspapers and networks?' asked Howie.

'You bet, H. And it's not just the dailies, I've got magazines, *Rolling Stone*, *Vanity Fair*, everyone wanting a slice of the action. It seems your antics in foiling Kelvin Kamani and the mob machinations has caught the public's attention. And that's before we get onto selling the series to the broadcasters. Then there's Hollywood, they'll want a piece of the pie, a dramatisation, the works.'

'Hollywood?' said Cassandra, unable to hide her excitement.

'That's right,' said Ed. 'I can see it now – the new face of Tinsel Town, Cassandra Troy. It all makes sense. And a second bite at the cherry for you, H. A triumphant return, the prodigal son, back where he belongs, at the top of the box office with all the frills. I wouldn't be surprised if there were calls to reboot all of your old franchises too. Very lucrative. We'll get your people involved of course but you both should be very, *very* proud of yourselves. This is the start of something massive. For all of us.'

'And what about the sheikh?' asked Howie. 'Isn't he mad about what happened to *The Regal Secret*?'

'Please,' Ed snorted. 'The man is a businessman. As soon as he realises it was *his* boat on which the action took place, he'll roll over and have his tummy tickled like everyone else. Trust me on that one, H. He'll crowbar up that precious wooden deck and sell it off plank by plank to the highest bidder, I bet.'

A waiter appeared beside them carrying a silver tray with a bottle of chilled Dom Pérignon and three glasses. Ed took up the flutes as the waiter prepared the bottle.

'Won't you join me?' he asked, flashing that welcoming, charming smile of his.

Cassandra looked at Howie sympathetically.

'One glass can't do us any harm, can it, chuck?' she asked.

'Maybe one would be fine,' he said. 'It sounds like we've got something to celebrate.'

The glasses had already been filled. Ed held his aloft as Howie and Cassandra joined the toast.

'Here's to you both,' he said. 'Temple and Troy, detectives of the high seas.'

Chapter 38

The hotel room was dark. It was to be expected at two in the morning. Cassandra had had great difficulty in opening the door. And now that she was in, she was fumbling along the walls trying to find a light switch.

'I can't see a thing,' said Howie, stumbling in behind her.

'I'm trying to find the button,' she shouted back at him.

'Well hurry up would you? My side hurts and my feet are on fire.'

'*Your* feet are on fire? I've been wearing Louboutins for six hours straight. It'll be a pig's foot in the morning, literally.'

'I don't know what any of that means,' he said.

She found a switch and flipped it. The whole room lit up immediately. The air conditioning flipped into life and the automatic curtains withdrew, revealing the glittering skyline of Monaco on the other side of the glass. No expense had been spared in putting up the celebrity crew. Cassandra had just been relieved not to be in cabin bunk.

She pulled off her heels and collapsed on the bed. Howie closed the door of the room and staggered a little over to where the minibar was waiting. She looked up at him, propped herself on her elbows.

'I thought you weren't supposed to be drinking?' she asked, mouth dry and tongue heavy.

'I'm not,' he said. 'But it's a bit late for "supposed to" now, isn't it?'

He scooped up all of the miniature liquor bottles and grabbed two glasses. Plodding over to the bed, he dumped his bounty down beside her before collapsing himself.

'What do we have here then?' He drunkenly eyed up the first bottle. 'Ah, Captain Morgan, how appropriate. I feel like we've been stuck at sea with a bunch of pirates. I'll drink to that. Aye, aye cap'n.'

He went to give a salute but missed his forehead. He fell backwards onto the bed, the rum spilling out all over his face. Cassandra snorted with laughter. Howie did the same. He lay there, wiping the alcohol from his eyes as she fetched him a towel.

'You've had enough for tonight,' she said. 'How about a nice cup of tea.'

'Ah, tea,' he said ruefully. 'You Brits absolutely love the stuff. I think it tastes like drain water.'

'That doesn't surprise me,' she said. 'But I think you should have a cup anyway, it's good for the soul.'

'Soul?' he asked, eyes closed, hands resting on his stomach. 'What's one of those when it's at home?'

'You're too hard on yourself.'

'No, I'm not. I've just spent too long in showbusiness to think that souls and decency still exist outside of birthdays and Christmas cards.'

'That's maybe the saddest thing I've ever heard anyone say.'

Howie sat up. 'It's true though,' he said. 'Just look at this trip, look at tonight. Do you think anyone upstairs really cared that Captain Rolando was dead? That his body was burned by a disgraced politician up to his neck with the Mafia? No, they didn't care, of course they didn't. They were having a nice time in one of the most expensive places on the planet.'

'I'm sure Ed cared. And Ms Sachiko cared enough to thank me earlier for the work we did.'

'Ed cares about one thing – money,' he scoffed. 'Okay, two maybe: money and fame. And that's fine. But once I've got my cut, I'm not chasing any more. We'll get nice big juicy royalty cheques and I'll have my stitches out. You'll be set up for life and we won't have to worry about suspects, motives, murderers and MPs ever again.'

The kettle's switch clicked off as the water boiled. Cassandra made two cups of tea. She poured the milk and was stirring. But she kept on stirring. And stirring. And stirring some more. Only when Howie called over to her did she realise what she had been doing.

'Are you alright there?' he asked her.

Cassandra blinked as she turned around. 'What's that?' she asked.

'You, are you alright?' he asked again. 'You've been stirring that tea on repeat. I think it's stirred.'

'Sorry.' She looked down at the mugs. 'I was just thinking, that's all.'

She took the mugs over and handed one to Howie. He sipped at the tea and winced.

'Like I said, drain water.' He put the mug down on a side table.

'I was thinking,' she said. 'It's been bugging me for the past week. This whole business with Rolando being a police spy. If he was working for Sal and the cops, wouldn't he have been more protected? I mean, isn't that the whole job of the police – to protect and serve.'

'Everyone makes mistakes.' He shrugged. 'You don't know who snitched on the snitch. Could have been a dirty cop, could have been somebody else. Also, they probably didn't think he was going into the lion's den – a bunch of celebrities don't seem like the most dangerous of crewmates. Even if you read up on Kelvin's background you'd think he was more likely to bore you to death than murder you. They probably thought Rolando was in danger of nothing more than being in a few more selfies than usual.'

'Yeah, that's true,' she said. 'But he was dead before the Serafinas' hitman could do the job. That's what Scorpione said, wasn't it? He said he'd found him dead already and stuck the knife in to make it look like he'd done his job. That's what's bothered me about all of this, Howie. If Scorpione didn't kill Rolando, then who did?'

'Kelvin,' he suggested. 'You saw how he was reacting. Maybe the Serafinas got to him first, told him to whack Rolando when he was on the ship for the show. Then when Scorpione shows up, he has to take him out too. Nice and easy, two birds and all that.'

Cassandra sipped at her tea. 'Yeah, I guess that makes sense,' she said, still thinking.

Howie rubbed his face. He kicked off his shoes and pushed himself up the bed, stretching out and unfastening his bow tie.

'Make yourself at home, why don't you, chuck,' she said, eyeing him.

'Thank you, I will,' he said, closing his eyes.

Cassandra got up and rounded the bed. She fluffed the pillows on the other side and climbed back on, still sipping her tea.

'But how would the Serafinas and Scorpione know where we were?' she asked out loud. 'And that Rolando and Kelvin were onboard.'

'Know where we were when?' asked Howie, his eyes closed, hands crossed on his injured stomach.

'The yacht was a private charter, Ed told us as much. That sort of stuff wouldn't be public record, surely?' she said. 'The mob ran a big risk of bumping off Rolando and Kelvin, he was a former defence minister for goodness' sake. People would know that he had been killed. And Rolando was a spy. That sort of stuff doesn't go without repercussions from the police. It's all very complicated.'

'Complicated, yes,' said Howie, dozing off. 'Not our jobs anymore, Cassandra. Let the police worry about it. We can just take the money and run.'

'I guess you're right about that,' she said.

Howie began to snore gently, but she wasn't ready for sleep. The thoughts that had been nagging her throughout the whole investigation were swirling through her mind. She wasn't sure why. Howie's advice had been the best she'd received in ages. Let it go, take the money and leave the responsibility, the *real* work, to the professionals. She'd done her bit. Now a whole new life of celebrity and status lay ahead. She should just enjoy it for as long as it lasted.

'And then there was that argument, do you remember?' she asked Howie's snoring form.

Howie didn't say anything.

'Remember, we saw them, the first night, Ed and Rolando, they were fighting. A heated exchange. Ed said it was nothing, that Rolando was just passionate, something like that. We never got to the bottom of what that was about, did we, babe?'

As if to try and silence her, Howie rolled over onto his side. His broad back faced Cassandra. She took another sip of her tea but it had gone cold.

She had the bit between her teeth now. An evening drinking and dancing felt like a declogger for her imagination. She quickly got out of bed and fetched her phone. Scanning through the recent media coverage, it was all the same story – how the show's production had been halted because of the alleged murder of the captain. Pictures of her, Howie, and the rest of the crew had all been provided to the media, along with statements from the police and Ed, as director and showrunner.

Then there were articles on what was going to come next. Ed, again, was ever present, talking about the planned documentary on Howie and Cassandra's investigations. There were tributes to Captain Rolando and talk of donations to charities in his name. All of this in just under a week, a few days.

Cassandra locked her phone. She rubbed her forehead, the sour taste of drink in the back of her throat. The fuzziness of the alcohol was still lingering over her but she pressed on, thinking of what to do. Or, even, if there was anything *to* do.

Then an idea struck her. She looked up and out at Monaco shining beyond the windows of her room. There was an outside chance, a slim possibility, that somebody knew something that might clear things up, for better or worse.

'Howie,' she said, turning back to the bed.

He was sound asleep. Rattling, loud snores were coming from him now, the kind that would keep her up all night anyway. She supposed she could find his key card and let herself into his room and sleep there . . . or she could go where her imagination was pulling her. She pulled the duvet free from her side and threw it over him, making sure he would be warm. Grabbing the trainers that Inspector Sal had given her, far comfier than the Louboutins. she pulled them on and hurried for the door. She turned the lights off and left Howie to sleep. She thought about leaving him a note. But she would be back soon enough. She hoped.

Chapter 39

Marjorie Bryant was bleary eyed when she opened the door. Australia's foremost alternative thinker was not at her best. Blinking in the brightness of the hotel corridor, when she was finally able to get her glasses on and realise who had woken her up, her already sour mood worsened.

'What the hell do you think you're doing, knocking on my door like this,' she rasped. 'Do you have any idea what time it is? I'm not some drunken stay-out-all-night floozie like you. Do you realise it's the dead of night?'

'I do, Marjorie, and I'm sorry,' said Cassandra, out of breath from climbing six flights of stairs. 'I wouldn't do this unless it was urgent. Can I come in?'

Marjorie barred the door.

'Certainly not,' she said. 'It's the small hours of the morning and I'm in my bed. It's been a terrible couple of weeks and I'm trying to enjoy some rest and relaxation in a place you wouldn't see me dead in unless somebody else was paying. And thankfully somebody else *is* paying. So you can sod off.'

She went to close the door of her room. Cassandra jammed a trainer-clad foot in the way and stopped it. Marjorie looked appalled.

'What are you doing, you silly girl?'

'Please, Marjorie, it'll only take a minute.'

'No.'

'Please.'

'I said no.' She tried to close the door again but Cassandra wouldn't move. 'Would you get your foot out of the way? I'm going back to bed.'

'It's life or death, Marjorie. Please let me in for a couple of minutes. Five.'

'Are you drunk or deaf? I said no and I mean no.'

She pulled the door back, ready to give Cassandra's foot one more almighty whack. But the younger woman stopped it, arm straining to keep it open. She muscled her way into the doorway.

'Look, I know this is highly unusual, babe,' she said. 'And believe me, if I didn't have to come begging to you, of all the people in the world, I wouldn't. But I need your help to put something to bed. And you're the only person who can give me what I need.'

'You're mad,' sneered Marjorie. 'You *have* been drinking, I can smell it on your breath.'

'Marjorie, I'm serious here, you have to let me in.'

'Marjorie!' A voice came from behind her, deep within the room. Cassandra peered over her shoulder and then back to the older woman.

'Is there somebody in there with you?' she asked her.

'What? No, of course not.' Marjorie suddenly seemed jumpy.

'There is,' she said. 'I heard somebody calling your name just then.'

'You're hearing things then.'

'Marjorie!' The voice called her again. This time there could be no denial. Marjorie knew this, her face flushing red.

'Who is that?' asked Cassandra, although she already knew the answer, she recognised the voice.

Before Marjorie could answer, Matthias appeared out of the darkness of the room. Bare chested, his lower half covered by a towel, he shaded his eyes from the light from the hallway as he neared the door.

'Cassandra?' he asked.

'Hi Matthias,' she said, unable to hide her smile. 'Lovely to see you. Unexpected too.'

'Are you alright? It's the middle of the night?'

'Yes, I'm fine, quite fine, chuck, thank you,' she said. 'I just wanted to speak to Marjorie for a moment about something a bit delicate.'

'She was just leaving,' said Marjorie vindictively, her secret exposed.

'It won't take a moment, honestly,' she said.

'If it won't take a moment then come on in,' said the former footballer warmly. 'I'll make us some coffee.'

'Matthias.' There was a strictness in Marjorie's voice that made it sound like she was addressing her dogs. 'It's the middle of the night.'

'And Cassandra is a friend. After everything we've been through I think we can give her a couple of minutes. You know, I was thinking about this the other day, how we're all bonded together, like a team, a shared trauma if you will. We had something similar on a trip to Bangkok before the World Cup we won and—'

'Matthias!'

Marjorie's severity was enough to quieten him down. Not that it mattered anymore, Cassandra had eased herself into the room already. Matthias started making coffee, completely at ease with wearing next to nothing.

Marjorie slowly came into the room. Her face was beginning to turn back to a normal colour but she was mad as hell. Cassandra knew she had to keep this short and sweet if she wanted to get what she needed from her.

'Tell us then,' she said. 'To what do we owe the pleasure of being woken up at three in the morning? You said it was life or death.'

'Life or death? Not again,' said Matthias.

'Yeah, I need to know more about before you boarded, I'm afraid,' said Cassandra.

She tried to untangle the jumbled ideas, thoughts and theories that were scrambling her brain. She felt like she was drowning in everything she wanted to say and do, or was that just the after-effects of the Dom Pérignon? She took a deep breath and tried to relax. Matthias handed her a mug of coffee but she didn't touch it. She needed answers even more than she needed caffeine.

'Marjorie, you said to Howie that your assistant had carried out extensive research on all of the crew before you set off for the production,' she said.

'Yes, she did,' she said. 'I like to know who I'm spending time with.'

'Did she do the same for Ed and the production company as well as your crewmates?'

'Ed?'

Matthias slurped loudly from his own mug. 'Why Ed?' he asked.

'Did you have any background material on him at all?' Cassandra asked again.

'I can't remember,' said Marjorie. 'But yes, I should think so, probably. Why?'

'Did anything flag up in that research? Anything out of the ordinary?'

'I can't recall anything. I wasn't as interested in the professional CVs – it felt more like reading LinkedIn than finding out the truth about my fellow so-called celebrities. What's this all about, Cassandra?'

'Please, Marjorie. I know it's late and I know I've stumbled upon your little liaison with Matthias. Honestly, I'm delighted for you both. But I need you to think hard. Think long and hard about that research, those documents and dossiers your researcher put together. Was there anything, *anything* at all that stood out from Ed's files.'

Marjorie gave Cassandra a dirty look. She readjusted her dressing gown, tightening the belt. Matthias, on the other hand, seemed perfectly comfortable lounging around in just a towel.

'It all seemed perfectly staid, Cassandra, if I really think back to it,' she said. 'He's been running this stupid *Sail or Fail* programme for years now, to moderate success. There are a litany of other shows he's credited, some cult, some classic, and if you dig back far enough you'll find he got a break in the industry through some friend of his father's, all standard industry stuff.'

'The other shows, what were they? Did you research that at all?'

'No,' she said flatly. 'Listen, I think I've been more than fair here. Can you please let us get back to sleep, it's very late, so late, in fact, that it's early and—'

'I've got the list here,' said Matthias.

He passed Cassandra his phone. A full credit list for Ed Wells was waiting for her. She quickly scrolled through the list, not recognising any of them.

'Thank you, Matthias,' she said, still searching.

'Not a problem, *fräulein*,' he replied. 'Is there something you're looking for specifically?'

'I'm not sure yet,' she said. 'But I'll know it when I see . . . it . . . ' She trailed off. One of the credits stood out from the others. And it made Cassandra's skin crawl. 'I think I've found it,' she said.

Marjorie and Matthias joined her. They looked over her shoulder at the screen as Cassandra clicked on the link.

'*Italy's Most Wanted*,' said the older woman. 'Hardly the most original title.'

'Forget about the title, listen to this,' said Cassandra. '"Fly-on-the-wall documentary series following the investigations and exploits of Italy's Carabinieri and the Polizia di Stato. Join officers as they battle with some of the notorious crime families and syndicates from the north and south, exposing drug networks, people trafficking and more."'

She looked up from the screen, her mind working overdrive.

'Do you think this has something to do with what's going on?' asked Marjorie, suddenly interested.

'I don't know.' Cassandra gritted her teeth. 'It could be nothing. It could be something. He's credited here as some researcher, and that covers all sorts in the biz. But supposing, just for a second, that he had some connection to the Serafinas through this show, long before we all set foot on deck, supposing there was even a sliver of a chance, that he was involved in some way. Shouldn't the authorities know about it?'

She turned to face the others. They both looked grey, and not just from the lack of sleep.

'These are serious accusations,' said Marjorie. 'And you don't have a shred of proof.'

'And what about that lump on the back of his head,' said Matthias. 'I carried him down to the guest suites after he was knocked unconscious. He seemed pretty out of it if you ask me.'

'So,' Marjorie asked. 'What are you going to do?'

Cassandra had been dreading that question. And now that it was out there, she still wasn't sure what the answer was going to be.

'I need to fetch Howie,' she said, heading for the door.

Chapter 40

Howie woke up with Cassandra standing over him, jostling his shoulder until his eyes were open. Not for the first time in his life was his sleep interrupted by a beautiful woman forcing him to get up. Usually it was followed by words like 'my husband is coming home' and 'what the hell are you still doing here?'

This time it was different. This time he was glad to see it was Cassandra Troy standing over him.

'Is it morning already?' he asked numbly. 'That was a reasonably good sleep. I even had a dream where I was back in LA and had been offered a part in the new James Bond film. Admittedly it was the villain not Bond himself but I'd take that—'

'We have to go, right now,' said Cassandra. 'Come on, get your shoes back on, we have to get out of here,' she said.

'Cassandra,' he asked, using all of his strength to sit up. 'What the hell is going on? What time is it?'

'Never mind all that now, we have to go.'

'Go? Go where? Has Ed's cheque bounced or something? Are the hotel throwing us out?'

He looked over at the huge windows of the suite. It was still dark outside. A little digital clock on the bedside table gave him some information.

'Hey, hold on a minute,' he said. 'I've only been asleep for like an hour. It's the middle of the night. And isn't this your room?'

'It doesn't matter, we have to go and we have to go right now,' she said, throwing his shoes at him.

He caught them clumsily. Throwing his legs off the edge of the bed, he tried to unscramble his haggard mind. He was still in his tuxedo, belly straining against the vice-like tension of his cummerbund.

Cassandra was hurrying about the room, gathering things up and shoving them into a suitcase. She grabbed her jeans and a T-shirt and skipped into the bathroom.

'Cassandra, do you want to tell me what's going on here?' he asked her.

'I'll explain when we're out,' she shouted back at him.

'Yeah, okay, I get that. But a little reasoning now, before I put my shoes back on might help get me moving. As actors who are better than I am might say, what's my motivation?'

She reappeared, fully changed, the expensive dress bundled up in an ball. He winced as she shoved it into a bag with all the care and grace of dirty gym gear.

'We have to try and speak with Ed, immediately,' she said. 'And if he reacts the way I think he might, a hasty exit on our part might be the best course of action.'

The mention of Ed seemed to blow away some of Howie's cobwebs. He stood up, instantly regretting it.

'Ed? What's wrong with him? He's not had another turn has he? I know he hadn't signed any contracts with networks and things. And as much as it pains me to say it, I'd quite like him to stay alive long enough to see us get paid the fortune we've been promised.'

'He's not dead, chuck,' she said gravely.

'Then what's the matter?'

Cassandra stopped her packing. She bowed her head and let out a long, frustrated sigh.

'This has been a nightmare, Howie. From start to finish, it's been an absolute shambles, a total catastrophe,' she said. 'This trip, this job,' she went on. 'From your seat on the plane getting messed up and me dropping my duty-free into the drink. And obviously everything else that happened after that, right up until now. I've felt like I've been cursed, really I have. It's like Mr Shig said.'

'You're not cursed, Cassandra,' he said, trying to offer some solace. 'It's been an absolute disaster, I'll give you that. But we're out of it now, we're on the other side. We can enjoy the fruits of our labour, that's what Ed said wasn't it?'

'See, that's just it,' she said. 'We can't, we can't, Howie.'

'Why not? What's the problem here? We're in the clear, we've done nothing wrong. We're heroes for god's sake!'

She slumped down into one of the luxurious chairs of her room. Sinking her head into her hands, she prepared for the worst.

'It's Ed. He's the problem,' she said. 'All this time, he's been the problem.'

'Ed?' Howie snorted. 'I know the guy is a pain in the ass, but—'

'No, he's more than that,' she said, looking up at him. 'I think he's behind everything that's been going on.'

'What?' Howie laughed a little. Cassandra was in no laughing mood.

'Where the hell are you getting that from?' he asked her. 'You think he's involved with Rolando's murder?'

'I think he's more than involved, babe, I think he probably *killed* Rolando.'

If she hadn't looked so serious, he would have thought she was joking. The remnants of his tiredness were rapidly retreating.

'No, you've got it all wrong,' he said. 'Ed? Ed's not a killer. He's a lot of things, a show-off, a bad director and showrunner, a complete narcissist, but he's not a murderer, Cassandra. I don't believe that.'

'It fits too well,' she said. 'He's the only one who's had access to everything and everyone, this whole trip. He worked on a show, years ago, when he was starting out that followed the cops around Italy dealing with mobsters and gangsters, Howie. He's pulled us together, he knew Rolando, so he could have known about him being an informant. It's all there, it all fits. Means, method, all of it.'

'And what's his motivation?' he asked. 'Why would he do what he's done? Why would he murder Rolando and try and blame it on Kelvin Kamani or that Scorpione guy? Are you trying to say he knew all about these guys too?'

She nodded solemnly.

'Where's your proof?' he asked.

There was a finality in his question. He rounded the bed so he was close to her. Cassandra was chewing it all over in her mind. She looked up at him sadly.

'I don't have any,' she said.

'Great.' He rolled his eyes.

'Not yet anyway, that's why I need your help, that's why we have to go now.'

'Hold on, time out, Cassandra, let's not get too hasty here,' he said. 'We could be on to earn a whole load of money here if Ed's plans come to fruition. We go round calling him a murderer and if we're wrong, we'll never even get another reality show gig again. It'll be advertorials and OnlyFans at this rate.'

'I heard the sales speech from Ed earlier too, chuck, I know what's at risk here,' she said. 'But there's also justice to think about, there's also Kelvin, as deranged as he is, being sent down for a crime he likely didn't commit. I know he's not covered himself in glory – taking hostages, disposing of a body, almost turning you into one, too – but I don't think he's killed anyone. Scorpione too, to a certain degree. I mean I know he's no boy scout, but he came onboard to kill a man he claimed was already dead and I believe him. Innocent people shouldn't ever have to pay for the crimes of the guilty, that's a basic human liberty. You know that, Howie, you've always known that. Otherwise you'd have never stuck at this investigation for as long as you have done. You wouldn't have been knocked around by the cops and wouldn't have taken a knife for me.'

Howie could feel his insides clenching at all of this. And that was before he'd processed everything she'd been saying about Ed, Rolando, Kelvin Kamani and Scorpione.

'I don't like the sound of any of this,' he said.

'I know,' she agreed. 'I don't either.'

'If you've got it wrong, if you accuse Ed of all these things, of somehow being complicit in everything, we won't just never work again – he'll probably drag us through the courts.'

'I appreciate that,' she said. 'But that's only if I'm wrong.'

'And what if you're right?' he asked. 'What do we do then?'

Cassandra stood up. She reached over and took his hands. 'I wouldn't ask you to get involved in this if I didn't believe that I was right,' she said. 'And if it wasn't the right thing to do. That's the most important part, chuck. What are we, after all, if we don't do the right thing?'

Howie made a strange noise. It was somewhere between frustration, anger, melancholy and despair. He was so tantalisingly close to what he'd longed for during his years in the showbusiness wilderness – a second chance. He probably didn't deserve it but he'd kept his ambitions burning. Now, in typical fashion, here it was being cruelly snatched away from him before it had begun.

'My old man used to say something to me,' he said, pinching the bridge of his nose. 'He said that if something appears too good to be true, invariably it is.'

'Yeah,' she agreed. 'My dad tells me that all the time too.'

'I don't think I'd appreciated it until just now,' he said. 'I really, *really* wish I'd stayed asleep. Or better yet, gone back to my own room. That way I wouldn't be involved.'

'You don't have to be involved if you don't want to be,' she said. 'I just thought you would want to be. Like I said, justice is worth more than all our careers, and followers and pay cheques put together.'

'Yeah,' he clicked his tongue. 'Justice.' He puffed out his cheeks then clapped his hands together. Looking about, he fetched his shoes and pulled them on. 'Okay then, Miss Marple,' he said. 'What's the plan?'

Chapter 41

The lights of the grandiose villa were shining over the high fences as the hotel car pulled up to the gates. Surrounded by a thick woodland, the brilliant white building shone out through the darkness like a wedding cake perched high above the sand and the sea beyond its borders. Everyone, it seemed, knew this place. Fashion designers, publishers, celebrities of every kind had called it their home at some point during their stay in Monaco. Now it was the temporary home to Ed, enjoying his moment as the hottest showrunner in the industry.

'Not a bad shack,' said Howie, peering through the windscreen. 'Are you sure this is where Ed lives?'

'It is indeed, sir. Your friend is very lucky,' said the driver. 'This place is among the most prestigious, most sought after properties in the whole state. And the costs are through the roof, as you can imagine.'

He whistled as he parked up. Cassandra went to give him a tip from her purse. He waved her away.

'Please, mademoiselle, there is no need,' he said.

'Are you sure, chuck?'

'Yes, certainly, it's hotel policy not to take tips from guests,' he said.

'But you've been so helpful,' said Howie. 'I say that, we haven't found Ed yet.'

'He's definitely here, Mr Temple,' said the driver with a friendly smile. 'I picked him up myself before your party just this evening and I've been chauffeuring him since he arrived here in Monaco. This is where he is staying.'

Cassandra patted him on the shoulder and climbed out of the car. Howie did the same and lingered at the driver's window.

'Hang around for a couple of minutes, would you?' he said. 'We may need a lift back – and faster than we imagined.'

'Of course,' he said, switching the engine off.

Howie nodded and headed for the gates with Cassandra. The huge, three-storey mansion rose up ahead of them beyond the cast-iron barrier. The front door was open but there was no sign of any life from within.

'Do you ever get a feeling you're walking into a trap?' he asked her.

'Yeah, I do as it happens,' she said. 'Although there's no way that Ed could know we're on to him. I didn't even know until about an hour ago.'

Howie gave a less than convinced grunt of approval. Cassandra took hold of the gates. She gently eased them forward, the hinges creaking and moaning.

'Careful,' Howie hissed. 'I think they're meant to be electric, not shoved open manually.'

'Sorry,' she said.

She opened them just enough to be able to squeeze through. Howie remained on the other side, clearing his throat for her attention.

'You don't expect me to get through there, do you?' he asked, pointing at the narrow gap.

'You shouldn't have eaten all of that free lobster then, should you?' she batted back.

Again, he grumbled under his breath. Sucking in his gut, he managed to just about get through the gap. They carefully made their way across the front porch and to the main entrance. The door was still wide open and two large cases could be seen sitting just inside.

Cassandra went in first, Howie close behind. The inside of the villa was just as opulent as the grounds. Chandeliers hung from the high, cathedral ceilings and every picture and mirror that lined the walls was rimmed in elaborate, gold frames. The smell of fresh lilies wafted down through the hallway. Even the black and white tiled floor felt expensive under their feet.

'Nice place,' said Cassandra, marvelling at it.

'Seems a shame that Ed is apparently leaving so soon,' said Howie, pointing down at the suitcases.

'In a hurry to go too by the looks of things,' she said. 'It's just gone four a.m.'

The sound of breaking glass came from further up the hall. Loud cursing followed, Ed's distinctive voice confirming in an instant that their driver had been correct.

'Okay, get behind me,' he said.

'What?'

'Get behind me,' he said again. 'If this turns ugly I want to deal with it first before it gets to you.'

'That's very sweet and kind of you, babe,' she said. 'But it's also pretty condescending. I should be protecting you, old timer!'

'You didn't complain before with Kelvin Kamani.'

'That's because I couldn't stop you throwing yourself at him.'

'Alright, fine,' he said. 'We'll go in together.'

'That's better.'

They nodded to each other and started off further into the house. Ed was still cursing somewhere in the distance and they followed his voice to a door close to the rear of the huge villa. It was closed and they lingered for a little moment outside.

'You ready for this?' Howie asked, whispering.

'No, not really,' she said. 'But I guess we don't have much choice now, do we?'

'We could always just leave,' he said. 'The car is still outside, we could hop in it, head back to the hotel and be sound asleep before dawn breaks. Just forget about the whole thing and remain dumb celebrities.'

'Yeah, that's not going to happen, is it chuck?'

Howie cracked a smile at that. 'Not in a million years,' he said. 'Not with you in charge anyway.'

Cassandra nodded in agreement. They pushed the door open. The kitchen was bright and open, the far wall dominated by panoramic windows that looked out across the sea. The sun was starting to rise over the horizon, casting its glow on cruise ships and yachts floating lazily in the Med.

Ed stood to attention when he saw them at the door. He was holding his hand, a dish towel wrapped around it tight, a hint of blood seeping into the cloth. Something crunched under Howie's shoe as he stepped into the kitchen, a broken glass, what looked like white wine spreading in a puddle across the terracotta tiles of the room.

'Howie!' Ed smiled broadly. 'Cassandra! What are you two doing here?'

There was a friendliness to the showrunner's tone. But it rang a hollow note. Something was amiss, Howie could hear it. There was a lack of conviction, a slight falseness perhaps, like a smile that didn't reach the eyes. His pulse quickened as they made their way into the kitchen.

'Don't mind the blood,' he said, holding up his hand. 'Had a slight accident with some plonk. I probably shouldn't be drinking this late into the night but who cares, you only live once, right? And we've got lots to celebrate, haven't we?'

He wandered over to the Belfast sink set in the island that dominated the centre of the room. Running his hand under the cold tap, he winced, never taking his eyes from Cassandra and Howie.

'Have you guys just left the party?' he asked. 'Man, you're both too hardcore for my liking. I always knew you were a party animal, H, but even I would have thought four in the morning was too much for you.'

'Old habits die hard,' said Howie, smiling weakly.

'To what do I owe this pleasure?' asked Ed, switching off the tap. 'You guys haven't been kicked out of the hotel have you? Because if you have, I'll have serious words with the management. You're both superstars, you don't have to put up with that kind of guff anymore.'

'No, it's not that,' said Cassandra. 'We wanted to ask you a couple of questions, that's all.'

'Questions?'

Ed seemed perplexed at this. He re-wrapped the towel around his injured hand and sauntered over to another worktop. Howie spotted some documents, sheets of paper and a passport, sitting close by.

'What kind of questions?'

Cassandra took a step forward. 'There's just a couple of things I wanted to get straightened out before we moved forward,' she said. 'A couple of lingering little threads to do with what happened to Captain Rolando and Kelvin.'

'Rolando and Kelvin?' Ed laughed. 'What about them?'

'What were you arguing about the night Rolando died?' asked Howie.

'Arguing? Me?'

'Yes, we saw you, Ed, on the main deck,' she said. 'You and Rolando were having a pretty heated discussion. You said it was just him being passionate but he was killed, not long after.'

'By Kelvin Kamani,' said Ed. 'The cops have explained all of this to us, Cassandra. What are you getting at here?'

'That's the thing that's bugging me.' She clicked her fingers. 'The police, you, everyone seems so convinced that Kelvin killed Rolando, that he knew about our captain working for the police, but it just doesn't make sense.'

'Kelvin is disturbed,' said Howie. 'But I don't think he's a murderer. He had nothing to gain from it.'

'Nothing to gain?' Ed laughed. 'The guy is up to his eyeballs in debt with some really bad people. If he murders an informant, don't you think that would get him off the hook? Seems like a pretty sensible move to me, in the worst possible taste of course.'

'That's the thing, chuck,' said Cassandra, moving around the kitchen island. 'He was in debt to them, sure. He made some bad choices, he was running for his life, but it just doesn't add up to me. Why would he put himself in danger, why would he take part in a show in public, on the high seas, with a known associate of the mob family he's trying to evade. Why would he do that sort of thing? Why wouldn't he just stay at home and hide out, keep a low profile?'

'He was desperate for the cash,' said Ed. 'He needs the money and he needs to rebuild his profile, Cassandra. You've met him, he can't be trusted, nobody in politics can. I was happy to have him on the show, of course I was. People *love* disgraced public figures. Almost as much as they love a comeback story. And Kelvin's story is even better now – he's a murderer *and* a crook. Gangsters, poisonings, it's got the lot.'

'Yeah, it has the lot,' said Cassandra.

Howie moved around the opposite side of the island. Something caught his eye as he tried to stay focused on what Cassandra was saying.

'See, I don't think it was like that at all,' she continued. 'Kelvin told me he'd been contacted by the Serafinas, saying they wanted payment for all the favours they'd done him in the past, covering up the scandal, making sure he was still comfortable, that sort of thing. But I don't think that's what happened. I think he got a call from someone, but not the Serafinas. I think he was contacted by somebody who knew that claiming to be from the mob would put the frighteners up him good and force him to do anything they asked. He's a weak man, Ed, a really weak man. He's privileged and out of touch. A call from any random number saying the right things would be enough to make him putty in their hands.'

'Interesting theory,' Ed said with a smirk.

'Isn't it?' she agreed. 'Especially if that somebody had previous connections to gangsters in Italy, like, I don't know, the showrunner who had worked on a documentary about them in his early years.'

'Me?' Ed blurted. 'You think I had something to do with all of this? I was as much a victim as everyone else, Cassandra. Do I need to show you my hospital results, my concussion report?'

'Oh I think that part was real enough,' she said. 'I just don't think it was Kelvin who did it.'

'Then who? Pray tell?'

'Scorpione, or whatever his name is.'

'Ah, of course.' Ed folded his arms over his chest. 'The Mafia hitman, why don't you take your beef up with him? After all, he's the one who admitted to us all that he's little more than a contract killer.'

'Us all?' asked Howie. 'You weren't there for that, Ed.'

The first cracks in Ed's calm demeanour started to appear. He was sweating now, forehead shining under the lights of the kitchen.

'I heard through others what happened, Sachiko, Marjorie, they were there, weren't they?' he asked.

'They were,' said Howie.

'And that Scorpione guy, he's a hitman,' said Ed. 'He said as much, didn't he?'

Howie rounded to face him. 'Ed, I know a thing or two about acting,' he said. 'But I know even more about bad acting. Believe me, I've had a whole career perfecting it. And even at my worst, it was still a hundred times better than Scorpione when he was put on the spot.'

'Who is he really?' Cassandra asked. 'Some goon you hired?'

'I don't rate your scriptwriting either, as it happens,' said Howie. 'Yeah, sure I almost accidentally drowned the guy, but come on. He could have improvised a little better.'

Ed was twitching now. He ran his good hand through his hair. He was laughing, his face turning a little redder.

'You guys,' he said. 'I knew I picked the right two for the spin-off. You're good, both of you. Quite the double act. Who would have thought it, eh? The ham and the tart? Sometimes I amaze even myself with how good I am at this sort of thing.'

'You orchestrated it all, didn't you?' Cassandra asked.

'That's absurd!'

'Admit it, Ed, we've caught you bang to rights!' yelled Howie.

'How dare you!' he shouted back. 'You come in here, in the middle of the night, spouting all of this drivel about me manipulating things behind the scenes like some mad media Svengali. Need I remind you *both* that without me, neither of you would be anywhere *near* the relevance you are now. Without this show, without what happened to Rolando, you'd both still be skulking about scratching out an existence that was barely worth thinking about. You, the great Howie Temple, the man who can't even get a free ticket to the cinema anymore let alone open a box office smash. And as for you, Cassandra Troy, don't make me laugh. Flogging cheap make-up and clothes a harlot wouldn't be seen dead in is *not* a profession to be proud of. Believe me!'

'How dare you!' Cassandra lunged forward.

Howie was close enough to stop her before she got anywhere near Ed. She was flailing her arms, her temper finally broken. Howie pulled her back and stood between them. Ed was laughing, loudly, mocking them both.

'There we have it, eh?' he scoffed. 'You can take the girl out of Liverpool but you can't take the Scouser out of the girl.'

'Don't rise to it,' Howie whispered to her. 'Don't give him the satisfaction.'

Cassandra's eyes peered through the hair that was covering her face. He slowly let her go and she stood there, beside him, chest rising and falling with every angry breath she took.

'Quite the imagination you've got, Cassandra, I'll give you that,' he said. 'But that's all it is, just a story, just conjecture and imagination. And those things don't stand up in court. Meanwhile Kelvin Kamani and that Scorpione chap are rotting away in an Italian jail somewhere, ready to be locked away forever and forgotten about. Your friend burned Rolando's body, remember? That was all his own doing, I had nothing to do with that, even though it will make great TV. And without any evidence, I'd recommend you shut down your wild accusations. Case closed, as they say.'

Cassandra gritted her teeth. As much as she hated to admit it, Ed was right. She had no proof, no evidence that had anything to do with all of this. And worse still, he knew it. He stood across the kitchen from them, smiling smugly. He knew that they knew what had happened. He was goading them, happy and fulfilled at his work.

'You're a coward, do you know that?' she levelled at him. 'A coward and a rat. That you would create all of this, a horrible ruse, for what? TV ratings? A stupid reality show? You must be out of your mind.'

'Evidence,' said Ed. 'Show me your proof that backs up your theory. I'm here, waiting. And I'll always be waiting, Cassandra. I made you, both of you. My suggestion is that you sit back, enjoy the ride and enjoy the spoils of what you're about to become. All thanks to me.'

Cassandra felt sick. Her stomach was flipping, her heart thumping in her ears loud enough that it was giving her a headache. She felt like a great weight was pressing down on her chest. She had been beaten, so close to the end. Then Howie spoke up.

'I wouldn't be so sure about that,' he said.

Ed lazily turned his gaze to the actor.

'You have something you want to add to this, H?' he asked. 'Better make it quick, I've got a plane to catch.'

'Yeah, just a little something,' he said, walking around the island and back towards the kitchen door.

He bent down with considerable discomfort and picked up a fragment of the broken glass. Holding it up to the light, he smiled.

'These are some lovely wine glasses, Ed,' he said. 'Beautiful even, a shame that you broke one. Smells like it was a lovely Château Latour that was in it too.'

He sniffed at the broken glass. Cassandra and Ed were watching him closely.

'You never fail to surprise me, H,' said Ed. 'I didn't have you down as a wine connoisseur. I didn't have you down as an expert in *anything* really, given how thick you are.'

'Very true,' he said. 'I'll tell you both how I know the wine another time, it's quite an interesting story involving the band Right Said Fred. But it's the glass that's caught my eye this time around.'

He placed the broken piece on the worktop of the island. Cassandra leaned in, staring down at it. Ed remained perfectly still, a growing concern etching into his tanned face.

'See, I thought I saw something when I was over there, by your cupboards Ed,' he said. 'More of these lovely glasses. And I thought I'd take a closer look, while Cassandra here was laying out her theory, as you put it.' He tapped the worktop with his finger. 'You're right about evidence. We don't have any for our thinking,' he said. 'Or at least we didn't until we came in here, just now.'

'What are you talking about, you idiot?' said Ed.

'The glasses, they have a brand mark on them,' said Howie. 'Brand recognition and all of that, I know how important it is to these big cruise liners and yachts. I think you might have even said so yourself.'

'There's a word here, a brand on this glass,' said Cassandra, twisting to read it. '*Meridian Sunset*. That's the same name that was on the knife in Rolando's back, the one that Scorpione said he stuck there when he realised the captain was already dead.'

Despite his tanned features, Ed was starting to turn pale.

'Why, that's right, Cassandra,' said Howie, putting on a show now. '*Meridian Sunset*, another ship perhaps, something else anyway. We saw that name on the knife as you said. And it's here, on these wine glasses that Ed has in his kitchen. Now I don't believe in coincidences, and this is no exception. I wonder, Ed, if you'd like to explain why there is branding from a seemingly random yacht that matches a weapon brought onboard *The Regal Secret* and used in a staged murder here, with you, where you live?'

'You don't want to show us your knife collection by any chance, do you?' asked Cassandra, now smiling broadly.

Ed looked ill. He was propping himself up against the worktop, his eyes moving furiously across the room, anywhere but meeting them. He tried to say something but couldn't, the words sticking in his throat.

'Well?' asked Cassandra. 'Do you want to explain any of this? Or shall we just call the police and be done with it?'

'Do you know, Cassandra,' said Howie. 'I think this might be the first time I've ever seen Edward here speechless.'

'Except when he was unconscious of course.'

'Oh yes, that's right. Although that's clearly a lie too as he knew what was going on the whole time.'

'Yes, true.' She tapped her chin. 'I wonder what the police and press will think when a ham actor and a tart are revealed to have caught the real killer? Any ideas, chuck?'

'I've got a few,' he laughed.

Ed wasn't laughing. He was just standing there, staring off into space as his world came crashing down about him. Cassandra and Howie gave him a moment, then decided it was time to move things along.

'Alright, come on, Ed,' said Howie. 'Time to go. We've got a car waiting and the cops will meet us at the hotel.'

'You might as well come clean about it now, babe,' she added. 'The game is up.'

Ed nodded slowly. He pushed himself off the worktop and trudged around the island. 'Do you know, it's funny,' he said. 'I remember reading about Kelvin Kamani when his whole scandal broke. He said something about doing *anything* to get what he wanted, even if that broke the law.'

'I heard that one too,' she said.

'You don't think you can stoop to that kind of level, not really. Until the wolves are at the door and you're facing the prospect of being without a job, without any money, without a future. Nothing. Such is life, I guess, especially in showbusiness. Howie can tell you that.' He drummed his fingers on the island.

'Come on, let's go,' said Howie. 'I don't need to hear another sob story about showbusiness, Ed. I've lived enough of them as it is.'

'True,' he said. 'Very true. You won't mind me doing this then, will you?'

He lunged forward and grabbed the shattered piece of wine glass that had been lying on the worktop. Swooping around Howie, he pulled him backwards, the shard jabbed into his throat.

'Howie!' Cassandra screamed.

'Take it easy, sweetheart,' said Ed. 'I won't hurt your boyfriend if you just back off.'

'Boyfriend?' Howie choked. 'I'm old enough to be her father.'

'Shut it!' he sneered. 'Just keep your trap closed and nobody gets hurt. You said there was a car waiting outside yeah?'

Cassandra nodded.

'Right, move it then, old man.'

Chapter 42

Ed backed slowly out of the kitchen. Cassandra followed them, keeping a safe distance. They stuttered along the hallway, past the suitcases and out of the main door. Howie was staying remarkably calm, despite having a piece of broken glass held at his throat. Ed kept tugging at him, pulling him backwards as they made their way across the porch. He kicked the gates open and the driver climbed out.

'Easy now,' said Cassandra. 'Just do as he says.'

The driver took a deep gulp. The inky sky was turning a paler shade of blue as the morning sun started its shift for the day. Not even the gloom could hide his fear. Cassandra could see it a mile off. She wondered, briefly, what she must look like, following Howie and Ed out of the door. Did this sort of thing happen all the time for drivers in Monaco?

'The keys, where are they?' Ed asked him.

'They're . . . they're in the ignition, sir,' he said.

'Get out of the way.'

'Don't let him get in the car,' said Howie.

'Shut up!' snapped Ed.

'Babe, maybe stay quiet just now,' said Cassandra.

The poor driver didn't know what to do. Ed sensed this and drove the shard of glass a little deeper into Howie's throat, a bead of blood appearing at its point. The actor let out a yelp.

'Give me the keys!'

The driver had no other choice. He reached back into the car and pulled out the keys. Standing back up, he held them out towards Ed and Howie.

Cassandra wished she had precognition. Her old great grandmother had always said she had a knack for seeing things before they happened. It was an old family trait, she had insisted. Being a student of logic, Cassandra had never really believed in any of that. Now, however, she wished she'd had just a little bit of insight into what the driver was going to do.

He reached out to hand the keys over to Ed. As the director did the same with his injured hand, the driver curled his fist tight and hurled the keys as hard as he could into the forest that surrounded the villa. The throw was so hard that none of them heard when or where it dropped down. Howie let out a little gasp of delight. Ed was not so pleased.

'Not smart,' he said.

He tightened his grip on Howie and began backing off down a little path that led from the front porch. Lights lit the way down a wide set of stone steps that curled around to the front of the villa.

'Stay there!' he demanded of the others. 'Or so help me I'll cut his throat open right here!'

Cassandra and the driver remained perfectly still. Ed vanished around the outer wall of the villa, Howie dragged with him. As soon as they were gone, she urged the driver on.

'Call for help,' she said. 'Call the police, right now. Tell them it's to do with the Rolando and Kamani case, an Inspector Dorotea Sal is leading the investigation in Italy. Hurry up, please, they'll need to send backup too.'

'Yes, of course, mademoiselle, right away.'

'Please hurry,' she said, sprinting off towards the staircase.

'And what are you going to do?' asked the driver, quivering hands reaching for his phone.

Cassandra didn't answer him. She didn't even hear him. They weaved through the garden and snaked around the property, a high cliff wall rising up to her left. At the bottom, the beach opened up in front of her, two dark spots staggering towards the waterfront.

She bolted across the sand.

The closer she got to Ed and Howie, the better she could hear them. Howie was shouting and swearing, Ed was giving as much, if not better back. The bigger man was struggling now, every step Ed took taking twice as long as it had to. Cassandra thought that if she put her head down and charged, she might stand a chance at something, anything, that would free her friend.

Unfortunately, Ed heard her long before she could reach him. The wind was blowing from behind her carrying every sound towards Ed. He spun Howie around, the shard of glass still at his throat, and demanded she stop.

'That's close enough,' he gasped. 'I'm not kidding around now Cassandra. I'll do it, I'll kill him, I've done it before and I'll do it again. It's just that easy.'

'You admit it then,' she said, panting for breath, her thighs burning. 'You killed Rolando, you poisoned him.'

'Overdose,' said Ed. 'That's what the autopsy report will say if Kelvin's kerosene party hasn't rendered that impossible. An accidental overdose of sleeping tablets. Hardly the most glamorous way to go but he wasn't the most glamorous guy. The opposite in fact. A small-time hustler with a taste for horses. He was a snitch, a rat, a grass, whatever you want to call it.'

'That didn't mean he had to die,' she said. 'And for what? So you could make a good TV show.'

'Correction, a *great* TV show. The best reality show that's ever been screened. And why not, eh? Who the hell is going to miss a chance to see a real life murder solved in front of their eyes, across eight episodes at forty minutes a time? You know what viewers are like, Cassandra, they're fickle, they're scandal-hungry and above all else, they want something bigger, twistier and more outrageous every year. Somebody had to die, why not him?

'You're a monster,' she said, her breath coming back to her.

'Maybe,' he said. 'But I'm nothing, *nothing*, compared to those animals in the network boardrooms. They'd sell their grandmothers' souls for good ratings. And I'm giving it to them, with the most original cast, crew and concept since somebody put a bunch of misfits together in a house full of cameras. I'll be hailed as a genius, I'll have revolutionised TV forever. My name will go down in industry history as *that* guy.'

'Yeah, the guy who took a life for a programme and put others at risk for no good reason,' she said.

'You're nuts,' said Howic.

'Shut up you!' Ed hissed in his ear.

'You are, you're completely crazy,' he said. 'Who the hell do you think you are anyway? You're not a revolutionary, you're a murderer. And I've got news for you pal, nobody remembers cowardly criminals like you.'

'Shut up! Shut up!'

Ed was getting more furious by the second. The dawning morning light glistened off the shard of glass at Howie's throat.

'You'll get your moment in the sun, sure, when the cops arrive and throw your ass in jail,' Howie went on. 'But you must be joking if you think you'll get beyond a few column inches in a newspaper.'

'Shut up! I'm a visionary!'

'You're a chancer, Ed, you always have been and you always will be. You've ruined countless lives with your antics, manipulating people's lives on camera for cheap thrills. Nobody will remember you, not even me and Cassandra.'

'No! No! Shut up!'

'As soon as we're done here we're going straight home and then you'll be nothing more than a bad dream, a distant memory, a footnote to our careers. Nobody remembers two-bit crooks like you, Ed. You're just not worth it! You can't even kill me as it wouldn't be in line with the plot you've always sketched out for this story. I'm meant to be the comeback kid – not the next corpse.'

Ed screamed. Cassandra knew now was the time. A fury flashed in Ed's eyes and he adjusted his grip on the glass. Crouching down, Cassandra scooped up a handful of sand. As the wind gusted, she threw it as hard as she could at both men, catching them both full in the face.

It only blinded the pair for a moment. But it was enough. Cassandra saw Ed loosen his grip on Howie and the bigger man tumbled away, clutching his neck. Cassandra saw her chance and she took it. Charging forward, she remembered what her father had taught her about self-defence when she was just starting to go out round Liverpool as a teenager.

'Kill the body and the head will die,' she shouted to herself.

She plunged two fists into Ed's stomach with as much force as she could muster. He doubled over like a pillow, the air punched out of his lungs. The shard of the broken glass from the *Meridian Sunset* dropped onto the sand as he sunk to his knees. She kicked it clear and then volleyed another shot, this time into his ribs. Ed tumbled away in agony, teeth clenched, arms wrapped about his stomach.

Cassandra straightened up and surveyed the damage. She was short of breath and she felt like her heart was going to burst through her chest. But she was alive, and so was Howie.

He made a strange groaning sound as he uneasily got back to his feet. One eye closed and the other teary, he hobbled over to Cassandra and steadied himself on her shoulder.

'Good work,' he said. 'I thought I was in for it there, for a moment.'

'So did I, babe,' she said.

He looked down at his stomach. A dark red patch had formed on his filthy white shirt.

'Not again,' he winced. He pressed it hard, the stitches burst from his slashing.

'We need to get you to a doctor,' she said, helping him.

'What are we going to do with this asshole?' he asked, nodding down at Ed writhing on the beach.

Before she could answer, the flashing red and blue lights of the Monaco Police Department shone through the dwindling darkness. Figures appeared on the clifftop, the villa looming over the beach like some unforgiving headstone.

'Right on time,' she said, relieved.

'We'll probably have to give more statements,' said Howie, the pair of them limping back towards the staircase and the cliff.

'Yeah, I reckon you're right,' she said. 'Who needs Macbeth soliloquies when you can give nightly performances to the police?'

Police officers reached the sands and came bounding over, running to meet them. Cassandra and Howie directed them in the way of Ed behind them as a paramedic appeared to help them.

The morning sun cleared the horizon of the Mediterranean Sea, bringing with it a sense of renewal and hope. Another day had dawned in Monaco, a chance for people to spend money they didn't have or talk about what they would do if they did have it.

For Cassandra and Howie, however, there was a sense of finality about that blazing red sun. For the first time since they'd met each other, this finally felt like the end. There was closure here, at last.

'Cut!' said Cassandra, and they stared out at the sea.

Chapter 43

'Just one day, that's all I'm asking for. One day where I can just sit, relax by a pool or on the beach and not have murderers, maniacs and all other kinds of ridiculousness come at me by the boatload.'

'Oh, far too soon, chuck,' said Cassandra, sipping on her exotic cocktail.

'What's too soon?'

'That joke, about boats.'

'Boatload? That's a well-known phrase, Cassandra,' said Howie. 'It's used in polite conversation and high society all the time.'

'And what, Mr Temple, would you know about either of those things?'

'More than you could possibly imagine,' he said. 'Did you know that I was once complimented on my small talk during a party at Selma Blair's house?'

Cassandra tipped her sunglasses down onto the end of her nose. Howie ignored her, taking up his Bloody Mary and stirring the drink with the stick of celery. He lifted it out, let the tomato juice drip off, then took a big, ugly crunch.

'Oh for goodness' sake, babe,' she said. 'Here.'

She flapped out a napkin and handed it across to him. He took it and, between chews, dabbed at the corners of his mouth.

'Bloody Marys, they always bring out the worst in me.'

'Wasn't your first wife called Mary?'

'She was,' he chuckled.

A warm breeze wafted in from the ocean. The pair had found a quiet, comfortable cafe that overlooked Monaco's main marina. They had been told by the staff that this was on the main route of the annual Grand Prix. Now, however, it was peaceful and almost serene. The tourists and the locals all went about their business quietly. Beyond them were a fleet of multi-million pound yachts and ships, all moored and ready for their masters' bidding.

Had things gone to plan, *The Regal Secret* would have been among them today, the last of the filming having just been completed. As it was, Howie and Cassandra found themselves at a loose end at their final destination in much stranger circumstances.

Neither had really spoken about what had happened since they left the beach. It was all too fresh in the memory still. But once Inspector Sal had arrived to officially sign them off as no longer being part of an active investigation, that would be it, finished. Forever.

'I thought you weren't supposed to be drinking when you're on painkillers.' Cassandra nodded at his cocktail.

'The measures this place gives, there's more alcohol in the hand wash in the toilets, believe me.'

'Touché,' she said.

'What time did Sal say she'd be here?' asked Howie, glugging down his cocktail.

'Eleven,' said Cassandra, touching up her make-up.

'And what time is it now?'

'Don't you have a watch?'

'I haven't bought it yet,' he said. 'I'm treating myself to a new Rolex, an Explorer, if you must know. Like James Bond.'

'I thought he wore a Seamaster. An Omega.'

'How do you know that?'

'I know my movies,' she said. 'The classics as well as the new stuff, I'll have you know. You have to be a pop culture encyclopedia when you're a darling of social media like me.'

'Really?' he scoffed.

'That and I did a thing with Omega the other year there. They sent me one of those Seamasters to feature on my channels.'

'I'm impressed. The Seamaster is what he wears in the movies,' said Howie. 'But I'm a purist. I've always wanted one, like Fleming himself. So I'm treating myself. And until then, Cassandra, I don't know the time. And I quite like it that way.'

'It's literally only just gone eleven, so Sal will be here any moment,' she said, clicking her mirror and foundation case shut. 'And speaking of exploring and masters of the sea, don't think I've forgotten about the duty-free money that you owe me.'

'What are you talking about now?' He took off his sunglasses and massaged his temples.

'Before we started this sorry affair, back in Livorno,' she said. 'You made me drop my duty-free booze into the drink. You owe me, Howie Temple.'

That last remark gave them both pause. She had saved his life. And he had saved hers. She had lost count over who was winning in that bizarre tally. She winced a little.

'Sorry,' she said.

'Sorry for what?' asked Howie. 'I do owe you, Cassandra. I owe you a great deal. My life, for one, but a whole lot more than that. And while you're painfully young, I don't understand half the things you say and you're constantly on your phone when you have one, I hope you know how fond of you I've grown. You've become a true friend. And I'm grateful for that friendship and everything it means.'

He reached over and took her hand in his. He rubbed the back of her skin with his thumb and smiled at her.

'Oh stop it,' she said, a lump forming in her throat. 'You're going to set me off now and I've only just gone and done my face again, chuck.'

She sniffed. He handed her the napkin marked with his Bloody Mary remnants.

'And then you go and spoil it all by doing something stupid,' she said, fetching her own napkin.

Howie shrugged. He let go of her hand. He looked relaxed, comfortable, at home among the opulence and gaudy brilliance of a place like Monaco. And for the first time since she had known him, Cassandra could see that Howie had once been not just a Hollywood star, but *the* star of an era, an A-lister, the man to be seen around, to be with, to be part of his entourage. Amazing, she thought, that it had taken all this to show her how fickle fame was – you could be getting million pound fees, or posting to millions of followers – but it could all be taken away from you too. She realised now however big your fame got, you couldn't let it be what defined you, or you'd be lost at sea.

She settled in too now, replacing her sunglasses and taking another sip of her cocktail. A large, black, sleek car pulled up in the street in front of them. The door opened and Gianluca, the muscular officer from the La Spezia police, stepped out.

Gianluca was immaculately presented as usual and looked perfectly at home here among the playboys and the idle rich. He rounded the car, removed his sunglasses, which looked far more like designer ones than standard police issue, opening the passenger door. Standing to one side like a bodyguard, he let Inspector Sal climb out from the sedan.

'Lights, camera and action,' said Howie, getting to his feet.

Cassandra did the same as Sal walked briskly through the clutter of tables in the cafe and came to a stop in front of them.

'Mr Temple, Ms Troy, it is good to see you again.'

There was no friendliness in the inspector's tone. She gestured for them to sit down and she joined them.

'Would you like a drink?' asked Cassandra. 'We can order you something.'

'No, thank you,' she said. 'If you don't mind I'd very much like to get straight down to business. In short, the Polizia di Stato in La Spezia would like to officially thank you for aiding our investigations into the murder aboard *The Regal Secret* and we formally release you of any obligation to further aid in any future enquiries that may be made. Sign here please.'

She produced two letters from the inside pocket of her blazer and clicked a pen for each of them. Laying them out on the table, she pointed at where the signatures should go. Howie and Cassandra duly obliged and the inspector thanked them again. She folded up the paperwork, returned them to her pocket and made to leave.

'Thank you,' she said for a third time.

'Hold on, wait a minute,' said Howie, Sal turning away from them.

She stopped and looked back at him.

'That's it?' he asked. 'That's all there is.'

'Did you expect something else?' she asked, seemingly genuine.

'Well . . . I . . . '

'You're not going to ask her to dinner, are you babe?' Cassandra whispered with a devilish grin. 'Because I think that ship has sailed. No pun intended.'

'What? No, of course not,' he said. 'I wanted to know what was happening with Kelvin Kamani and that Scorpione guy. And Ed, for that matter.'

Inspector Sal's lips tightened. She cocked an eyebrow at both of them and then looked over her shoulder at Gianluca standing by the car. Not that she needed his permission, she seemed to be making sure he wasn't listening. She shouted over to him.

'You said you had someone to see, Gianluca. Go on – I can drive myself back to the station.'

Once Gianluca had lumbered off she leant in. 'The matter is being taken care of,' she said.

'That's all we're getting?' Howie sneered. 'We risked our lives to bring that dirtbag in. The same dirtbag, I may add, that you let slip right through your fingers. Come on, Dorotea, we're owed a little bit more than that.'

'Inspector Sal to you, Mr Temple,' she said.

The hardness in her face relented a little for a moment. For the briefest of seconds, Cassandra saw that she was human again, like she had shown back in La Spezia. She leaned down and spoke conspiratorially to them.

'Kelvin Kamani is receiving psychiatric help,' she said. 'He'll return home to Great Britain, a free man. A stupid man, perhaps, after he burned the body, but he hasn't committed any crimes beyond that.'

'That's good to know,' said Cassandra. 'He was a pawn in all of this, wasn't he? He was just the high-profile name and face that Ed needed to make that stupid show get buy in with the viewers and the networks.'

'It would seem that way.'

'And what about Scorpione?' Howie asked.

'A petty thug from Turin,' said Sal. 'Gavino Gelli is his name. Mercenary is probably too strong and competent a word to describe him. He has never had any dealings with the Serafina family or their operations. It would appear that Edward Wells merely used him as another part of his ruse. Gelli claimed that he'd met Wells in a bar somewhere and they'd gotten talking. The plan was for Gelli to claim to be a hitman for the mob, sent to kill Mr Kamani while onboard your yacht. Captain Rolando's death was merely the catalyst to start the whole thing.'

'And the argument, between him and Ed?' asked Cassandra.

'We may never know for sure,' Sal shrugged. 'They had known each other for years, that much was true. But I can safely assume that friendship was how Wells knew that the captain was one of our informants. I suspect Ed had let on that he knew Rolando's double-life. *His* connection to the Serafinas was very much real, Ms Troy. He was a good man.'

'He seemed that way in the short while I got to spend with him,' said Cassandra. 'What an absolute tragedy all of this is.'

'Indeed,' said Sal, straightening up. 'As I mentioned before, your involvement and your help have been greatly appreciated. There is talk of medals, although with budget restraints and cuts across every department, I cannot promise this.'

'Medals? Bloody hellfire,' laughed Cassandra. 'I've never won anything in my life. Not even Rear of the Year.'

'And what about you, inspector?' asked Howie. 'What will you do now?'

'My work never ends, Mr Temple,' she said, with just the hint of a smile. 'I am a policewoman, a detective. I won't stop, just as the drug dealers and criminal gangs will never stop. And that is the way of things in this part of the world. Spare me a thought the next time you are on set, sir.'

She held his gaze a little longer than expected before the stubborn, serious mask returned. She patted her pocket to make sure she had her documents and gave the slightest of bows before returning to the car. It sped off into the late morning traffic and was gone.

'"And what about you, Inspector?"' Cassandra puckered her lips. 'Was that really the best line you could have come up with? You might as well have asked her what colour of socks she prefers as a Christmas present.'

'Never underestimate the long game, kiddo,' he said, taking up his cocktail again. 'I know what I'm doing.'

'Oh yeah? Well, there's a first.'

The comfortable sea breeze picked up again as it rolled in off the Mediterranean. The morning had been warm and, once again, the weather gods were promising another glorious day in Monaco. Paradise. Unless you looked closely. Any casual observer who had spotted the couple down below at the marina furtively loading equipment onto a small launch wouldn't have thought twice. There was always something being filmed in Monaco – from big money ads to blockbuster films. This was no different, just a man and woman loading cameras onto a small vessel.

But if Howie had turned or Cassandra moved to one side, either would have noticed Gianluca walking up, handing over a holdall and waving off two people who looked remarkably like Ben and Geri.

Chapter 44

Sunset Strip was where old Hollywood glamour met new Hollywood fame and fortune. The buildings were disjointed and varied wildly from block to block. From souvenir shops and tat vendors to historic music venues, bars and restaurants that charged hundreds of dollars for a burger and fries, it was a cultural melting pot that attracted the rich, poor, famous and infamous, all at the same time.

Cindy Czarniecki had driven down this stretch of road a million times. None of the neon flashing lights, the endless tour guides, the luxury cars and paparazzi bothered her anymore. In fact, she barely even *saw* them anymore. This was just another place between points A and B. And she was usually late.

The only time she'd look up from the road ahead would be if a billboard took her attention. And only then if she had a client whose face was plastered across it. A quiet acknowledgement that, as a talent manager, she had done her job, was all she would afford herself. There was always another contract, another pay dispute, another moaning actor, singer, band or artist who needed to be talked down from the hissy fit of the century.

Hers was a thankless world of backroom politics, late night deals and ducking and diving just to keep the tax collectors at bay. If she stopped to marvel at every little wonder that living in Los Angeles afforded her, she'd get nothing done. And nothing cost money.

The phone rang. An unknown number flashed up on the screen in her convertible Mercedes, the roof down, the most up-to-date model. Cindy was always reticent to answer numbers she didn't recognise. As a Hollywood agent for the better part of two decades, she was confident there was nobody in the industry, or any related industry, that she didn't know. And if she didn't know them, they weren't worth knowing.

The ringer kept going as she passed the famous Rainbow Bar & Grill, a queue stretching from its door a mile long. Cindy couldn't remember the last time she had to queue for something. She zoomed past the poor saps waiting to be gouged mercilessly, all for a quick snap on social media that would be forgotten about in the week.

Against her better judgement, she pressed the answer button on the steering wheel. The phone clicked on through the surround sound speakers.

'CC,' she said, no time to say the mouthful that was her full name.

'Cindy, how the hell are ya?' came a bold, brash voice from the other end of the line.

'Who is this?'

'Cindy, you minx, you know who this is.'

'No, I really don't,' she said sternly. 'And you have about point five of a second to explain why you're phoning me from an unknown number and, more importantly, how you got my cell. Tick tock, time is ticking.'

'Oh Cindy, you always were a venomous viper. So glad you haven't changed a bit.'

Cindy's mind started ticking over. She didn't recognise the voice, the accent was throwing her. Boston, certainly, with the confidence and over familiarity that could only mean one thing. A movie producer.

She began poring through the library that was her memory, thinking where each and every one of her hundred clients was in the world. Had something happened on set? Was this a lowlife filmmaker trying to squeeze an extra few cents out of a deal? It could be anything.

'I won't ask again,' she said.

'You don't remember me, do you, sweetheart?' asked the man.

She could hear him smiling, even on the phone. It made her skin crawl.

'Call me sweetheart again, buster, and I won't just hang up, I'll have my army of lawyers on your case so fast you'll wish you'd kept your birthday money from grandma.'

'Wow, okay, slow down,' he said. 'I'm just messing with ya.'

'If this is some sort of prank, it's not funny.'

'It's not a prank, Cindy.'

'I'm hanging up now. Goodbye.'

'Wow, wait, hold on!' He was shouting now. 'Hang on, just a second.'

'Bye now.'

Her finger was hovering over the cancel button. Then he dropped his bombshell.

'I want Howie Temple!' he shouted.

Cindy almost crashed her car. She swerved, regaining control and her concentration. She fished around, pawing blindly for her phone. Finding it, she snatched it up and turned off the speakerphone mode.

'Howie Temple,' she said. '*The* Howie Temple?'

'Yes, Howie Temple, the actor,' said the caller. 'The actor, or at least he used to be. You're his agent, aren't you Cindy? At any rate, it says so on your website.'

'Yes, that's right,' said Cindy.

It took a lot to surprise Cindy Czarniecki. She had built up a thick skin that she wore like a suit of armour. You had to in showbusiness. Any sign of a crack and your rivals would be all over you, carving up the corpse and stealing away your business. If Cindy Czarniecki wasn't ten moves ahead of everyone else then something was severely wrong. And she had to get back ahead of the game as quickly as possible.

Howie Temple was a strange exception to this rule. He was so remote, so out of the loop that she'd not given more than a moment's thought as to what happened to him in years. He hadn't delivered a successful project for over a decade. He hadn't turned her a profit in even longer. They had barely spoken recently. There had been something about a reality show in Italy but one of her assistants had taken care of that. He was a dead rubber. She'd thought about cutting him loose plenty of times but some things were best left to wither. Now she was getting phone calls about him. To her well-trained nose, something about all this smelled off.

'What's he done?' she asked. 'Has been arrested? Is he dead?'

'Dead? No, no he's not dead, not yet at least,' laughed the man on the other end of the phone. 'Quite the opposite in fact. It would appear that he's been mixed up in something of a murder mystery in the Ligurian Sea,' said the man.

'Murder mystery?' She wrinkled her nose.

'Yeah, some big deal involving Mafia types and a luxury yacht owned by a Saudi prince.'

'Now I *know* you're yanking my chain, buster.'

'No, no, it's all true, all straight,' he laughed. 'It's all over press. You should get your staff to keep you better informed, Cindy. Your man is a rising star again over with the Europeans. He's even got himself an attractive young sidekick, a Limey.'

'Howie Temple? *The* Howie Temple?' She could barely believe what she was hearing.

'That's what I said.' He coughed. 'He's paired up with some young influencer; her name is Cassandra Troy. She used to be a big thing with the kids, but she's getting on a bit now, almost thirty. He's a hero,' he said.

'Hero?' Cindy said. 'Howie Temple? A hero? The man is a drunk. A penniless drunk at that. How the hell could *he* ever be a hero again?'

'It's true,' said the man. 'He's very much the toast of the town over in Europe. He's gone viral. And I don't mean the flu. Him and the "content creator" or whatever she styles herself as, have become something of an unlikely sleuthing duo. And everyone wants a piece of the action. Including me.'

Cindy was giving serious consideration that this might, in fact, be Howie on the other end of the line. Although the accent was too good, too genuine to be his. He'd never been very good with voices. Then she thought about it being a crank call or a wind-up again. Was she being sent up by MTV or a disgruntled ex-client?

'What do you want, mister . . . ?'

'It's Roger, Cindy.'

'Roger who?'

'Roger Lewden. Come on, don't be like that, you remember, we met at that big thing up in the Hollywood Hills a few years ago, remember.'

Cindy went to lots of 'big things in the Hollywood Hills'. So many, in fact, she couldn't remember three quarters of them. Which was usually a mercy.

'Okay, right,' she said. 'What do you want Howie for, exactly?'

'Straight to business, that's what I've always loved about you, Cinders,' rasped Lewden.

She decided to let 'Cinders' pass.

'Look, I'm putting together a bit of a soiree at my place in Malibu,' he said. 'There's going to be a lot of influential people there. I've got a couple of really prime pictures I want to get off the ground and the kind of guys and gals coming along are the sort of folks who like to be impressed, entertained, you know what I mean?'

'Go on,' she said.

'Yeah, well, this is where your boy Howie fits in,' Lewden went on. 'I'm thinking about having a little murder mystery night, have people come along and play characters, you know the deal. Everyone has a role to play and we uncover the killer at the end. You know the thing, somebody is the butler, somebody is the maid, another schmuck is the old army colonel who's got a grudge against everyone else. It's just a chance for everyone to get tanked up and get loads of pictures greenlit. But I thought if we had a real life detective, a sleuth, a gumshoe, whatever you want to call it, then it would make things that little bit more, y'know, real. You never know, Howie might even get a new screen role out of it.'

Cindy felt the cogs whirring around in her brain.

'Alright,' she said. 'But we're talking serious money for an appearance like that. An evening's work, a private party with what did you call him, the viral sensation? Six figures, baby. Take it or leave it.'

There was silence on the other end of the phone. Cindy was congratulating herself. Everything was all well and good until money was involved. That usually separated the big game hunters from the small fry.

'Dollars?' asked Lewden.

'No, Deutschmark,' she groaned. 'Of course dollars. US.'

'Seems a bit steep to me.'

'You get what you pay for, Lewden,' she said, slipping back into agent mode and finally, for the first time in this conversation, feeling comfortable.

'Okay, okay,' he said. 'Over a hundred K for one night's work. You drive a hard bargain Cinders, but I like your style. I need the girl too, of course. Your boy Howie isn't lighting up the internet on his own. I need him *and* her. Stick a little deerstalker on his head, truss him up like Sherlock Holmes and we'll have a great time.'

'Send through all the details to my people and we'll make sure that Howie pulls himself together, combs his hair, the works.'

'Excellent, thank you Ms Czarniecki. A pleasure doing business with you as always,' Lewden cackled.

'And you.' She smiled. 'Oh, and before you go. Did you say he's been involved in a *murder* case over in Europe?'

'Yes, that's right,' said Lewden. 'Seems Mr Temple and this Cassandra Troy have solved one murder and foiled another while filming a reality show between Livorno and Monaco. I understand they could be getting commended by the Italian police force for their efforts.'

'Commended? You mean like a medal?'

'That's correct.'

'Alright, it's 250 then.'

Lewden was speechless. Cindy held firm.

'You phoned me, remember?'

'Yeah, I know that.' The smile had gone from his face, Cindy could hear it. 'Although I'm beginning to regret picking up the phone now.'

'Hey, if you want to make money in this town, you've got to spend it first, right?'

'Right.' The stuffing had been knocked out of him.

'You do what you need to do to get this done.' It was Cindy's turn to leer like a crocodile. 'Call me back when you've come around and seen sense.'

'Yes, but—'

She hung up the phone. Howie Temple, that old dog. Quarter of a million for showing up to a party with some co-star. She totted up her commission. Not bad for ten minutes of work that she didn't even need to chase.

Whatever Howie had been up to while in Europe was nothing to do with her. But if she could still make money out of him then all the better. He could dress as a chicken and do a handstand on the Eiffel Tower for all she cared. As long as these kinds of calls kept coming in.

Now all she had to do was find him. And what was the name of that other woman? Cassandra Troy, was it? Cindy had never heard of her. Lewden had said she was English. That would be why. She was queuing in traffic now and grabbed her phone and looked up her profile.

There was no agent listed on her socials. Instead it just had one line:

FOR ALL ENQUIRIES, CONTACT MY REPRESENTATIVE – MR A SHIG

Cindy scoffed. She knew all the best media lawyers – who was this guy? She wondered if she could persuade this Cassandra to sign with her. She already thinking about buying herself a new client treat when the flashing blue and red lights of the police distracted her. She looked in the rear-view mirror to see a bike cop urging her to pull over.

'Damn it,' she said, guiding her car to a slow stop close to the end of the Sunset Strip.

The cop parked behind and walked up to her. He pulled off his shades, Cindy didn't offer him the same courtesy.

'A little fast there, ma'am. And did I see you on your cell while driving this vehicle?'

Cindy didn't answer.

'Licence and registration please,' he said, tone flat and monotonous.

This wasn't meant to happen in Hollywood, Cindy thought. She was already dreaming up who to pitch Howie to. A guest spot on *Saturday Night Live*, perhaps? Jimmy Kimmel or Oprah? She was too busy thinking about who would write the biggest cheque to have Temple and Troy on their show. She could practically taste the money, the deals, the brands. She'd recognise that sweet buzz of adrenaline and ambition anywhere – it was the taste of fame. So, no, she couldn't stop for anyone today, traffic cops, priests or acts of god – nothing was mighty enough to get in the way of a star being born, or reborn in this case. It was time for her to play her favourite trump card:

'Come on officer, don't you know who I am?'

EPILOGUE

Ben and Geri heaved the metal case over the side of the boat. It bobbed for a moment then sank swiftly, leaving nothing but a glittering line of bubbles for a few moments. There was no glug, nothing. Just silence. Exactly what they wanted, in more ways than one.

Their bosses had given them strict instructions. Let that fool, Ed Wells, think he was pulling all the strings. But if he even mentioned the Serafinas' name on camera, then that footage could never see the light of day. As a family, they preferred infamy to fame. Let the TV execs fight over clips of the discovery of the body, or the camera-hungry crew trying to get suntanned while trying to stay alive. No, all of that could air. But just not that night where Ed told Rolando he knew everything. Those shots had never been uploaded, the memory cards wiped and were now gently falling to the seabed. Let the vain director think he'd made up the Mafia links for views and drama. It suited the Serafinas to watch unnoticed. Ben and Geri had played their part well. It was, after all, the quiet ones you had to watch.

Acknowledgements

There's always a degree of trepidation when you try something "different". Longtime readers will be familiar with my work being in the distinctly NON-sun soaked, celebrity populated world of Cumbria and the Lake District. To transport, not only a murder mystery but myself, to the glitz and glamour of the Med and Monaco was something of a culture shock. But change, as Heraclitus once quipped, is the only constant. I hope that you, the reader, felt just as transported to this world away from bingo clubs, vats of tea and fold up tables.

As is always the case, there are far too many people to thank and not enough editorial space. I've always been minded to say that a book takes a village. And while it may be my name on the front cover, it couldn't come to life anywhere near the way you've just read without a litany of dedicated, hard working and simply wonderful individuals and professionals. All of which I'm forever indebted.

A huge debt of thanks goes to Elizabeth Counsell. Without her support and encouragement to try something new, there would be NO *All At Sea*. Her constant championing of my work has been steadfast and perennial over the last three years. And I'm indebted to her for her faith. The same goes for Marissa Constantinou who has also shown me nothing but enthusiasm, not just with this book, but my career as a whole.

I'd also like to extend a special thanks to Genevieve Pegg. Her devotion, patience and unflappability when it comes to editing the miasm that is my first drafts have become the reassuring hug that makes writing so bloody enjoyable. And her faith in me to write something different, in a completely new, less "homely" setting, was the shining light that got me through those long days and nights of self doubt and endless nail biting.

My thanks as always to Alice Murphy-Pyle and Jess Haycox who work so tirelessly in shouting about and waving the flag for my work. I'm always immeasurably excited when I see their names pop up in my inbox or screen as I know there's some brilliance on the other end of the message. It's one of the absolute privileges of my career to be able to work with such special, brilliant people and HarperNorth is bursting at the seams with them.

Gratitude also to several writer friends who were on hand to support me during this process – many of which have said such lovely things both privately and publicly about the book. Jonathan Hall is not only a fabulous author but a dear friend. His confidence in my writing never ceases to amaze me. Steven Kedie is always at the end of a text message to remind me why I love writing so much. And last, but by no means least, Mark Buckland – a wonderful writer in his own right and a good friend for what feels like a very, very long time.

I'll close before I'M thrown overboard, by saying thank you to my family, near and far. I don't get to play with imaginary goodies and baddies without their care, consideration and sheer willingness to put up with me. It's not easy, but hopefully I still make you all smile.

**Have you read Jonathan
Whitelaw's other unmissable novels?**

**Check out the first chapter of
The Bingo Hall Detectives here...**

Chapter 1

KELLY'S EYE

"We're not Starsky and Hutch. Would you *please* slow down!"

Jason gritted his teeth. His mother-in-law was a notorious backseat driver. Too fast, too slow, too close to the curb, watch out for that cyclist, wasn't that the turning there, are we there yet? She had mentioned them all. It should have been a scenic drive through the lakes to the peaceful town of Penrith – not the Cannonball Run.

His grip on the steering wheel tightened. "I'm going at the limit, Amita," he said, trying to keep his voice light.

"I don't care what that thing says, you're going too fast," she fired back. "I'd like to be able to see my grandchildren at least once more, if that's alright with you? Which reminds me, do you drive like a maniac with them in the car and I'm not here? Does your wife know about your lead foot?"

"I know where I'd like to put my lead foot," he muttered.

"What?"

"Nothing," he sighed.

Silence descended in the car. Jason had been spending a lot of time with his mother-in-law recently. And it wasn't through choice. It wasn't that he disliked her – Amita Khatri could be very warm and generous when she chose to be. It was when she chose *not* to be that he had a problem. With everything that had been going on, he had enough problems to worry about.

"Bugger, did I bring my glasses?" she said, reaching for her handbag.

"They're on your head," said Jason, concentrating on the road.

"So they are," she tutted. "Rats, have I brought my pen?"

"Front pocket of your bag."

"Yes, so it is," she said, finding her bingo blotter. "Now I can't remember if I have the money to pay Georgie for that magazine subscription –"

"You've rolled up a tenner and put it in the pocket of your cardigan."

Amita patted her tummy where the pocket was. She cocked an eyebrow at Jason.

"Anyone would think you were spying on me."

He thought about answering her back. He thought about saying how she'd spent the last hour before leaving the house going through a very vocal checklist, as if she was packing for an attempt on Everest rather than an evening with Penrith Bingo Club. He thought about telling her that he'd missed most of the news and all of the weather because of the racket she'd been making. Jason thought about lots of things before deciding it wasn't worth the argument.

"Just looking out for my favourite mother-in-law," he said with a forced chirpiness.

"And if I believe that, I'll believe anything," she snorted, a hint of a smile behind her frown.

Jason smiled. He let his grip on the wheel loosen and reached down to the radio.

"You're not putting that on, are you?" asked Amita. "I can't listen to *anything* before the bingo," she said sharply. "It's one of my superstitions. You know this, Jason. You know that I've got to be absolutely in the zone, completely focussed, ready to pounce when those balls come out of the machine."

"Isn't it all electronic now?" he asked. "Don't they have a big screen with a random number generator doing all the hard work?"

"You don't know what it takes to play the numbers," she said. "No radio."

To make sure he had understood, she slapped his hand. He gritted his teeth.

"Fine," he huffed, adjusting himself. "But I want it put on the record that I think you take this bingo far too seriously. It's not the World Cup, you know. It's a load of old folk gathered in a church hall, gossiping about the neighbours."

"How dare you," Amita gasped. "We do *not* gossip. We're there to win."

"Oh, come off it, Amita," he laughed. "You go in there, every week, and talk about everyone who hasn't turned up for half an hour. You play a bit, then you stop for free tea and a Digestive biscuit before kicking off the second half for a right proper bitching session. The clock strikes nine and you all shuffle back out, ready to gather up as much gossip as you can in the week. Cutthroat competition is not the name of the game."

"It is more competitive than you'll ever know," Amita huffed. "Just last week Margaret Cullin won fifty pounds on a full house."

"I'm sure the *Financial Times* was relieved to get a front page that night."

"And then there was last month, when Madeleine Frobisher went home with the rollover jackpot."

"How much was that then?" asked Jason.

"Seventy-five pounds and forty-six new pence."

Jason rolled his eyes. "The excitement never stops," he said. "Look, I never said you didn't play *any* bingo. Obviously you do. All I *am* saying is that you spend an awful lot of time talking about people behind their backs. Is that or is that not the case?"

Amita considered her words carefully. She chewed them over, thinking about the accusations levelled at her. She always did when Jason was the one pointing the finger. She hated to give him an inch. He always took the mile and then some.

"No comment," she finally said.

That made Jason laugh. "No comment?" he said. "No comment? What's that supposed to mean?"

"It means no comment, that's what it means. You're supposed to be a journalist Jason, you should know what 'no comment' means by now."

"I *am* a journalist," he fired back.

"Oh yes, sorry, I had forgotten," Amita folded her arms. "I'd forgotten that watching daytime television in your pyjamas and the latest from the frontline of vacuuming the stairs were cutting-edge reporting these days. How silly of me."

There was a noticeable chill to the air between them now. While Jason knew he'd probably gone too far with his criticism of the bingo club, he thought she was being more than cruel now.

The Musgrave Monument in Market Square loomed through the darkness. Jason felt its clock face was watching him as they drove beneath its glare, almost egging him on to say something. The nineteenth century tower was the focal point of the town; every road seemed to lead to it in the end. If Penrith had a skyline, the Monument's pyramidal peak and bunting would be the highlight.

"No need to kick a man when he's down," he said, his voice like muted thunder. "I'm out of work, you know."

"I know it all too well, Jason," said Amita in that snippy, condescending manner he hated with a vengeance. "I know that, while my daughter is out breaking her back to keep your family afloat, you're messing around on that computer of yours, playing games and watching football highlights."

"I'm trying to find a new job," he said, teeth clamping together, jaw tight. "I was made redundant, Amita, you know this. I'm trying my hardest to get another reporter gig, but it's a very tough market."

"I've told you a million times, Jason," she sniffed. "You should go freelance and make your own work."

Jason had heard this all before – from Amita, from his family, from everyone who cared to have an opinion. The only thing worse than being out of work was being told how to get another job. It made his blood boil.

He was about to launch into a furious tirade when Amita screamed.

"Look out!" she yelled, slamming her hands onto the dashboard.

Jason panicked. He fumbled with the steering wheel as the headlights flashed across the street. A gathered pack of anoraks, corduroy trousers and sensible walking shoes appeared then vanished into the darkness as he wrestled the car out of the way. He slammed on the brakes and they came to a halt – no harm done.

"Bloody hell," he breathed. "They came out of nowhere."

"You weren't concentrating," said Amita, unclipping her seatbelt. "And you were going too fast, like I said!"

He started to plead his case but she was gone, out of the car door, before he got the chance. He caught his breath, pinching the bridge of his nose.

"The Sheriff of Penrith is off to greet her citizens," he said to himself.

But just then he noticed Amita had left her handbag. She was not a woman usually parted from her weapon of choice, and he thought he'd better deliver it to her before he got accused of rifling through its mysterious contents.

Mustering the energy, he got out of the car, stopping first to make sure he definitely hadn't run over any lagging members of the bingo club. The chilly autumn air made his face tingle and woke him up a little. He felt guilty for being so snippy with Amita – she'd hit a sore spot when it came to work. He had little to show for an afternoon of emails and job-hunting. He'd make it up to her with her bag by way of a peace offering.

The gathered group was making quite a noise outside the church hall. Even in the dim light of the evening he could make out Amita at the centre of the action. Something was clearly up.

He pressed the button to lock the car, and it bleeped with a satisfactory chirp as he walked casually over to the assembled gang of elderly Penrith locals.

"What's going on then?" he asked Amita, but before she could answer, a tall, broad-chested old man spoke to him without looking away from the centre of the crowd where Amita was holding court with another well-dressed septuagenarian, both of them vying for supremacy.

"Madeleine's dead," he said bluntly. "Broke her neck."

"Madeleine who?" asked Jason.

"Frobisher," said the old man.

"Is that her that won the monthly jackpot?" asked Jason.

"Aye," said the old man, his moustache twitching as he sneered at him. "That's her."

"Guess she didn't have time to spend it then, eh?" Jason elbowed the pensioner in the ribs, egging him on for a laugh.

The crowd fell silent. Suddenly every pair of bespectacled or laser-surgically-enhanced eyes was on Jason. He could almost taste the contempt hanging in the air as he tried to back away. But Amita pushed her way out to the edge from the centre of the group, grabbed her bag, and locked eyes with him.

"And you are going to write the story?' she said in a voice that Jason knew would lead to trouble.

Harper
North

Would like to thank the following staff and contributors for their involvement in making this book a reality:

Fionnuala Barrett
Sarah Burke
Alan Cracknell
Jonathan de Peyer
Anna Derkacz
Tom Dunstan
Kate Elton
Sarah Emsley
Laura Gerrard
Simon Gerratt
Imogen Gordon Clark
Lydia Grainge
Monica Green
Natassa Hadjinicolaou
Emma Hatlen
Jess Haycox

Megan Jones
Taslima Khatun
Holly Kyte
Rachel McCarron
Millie Morton
Alice Murphy-Pyle
Genevieve Pegg
Amanda Percival
Dean Russell
Eleanor Slater
Hilary Stein
Katherine Stephen
Katrina Troy
Claire Ward
Poppy Loughtman

For more unmissable reads,
sign up to the HarperNorth newsletter at
www.harpernorth.co.uk

or find us on socials at
@HarperNorthUK

ABOUT THE AUTHOR

Born and raised in Scotland, Jonathan Whitelaw is an author, award-winning journalist and broadcaster.

After working on the frontline of Scottish politics, he moved into journalism. Subjects he has covered have varied from breaking news, the arts, culture and sport to fashion, music and even radioactive waste – with everything in between. His work has appeared in *The Sun, Daily Mail, Scotsman, STV* and *The Scots Magazine* as well as numerous international newspapers and websites.

Jonathan also regularly contributes to book events and festivals, with appearances on the Blood Brothers podcast, the Bloody Scotland Book Club, and presenting the Desert Island Crooks panel at the Bloody Scotland crime writing festival.

The author of more than ten novels, his work includes the award-winning Bingo Hall Detectives series.

He now lives in Canada with his family.